ANDREW STICKLAND is a
story writer whose work has vario
Fantasy Society, Games Worksh
and *The Economist*. He studied lav
then creative writing at the Unive
lives in Cambridge.

THE ARCADIAN INCIDENT

THE
ARCADIAN
INCIDENT

ANDREW STICKLAND

Published in 2023
by Lightning Books
Imprint of Eye Books Ltd
29A Barrow Street
Much Wenlock
Shropshire
TF13 6EN

www.lightning-books.com

ISBN: 9781785633485

Cover by Ifan Bates
Typeset in Centaur and Zona Pro
Printed and bound by CPI Group (UK) Ltd, Croydon, CR0 4YY

British Library Cataloguing in Publication Data

A catalogue record for this book is available from the British Library.

For James

PROLOGUE

IT WAS NIGHT. And on Luna, the night lasted for fifteen days.

On the far side, away from the prying eyes of Earth, the temperature had dropped to minus 150 degrees Centigrade and the four figures bounding their way across the regolith-dusted craters of the Korolev Highlands were already beginning to feel the cold. Their environment suits were thin, flexible, designed for short-duration work, and the internal heating systems were already struggling. Another hour would see the air tanks and power cells begin to run dry and at that point, the journey would very quickly become very unpleasant.

But there was no need for worry. At the lip of the next crater the group's destination came into view, nestled in the centre of the depression and no more than half a kilometre ahead. They paused and their leader scanned the distant structures. It was a standard-construct field camp, with a pair of expanded kevlar domes linked together at its centre. A small rover and a larger transport were backed up against the airlock of one of the domes, and off to one side was a third, smaller dome linked to a communications array. Two plasmalights set on masts at either side of the site bathed the whole area in a ghostly blue-white glow.

The four figures continued down the slope, taking long, bounding strides that allowed them to cover the distance in no more than five minutes. At the edge of the camp the leader indicated for one of his men to search the communications dome. The man drew a pistol from his holster, but the leader clamped a hand around the weapon and shook his head.

Meanwhile, one of the others set about opening the airlock door on the nearer dome, overriding its electronic locking mechanism with the microputer attached to the back of his glove. The three men squeezed themselves into the compartment, resealed the outer door, and waited while clean air was pumped in. When the process was complete and the inner door opened, they stepped cautiously into the first of the linked domes.

It was smaller on the inside, its metallic skeleton creating a room no more than three metres wide and six or seven metres long. It appeared to be part research lab and part repair shop. A makeshift table in the centre was strewn with twisted pieces of metal and broken-down electronic components. The rest of the space was taken up with tiny workstations, each crammed with stacks of equipment, monitor screens and endless trailing wires and cables.

Only one workstation was occupied. A young woman sat staring at her monitor as column after column of numbers scrolled slowly down the screen. With her back to the airlock, she was oblivious to the intruders until one of them shoved her on the shoulder. She turned, saw the looming figure and screamed, stumbling away and tugging out the ear buds that had prevented her from hearing the airlock activation alarm.

'Sam!' she yelled, edging back towards the end wall. 'Sam! Get in here, quick!'

The far door slid open and a young man stumbled through, rubbing his eyes sleepily. When he saw the black-clad newcomers and their weapons he hesitated, then rushed forward to try and protect the terrified woman. She grabbed his arm, squeezed herself behind him and tried to drag him back towards the door, but already another of the intruders had cut off their escape.

'Who the bloody hell are you?' the young man stammered.

The group's leader stepped forward. He was a giant of a man, broad and muscular, but without the awkwardness that often comes with such a build. He moved easily, even in the low Lunar gravity, and towered over the frightened figures, gazing at them from behind his dark visor.

'Who...' the young man began again, but the tall figure raised his hand and cut him off. Slowly, he reached up, unsealed his helmet and removed it.

'Where is the professor?' he asked. For such a large man his voice was strangely quiet. Quiet, but not soft. It was a harsh, grating whisper, more like the growl of a hungry beast than the voice of a man, and the reason for it was clear – a thick scar that began somewhere behind the dark glasses he wore even inside his helmet, and continued down his right cheek before twisting awkwardly across his throat and disappearing beneath his collar.

'Where is the professor?' he asked again.

'She's right here,' came a new voice from the doorway, as a woman came storming into the room. She pushed her way past the others and placed herself directly in front of the giant, hands on her hips and a scowl on her face. He recognised her from the files he'd studied. An unremarkable woman, at least physically; early fifties, medium height, brown hair losing its colour, olive skin the

11

same.

'How dare you barge in here like this, terrifying my staff and dragging me out of bed in the middle of the night? Who the hell are you, and what the hell are you doing in my camp?'

She was a thin woman, her features drawn, the skin tight across her cheeks. But she was not frail. It was anger the man could see in her eyes, not weakness, not fear. He would have to change that.

'Who are they?' he asked, indicating the two people behind her. 'Students?'

'My research assistants,' she snapped back. 'Now I'll ask you again. Who are *you*, and what are you doing in my camp?'

'I am Mr Archer. I am here to collect you.'

'Collect me? What are you talking about, collect me? The plan is for us to be out here for six more weeks, not pack up and come home now. I haven't had time to do half the things I have planned yet, and I have absolutely no intention of going anywhere, with you, or with anyone else for that matter, until I'm good and ready to go.'

Mr Archer drew a huge knife from a sheath attached to the back of his suit. One edge was smooth and sharp, the other jagged-toothed, like a saw. He held it casually by his side. 'It is not a request.'

The professor took an involuntary step backwards but then checked herself, took a deep breath and forced her gaze away from the huge blade and back towards the man's scarred face. Slowly she shook her head. 'If you're here to collect me, then it's because you want me to do something for you, yes? You have something particular in mind. So I don't think you have any intention of actually using that knife, do you? It's there for intimidation. And I am not easily intimidated, Mr Archer. So why not put it away and we can talk about this like civilised people? I'm assuming here that you are actually a civilised man, Mr Archer?'

Mr Archer grunted. 'Nice speech. Now listen to mine.' He stepped forward and leant down so his face was directly above the professor's. 'Yes,' he hissed. 'I need you for something. And you are right, I will not be using the knife on you.' He brought the weapon up and let the sharp point hover between them, no more than an inch or so from her face. 'But I am not so concerned for your…' he glanced behind her briefly, '…research assistants. They will accompany us. And the first time you refuse to do exactly what I tell you to do, I will take one of them, I will slice them open from throat to groin and I will gut them like some helpless animal. And I will make you watch as they bleed slowly and painfully to death in front of you. Because no, Professor, I am not a civilised man. Do you understand?'

The woman nodded quickly, and Mr Archer was pleased to see that the fear was now firmly in control. 'Good,' he continued. 'So go and put on your E-suit. You work for me now, Professor Fischer.'

PART ONE

LUNA

1

THE SHUTTLE TO LUNA

LEO FISCHER GRIPPED the waxed paper bag, pressed the lemon-scented opening against his mouth and threw up as quietly as he could. Nothing came out. Nothing had come out last time either, and Leo began to hope his empty stomach had finally decided to settle down and stop trying to turn itself inside out. It was empty. It had been empty for the past twenty minutes, ever since the last of his strawberry and banana GalactaMax had come back up and spectacularly failed to make it into the so-called convenience bag he was now breathing in and out of. It had been awkward and embarrassing and had involved a lot of apologising to his neighbour – an overweight, middle-aged man with a permanent scowl on his face who reminded Leo of his history teacher – but at least he'd been able to collect the floating blob of pink goo and steer it into the bag before it wandered away down the compartment and caused some serious chaos. There were, Leo thought, at least some advantages to throwing up in zero gravity.

But worse than the dry heaving and the apologising and the sour-faced tutting from his neighbour was the fact that the whole messy and embarrassing performance was being watched with great delight by the girl sitting across the aisle. She was reading a book – an old-fashioned, actual paper one – but she was holding it in front of her face and peering at him around the side. Whenever he groaned into the convenience bag, the book would shake with silent laughter, just like it was doing now. Leo leant across and the face disappeared behind the book once more.

'I know you're not really reading that,' he said. 'You haven't turned the page for at least five minutes.'

For a moment the girl didn't respond, except to very deliberately turn the page, but then she lowered the book and left it floating by her knee. 'Sorry,' she said, still smiling. 'But it is kind of funny.'

'Hilarious,' Leo replied. He sat back and took a deep breath of the scrubbed and faintly lemon-scented air – the only kind he would be breathing for the next few weeks, now that he'd left Earth behind – and tried to relax. It felt like his stomach was finally coming round to the idea that it was floating, and completely empty, so he sealed the half-full convenience bag and tucked it into the pouch on the side of his seat.

'First time off-planet, huh?' the girl asked.

'How can you tell?' Leo said, giving her his best attempt at a sarcastic smile. He turned away and tried to stare out of the tiny porthole window beyond his disapproving neighbour, but already Earth was behind them and all he could see was empty blackness. No planet, no stars, just his own reflection staring back at him and a single, tiny bright dot that was probably another spacecraft, too far away for him to identify.

She was right, it was his first time off-planet. And yes, he was nervous and nauseous, but hadn't he been pretty relaxed about the whole thing on the way up? He hadn't been pressed against the window for every second like many of the obvious first-timers, or stayed gripping the armrests with tightly shut eyes like some of the others. He'd been excited, sure. What fifteen-year-old wouldn't be excited to spend their summer holidays on the moon? But he thought he'd been playing the seasoned space traveller pretty well – right until the moment when his stomach had betrayed him and shown him up for the hopeless newbie he really was.

'You know,' continued the girl, obviously failing to notice Leo's attempt to ignore her. 'You can get pills to help with the barfing. Didn't they offer you some back at the station?'

'I said I didn't need any.'

'Guess you're regretting that now, huh?' She reached into her jacket, brought out a packet of travel sickness pills and sent them spinning across to him. 'Here. I always take some, even though I never need them.'

'Thanks.' Leo caught the packet, carefully read the instructions and then popped out two tablets, swallowing them with difficulty and wondering if they would stay down or come straight back up.

'They work pretty fast. Give it five minutes and you'll be as good as new. So, what's your name?'

'Leo,' he replied. 'Leo Fischer. And that's Fischer with a *c*,' he explained, because sooner or later he always ended up having to do it anyway.

'Nice to meet you, Leo Leo Fischer with a *c*. I'm Skater.'

'Skater?'

'Yep, just Skater.' She gave him a self-satisfied smile. 'Kind of memorable, don't you think?'

'I suppose.'

'So, how old are you?'

'Fifteen.'

'Really? Me too. Although people say I look much older. What do you think?'

Leo looked across, met her gaze and quickly looked away as he began to blush. He could feel his cheeks growing hotter and hotter, but there wasn't anything he could do about it. It always happened at times like this, and he hated it. More than just about anything. It was so humiliating.

And anyway, he already knew exactly what she looked like, having spent a good fifteen minutes staring at her in the departure lounge before boarding the shuttle. She'd bustled in extremely late, had a brief argument with the company chaperone while emptying out and then repacking her shoulder bag, then sat with her boots resting on the table in front of her while she listened to music, read her book and ignored everything and everyone around her until it was time to board. At which point she'd grabbed her bag, pushed her way confidently to the front of the queue, right in front of him, and been almost the first through the gate.

Mostly, he was interested in her because she was interesting, Leo told himself. But she was pretty too, in a lazy, slightly chaotic sort of way, and that made her worth looking at as well. She had long blonde hair, tied up at the back with a piece of string, that kept floating up in crazy swirls whenever she leant forward in her chair. He had no idea what colour her eyes were, even though that was one of those things you were supposed to notice about people. Blue, he guessed, if the excessive eye liner was anything to go by, but it made very little difference anyway. When he looked at people, it was always their mouths, not their eyes, that he looked at, and Skater's mouth was a lot more interesting than her eyes because for some reason she'd decided to paint her lips a really odd shade of green.

Her clothes were old-fashioned, but the way she wore them made them look stylish; tight black trousers torn at the knees, a grey top with a logo he didn't recognise, an old uniform jacket of some sort and the clumpy boots she'd had perched on the table earlier. Leo glanced down at his own clothes — a dull blue, all-in-one under-suit he'd chosen because that was what his guidebook had suggested would be most comfortable for the shuttle, and a jacket that was clearly designed for carrying things in its pockets, not for style — and really wished he didn't look quite so…normal.

'So?' Skater asked.

Leo looked up. 'Sorry. What?'

'So, do I look older than fifteen?'

'Uh, yeah, I guess.' Leo mumbled, his cheeks still burning. 'Especially with all the make-up and stuff.'

'Hey.' Skater leaned out across the aisle and motioned for Leo to do the same. 'Please tell me that's not your dad you're travelling with,' she whispered, glancing across at his fat, unfriendly neighbour.

'God, no,' Leo exclaimed, horrified that she could have thought such a thing. 'He's just the guy I got stuck sitting next to. No, I'm travelling on my own.'

'Oh right, so you're another one of Pam's prisoners then, like me?'

'Who's Pam?'

'She's our wonderful chaperone.'

'The one you were arguing with, back in the spaceport?'

'You saw that? Well, that's her. We really don't get on.'

'Yeah, I got that impression. So what were you arguing about?'

'Oh,' Skater waved her hand dismissively. 'You know, just stuff. It's always the same, every time I fly.'

'I take it you've been to Luna before then?'

'Yep. I come up every six months, pretty much. This is my tenth trip so far. And I went to Mars once as well.'

'How come? Are you seriously rich or something?'

Skater laughed. 'Dreamland! No, my dad's a pilot. He works for MarsMine, flying short-haul stuff out of Luna mostly, but sometimes he gets to take one of the big supply trains out to Mars or wherever. Anyway, it's part of his contract that he can bring his family up to Luna for free twice a year, so I always make sure I'm free whenever he can arrange the flights.'

'On your own? What about your mum?'

Skater's smile dropped. 'My mum and dad are divorced. Mum came up with me the first couple of times, but she hated it. She and Dad hardly spoke to each other, and she spent the whole time in the hotel room, refusing to go out and do anything, just waiting until she could go home again. Also, she was a bit like you.' She motioned to the side of Leo's seat, where the convenience bag was tucked away. 'She couldn't cope with the zero g. So now I get to travel on my own, and I try and spend as much time as I can up here – just me and Dad – and it's absolutely beyond beyond. Every minute of it. Sometimes we go out trekking into the crater fields, camping out and stuff, or sometimes we go off to one of the other cities for a change. And whenever he can, he lets me ship out with him, like when I got to go to Mars. He had to get special permission from the company for that one, and of course Mum went totally supernova because it meant I had to miss, like, half a term of school, and in the end the only reason she let me go was because I had a complete flip-fit and told her that if she didn't let me go, I'd go anyway and never come back, and I think she really believed I'd do it so she gave in.'

She took a deep breath and plunged straight on. 'So what's your story? How come you're heading off to Luna all on your own?'

'I'm going to meet my mum,' Leo explained. 'She's been working up there for the past few weeks and she's arranged for me to come and help out for a bit. Kind of like work experience.'

Skater grimaced. 'Your first trip to Luna, and you're going to be spending your time working? That's just wrong.'

'It won't be for the whole trip, just for the first couple of weeks. After that the plan is to spend some time sightseeing.'

'Just you and your mum? What about your dad?'

Leo shook his head. 'I haven't got one.'

'Divorced as well?'

'Nope, just never had one.'

'Explain.' Skater looked confused. 'I mean, you must've had a dad at some point.'

'Okay, well technically yes, I did have a dad for a while. But apparently he ran off with one of my mum's bridesmaids, some time between the wedding and me being born.'

'Harsh.'

'I suppose.'

'Do you ever see him?'

'No.'

'Do you want to?'

'No.'

'And your mum never remarried or anything?'

'No.'

'Wow. So does it bother you, not having a dad?'

'Not really,' Leo said with a shrug. 'I mean, look at me. I'm not exactly the kind of person who wants to be spending all day kicking a ball around the park with their dad, or whatever it is kids are supposed to do with their dads.'

'True, you're really not the sporty type.' Skater looked across and laughed.

'What's so funny?'

'Sorry, it's just…you're not exactly the SAT type either, are you?'

'SAT?'

'Socially Aware Teen. And no, if you don't even know what it means, you're really not one of them. Nor am I, by the way. I'm way too much of a Retro to be a SAT. In fact, I'm like the ultimate anti-SAT.'

'Well I'm not a SAT or a Retro,' Leo admitted. 'Or anything else with a smart name. I'm just a boring old nerd, with a boringly sensible haircut and boringly sensible clothes.' And then, mostly to himself, he added, 'and not many friends either.'

'Yeah,' Skater agreed. 'There are a few kids like that at my school, but I honestly don't know much about them. They always seem to be doing homework, or going to after-school clubs, and you never see them hanging out in the malls and coffee shops, or going to parties and stuff, so you never get to find out what they're really like. And everyone hates them anyway because they always come top in all the exams. And I mean, like, *all* the exams.'

'Yeah, that sounds exactly like my life all right.'

'So are you clever?'

'Yes,' Leo said, without embarrassment. 'That's one thing I definitely am.'

'How clever? Never mind,' Skater added, before Leo could answer. 'You can tell me later. Look who's about to come and ruin our day.'

Leo looked round and saw that the chaperone, Pam, was gliding her way along the aisle towards them, a cheery grin fixed on her unpleasantly over-made-up face. When she reached their seats, she came to a graceful stop and the smile grew even wider.

'Hi, Leo,' she beamed. 'And welcome to space. How are you feeling?'

'Yeah, okay,' Leo replied, automatically. But in actual fact, he was feeling okay. His stomach felt like it had finally remembered where it was supposed to be and actually, it was even trying to suggest he might like to put something back inside it.

'Wonderful,' Pam replied. 'Wonderful. Excited?'

'I guess.'

'Of course you are. Now...' She glanced at the small screen she wore on her wrist. 'It says here that your mother will be collecting you in Atlantis. Is that correct?'

'That's right.'

'Wonderful. Well then just you sit back and enjoy the trip and I'll pop back a bit later to run through all the immigration details with you. Okay? Wonderful.' She turned to Skater and it was clear she had to work hard to keep her smile in place. 'And Lisa Kate. A pleasure as always. No need to ask if you need anything, is there? I'm quite sure you're well able to look after yourself, yes?'

'Hi, Pam,' Skater said, returning the forced smile. 'You know you can call me Skater if you want. Everyone else does.'

'Well everyone else can do as they wish. But I think I'll stick to Lisa Kate, if you don't mind. You know where to find me if you need me. Do have a pleasant flight.' And with that she pushed off and continued her graceful way along the cabin.

'Lisa Kate?' Leo asked.

'You hungry yet?' Skater asked, ignoring the question.

'Yeah, I think I am, actually.'

'Good. Let's go find some food.' She tucked her floating book away, unclipped her seat strap and let herself glide out into the aisle. 'They've got this great viewing gallery a bit further along where you can stare out at space, and there's a food bar there as well. Come on, it'll be fun.'

'Okay.' Leo unclipped his own strap and pushed himself out of his seat. Immediately he shot upwards, crashed painfully into the roof of the cabin, spun around, and found himself back in his seat, only now it seemed to be sitting on him instead of the other way round. He could hear laughter from some of the nearby seats, and the grumpy man beside him – now upside down – began his tutting once more.

Skater reached across. 'Come on,' she said with a grin. 'I'll give you a hand.'

Blushing furiously, Leo let himself be pulled along, floating just above the other passengers. There were handholds all along what had previously been the ceiling, and Skater easily propelled the two of them the entire length of the cabin in just a few pulls.

'I thought it would be like swimming under water,' Leo explained. 'But without the getting wet bit.'

'No, everything's a lot slower under water, because of all the resistance.'

'Yeah, I get that now.' He let go of Skater's hand and floated free, watching as she effortlessly glided through the narrow entrance into the next compartment. He hesitated for a moment, took a firm grasp of the nearest handhold, and gave himself a gentle push, this time managing to control his movements much more successfully. He bounced, almost gracefully, on the floor and then floated back up to where Skater was waiting for him, standing upside down with her feet tucked into one of the handholds. 'This is amazing,' he told her. 'I think I'm already beginning to get the hang of it.'

'And how's the stomach doing now?'

'Pretty good, actually. I guess those tablets really do work.'

'Supreme. Let's go get some food then.'

They continued through the second cabin and into the viewing gallery beyond. This was wider and taller, with a domed roof filled with large triangular windows. A long, well-stocked food bar curved along one wall, and tiny tables filled the remainder of the floor area.

There were no seats, but soft, stirrup-like hoops were attached to the floor so customers could tuck in their feet and stop themselves drifting away. Most of the tables were already occupied.

'I'll get the food,' Skater announced, joining the small queue. 'What they sell here is so much better than the free stuff they'll come round with later, and Dad always tops up my credit before the flight so I can afford to blob out on whatever I want. Go find somewhere to perch. But don't bother with the tables, try and grab us a window.'

Leo pulled himself along one of the guide wires and made for a window near the centre of the dome that a young couple had just abandoned. While he waited for Skater, he took his first proper look at the amazing view outside the ship.

The first thing he saw was Earth, huge and bright, directly behind the ship. He could clearly make out the bottom half of Africa, upside down, as it began to disappear into the darkness of its nighttime. It was incredible – so much more incredible than he'd ever imagined it would be. He'd made the journey dozens of times on his computer, zooming up from London Spaceport, through the clouds and the upper atmosphere, out into the darkness, until the Earth was far behind. But even when he'd run it through the holo-helm, it hadn't been anything like this. 'Wow,' he whispered, feeling slightly foolish for saying it out loud, but too amazed to stop himself. He glanced round sheepishly, but no one was paying him the slightest bit of notice. They were all too busy doing exactly the same thing.

He'd always planned to go into space at some point, possibly even live off-planet for a while, but certainly not while he was still fifteen. Maybe only three or four other kids in his school had been up even this far, and here he was, about to spend his entire summer holidays on the moon.

He twisted round, looking for Luna itself, but the front section of the ship was blocking his view. It was a giant revolving cylinder, three times the diameter of the rest of the ship and had – in Leo's opinion – no business being this close to the viewing gallery.

'That's First Class,' Skater said, floating up next to him and eating something from a long silver package. 'They have gravity in there.'

'Yeah, I can see that,' replied Leo. 'Though I don't really get the point. I mean, it's only for a few hours, and I'd have thought they'd enjoy floating about for a bit. It's a lot of fun.' He eyed the silver package suspiciously. 'What's that?'

'Heated plant protein cylinder secured inside a soft-carb envelope.'

'Huh?'

'Hot dog.' Skater floated a second packet across to Leo and took another bite of her own. 'Mop bab, apfuwee.'

'Excuse me?'

She swallowed. 'Not bad, actually.'

Leo opened the pack and peered inside. It really was a hot dog, complete with onions, cheese and some variety of brownish sauce. It smelt good, and as his stomach was now trying to tell him that it felt much better and hadn't had anything solid inside it for most of the day, he took a bite. Then another. And another.

'I think it's mostly so they can eat and drink properly,' Skater said, indicating the First Class section with a flick of her head. 'You know, sit with a nice glass of wine, in a proper glass, and not have to drink it through a straw. And the whole going to the toilet thing as well, I guess. Oh – here – I got us these as well.' She reached into her jacket and produced two cartons of Slake. 'Sorry, they only had citrus, which is kind of meh, I know, but at least it'll wash the dog down. And there's chocolate as well, to take the taste away afterwards.'

Leo popped the carton and squeezed some of the drink into his mouth. It tasted fine. 'Okay,' he said. 'So you were going to tell me about the Lisa Kate thing.'

'There's nothing to tell,' Skater said with a shrug. 'Lisa Kate Monroe. That's my real name.'

'So where does Skater come from? Are you a skater?'

'Well, yeah, sometimes. But that's not where I got the name. It just comes from Lisa Kate if you say it really fast. Lisakate. Lisekate. Li-skate. Skate. But Skate makes me sound like a fish, so I made it Skater instead.'

Leo laughed. 'Good explanation.'

'I know, right? I make it a lot.' She finished her hot dog, finished her drink, stuffed the empty packets in one pocket and produced two bars of chocolate from the other. 'Now my turn to interrogate you.'

'Okay.'

'So what's the deal with this work experience thing you're doing? What kind of work does your mum do anyway? And are you going to be staying in Atlantis for the whole time?'

'Actually, we're not staying in Atlantis at all.'

'Oh.' Skater sounded disappointed.

'Well, not for the work bit, anyway. We've got some sightseeing planned for our last couple of days before leaving, but when I arrive, Mum's taking me straight off to Reynes. That's where she's based.'

'So, you'll be living out on the dark side, eh? Spooky.'

Leo paused as he was about to bite his chocolate. 'You do know there isn't really a dark side of the moon, don't you? We only ever see half of Luna because its rotational speed matches its orbit around Earth.' He showed Skater what he meant by slowly orbiting his chocolate bar around his Slake carton. 'But both faces still get just as much sun as each other.'

Skater gave him a pitying look. 'Hands up who's actually been to the *far* side of the moon?' She raised her arm. 'And hands up who's actually watched a sunrise over the lip of a crater while they were on the *far* side of the moon? Only me? Okay, so hands up who actually has a sense of humour and knows what a joke is?'

'Sorry. I just thought you might not know. Some people don't.'

'I don't see you putting your hand up.'

Leo raised his hand. 'There. Yes, I know what a joke is.'

'Are you sure?'

'Yes, I'm sure.'

'Good, because... Oh, look!' Skater pointed out through the window to where another ship had come into view. 'That's one of the Zodiacs. They're Chinese-built super-liners, massive great cruise ships, that go between Luna and Mars. There's four of them, but they're building a load more so they can run to the outer colonies as well. That one's—' She paused for a second, staring out at the great ship. 'The *Ox*. You can tell by the coloured strips along the outside. On the *Ox* they're yellow. See? People call them the Canton Cartwheels — because of their shape, obviously — and Dad says they're really, really, beyond supreme; not just for the passengers, but for the crew as well. Full gravity and everything. And fast. They can go dock to dock in under six weeks when Mars is close, like it is now.'

Leo knew most of this already. By chance he'd come across a docu-feed about the Zodiacs a few months back. It had seemed interesting, so he'd expanded it and watched the whole thing. In fact, he probably knew more about them than Skater did, but he wasn't about to point this out and risk another round of sarcastic comments. So he let her ramble on enthusiastically while he gazed at the magnificent spaceship, spinning gracefully off on its journey.

It might have been a hundred kilometres away, or it might have been several thousand. With nothing but empty blackness between the two ships, it was impossible to tell.

'...and the outer rim is so long they have this little shuttle that runs around it. And it's packed with shops, and eateries, and cinepods and stuff, and apparently some of the VIP cabins are like whole apartments. And the whole thing is powered by four huge Bannax-Tori ion-thrust engines that were designed especially for them.' She sighed. 'Sweet Sol, how I would so love to pilot one of those.'

They watched until the Ox was too small to be of any more interest, and Skater told Leo about her plan to become a pilot, working for one of the big companies until she could afford her own ship, then spend the rest of her life as a trader, travelling between the planets and stations until she'd visited every single inhabited place in the Solar System. And after that, she explained, she would turn around and do it all again.

They ate more hot dogs, drank more Slake, and continued gazing out of their window while Skater told Leo about all the places she'd been on Luna, what they were like, and which ones she would definitely be going back to this time. They talked a little bit about him as well, but after he'd explained that he loved computers, that his mother was an academic and that they would mostly be spending the next several weeks staring at screens full of numbers, Skater lost interest and went back to telling him about camping in the regolith desert.

Eventually their conversation was brought to an end by an announcement requesting that everyone return to their seats as the ship was about to commence deceleration procedures. Reluctantly Leo abandoned the window, still without having seen anything of their destination, and followed Skater back through the ship.

'Never mind,' she called across, as Leo strapped himself back down beside his grumpy history teacher look-alike. 'Watching out the window is nothing compared to actually putting your feet on the surface. I guarantee that even if you're only coming up here to work, it's going to be beyond ultimate.'

'I know,' Leo agreed. 'This is definitely going to be the best trip ever.'

2
AN UNEXPECTED MEETING

'**LOOK, THERE'S MY DAD!**' Skater called out, as soon as the doors into the arrivals hall hissed open. She pointed towards the large collection of waiting people and began to wave furiously. A tall, fair-haired man waved back just as enthusiastically. He looked so like Skater he couldn't possibly have been anyone else's father.

Skater turned to Pam, who was standing beside her two charges with the same fixed smile she'd had on her face, as far as Leo could tell, for the entire eight-hour journey. 'There's my dad,' Skater repeated. 'Okay, seeya!' And without waiting for a response, she launched herself across the hall. She bounced once, halfway across, and was enveloped by the open arms waiting for her before she'd even hit the floor for a second time. Leo was impressed. Pam simply shook her head.

'That girl. Honestly,' she muttered. And then, a little louder, 'Now then, Leo. What about you? Any sign of your mum anywhere?'

The hall was busy, but a quick scan confirmed Leo's suspicion that his mother was not among the scores of people milling around. She was late. And honestly, he wasn't surprised. She was the typical absent-minded professor – a genius in her own field, but little more than useless in the real world. She was always forgetting appointments, birthdays, the names of people she'd been introduced to several times. Now it looked like she'd also forgotten what time his shuttle was due in.

'She'll be late,' Leo said, matter-of-factly. 'Unless she's completely forgotten that today's the day of course. In which case, she'll be really, really late.'

'Oh, I doubt that,' Pam said, searching around for anyone who looked like they were about to come and take Leo off her hands. 'I'm sure she must be here somewhere. Can't you Tracelink her?'

'She doesn't wear one.'

'She...' The smile was slipping. 'Oh. Well, then we shall have to do it the old-fashioned way. Eyes peeled.'

Leo gave a sigh and began a more detailed examination of the arrivals hall. It was long and wide, but nothing like the glass and steel domes of the spaceport back in London that had risen for thirty storeys into the sky. Here, the roof was no more than fifteen metres above him, and even though the entire thing was covered with huge banks of natural daylight glow-lights, Leo was still very much aware that he was deep underground, with thousands of tonnes of lunar rock pressing down on him.

The place was filled with the usual shops and food stalls. Some of the names were different, but they looked the same as the ones back on Earth, with their glowing signs and adver-teaser screens, and the annoying jumbled drone of their competing welcome call-outs. And as far as he could see, his mother wasn't in any of them. He checked again, to be sure, and then he checked once more, because he couldn't think of anything else to do, and then he decided to check his phone, in the unlikely event that she'd actually thought to leave him a message.

He slipped the device into his ear and brought the screen round in front of his right eye. 'Messages,' he said. 'Mum.' A list of dates appeared on the tiny screen, the most recent being May 28 – just over six weeks ago. He closed the screen and tucked the phone back into his pocket.

'...somewhere...somewhere,' Pam was muttering, as she continued to search the room. 'Ah-ha!' she exclaimed after a moment. 'Here we go. This must be for us.'

Two men were heading towards them. The first was dressed in the same purple uniform as Pam and the two clearly knew each other.

'Evening, Pam,' he said with a quick, nervous smile. 'I take it this is young Mister Fischer?'

'It is indeed,' Pam replied. 'But we were expecting his mother to be collecting him, not...' She glanced down at her wrist screen. 'I don't seem to have any other contact listed, Mr, uh, Mr...'

The second man ignored her and held out his hand for Leo. He was small, a little shorter than Leo, with a stocky build and a strong, confident handshake. His dark hair was so short it was only just longer than the stubble covering his chin and this, together with his worn and creased jacket, gave Leo the impression he'd just woken up from a long sleep.

'Leonard Fischer?' he asked.

Suddenly Leo was nervous. Nobody called him Leonard unless it was for something really important. Or if he was in trouble. 'Yes,' he replied. 'But everyone calls me Leo.'

'Leo. Of course.' The man nodded, making a mental note. 'My name's Aitchison. We need to talk.'

'But—' Pam began. The man cut her off.

'Thank you…Pam, isn't it? I'll call you if I need anything else.'

'But—' Pam tried again. This time the uniformed man took her arm and gently steered her away. 'It's fine, Pam. It's all been arranged. Come on, I'll fill you in.'

Now Leo was really starting to get worried.

'Right,' the man called Aitchison said. 'Why don't we find somewhere to sit?' He set off towards the nearest place with free tables, making no effort to help with the two large bags Leo had brought with him. They weren't heavy – the low gravity saw to that – but they were awkward, and Leo lost his balance and stumbled twice before making it to where Aitchison was waiting for him.

'Did my mum send you?' he asked as he settled himself into the chair.

'Not exactly, no.'

'You don't work with her?'

'No.'

'So you're not here to take me out to Reynes?'

'You know, usually I'm the one who gets to ask the questions.' He gave Leo a small, humourless smile. 'But no, I'm not here to take you out to Reynes.'

'So who are you?'

'I told you. My name's Aitchison. I'm…' He paused, searching for the right word, '…a policeman, if you like.'

'A policeman?' Leo could feel his heart pounding in his chest. His mouth had gone dry. 'Is this something to do with my mum? Something's happened to her, hasn't it? That's why she's not here.'

'Well.' Aitchison sat back in his chair. 'She's not dead, if that's what's worrying you.'

Yes, that was exactly what was worrying him, and hearing the words gave him a huge sense of relief. Without realising it he'd been clenching his fists, and now he relaxed, wiping his palms down his trouser legs.

'Or injured, in fact,' Aitchison continued. 'As far as we can tell.'

'As far as you can tell? What does that mean?'

'It means exactly that. We don't know for sure.'

'I don't understand.'

'Your mother's gone missing, Leo.'

'Missing?' He didn't understand. But before he could ask Aitchison to explain, someone behind him slapped their hands down onto his shoulders and the shock sent him shooting out of his seat with a yelp.

'Gotcha!' Skater said, triumphantly.

'Holy crap!' Leo cursed, as he picked himself up off the floor. 'You nearly gave me a heart attack.'

'You'll get over it. Anyway,' Skater continued, pulling her father forward by the arm. 'This is my dad. He didn't believe me when I said I'd actually made friends with somebody on the shuttle, so I told him he had to come over and say hi, to prove you were really real. Also, I thought we could make plans to meet up – you know, once you're back in Atlantis after doing all your work stuff. But maybe you need to check that with your mum first? Where is your mum, anyway?'

'She's. . .' he began, looking across at Aitchison expectantly. But the man said nothing. 'Not here yet,' Leo finished, weakly.

'Well, whatever. Dad, this is Leo. Leo, this is my dad.'

Skater's father stepped forward, gave Leo a broad smile and held out his hand. 'Hi, Leo. Pete Monroe. Nice to meet you. I'm glad you and Skater got to chat on the flight up. As far as I can tell, she usually spends her time picking fights with the cabin crew.' He turned to Aitchison, offering the man his hand and the same warm smile. 'Pete Monroe. And you are?'

'Having a private conversation,' Aitchison replied, folding his arms and ignoring the outstretched hand. For a few seconds there was an awkward silence as the men stared at each other, but finally Pete drew back his hand and turned back to Leo.

'Everything okay here, Leo?'

'Everything's fine,' Aitchison said.

'Leo?'

'Um, yeah,' Leo replied. 'It's okay. Really.'

Pete looked around the arrivals hall and nodded towards a juice bar a few shops away. 'Skater and I are going to sit and get something to drink. Why don't you come over and join us, when you've finished up here?' He looked back at Aitchison. 'Perhaps we can wait for your mum together.'

'Okay,' Leo said doubtfully, unsure if Aitchison would let him go or not.

'Friends of yours?' Aitchison asked, once Pete and Skater had moved off. He reached into his jacket, brought out a pocket slate, and began to tap on the tiny screen.

'Not exactly,' Leo replied. 'I met Skater on the flight. We talked a lot, but I don't really know her that well or anything. But listen, tell me what's happened with my mum. You said she's gone missing?'

'Interesting,' Aitchison said, not to Leo, but in response to what he was reading. He tapped some more. 'When did you last speak to your mother?'

'Actually talk to her? About two months ago, just before she came up here. We went through the arrangements for my trip and talked a bit about the work I'd be doing. That sort of thing. Then she left me a message, about two weeks after that, but it was just to let me know she'd spoken to the school and arranged for them to get me to the spaceport and stuff.'

Aitchison looked up briefly. 'School?'

'I go to boarding school.'

'I know. And does your school usually arrange your holidays for you?'

'Well, no. But this was a special case, because Mum was already up here and there was no one else who could collect me at the end of term.' Leo paused. 'But it's not exactly the first time she hasn't been there to pick me up,' he added.

'And you didn't try to contact her?'

'She was going to be out in the field, so she told me not to bother her unless it was an absolute emergency.'

'So no contact at all for six weeks? No messages? No failed calls? Nothing?'

'No, nothing.'

'Hmm, pity.' Aitchison drummed his fingers on the table. 'Still, it was a bit of a long shot anyway. Ah well.'

'So where is she?' Leo asked.

'I told you. I don't know.'

'Okay, so what's happened to her then?'

'I don't know that either.'

'So what do you know?' Leo snapped. He stood up, wobbled slightly and gripped the sides of the table for support. 'Are you going to tell me, or are you just going to sit there and ask me a whole load more stupid questions? Because if you don't know anything, then I'm going to go and find someone who does.'

'Sit down,' Aitchison said, calmly. 'You're making a scene, and that isn't helping either of us.' Leo remained standing. 'Leo, sit down.'

'Goodbye,' Leo said, and bent down to collect his bags.

'Fine,' Aitchison said with a sigh. 'Sit down, and I'll tell you everything I do know about your mother's disappearance.'

'Everything?'

'Promise.'

Leo sat down. He was shaking so badly he probably wouldn't have been able to walk away without falling over anyway. 'Please,' he said, no longer angry, just desperate. 'What's going on?'

'It was three weeks ago,' Aitchison began. 'Out at the camp your mother and her team had set up in the Korolev Highlands. Two of the team had taken the camp's hopper back to Reynes for supplies. They were away for a few hours, and when they returned, the rest of the team – your mother and two others – were gone.'

'Gone? Gone where?'

'Well, one of the vehicles was also missing, so at first it was assumed that your mother had taken the others off exploring somewhere, even though it was against protocol to leave the camp empty. But after twelve hours with no contact they suspected something was wrong and called it in as a missing persons alert.'

'Twelve hours? They couldn't even contact them by radio and they still waited twelve hours?'

Aitchison shrugged. 'Who knows? Anyway, the truck wasn't that hard to find. It was only a few kilometres from the site and the transponder was still running so they were able to get someone down to it straight away.'

'And?'

'Empty. Abandoned.'

'But there were other tracks?'

'Very good,' Aitchison said, with a nod. 'Yes, there were tracks. Unfortunately, a lot of them were blown away by the engine blasts from something taking off nearby, but we've analysed everything we could find and the results suggest that four people – probably men – flew in by shuttle, walked from the landing site to the camp and left using the truck, along with the three missing members of the science team. They all seem to have transferred onto a shuttle. And that, I'm afraid, is all I can tell you. Except that there were no signs of a struggle at the camp. No damage was done, and no shots appear to have been fired.'

'What about the shuttle?'

'Nothing. It wasn't logged. None of the tracking stations picked it up, either coming in or going out, and no one can give us any sort of visual ID because no one seems to have seen it. It's a dead end, I'm afraid.'

'Well what about…I don't know…radar logs? Or what about the prints its landing gear left in the dust? Can't you scan those and find out what sort of a shuttle it was – track it that way?'

'I'm very good at my job, Leo. If I tell you there's no way we can track the shuttle, believe me, I know what I'm talking about.'

'But…' But what? Leo didn't know what else to say. The man would have an answer to every suggestion he made, every idea he came up with, and to be honest, he was pretty much out of ideas anyway. If the man said he was doing everything possible, then Leo had no real option except to believe him. 'So what happens now?' he asked.

'Now?' Aitchison replied. 'We keep looking.'

'I mean about me. What am I supposed to do?'

'Yes,' Aitchison said to himself. 'What indeed?' He had gone back to reading his slate and spoke without looking up. 'You have an uncle, I believe.'

'Yes. In New Zealand.'

'Well, that's always an option.'

'Not a very good one,' Leo muttered.

'Why? You don't get along?'

'It's not that. It's just that I was hoping I could stay up here on Luna. I want to help. And I want to be here when we find Mum as well. My return flight's not for four weeks. Can't I stay here till then? Help with your investigation?'

'Where would you stay? Who would look after you? Taking the shuttle on your own is one thing, but you can't spend the next month living in Atlantis on your own.'

'Why not? I've done it before, back in Cambridge, when Mum's been off on assignment somewhere.'

Aitchison looked up from his slate and stared at Leo in surprise. 'Have you?' he asked. 'And did you know that's against the law?'

'It is?'

'Yes. Very much so.'

'Oh.' Leo looked down, remembering all those times he'd been left on his own over the past couple of years. At some point in almost every holiday, his mother would head off somewhere for work, usually with no more than a few days' notice, and expect him to look after himself until she returned. Sometimes it was no more than an overnight stay for a conference, or a few days working at some other university, but occasionally it was for much longer, like the time she'd spent two weeks in Antarctica, leaving him to enjoy Easter on his own. She had never actually left him alone for as long as a month – that two weeks had been the longest – but he wasn't about to admit that to Aitchison.

'However,' Aitchison said, interrupting his thoughts. 'I'd like to keep you around for a few days anyway, in case there's anything else I need to discuss. Let me give it some thought while you wander over and enjoy that juice your new friends promised you. I'll join you in a while.'

Leo looked over to Skater and Pete. Skater waved.

'What should I say to them?' Leo asked. 'About my mum and everything?'

'Whatever you like. But the truth would probably be best.' He gave Leo his humourless smile. 'And who knows? Perhaps they might even be able to help.'

3

THE OLD MAN

MR ARCHER PAUSED in front of the imposing doors and attempted to smooth down his suit jacket. It was expensive, tailored to fit the muscled bulk of his chest, but sometimes it had a tendency to ride up if he chose, as he had today, to carry more than one concealed sidearm beneath it. It was a small detail, but exactly the kind of thing the Old Man would notice. When he was satisfied with his efforts he picked up the slate from the table beside him, silently opened one of the doors and entered.

Carlton Whittaker, the old man in question, was seated behind an ornate wooden desk that occupied the centre of the room. But his chair was swivelled away from the doors to face a picture window that ran the full width of the end wall. Beyond the window, the sun was beginning to set behind the distant hills and shadows were creeping over the lake beneath them. On the near shore, a silver birch tree caught the fading sunlight – the perfect counterpoint to the crystal blue of the water.

Mr Archer walked to the desk, scanning the room on the way. It was the first thing he did whenever he entered any room and it was second nature now. Even here, where he knew there could be no hidden dangers, he still went through the motions: identify potential threats; locate all entrance points; take note of anything unusual or out of place. He stopped at the desk and made no further sound. The Old Man knew he was there. He would respond when he was ready.

'Beautiful, isn't it?' Whittaker said at last. It wasn't really a question, and Mr Archer knew better than to answer. 'All those different, subtle shades of blue in the sky and the water. That's what I miss the most. I couldn't give a damn about all their fresh air and green spaces. But that blue, that's really something.' He spun his chair round, tapped a small panel on the desk, and the scene dissolved, revealing instead a silver skyline of spires and domes. Beyond them, the Martian sky sat dull and yellow and lifeless. 'Sadly though, I suspect it's now going to be some time before I get to experience them firsthand, eh, Mr Archer?'

'Let us hope not, sir,' Mr Archer replied in his low, rasping voice.

'Anyway,' Whittaker said, clapping his hands as if to dismiss his daydreams. 'To business. How was your flight?'

'Fast.'

'And our new guests?'

'Randhawa's people can take care of them until I return.'

'Good. The sooner we can get them started, the better.'

'But this is not why I'm here.'

'You have other news?'

'We have found our missing pilot.' He handed the slate across to Whittaker who scanned the screen.

'So, the cunning Captain Duggan has finally surfaced. And on Luna, of all places. It's a pity you didn't know about this a few weeks ago, eh? You could have killed two birds with one stone, so to speak.'

'Yes.'

'And what exactly is he doing on Luna?'

'Hiding out. Waiting for safe passage back to Earth, most likely.'

'And he hasn't made any attempt to contact the authorities? Or the media?'

Mr Archer shook his head. 'It's possible, but unlikely. There have been no reports.'

'No? Well that's something, at least. I imagine he's going to be a lot more careful choosing someone to approach now, what with his last attempt having been so unsuccessful. And that's assuming he still has his precious data files, of course. There's always the chance he's gone and lost them and now doesn't have anything to back up his far-fetched theories. How convenient that would be.'

'He is still a threat, even without the files.'

'Oh, I think you overestimate him, Mr Archer.' Whittaker's smile dropped, and a menacing tone crept into his voice. 'Without those files he's nothing but a crazy old man, with a bunch of crazy ideas about some huge conspiracy he doesn't even understand. No one in their right mind is going to believe a single word he has to say, about this, or about anything else for that matter. But the files...' He slammed his palm on the desk. 'I want those data files, Mr Archer.'

'Then I will get them for you.'

'You have people you can trust?'

'Local contacts,' Mr Archer said with a faint sneer. 'I suppose they could do the job, but I would be happier to go myself. It would be less...messy.'

'No. Absolutely not. You've only just got back, and I need you here on Mars. With the election so close, I'm spending more and more time on the campaign trail, and the minute I step out of the building, I'm swarmed by news drones recording my every move. There's absolutely no chance I'll get any time to myself for a while so I'll need you to supervise things at the Facility and make sure everything is running to schedule. Besides, I'm impatient. Duggan is a loose end and I want him dealt with as soon as possible.'

'Permanently?'

'Not until we have the data files. After that, do what you think is best.'

Mr Archer nodded. He already knew what was best.

'Good. Well, I'm glad to see things are progressing,' Whittaker announced, in a businesslike manner that told Mr Archer the meeting had come to an end. 'Keep me informed.' He handed back the slate and Mr Archer rose and left without another word. 'Oh, one more thing I forgot to mention,' Whittaker called out. Mr Archer paused in the doorway. 'You know we're handing over the *Arcadian* to the Montgomerie Museum later this week?'

'I do.'

'Well, what do you think about this? They've invited me to come along and formally open the exhibition, maybe give a little speech.'

'How appropriate. What will you say?'

'Oh, I don't know,' Whittaker said, with a dismissive wave of his hand. 'I'll make something up. I'm quite good at that.'

Mr Archer stretched his twisted mouth into a smile. 'Yes, sir. You are indeed.'

4

A MISSING MOTHER

'**KIDNAPPED!**' **SKATER SHOUTED.** Several people nearby turned to look at her.

'Shhh!' Leo said, glancing across nervously to where Aitchison was sitting, making a phone call but still glaring across at them with his free eye. 'Try not telling the whole neighbourhood.'

'What do you mean, kidnapped?' she asked, more quietly this time.

'That's what he told me. She was out at the field site, some guys turned up and took everyone who was there, piled them into a shuttle and disappeared.'

'Who?' Skater asked. 'Who just turned up and took everyone?'

'I don't know. Four men. That's all he said. They took everyone from the base and left by shuttle.'

'When was this?' Pete asked.

'Three weeks ago.'

'Three weeks?' he said, stunned. 'I thought you were going to say three days. Why are you only finding out about this now? Why didn't anyone contact you back on Earth?'

'I...don't know,' Leo said, awkwardly. 'I didn't think to ask.'

'But how the hell could you not know something was wrong anyway?' Skater asked. 'Don't you, like, talk to her much? Didn't you notice she'd stopped casting?'

'She doesn't broadcast much, even at the best of times, and I was kind of assuming she'd be going dark while she was up here anyway.'

'And I just bet she doesn't wear a tracer either, does she?'

'Nope.'

'That figures.'

'Listen, Leo,' Pete said, interrupting Skater. 'Are you okay? I mean, you seem pretty calm for someone who's just been told his mother's been kidnapped. I'm worried you might be in shock.'

'I'm fine,' Leo replied. He was starting to get embarrassed and took a long suck on his juice pod to cover the awkward silence that had suddenly swallowed up the conversation. Pete was giving him *the look*. It was the one people always gave when they were concerned about him, when they were worried he was keeping everything bottled up and just needed a sympathetic ear, or a shoulder to cry on, or whatever. Then it would all come pouring out and he'd feel much better afterwards, once he'd 'got in touch with his deeper, emotional self'. That's what the school counsellors had said, in the psychological profile that made up part of his academic record and which he'd hacked into last year, partly out of curiosity, but mostly because the system security was so lax it would have been a crime not to.

'Really, I'm fine,' he repeated, when it became clear they were waiting for him to say something. 'This is just the way I deal with things. I love my mum, and I really am worried sick about what's happened to her and everything. And maybe you're right; maybe I am in shock and maybe later it'll hit me. But honestly, this is how I always deal with, you know, emotional stuff. It still happens, it just happens on the inside.' He gave them a smile. 'See?'

Skater was staring at him as if he had two heads. Obviously she didn't get it at all, which wasn't exactly a surprise, Leo thought. But it was clear Pete understood. 'Fair enough,' he said, and didn't follow it up with any sentence that began with the words, *but if you ever need...* And Leo decided there and then that he really liked him.

'But what I don't get,' Skater said, 'apart from the whole, keeping it all inside deal, is why anyone would want to kidnap your mum in the first place. I mean, it's not exactly like she's A-grade ransom material, is she?'

'No. She's an academic. I mean, she's fairly high up in her field and all that, but that doesn't make her rich or famous.'

'What exactly is it she does, Leo?' Pete asked.

'She's a techno-archaeologist.'

'Great,' Skater said. 'So what exactly is it she does?'

'It's the same as normal archaeology, but instead of digging up old pots and bones and stuff, she retrieves data from obsolete technology. So, say, for example, that someone discovers some old computer system somewhere, and they want to find out how it works, or what information is stored on it. Most of the time, you can't just switch it on, because the system will be too badly damaged, so you have to take the whole thing apart, clean it up, replace anything you can't repair and put it all back together again. And that's just to get it working. Once it's up and running, you have to find some way of accessing the data, and that can involve anything from running it through a series of translation programs all the way up to writing a whole new operating system for it.'

'Ancient computers?' Skater asked. 'So, you're telling me that's how they actually built the pyramids?'

'I didn't mean that ancient,' Leo replied, and then realised from the look she was giving him that she'd meant it as a joke. 'Just, you know, really old,' he finished, weakly.

'And that's what she was doing up here?' Pete asked. 'Searching for old technology?'

'Not really, no. This one is a basic data retrieval job on an old Russian satellite that crashed about fifty years ago. They've known about it all the time, but for some reason no one's ever bothered to do anything about it till now. But it's not secret or anything. To be honest, I think the only reason she agreed to work on the project was because it included a free trip to Luna. It's pretty straightforward work as far as I can tell.'

'Maybe she found something else out there?' Skater offered. 'Something that really was secret.'

'Yeah, maybe. I don't know.'

'Well, here's your chance to find out,' Pete said. 'Your mysterious friend has finally decided to come and join us, so maybe he can tell us what's really going on.'

Aitchison came across, sat down in the last free seat at the table and gave them a broad smile. 'Aitchison,' he said. 'Local law enforcement.'

'You're not a policeman,' Pete replied. 'I've dealt with the Police Authority up here and I know exactly what they're like. And they're not like you.'

'Well, perhaps not so much of the local then, but I am law enforcement.'

'Terran, or Inter-P?'

'Does it matter?'

'I suppose not. You're all the same really.'

'And you would know, wouldn't you, Commander?'

For an instant Pete looked startled, then he gave a shrug and slowly shook his head. 'If you've read the file, you'll know I'm retired. I work for MarsMine now.'

'Yes, you do. And I'm sure flying shuttles around Luna is every bit as exciting as patrolling the System as a Sentinel, huh? Jupiter Squadron, wasn't it? The best of the best?'

Pete looked over at Skater. 'I made my choice. I don't regret it.'

'Of course not. Whether it's a daughter you only get to see twice a year, or a mother who's suddenly gone missing, we all know how important family is, don't we?'

'Do you know why anyone would want to kidnap her?' Leo asked, feeling that he should be taking part in the conversation.

'I never said she'd been kidnapped.'

'But that's what you think,' Pete said. 'You wouldn't be here if this was a simple missing person case.'

'What I said was that four men arrived at the camp, didn't stay long, then left with the three scientists.'

'Sounds like a kidnapping to me,' Skater said.

'Well,' Aitchison replied. 'I think for the moment we have to assume you're right. The other possible scenarios are somewhat unlikely.'

'So why her?' Leo asked again.

'I was rather hoping you could tell me. I gather you know more about her work than just about anyone, and I really don't understand all the datapedia stuff I've been wading my way through over the past week. Maybe you could explain it to me, and maybe together we could look back over some of her recent projects – see if there's anything there that might help.'

'Okay. But—'

'I know. It'll mean you having to stay up here for a while. But actually, I've decided that's a good idea anyway. It means I've got you on call in case I need to know anything, and it gives you a little bit of time to do some sightseeing while you're here.'

'Sightseeing?' Pete asked, incredulously. 'His mother's been kidnapped.'

'And we're doing everything we can to find her. But even if Leo is going to be helping us, there'll be entire days when there's nothing for him to do. Are you going to insist he spends his time stuck in some dreary hostel and not get to see anything of Atlantis, on his first ever trip to Luna, just because his mother's missing?'

'You know that's not what I meant. If Leo wants to make the best of the situation and try to see something of Atlantis while he's here, I'm fine with that.'

'Good,' Aitchison said. 'I was hoping you'd say that, because I don't actually have a dreary hostel booked for him and I was wondering if you wouldn't mind looking after him for a while.'

'What?' Pete asked.

'Yes!' Skater shouted at the same time.

Pete looked at her, more surprised than angry, and shook his head. 'We can't.'

'Yes we can. I'll do it. I'll be like his tour guide, except I'll take him to all the really buzz places, not the boring tourist stuff. Or I could take him to those as well. You wouldn't even have to come with us, unless you wanted to, because I know my way around. And you're always saying it's a shame that whenever I come up to Luna I spend all my time with you and never get to hang with anyone my own age – which is completely dumb, by the way. I love just hanging with you. But anyway, now I have got someone my own age to hang with and it'll be wilder than wild.' She paused and calmed down slightly. 'And, you know, it'll help him take his mind off the other stuff.'

Pete took one of her hands in his own, gave it a gentle squeeze and turned to Aitchison. 'We can't.'

'Actually, you can,' Aitchison replied. 'It's just for a few days while I get things sorted out. You can hand him back before you leave.'

'Leave?' Skater asked. 'What do you mean, leave? Are we leaving? Where are we going?'

'Sorry,' Pete said, turning back to her. 'I was going to tell you over dinner.'

'Tell me what?'

'It's just something I had planned for the holidays. We'll talk about it later.'

'Mars. Please tell me you're booked to do a Mars run and you're taking me with you?'

'Not exactly, no.'

'Then where?'

'Later.'

'Come on,' she pleaded, pointing at Aitchison. 'He obviously knows about it already. How come he gets to know and I don't?'

'Anyway,' Pete said, and waited for Skater to finally stop talking. 'It's not really my decision to make. It's up to Leo, isn't it?'

'True,' Aitchison said. 'So let's ask him. Leo, do you want to spend the next few days stuck in some miserable little hostel on your own, or do you want to have a few days enjoying the sights and sounds of Atlantis with someone your own age, and her very sensible and responsible father?'

'I…' Leo didn't know what to say. Everything seemed to be happening very fast. People were making decisions for him, telling him how he should feel and what he should do, and it felt like he wasn't really part of the conversation at all. Obviously Aitchison wanted him to go with the others — that's why he'd made the hostel option sound so terrible — and obviously Skater wanted him to as well. And from the sound of it, Pete would agree if he said that was what he wanted.

Of course it was what he wanted; for the company, if nothing else. Normally he was perfectly happy on his own and never went out of his way to make new friends, but even he could see that, right now, being on his own was the worst thing he could possibly be. He needed to be distracted. And yes, maybe even to enjoy himself a little bit.

'I would like to go with you,' he said to Pete. 'If you really don't mind.'

'Of course not. I'd be happy to help out.'

'Yes!' shouted Skater, slapping the table with delight and knocking her drink over the side in the process. She stuck out her foot, flicked the falling carton with the toe of her boot and caught it as it flew back up past the table. 'I love low g.' She turned to Leo. 'It's almost as good as no g, and you had a lot of fun with that, didn't you? But you do have to be able to walk properly, otherwise getting around is going to be a complete mare, so first things first, we need to get you some skuff boots.'

'Skuff boots?'

She lifted up a leg, planted her boot on the table and showed Leo the sole. 'Skuff boots. They don't have to be boots, of course, but that's just what everyone calls them. All the floors up here are made out of this stuff called Resistolene – '

'Yeah, I know,' Leo tried, but Skater carried on anyway.

'And skuff boots have this stuff on the bottom that reacts with Resistolene and makes them more grippy. Walking properly still takes a bit of getting used to, but you won't be falling over every few steps like you are now. Actually, I'm surprised no one told you to get some back on Earth,. They're, like, must-haves for up here.'

Leo lifted up one of his own shoes to display the distinctive pattern of grey microfibres along the sole. 'I do have some. I just didn't know they were called skuff boots.'

'What? You're already wearing skuffs and you still walk like that? We have so got to get you grav-trained, Earth boy.'

While Leo and Skater compared shoes, Pete gave Aitchison their contact details, even though Aitchison didn't seem to need them. 'Right,' he announced, once they had finished. 'Skater, get your foot off the table. Leo, you're with us now. And if we're all ready, I suggest we head to the hotel and get ourselves sorted out there, then head out somewhere for dinner.'

As Leo was collecting his bags, Aitchison leant over the table and handed him a plastic call card. It was plain white, with the single word, *Aitchison*, printed in small, raised letters. 'Here,' he said. 'Keep it safe. But feel free to use it as often as you want. It will call through to me directly.'

Leo tucked the card into one of the arm pockets on his jacket. 'And you'll let me know the minute you find anything out?'

'Of course.'

'Mr Aitchison.' Leo paused, feeling foolish, but knowing he had to ask. 'This is all real, isn't it? I mean, my mum really has been kidnapped. It's not just some big joke, or misunderstanding or something?'

'No. I'm afraid it's all very real.'

'But you are trying to get her back?'

'Leo. I promise you, right now finding your mother is my number one priority.'

'Getting her back, you mean. Not just finding her, but rescuing her as well?'

'Of course,' Aitchison said, and gave Leo a reassuring smile.

But for some reason, Leo didn't feel at all reassured.

5

A LUCKY ESCAPE

AS SOON AS HE WAS round the next corner, Jack Duggan stopped running. He collapsed against the wall, gasping for breath and clutching his chest to ease the burning in his lungs. The air felt hot and dry – a mixture designed for tourists and casual shoppers, not for someone running for his life – and almost at once he began to feel dizzy.

'Hey, bud. You okay there?'

Jack lurched on, pushing past the startled man without looking at him. 'Great,' he muttered between gasps. 'Never better.' He wiped the back of his hand across his forehead to stop the sweat running into his eyes and cast a quick look back. Was he safe? Had he lost them? Unlikely. But making it into the Zhai Street lift just as the doors were closing had probably given him a couple of minutes and he was determined to put them to good use.

But no more running. For a start his old body wasn't up to it

— he already felt as if his knees would give way at the sight of a seat — but it was also attracting too much attention. People were staring. They would remember him, and what he needed more than anything was to blend in, to get lost in the crowds, to disappear.

A little further along the streetway another of the huge lifts was just arriving. Jack pushed his way into the small crowd of people waiting to embark, but at the last minute he squeezed out on the far side and made his way quickly down the passageway along the side of the giant machine. It brought him to a narrow staircase, and because the lift was going down, he went up.

He'd spotted the two men straight away, loitering outside the entrance to the run down hab-block he'd called home for the past couple of weeks. They were dressed as maintenance workers, but the disguise was so bad Jack had wondered why they'd bothered. Their orange work suits had been ill-fitting and much too clean. They hadn't brought any tools or equipment with them. And they'd spent way too much time watching the streetway, paying no attention to the building behind them.

He should have turned around there and then, abandoned his few remaining possessions and found somewhere else to hide out while he tried to find a way off this miserable rock and back to the relative safety of Earth. But there had still been one or two items he could use — the blank credit chips, a little food, a change of clothes — and he'd been certain he could be in and out without those two jokers spotting him.

There was a second entrance at the back of the building, and Jack had been relieved to find it had been left unguarded. Ironically, the sign on the tiny doorway read *Maintenance Access*, and one of the first things he had done after moving in was to make sure the lock was disarmed in case he ever had to make a quick getaway. A stairway just beyond led all the way down through the ten floors of the building and Jack had made it down, collected everything he needed and been out of the room in less than five minutes.

But that was when it had all started to go wrong.

'Hey, you!' someone had shouted from the far end of the corridor. 'Stop!' Jack had kept walking but had cast a glance over his shoulder and sure enough, there'd been two more of the orange-suited thugs coming towards him.

'Stop!' the man bellowed again, breaking into a run when it became clear his prey had no intention of obeying. But the building was so old that the floors had never been treated with Resistoline and almost immediately he'd stumbled and the man behind had crashed into him, sending them both sprawling. That was when the man had drawn his pistol and fired several shots.

It was a laser weapon, and Jack had felt the heat of the first two shots as they fizzed past his head. But the third had torn through the bag slung over his shoulder and burnt its way across the top of his left arm. The fourth hit a wall light that had exploded in a shower of sparks, but by then Jack was through the fire door and bounding up the stairway towards the exit.

He was starting to feel dizzy. The pounding in his chest wouldn't stop, and his left arm was throbbing like crazy. Was it the wound, or a heart attack? Either way, staggering along like this was doing him no good. There were fewer people up here, but he was still drawing too much attention, and his pursuers could reappear at any minute. If they did, it was all over. There was no way he could outrun anything right now.

He turned, and turned, always picking the narrowest, emptiest walkways and no longer caring which direction he was walking in. Finally, in a small passageway, poorly lit and filled with the stench of refuse pods long overdue for collection, his legs gave way and he collapsed, dragging himself behind one of the pods so he would be hidden from view.

The dizziness passed, and the pounding settled down to a dull thudding. Not a heart attack then, he thought, relieved, which meant the pain in his arm had to be from the laser burn. Carefully he peeled back the singed material around the wound and held his arm up to the dim light. A bright pink groove had been burned into the flesh below the shoulder and the skin was smooth and tight from the heat. A quick dose of derma spray would have repaired the worst of it and dealt with the pain. But that was too bad. There was no way he was going to risk a trip to a med-clinic. That would be the first place they'd go looking.

So they'd caught up with him again. Well, so much for thinking he'd be safe once he was off Mars. Clearly they weren't going to let this one go — whoever *they* were. He still didn't know for sure. Someone at the company was involved — they had to be, because they were the only ones who'd had access to his original report. But who else? The military? The Martian government? Even he thought that sounded a little paranoid. But with a gang of hired killers hot on his trail, he was allowed to feel a little paranoid.

He patted his side, feeling for the data pin tucked into the lining of his jacket. Maybe he didn't know who *they* were, but he knew exactly what they were looking for, and he was damned if he was going to let them get their filthy hands on it. But how could he stop them? He wasn't even a real person any more. They'd taken his job, sealed his credit account, wiped his identity. If he tried going to the authorities now, the first thing they'd do would be arrest him. But he couldn't keep running either. He'd been lucky this time — if you could call ending up in a garbage dump with a burnt shoulder lucky — but sooner or later his luck would run out. He needed help, and he needed it fast. But who was there to help him? Who?

6

ATLANTIS

LEO HAD TO ADMIT that the city of Atlantis was an impressive feat of structural engineering. It was a huge, bustling capital city, home to well over half a million people. Some of it was over two hundred years old. And the whole thing had been built entirely underground. On the moon.

But it was still just a city: noisy, bustling, crowded and dirty, with little going for it except a few vaguely interesting tourist spots and a couple of second-rate museums, no matter what his over-enthusiastic tour guide might say to try to convince him otherwise. And it wasn't just that it was old; it was old-fashioned. So many of the buildings were plain, rectangular boxes, squashed into awkward rows along the sides of streetways that seemed too narrow for them. It made the place feel oppressive in a way that no amount of fancy lighting and giant landscape screens could disguise, and it made Leo feel like he needed to find a window to open and let in some fresh air.

Old-fashioned, and outdated. The shuttle pods were maglev-powered and still ran along rails in the middle of the wider streetways, while building-sized elevators did the work of transporting people vertically. Here and there, Leo had even noticed actual static stairways. Skater argued that the place had soul, that it felt like a proper city where things were original and interesting, but to Leo it all felt quaint, as if the place was a historical theme-park, designed to show people what life had been like two hundred years ago. He would enjoy spending a few days here, but after that he would definitely be happy to get back to somewhere a bit more... contemporary.

'Hey, guess what?' Skater asked, interrupting his thoughts. She had a huge grin on her face and Leo sighed, knowing what was coming next. It wasn't the first time she'd asked the same question that morning, and the chances were it wouldn't be the last.

'Your dad's finally got sick of your non-stop talking and he's decided to sell you to a crazy old scrap miner for the price of a ticket back to Earth?'

Skater gave him a sharp dig in the side and glared at him. 'Guess properly.'

'Hmmm,' said Leo. 'Are you going somewhere, perhaps?'

The huge smile returned and Skater squealed with excitement. 'Yes! I'm going to Mars. Mars! On a Zodiac!' And she did the dance of joy again. It was a bobbing little dance that required a lot more balance and co-ordination than it appeared to, as Leo had discovered earlier when he'd been forced to join in. But only once. After that, they'd both agreed he could leave the dancing to her.

'It's going to be buzzing,' Skater continued. 'I mean, going to Mars is beyond unbelievable anyway, but going there on a Zodiac, that's like so beyond beyond, it's out the other side. And I am so going to talk Dad into getting us a total tour of the flight deck and the bridge as well.' She tilted her head to one side and stared right through Leo. 'It's a shame it's the *Dragon* though, and not the *Horse*. That's the newest one, and it's even bigger than the rest. And faster. But apparently it's being saved for the Europa run, and something tells me Dad would not be so wild up for a trip to Europa.'

Leo smiled. Even though he couldn't stop thinking about his mother and what might be happening to her, Skater made it difficult to stay gloomy for long. Which was a good thing. He'd decided the night before, when he couldn't sleep, that although he wasn't going to be able to stop himself from worrying, he could at least stop himself from moping and feeling sorry for himself. Moping wasn't going to help him find his mother, and that was exactly what he'd decided to do. He had just over a week with Skater and Pete before they were due to leave, and he was going to use the time to get to know Atlantis, learn what he could about how things worked on Luna and use all the processing power at his disposal to work out who might have taken her, why, and where they might have gone. Skater had said she would help, and right now she was doing exactly what Leo needed her to do – cheer him up, keep him busy, show him around Atlantis.

'You okay, Leo?'

'I'm fine. I was just, you know...'

'Yeah, I know.' She stopped smiling, looked serious for a moment and rested her hand against his arm. 'Sorry. It must be really annoying to have me going on and on about Mars and being so happy all the time. I know that's not what you want to be thinking about right now.'

'It's okay,' Leo said quickly. He felt embarrassed, but not enough to move his arm away. 'This is a sightseeing day, remember? You're supposed to be cheering me up, not feeling sorry for me.'

'Alright then, plans.'

'Plans?'

'Plans. We're not meeting up with Dad until dinnertime, so we have the whole day for exploring.' She held up her right hand, waving her first finger. 'Plus, I have a finger full of credit and I'm not afraid to use it. We are going to hit the shops.'

'And the museums.'

'Museum,' Skater corrected him, emphasising the singular. 'No more than one a day, that's the rule. And I am absolutely not going back to the Heritage Museum under any circumstances, no matter what you say. I'd rather chew my legs off.'

'What about the Museum of the Solar System then?'

'MOSS?' Skater shrugged. 'Meh.'

'Really? I thought it was supposed to be pretty good. That was one of the places Mum and I were going to visit.'

'It's okay for tourists. They've got a few old pods and rovers and stuff you can crawl around in, and the virtual travel dome is pass-grade, I suppose. But it's still a museum. Give me a trip round a proper, working shipyard any day. In fact, we could shuttle up to Port Vincent and have a look around there if you like. That's where they build a lot of the small freighters and non-military stuff. Dad knows loads of people up there and there's always someone he can find to give us a tour round the new builds.'

'Sounds great,' Leo said. 'Except that I'm not allowed to leave Atlantis, remember?'

'Oh, yeah. Well, that's too bad for you. Looks like it'll have to be MOSS then, and that's too bad for me. Come on, let's get it out of the way first.'

The museum trip was not a great success. They took one of the shuttle pods and it should only have been a ten-minute journey, but Skater insisted on getting out at almost every stop along the way to show Leo various things he might find interesting, and in the end it took them nearly two hours. To be fair, one or two of the places they stopped off at were actually quite interesting, and Leo had been particularly impressed with Armstrong Park. This was right in the centre of the old town and opened up over three levels, with the lowest covered in beautifully tended lawns of real grass. Statues and monuments to the pioneers of Lunar colonisation were dotted about, each floating in its own electro-mag stasis field, but for Leo, the most impressive thing about the park was the giant, slow-motion waterfall set against a bare basalt wall at one end. It was a masterpiece of technical engineering and Leo promised himself a second visit to examine it in detail, some other time. Possibly without Skater.

By the time they arrived at MOSS, Skater was already complaining about being hungry, and she continued to complain about being hungry for most of the following hour and a half, pointing out on several occasions that she would be happy to abandon the museum in favour of a nearby burger bar she knew as soon as he was done looking at old moon junk. Or possibly sooner.

Finally Leo had had enough. 'Look, this might be the only chance I'm ever going to get to see this stuff. Can't you keep your stomach under control for another hour or so?'

Skater put on a confused face. 'Stomach? Control? I don't get it?'

'Fine,' Leo said with a sigh. He knew when there was no point arguing, and with Skater, that seemed to be pretty much all the time. In fact, he hadn't been enjoying the museum anything like as much as he'd imagined he would. It was one of the places his mother had promised to take him, and it felt wrong to be going round without her. She knew so much about all this old technology, she would have made the trip so much more interesting than he'd managed on his own. So no, he thought. He didn't mind being dragged away before he'd seen everything. He'd come back sometime and do it properly, with his mother. Besides, he was hungry too.

'Wow, this is great,' he admitted fifteen minutes later as he took another bite of his burger. They were at a table nestled into the back of a small eatery called Big Joe's, an unassuming, poorly decorated food bar on one of the upper levels. The streetways were narrower here than in Central District, and most of the buildings seemed to be administration or manufacturing blocks. There were very few people – certainly no tourists – but Skater had insisted that Big Joe's was *the* place to eat.

'Dad brought me here the first time I ever came to Atlantis,' she explained. 'It's really popular with the dock workers, and a lot of the ship crews hang out between shifts.'

Leo looked around. Two tables away was a middle-aged man who might well have been a dock worker. He was grubby and unshaved, hunched over a carton of something he was obviously trying to make last for as long as possible, and he looked like he might even be trying to get some sleep. A few others were seated nearer the front of the eatery, alone or in twos, but from the look of their clothes they were most likely administration staff. There was no one who looked even vaguely like a shuttle pilot.

'Maybe the shuttle crews like to eat their lunch a bit later,' he said. 'Like at lunchtime?'

'It is lunchtime,' Skater protested. 'It must be, because they told me I was too late to get the breakfast. Anyway, if you're not hungry yet, don't eat.' She reached over and helped herself to one of his chips.

'I didn't say I wasn't hungry,' Leo replied, curling his arm around the top of his plate and sliding it towards him. 'And it's great. I love it.'

'That's because it's real fake meat, not that disgusting beetroot-veg-protein muck you get in Lunaburger's.'

'Actually, that's where I thought we were going to go.'

Skater grimaced. 'For real? Have you ever tried a Lunaburger?'

'No, of course not. This is only my second day on the moon, remember?'

'Well, don't bother. They're beyond yik.'

Leo took another bite. 'You know, when I told people at school that I was coming up here for the holidays, everyone said I had to bring them back some Lunaburger holo-tokens. There are different sets. People collect them.'

'Nerds collect them,' Skater corrected him.

'Well anyway, Lunaberger was one of the places Mum and I were going to go together.'

There was the look again. Skater was about to go all serious and Leo really didn't want to spend the rest of lunch not knowing what to say, so he carried straight on, trying to sound as cheerful as possible. 'But from the sound of it, maybe we shouldn't bother.'

'Big Joe doesn't do nerd tokens. You'll still have to go to Luna-B's if you want to keep your friends happy.'

'True.'

'Or don't bother, and get yourself better friends.'

'Listen,' Leo said, after a brief pause to finish his burger. 'Can I ask you something about my mum?'

'Yeah, of course. You know you can talk about her whenever you need to.'

'That's not what I mean. I mean I want to talk about what might have happened to her.'

'Go on,' Skater said, suddenly interested.

'Well. Have you ever heard of a spaceship called the *Arcadian*?'

'Yeah, of course. Everyone's heard of the *Arcadian*, haven't they?'

'I hadn't. At least not until yesterday, when Aitchison asked me about it.'

'What did he say?'

'He asked if I'd ever heard Mum mention the name.'

'And had you?'

'No. Like I said, I'd never heard of it. And if Mum knew anything about it, she certainly never said anything about it to me.'

'Did Aitchison say why he wanted to know?'

'No, he just dropped the subject. But there was something about the way he brought it up. I'm sure he thinks it's important.'

'Well it makes sense. I don't know why I didn't think of it myself. An ancient spaceship appears out of nowhere and then a world expert on ancient spaceships goes missing. There's got to be a link.'

'But she's not an expert on old spaceships, only on the computers that controlled them. And actually it's not even the computers themselves, it's the data stored on them. And that's the thing about the *Arcadian* — there wasn't any data there.'

'Explain.'

'I spent some time last night finding out everything I could about the *Arcadian*. You know the story, right?'

'Yeah. It was on its way to Alpha Centauri when it disappeared, somewhere out in deep space like a hundred years ago or something, and then for some reason it turned round and came back home again and no one can figure out why.'

'Not exactly. It didn't disappear, it malfunctioned: stopped sending back data. They tried to reboot it but that didn't work so after a few years of not hearing anything, they gave up and abandoned it. What they think now is that the reboot did actually work, but because some of the comms systems were too badly damaged, it turned itself round and came home to get repaired.'

'That's right, I remember now. It drifted right into the shipping lanes and nearly collided with one of the rock trolleys heading out to Jupiter. That's how MarsMine got hold of it. They managed to scramble a salvage tug out of somewhere or other and get to it before it made it as far as the inner system and actually hit something.'

'So anyway,' Leo continued. 'When they got as far as trying to analyse the data from its memory banks, they discovered there wasn't anything there. The reboot must have wiped them clean, and the original damage meant it wasn't able to record anything afterwards either. So there was literally nothing there except the original operating system software. And if there's no data, there's no need for Mum to be involved.'

'Then why did Aitchison ask you about it?'

'I don't know. Maybe he's just trying everything.'

'Or maybe there's something he's not telling you.'

'But even if there is, even if the *Arcadian* has got something to do with Mum, that still doesn't explain why someone would kidnap her. She doesn't know anything about it.'

'As far as you know.'

'Well, there's always a chance,' Leo conceded. 'She doesn't tell me everything.'

'Exactly. It's a clue, and we're detectives. So let's investigate.'

'Great. How are we going to do that? The *Arcadian*'s on Mars, not Luna.'

'Okay.' Skater gave him a sly smile. 'And do you know anyone who's thinking of going to Mars any time soon?'

'Oh no,' Leo muttered. 'Here we go again.'

'Because I do,' Skater continued. 'Me. I'm going there next week, in fact. On a Zodiac.'

'Yes. So I gather.'

'I'll be your contact. I'll check out the *Arcadian* and report back if I discover anything.'

'You do know it's in a museum now?'

'Really? Oh, well maybe I won't go and snoop it then. Sorry, but I'm not going all the way to Mars just to go to another museum.' She paused and put her serious face back on for a moment. 'You know I'm joking, right?'

'Yes, Skater. I know you're joking.'

'Good.' She reached over and stole another chip. 'Now, finish these and let's sort out dessert while I tell you all about the things I *will* be doing on Mars.'

And two tables away, his coffee forgotten and long cold, Jack Duggan continued to listen eagerly to every word they said.

7

A STRANGE MEETING

'**Don't look now,**' Leo muttered, 'but I think we're being followed.'

Skater instantly turned to look. 'Where?'

Leo grabbed her arm and tried to drag her into the nearest shop, but Skater was having none of it and slipped free, sending Leo sprawling backwards in the process. For a couple of seconds he struggled to keep his balance, then let himself fall slowly and painlessly to the ground.

'What part of don't look now did you not understand?' he asked, picking himself back up. 'Look, he's gone now.'

'Result,' Skater replied with a pleased grin. 'Now we're not being followed any more.'

'Skater! My mum's been kidnapped, we're trying to find out anything we can about where she is, and you go and scare away someone who's following us. I thought you were supposed to be helping me.'

'I am. Sorry, but I didn't think turning round would be such a big deal. Who is it, anyway?'

Leo glanced back along the crowded walkway. After lunch Skater had brought them back downtown so she could show him all the best places to buy a lot of things he wasn't interested in buying, and the streetway was busy with afternoon shoppers.

'There,' he said, after a few seconds of searching. 'And don't make it so obvious this time. It's the guy in the dark jacket, standing over by that information holo-screen. The one with the big bag over his shoulder. Do you see him?'

'Him?' Skater asked in surprise. 'He looks like a junker. Honestly, Leo, I don't think he's the one who kidnapped your mum.'

'Don't be stupid. Of course I don't think he's the kidnapper. But I bet he knows something about it. Why else would he be following us?'

'I don't know. Maybe he's looking for a handout and thinks we'll be a soft touch. And how do you know he's even following us?'

'Because I've been paying attention. He goes wherever we go and stops whenever we do. And he hid when you looked at him.'

Skater shrugged. 'Maybe he's shy.'

'Also,' Leo said, realising that Skater wasn't going to pick up on the most obvious point. 'He was sitting two tables away from us at lunch.'

'For real?' she asked, trying to stare at the man and not stare at him at the same time. 'In Big Joe's? Are you sure?'

'Positive. I thought he was asleep, but if he wasn't, he must have heard everything we said.'

'Wild. And top detective work as well. I didn't even realise there was anyone sitting anywhere near us.'

'No, you were too busy stealing my chips.'

'Okay, so let's go and talk to him, find out what he's playing at.'

'No, not here. It's too busy. Let's lead him somewhere quieter.'

'What, like a dark alley, where no one will see when he pulls out a knife and makes us hand over everything we own?'

'Hey, you were the one who said he looked like a junker.'

'Yes, but I didn't say he was a *harmless* junker. He can still be a crazy old murderer, even if he isn't a kidnapper.'

'Then let's call the police.'

'No, I've got a better idea.'

'A better idea than calling the police? That's the best idea possible.'

'Fine, then call them. I mean, look at the great job they've done of finding your mum so far.'

'Well, what's your plan?'

'Follow me,' Skater said, linking arms with Leo and steering him quickly down the nearest turning. It was a short streetway, too narrow for a shuttle rail. The shops were smaller, too, and Leo didn't recognise any of them from the malls back on Earth. But there were still plenty of shoppers. 'Still too busy,' Skater said. 'Come on.'

'So what's the plan,?' Leo asked as Skater pulled him along. 'Are we looking for somewhere quiet?'

'Yes.'

'But that was my plan, and you said it was stupid.'

'I didn't say it was stupid, I said it might be dangerous.'

'Is your plan dangerous?'

'Course not. My plan is beyond brilliant.' She stopped suddenly in front of a brightly lit adver-teaser screen that was currently showing a young woman spraying different parts of her face with what appeared to be rainbow paint. 'Is he still following us?' Skater asked.

Leo moved round so he could get a better view of the streetway behind them. 'No. Wait...Yes. Here he comes.'

'Good. Let's keep going then.' They moved off, and at the end of the row of shops Skater paused, looked both ways, and decided to go right. 'Yes,' she said, as they rounded the corner. 'This will do fine.'

They were in an even narrower streetway and Leo felt as if he'd stepped back in time. The shops were hardly shops at all – more like expanded market stalls. They were tiny, single-storey buildings painted in bright, bold colours. Some had awnings above their doorways, others had racks full of products in front of their cluttered windows, or hanging from metal frames built out onto the walkway.

'Wow,' Leo said. 'What is this place?'

'It's called Flea Market,' Skater replied, quickly. 'I love it. Best shopping in the whole of Atlantis. We'll come back some time, when we're not so busy.' She gave him a slight push. 'You go on. Look at some stuff. Take a couple of minutes and then turn back when you're about halfway down.'

'Wait. What? What am I supposed to do?' But there was no reply. Skater was already disappearing into the nearest shop.

Leo walked on, confused. Was he supposed to hide, or just stand there? Turn back, she'd said. Did that mean he was supposed to confront the man? And what was Skater going to do? Presumably she had some sort of plan, he just wished she could have let him in on it. As casually as he could he wandered along the row of shops, pretending to be interested in the women's clothes, hand-crafted ornaments and specialist foods that seemed to flow onto the walkway from every store front. But after a while he found a store that did interest him – a souvenir shop. He paused to stare at the window display of floating models of Luna, moon rocks, model spaceships and little holo-statues of smiling, waving aliens.

These were exactly the kind of thing he'd imagined bringing back for his friends at school, but now they seemed tacky and overpriced.

He glanced back up the street, and sure enough, there was the mystery man, looking into one of the shops and waiting for him to move off again. Beyond him, Skater had reappeared to cut off his escape so Leo began to walk back towards them, desperately trying not to imagine the huge knife the man might be carrying beneath his jacket.

When he realised what was happening the man turned back, but found Skater blocking his way. He tried to step around her, but she moved to block him again and he was forced to try to push her aside. As Leo rushed up, he saw Skater drop to the floor, slide her legs between the man's feet and twist, tripping him and knocking him onto his hands and knees. By the time Leo reached them, Skater was already back on her feet, standing in front of the man and looking ready to do the whole thing again if he tried to run.

'Wow. Good job,' Leo said.

'I thought so,' Skater replied with a quick smile. 'Never tried that outside the practice ring before.'

'You can do judo?'

'It's called Brazilian jiu-jitsu. Same kind of thing though.'

Leo looked around. A few shoppers had stopped to see what was happening, but none of them seemed eager to get involved. He reached down, took hold of the stranger's arms, and helped him onto his feet, ready to spring back if the theoretical knife made a sudden appearance.

'So,' he said, in what he hoped was an authoritative voice. 'Are you going to tell us why you're following us? Or will we call the police and let them sort it out?'

The man began to laugh, slowly at first, but quickly it became more uncontrolled. Leo had been expecting him to put up a fight, or try to run, not burst out laughing. He looked at Skater questioningly, but she was as confused as he was.

'Stop it,' Leo demanded. 'This is serious.'

'I know, I know,' the man replied, taking a deep breath and forcing himself to calm down. 'But you gotta see the funny side. After everything I been through, and then to be overpowered by a couple of kids. I'm fine,' he added, waving his free arm and smiling at the staring shoppers. 'Just messin' with the kids. Everything's fine.'

'Is it?' Skater asked. 'Is everything fine?'

The man looked down to where Leo was still gripping his arm. 'I won't run, if that's what you mean. Not from you two, at any rate.'

'What does that mean, not from you two?' Leo asked, releasing the arm. 'And why were you following us?'

'Long story.'

'Short version then,' Skater demanded. Her fists were clenched. She was still expecting trouble.

'Alright.' The man straightened his jacket and Leo noticed him patting the side, as if checking for something in the pocket. 'I heard what you were saying, back at the diner. Not deliberate, but you weren't exactly whispering, were you?'

'So?'

'So I heard you got a problem. Well, I got a problem, too, and I reckon maybe we might be able to help each other out.'

'How?'

'How's about I discuss that with your parents?'

'If you were listening to us,' Leo said, 'then you know we're kind of short on parents right now.'

'Yeah,' Skater added. 'So it's us, or the police. Your choice.'

'Fine.' The man glanced around. 'But not here. Somewhere quiet.'

Leo stared at the man. Did he really know something? He

didn't look like he could possibly have had anything to do with the kidnapping, but when he talked, he sounded a lot more convincing than he looked. There was only one way to find out. 'Okay,' he said. 'Let's go somewhere quiet.'

'Bad idea,' Skater muttered, shaking her head at Leo.

Leo took a step back so he could whisper in Skater's ear. 'I really want to hear what he has to say. We'll be careful. I've thought of somewhere we can go that'll be safe, and if he tries anything, you can use your jiu-jitsu on him again. It was amazing, by the way.'

'Thanks. And Sweet Sol, I hope you know what you're doing.'

'Yeah,' Leo said. 'Me too.'

8
PIECES OF THE PUZZLE

AN HOUR LATER they were back at the Museum of the Solar System, sitting in a quiet corner beside a particularly unexciting, non-interactive display about early asteroid mining techniques. In the few minutes since they had sat down, not one visitor had done more than glance their way and walk past. Even Leo thought it looked boring. It was the perfect place to continue their conversation undisturbed.

They'd taken the shuttle across town. At first, the man had said little, preferring to sit silently with a flight cap pulled low to hide his face from the other passengers. But Skater had wanted answers, and hadn't been prepared to wait. Reluctantly, he'd told her his name was Jack Duggan and that he was, or at least had been, a freight pilot with MarsMine. That was enough for Skater. She'd spent the rest of the journey pestering him for details: which ships he'd piloted, the routes he'd run, his trips to the outer colonies.

When she asked if he'd ever been attacked by pirates, he'd given a small laugh and replied, 'only once,' then refused to give any details. By the time they arrived at MOSS, Leo was finding it hard to remember that this was the same man Skater had been convinced was out to murder them just an hour before.

'Okay,' Jack Duggan said. 'This seems quiet enough. Now, before you start bombarding me with more questions, let me ask you one.' He reached inside his jacket, thrust his hand through the pocket and brought out a tiny silver object that must have been hidden in the bottom seam. 'You got anything you can plug this into?'

'Let me see.' Leo examined the data pin and nodded. 'It'll fit in my slate. What's on it?'

'Video files. Raw footage from the external cams on my last ship.'

'Nothing holo? Should work fine then.' Leo took out his slate – the small one he always carried around for gaming – and plugged in the pin. After a few taps the video began to play, showing an empty patch of space and a distant star field.

'Details?' Skater asked.

'Right,' Jack began. 'This is part of the vid log from *Erebus*. She was my last ship. Cargo freighter. I used to run the long haul out to the Jupiter colonies, dropping off supplies and hauling ore trains back to Mars.'

'What was she?' Skater asked. 'Armadillo Class?'

'That's right.' Jack looked impressed. 'How'd you know a thing like that?'

Skater smiled. 'I'm kind of interested in spaceships.'

'Okay,' Leo said. 'So what exactly are we looking at here?'

'About ten months back. We're out past the Belt, heading for Europa, when we're picked up by pirates.'

'Pirates? Really?' Skater asked, unable to keep the excitement out of her voice. 'So this is the time you were telling me about?'

'The very same. There were two of them. Must've been out hunting and picked us up on the long range. Just our bad luck I guess. Anyway, suddenly there they were. They were faster than us, they had weapons, and we were days away from the nearest station.'

'So what did you do?'

'The only thing we could. We ran. And that's what you're looking at now. This is the view from the rear cam. You can't really see the pirate ships at this mag, but they'd already fired a couple of warning shots and me and Ayo — he was my co-pilot — were arguing about whether we should ditch the cargo and hope that was all they wanted. In all my years hauling freight I never lost a single shipment, and I wasn't about to start then. But Ayo, well, he'd got himself into a nasty scrape with pirates a few years back and was in no mood to try that again.'

'So what happened?' Leo asked.

'Keep watching. It's coming up.'

They continued to stare at the screen. 'They're using bullets?' Skater asked, as lines of tracer fire burst out of the darkness and flashed past the camera. The star field began to spin rapidly. 'And that's the ship taking evasive action, right?'

Jack tapped the screen, pausing the video. 'Evasive action's right. But not from the pirates. At that range their cannon weren't going to hit much of anything. And if you know what an Armadillo is, you'll know their hulls can stand up to a fair old pounding before taking more than a scratch or two. No, what she was evading was something else. Something a lot more interesting.' He tapped the screen again and the video continued.

After a few seconds the camera view changed and Leo found himself looking along the top of a series of linked white modules that seemed to stretch out forever.

'Wow,' he said, impressed. 'Exactly how long is an Armadillo?'

'That ain't the ship,' Jack said. 'That's twenty-five kays of cargo pods. The ship itself is behind the camera, pushing them along. But never mind the pods, it's what's above them you need to be looking at.'

At first Leo couldn't see anything except the stars. He leant in, trying to spot whatever he was supposed to be looking at. And then he saw it – a patch of blackness, moving along the length of the cargo pods and blocking out the stars behind it.

'Woah!' Skater said as she also noticed the black shape. 'No wonder the ship took evasive action. Where the hell did that come from?'

'Is it an asteroid?' Leo asked.

'No. Look.' Skater paused the video once more and studied the black shape. 'You can tell it's machine-made because the edges are so straight, and all the surfaces are completely smooth.'

'So it's another ship, then?'

'Not like anything I've ever seen.'

'Me neither,' Jack said. 'No lights, no windows, no markings.'

'Could it be a drone?'

'Not at that size,' Skater said. 'You could fit a crew of fifty in there, easy.'

'Okay, so it's a mysterious ship that nearly crashed into you. So what?'

'So watch what happens when it gets too close to the pirates. It's heading right for them, remember.'

Leo continued to watch. The camera was tracking the dark shape as it passed above *Erebus* and on towards the pirates. The cannon fire increased, but after a few seconds it was clear they were now targeting the black ship speeding towards them, not the much larger freighter. The camera zoomed in, so that the hulking pirate ships were just visible behind the blue flashes. And suddenly the firing stopped and the ships were gone.

'What happened?' Skater asked. 'They just disappeared. Did the black ship fire at them?'

'Did you see any return fire?' Jack said. 'Any explosions? Nope. That ship just carried straight on ahead, soaking up all that fire like it didn't matter, then just like that, it's on its own. No weapons fire, no pirates, no nothing. And you know what? We scanned for wreckage, scanned the whole damn area with everything we had, and there was nothing. Zip. Like they never existed.'

When the video footage finished, Leo unplugged the pin and handed it back to Jack. 'So it's a military prototype, something secret. It's obviously stealth-enabled, and it has some sort of new weapon that isn't visible. Pretty impressive. But what makes you think this has anything to do with my mother being kidnapped?'

'Maybe it does, maybe it don't,' Jack said, leaning in and lowering his voice, even though there was still no one nearby. 'But it has everything to do with the *Arcadian*, and from what you were saying at the café, that might have something to do with your mother.'

'What's it got to do with the *Arcadian*?' Skater asked.

'You know the story, I heard you talking about it; how it drifted into the shipping lanes, nearly collided with a freighter on its way out to Jupiter…'

'Sweet flaming Sol,' Skater exclaimed, suddenly making the connection. '*Erebus* was the freighter it nearly hit.'

'Exactly. And according to the official report, that's what you just been watching.'

'What? That black thing didn't look anything like the *Arcadian*. I've seen it on the news feed. It's way smaller, and way older, and way…uglier.'

'Yep, all of that. But you do some digging, search for the original vid files for the collision, and what you'll find is exactly what you just saw, except that instead of the black ship, you got the *Arcadian*.'

'They altered the vid files?' Leo said. 'But that's impossible. Well, no, that's not true. It's actually quite easy. Anyone can do it with the right software and a good enough computer. But what you can't do is overwrite a ship's AI unit, and all the data from the cameras would have passed through the AI before being stored. It would know if the files had been altered, and AIs can't lie.'

'Funny thing. Seems *Erebus* was due a spell in the dockyard. After I brought her back from the Europa run they took her in and gave her a complete refit — including swapping out both AIs.'

'At the same time? But that's illegal, isn't it?'

Jack shrugged. 'It's MarsMine. Who's gonna know, and who's gonna stop them, even if they did know?'

'But I still don't get it,' Skater said. 'Why would MarsMine want to swap the files anyway?'

'My guess? They know all about that mystery ship and they wanna make damn sure no one else does.'

'You think MarsMine built it? Why? I mean, I know they've got their own defence fleet, but this looked way more hi-tech than anything they would need. It looked more like some top-secret government spy ship, not a defence cruiser.'

'Yeah? Well whatever it was, I wish to god I never set eyes on the thing. Thirty-four years I worked for that company. It was my whole life. And now it means nothing. They took my ship, my job, even my identity. They wiped my account, my history, everything. I try to access anything now, all it does is tell them where I am so they can send a hit squad after me.'

'They're trying to kill you?' Skater asked. 'For real?'

'They got Ayo. Back on Mars. Said it was an airlock malfunction, but no way was that what happened. And I know they were planning the same for me if I hadn't got off Mars when I did. Thought I'd be safe enough here, but I guess not. So it's time for me to run again. Figure Earth is my best bet now. I still got me a few contacts down there, could probably hide me for a while till I can sort out this whole goddamned mess.'

'So what's the deal?' Leo asked. 'You'll give us the pin in return for us buying you a ticket back to Earth?'

'Tempting,' Jack laughed. 'But I don't think so. Could you even afford it? No, I can get myself back to Earth from here easy enough if I'm careful. I know how to play the system.'

'What do you want from us then?'

'Time. Somewhere to hide out for a few days, catch my breath, so to speak.'

'Oh, so no,' Skater said, emphatically shaking her head. 'So way beyond no.'

'Look,' Jack said. 'I don't expect you to trust me, and I don't even expect you to believe my story. It sounds so crazy, even I don't believe it sometimes. But I'm desperate. I got nowhere else to turn, and I really do think it might be tied in with this kidnapping thing of yours. Just give me one chance, okay? You told me earlier your dad was a pilot. Let me talk to him, show him the vid, and see what he thinks. If he says no, then that's the last you'll see of me. Word of honour.' He looked at Leo. 'Please. One chance. For your mother's sake.'

Leo turned to Skater. 'What do you think?' He tried to keep the excitement out of his voice, but it must have been obvious what he was thinking. Yes, they should give Jack Duggan a chance. It was too good an opportunity to miss. His story was the closest thing they had to a lead, and this was exactly what they'd been trying to do – find clues, follow leads, help solve the crime. And what did they have to lose? Now that they'd seen him up close, spent some time with him, he didn't seem all that scary. If he'd wanted to attack them, he'd have tried it on their journey across town. 'We'll be safe enough with your dad there,' he muttered.

'Maybe. But it still ranks top three on the stupid ideas list. And that's just today.'

'Anyway,' Leo said. 'There's someone else I want to show that vid to.'

'Aitchison?'

'No, not him.'

'Who then? I didn't think you knew anyone else up here?'

'I think it's time I introduced you to Daisy,' Leo said with a sly grin.

Skater stared at him blankly. 'Who the Sweet Sol is Daisy?'

9

MARTIAN INTRIGUES

'FAILED?' CARLTON WHITTAKER asked.

'Yes, sir,' Mr Archer replied in his harsh whisper.

'Four men – trained professionals, I assume – and they failed to deal with one helpless old fool of a space pilot?'

'Yes, sir.' He hated having to say the words, to take the blame for something he hadn't been responsible for, but long experience had taught him there was absolutely no point in trying to justify himself to the Old Man. It only made matters worse, and right now, worse would not be a good place to go.

'Are they going to try again?'

'They have surveillance on the building where Duggan was staying. He has not returned. I do not think he will.'

'Oh really? You surprise me, Mr Archer. I'd have thought going back to the place where he was shot at would be the first thing he'd want to do.' Mr Archer said nothing. The Old Man didn't like

86

having his insults brushed aside, especially with pointless excuses. 'And that's it?' Whittaker continued. 'That's your whole report?'

'For the moment, yes. I thought you would want to know as quickly as possible.'

'I don't know why. My day would have been a whole lot better without knowing how many incompetents are working for me.' Whittaker sank back into the soft leather of his chair, took a deep breath and released much of his anger along with a sigh. 'I shouldn't get angry. It's not good for my heart. And it's not as if you didn't offer to go and sort out matters yourself. Yes, I do remember that, Mr Archer, and I'm quite sure that had you been there in person, the whole thing would have been handled a lot more effectively.'

Mr Archer said nothing, but gave a slight nod to acknowledge the rare concession. The Old Man looked worn out, he thought, and he made a mental note to make sure he was getting all the medication he needed. It wouldn't do to have the possible future president of Mars looking exhausted in front of the cameras.

'Anyway,' Whittaker continued. 'At this point Duggan is nothing more than a side issue. He's already missed the chance to have his story taken seriously, at least by anyone except a handful of conspiracy-obsessed fools. If he goes to the news channels now, they'll just laugh at him.'

'But we continue to hunt him?'

'Most definitely. I've told you before, Mr Archer, I dislike loose ends. I like my affairs to be tidy. And speaking of tidy, I want you to make sure those incompetents on Luna never have the opportunity to work for us again. Ever.'

'I understand.'

Whittaker began to cough. He took out a small, ornate silver case from his jacket and helped himself to several capsules, washing them down with sips of water between coughs. Yes, Mr Archer thought. He would definitely have to look into the Old Man's health. Tired was one thing, but a dose of Martian flu would be a different matter. Bed rest would not be an option for the next few weeks.

'Now,' Whittaker continued eventually. 'While you're here you can give me an update on what's happening with our professor. I'm impatient for results.'

'She is still settling in. Does very little work. One of her assistants – the girl – is sick.'

'Is it serious?'

Mr Archer shrugged. 'If she dies, it's not important.'

'Oh, but it is, Mr Archer. It's important to the professor, and that makes it important to us. I suspect once she understands the nature of the work I have planned for her, she'll be a willing enough captive. But in the meantime I'm quite sure we'll get more out of her – out of all of them – if we treat them with a little kindness. I assume you are capable of kindness, Mr Archer, when the need arises?'

Mr Archer said nothing. Kindness was not something he'd ever felt the need to add to his skill set. It led to weakness. It was said that you could kill someone with kindness, but as far as he was concerned, this seemed like a slow and inefficient method. No, he was content to stick with what he knew best and leave the kindness to others.

'I'll see to it,' he said, without conviction.

'Excellent. Then that will be all for now. On your way out, you might like to show the Admiral in. I suspect he's come looking to raise his monthly…consultancy fee. I understand he's had a run of bad luck with the cards recently and I'm not sure he's mentioned it to his wife.'

'So I hear. Do you want me to get rid of him?'

'No, Mr Archer. I think I can handle this one. He's nothing but a greedy, stupid, drunken old fool and it does cheer me up to watch him grovel and beg for his pathetic allowance. And besides, I was thinking of asking him if I could borrow one of those lovely new attack cruisers he's just taken delivery of. They look like they might be a lot of fun, eh?'

'Yes, they do,' Mr Archer replied, before closing the door.

In the outer office he found the Admiral lounging on a sofa, a large glass of Whittaker's specially imported Scotch whisky in his hand. He was a fat, balding man, very much at the end of his career. His fancy uniform, with its medal ribbons and gold braid, was barely able to cover the belly that pressed against it.

For a moment the two men stared at each other silently, like circling fighters trying to appraise their opponent's skill. Mr Archer did not need long. 'Admiral,' he grunted. 'Always a pleasure.'

'Archer. I wish I could say the same.'

'A little early in the day for that, isn't it?' Mr Archer asked, indicating the man's glass.

The Admiral gave a sneer. 'I'm on Terran time.'

'Mr Whittaker says you can go in now.'

The Admiral drained his drink in one large gulp, struggled to his feet and thrust the empty glass at Mr Archer as he passed. 'Thanks.'

Mr Archer said nothing. Instead he imagined the many enjoyable hours he would have giving this pathetic man the slow, agonising death he so richly deserved, just as soon as the Old Man no longer had any use for him. And that time was fast approaching.

Mr Archer smiled.

10
DAISY

HAVING NEVER HAD one of his own, Leo didn't really understand fathers. As far as he could tell from the kids at school, fathers were authoritarian figures, preoccupied with having too much work and not enough money. They were never free when you needed them and spent most of their time shouting at their kids for no reason. To be fair, he hadn't heard Pete do any shouting yet, or even complaining for that matter, but Leo was still dreading the scene at the hotel when Skater, along with the friend she'd only known for a couple of days, introduced an unwashed, unshaved homeless man who claimed to be on the run from killers and who seemed to be mixed up in a system-wide conspiracy into which he'd now dragged all three of them. Leo could imagine the anger and shouting and endless explanations. There might even be tears.

He was so wrong. After the introductions, Pete sat quietly while Skater gave him a typically long and detailed run-down of- the day's events. He asked Jack Duggan a few questions about his situation, a lot more about his career as a MarsMine pilot and then announced that he wanted to see the video footage of the incident for himself. Jack handed over the data pin and Pete went to plug it into the room's wall-mounted monitor.

'No, wait,' shouted Leo. 'Not in there.' The others looked at him in surprise.

'Why not?'

'It's not secure.'

'Secure?'

'Yeah. All public-access networks, like this hotel's, automatically record everything that happens on the network. So if you message someone, or request a search for information, or watch a vid clip, the system records what you've done. It then runs all the data through filter algorithms that identify anything illegal, and reports everything it picks up to the authorities.'

'But what we're doing isn't illegal,' said Skater.

'No, but it doesn't have to be. All you need is access to the network's system and you can tell it to filter for anything you want – like the name *Erebus*, for example. If the vid file comes straight from the ship's AI unit, it'll have an identification code built in. That would be simple enough to track.'

'But you'd still need access to every single public network, wouldn't you? Even here in Atlantis, there must be thousands of them.'

'Governments do it all the time, and most of the mega-corps as well. Someone like MarsMine could do it no problem.'

'But I've already watched the film dozens of times,' Jack said.

'On open networks?'

'Well, yeah, sometimes.'

'Then that's probably how they've been able to track you,' said

Leo.

'Dammit,' said Jack. 'I should have thought of that.'

Leo sighed, wondering how so many seemingly intelligent people could be so clueless when it came to dealing with computers.

'So we avoid the networks,' Pete said. 'But we can still use a slate?'

'Yeah. As long as you're not linked in to a network that's fine. But actually, I have a better idea.'

'Does it involve introducing us to the mysterious Daisy?' Skater asked.

Leo smiled. 'Wait here.' Two minutes later he was back from his own room carrying his rucksack, and while Jack had a shower and Pete sorted out some spare clothes for him, Leo unpacked the contents onto the desk beneath the wall screen.

'What's that?' Skater asked as Leo produced a dull, metallic box and a handful of cables and began to connect them into the side of the wall screen.

'I have my own computer,' he said.

'That's a computer?' Skater laughed. 'But it's huge. And ugly. Please tell me you didn't actually buy that? Someone just paid you to take it away, right?'

'As a matter of fact, I built it myself.'

'Nice. Look.' She held out her arm to show Leo her watch. 'like.'

'Great,' Leo replied, without looking.

'And I didn't have to build it myself either. I just bought it. Well, actually, Dad bought it for me. But I chose it. It's a VelociT.' She paused, uncertain. 'They're pretty good, aren't they?'

'Yeah, the VelociT's a good computer when you want something to carry around with you. I've got one as well, though I tend to use the slate more, because it runs a better 3D interface. But this is a little bit better than a VelociT.' He switched on the power, plugged in the data pin and stepped back. After a few seconds a small light on the side of the box changed from red to green. Nothing else happened and the screen remained dark.

'That's it?' Skater asked. 'Impressive.'

Pete wandered in, accompanied by a somewhat cleaner and fresher Jack, dressed in one of Pete's spare MarsMine uniforms.

'Hey,' Skater announced sarcastically. 'Great disguise, Dad. No one will ever recognise him now.'

'It's only temporary, until we can get his other stuff cleaned up. Anyway, are you all set up here?'

Skater looked at Leo. 'Are we?'

Leo nodded. 'We are.' He turned to the screen. 'Hi, Daisy.'

Hi, Leo. How's it going? It was a young woman's voice, casual and relaxed and with a strong accent.

'That's Daisy?' Skater asked, confused. 'A big ugly computer with a really bad Australian accent?' She paused and looked suddenly worried. 'Or are we just using the box to actually talk to someone in Australia, in which case, I think the accent's great?'

'No, we're talking to the box, but the voice is just something I was working on at school.' He turned back to the blank screen. 'Daisy, I've got some friends here who'd like to meet you. Why not come and say hello?' Leo glanced round at the others. 'Better make it something smart,' he added quietly.

After a few seconds the wall screen came to life to show what appeared to be the inside of a study, with row upon row of book-lined shelves set along dark wooden walls. A real fire was burning in a huge fireplace, and beside it was a desk piled high with old books and papers. A pretty, smartly dressed young woman rose from the chair behind it and walked towards the screen, smiling and motioning to her surroundings.

How's this?

'Very nice,' Leo replied. 'You haven't done this one before.'

You weren't specific as to the nature of your guests. I thought this would cover most eventualities. The Australian accent had been replaced by a more clipped, precise English one.

Leo turned to the others, who were staring at the screen in amazement. 'Guys, say hello to Daisy.'

'Leo,' Pete managed after a few seconds. 'That's an AI.'

'Yes it is.'

'And a fairly advanced one, from the look of it.'

'Yep.'

'No way.' said Skater. 'You have your own AI?'

'Yep.'

'And you built it yourself? What kind of a genius nerd are you, Leo Fischer?'

Leo began to blush. 'Thanks, Skater. That's the nicest thing anyone's said to me all week. Or ever, in fact. But I didn't actually build it myself in that sense. I'm not even close to being able to create an AI from scratch. What I did was just collect the bits and put them together in the right order. Actually, the basic intelligence core came from a research project my mum was working on a couple of years ago. She gave it to me as a birthday present.'

'A birthday present? For real?'

'Isn't that illegal?' Pete asked. 'I thought all artificial units of anything like this level had to be registered through a government.'

'This one is. Technically, she belongs to the University of Cambridge.' He smiled. 'She's on extended loan for research purposes.'

Skater walked to the screen and stared at the image of the woman. Even up close it was difficult to tell whether or not it was a real person. 'Can it see us?'

Perfectly, replied the woman on the screen and Skater stepped back, startled. *I have full access to both the cameras built into this display unit.*

I have already stored your image and I am now attempting to identify you.

'Buzz.' She turned to Leo. 'But also, just a little bit on the creepy side, don't you think? And did you really have to make her look like such a floozy?'

Actually, it was my choice to appear in this manner, not Leo's. Would you be happier with this?

Skater turned back to the screen to find that the young woman had been replaced by a much older, more kindly and maternal version of herself. 'Yeah,' she said, satisfied. 'Now you look more like a Daisy.'

'It's an acronym,' Leo explained. 'It stands for Dedicated Artificial Intelligence SYstem.'

'Cute.'

'So,' said Pete. 'Can she play us the vid file safely?'

Yes, I can. The memory pin is confirmed clean and I am currently working outside the local network. Leo, would you like me to play the contents of the data files for your friends?

'Yes please, Daisy.'

Daisy played the film of *Erebus*'s near miss with the mysterious vessel and Pete watched it over and over. He discussed his opinions with Jack, and the pair of them bombarded Daisy with questions about spaceship construction, military vessels that looked even vaguely similar, and any information she could find about the *Arcadian*, both now and when it was launched. After half an hour, Leo had lost interest. He wandered off and sat on his own with his pocket slate. After another twenty minutes, even Skater had got bored. 'Hey,' she suggested. 'How about me and Leo go get us all something to eat while you two find out what you can about how to build a spaceship?'

'Okay,' Pete answered, without looking away from the screen. 'Good idea.'

Back on one of the lower street levels, Skater led Leo to a food bar designed like a child's idea of a space rocket, all purple and sparkly, with a friendly astronaut leaning out of a portal window and waving a mechanical arm at a cute, smiling alien perched on top of the rocket.

'Marmaduke's,' she announced. 'Tacky, kitsch, overpriced.'

Leo laughed. 'What's not to like?'

Skater went straight to the counter and began tapping out their order, selecting various odd-sounding items and forcing Leo to delete the perfectly nice-looking sandwich he'd chosen for himself, choosing instead something called a Moon Mountain. 'You'll love it,' she said. 'And it's a lot more fun than that blandwich you wanted.'

When it arrived, Leo discovered that the Moon Mountain was well named, seeing as how it was only just smaller than his head. After a moment trying to decide how he was actually going to deal with it, he succeeded in filling his mouth with a huge chunk of something that was sticky and chewy and almost certainly had something to do with cheese. Skater loaded him up with more of the same for the others.

On the way back, while Leo battled with his Moon Mountain, Skater was unusually quiet. In the hotel lobby, waiting for the lift, she turned to him. 'Listen, Leo. You have to come to Mars with us. I know you say there's no proof that's where your mum's been taken, but it's starting to look pretty damn convincing to me. The *Arcadian*, that black ship, Duggan. They're all linked, and they're all linked to Mars as well. Let Aitchison keep searching here on Luna and if he finds something, great. But you can't stay here anyway. He's going to send you back to Earth as soon as we set off for Mars next week and you most definitely aren't going to be any use to your mum stuck in New Zealand. Me and Dad, I promise we'll do what we can, but I'm sure we'd get a lot further if you were there as well.' She paused and smiled, and it was the first time Leo had seen her looking even slightly embarrassed. 'And besides,' she continued, 'I kind of wish you were coming with us anyway. I reckon the trip would be a lot more fun if you came along.'

Leo blushed. He wanted to say something but couldn't think of what to say. Besides, his mouth was full of sticky, cheesy mush. He forced himself to swallow and nearly choked in the process. Skater offered him a carton of something fizzy and turquoise to wash it down. 'I can't,' he said once his mouth was finally empty.

'Why? Because some stupid official says you have to go back home? That's just beyond dumb. This is your mum we're talking about. Don't you want to find her?'

'I can't,' Leo repeated. 'Because I can't. Even if there was some way I could get away without Aitchison finding out — and honestly, I don't think there is — and even if I could get my hands on a huge amount of credit so I could afford a ticket — which I can't — there aren't any tickets to buy. The *Dragon* completely sold out months ago. Even the waiting list is full.'

'Oh.'

'And before you ask, there's nothing else going out to Mars for at least the next month either, except a couple of slow freighters, and even they're booked out.'

'And you know all this, how?'

'Because that's what I was doing after I got bored watching the same piece of film over and over again. I had a look to see if there was any way I could come with you.'

'Oh.'

'And you know what? I think you're right. I think my mum is on Mars. And it makes me mad as hell to think that I can't go out there and try and find her myself.'

'You can. We'll think of a way.'

'How?'

Skater gave him a reassuring smile. 'Come on. Let's go talk to my dad. I absolutely guarantee he'll be able to think of some way to get you to Mars, even if he has to fly you there himself.'

11

A PASSAGE TO MARS

THE CARGO DOCK was almost empty, most of the supplies having been loaded during the previous week. Robotic loaders, known as steves, were ferrying the final few containers along the short tunnel that led into one of the *Dragon's* smaller holds, their skeletal arms easily controlling and directing bulky crates that, back on Earth, would have required a reasonable-sized crane to move.

The duty supervisor, floating off to one side beside a large control panel, looked with satisfaction as the last container was collected from its storage pallet. Another ten minutes would see it stowed and then he could power down and clock off. And not before time. His shift was supposed to have ended half an hour ago, but with departure so close it was a case of all hands till the job was done. Now, finally, it was job done.

Then he noticed the two men bobbing towards him, pushing a small crate. They were MarsMine employees, judging by their uniforms, but they looked more like flight crew than freight haulers. And they certainly had no business bringing him extra cargo just as he was getting ready to go home – because that was clearly their intention. He checked the manifest on the screen just in case, but there was nothing listed as outstanding. So he took a deep breath, let out a long sigh and turned to face them with a scowl and a shake of the head.

'No. No. No,' he announced as the men brought their crate to rest beside the entrance to the tunnel. 'We've closed. That's the last one just going on now. And besides, you're not on the list.'

'Hi,' said one of the men cheerfully, holding out his hand. 'Lieutenant Tony Nixon. Co-pilot on *Erebus*. She's a freighter, works out of Mars Central. Does the deep run out to the colonies.'

The supervisor knew what was coming. This kind of thing happened all the time – adding a bit of 'private' cargo at the last minute – but he was damned if he was going to make it easy for these two jokers. He shook the outstretched hand, but made sure he kept the scowl on his face. 'Anyways,' the man continued. 'The thing is this. There's some bigwig from MarsMine booked on the *Dragon* and he wanted all this personal stuff shipped along with him, so we got the order to sort it out.'

Still the supervisor said nothing.

'Problem is, some of it was coming from Earth, see, and we had to wait till it was all together before we could pack it and get it loaded. We ended up running a bit late.'

'Personal possessions go on with the passengers up at the main departure gates. We're stores and heavies only.'

'Yeah, I know it. But apparently he ain't supposed to know about it. It's a birthday surprise or something and we were told to keep it away from the passenger departure terminal just in case. We were hoping we'd be able to get it aboard here. You know, without any fuss,' he added, giving the final words a particular emphasis.

'What name?'

'Monroe,' the second man said. 'Cabin 1046.'

'Documents?'

The man handed over a couple of official-looking sheets but the supervisor barely looked at them. He knew they'd be official enough. 'There's nothing on the list for any Monroe,' he said with a shake of his head. 'And anyway, you're too late. My shift's already over. Right now I've got things to do and places to go.'

'Ah, ain't that a shame,' the one called Nixon said. 'And it leaves us with a huge problem, 'cos we're gonna be looking at getting into a whole heap of trouble if we don't get this here crate onto that there ship. So I don't suppose you'd know any way we can find a solution to this huge problem, do you? It would mean a whole lot to us.'

The supervisor gave a grunt. It was a terrible story. Not the worst he'd been told, but close. Still, what did it matter? What came now was the good part. 'I guess I might be able to do something for you. Maybe. As you can see, we're not sealed up yet. But it would mean me having to stay for another twenty minutes, which I'm not so happy with. Like I said, places to go. And it would still have to be checked over by the Candimen. I can't do nothing about that.'

'Oh, there ain't nothing illegal in here,' Nixon replied, a bit too quickly. 'Look.' He and the second man unclipped the two catches on the side of the crate and swung open the lid to reveal a carefully packed collection of what seemed to be common personal items – clothes, electronic goods, ornaments, even a stack of old paper books. The supervisor peered in unenthusiastically until something caught his eye. 'What are those?'

'These?' said Nixon, picking up a couple of packages carefully wrapped in gold paper. 'These, my friend, are boxes of chocolates.'

'Chocolates?' said the supervisor, suddenly taking more of an interest.

'Chocolates,' Nixon repeated with a sly smile. 'Proper Terran imports, mind. Very expensive. The kind of thing you might think of giving as a present to someone special. You know, if you wanted to *really* impress them.'

'Is that a fact? Terran imports, eh? Not the fake stuff they knock out up here?'

'The very best.' The two men closed the lid again. 'Anyways,' said Nixon. 'I can see you're a busy man and we mustn't take up any more of your valuable time. We'd be happy to drop this off ourselves and then head out through the passenger gate if you like. That way you wouldn't even have to wait for us. And of course we'll check it in with the Candis ourselves. That's only fair.'

'Doors are closing in two minutes,' the supervisor announced, turning back to his console. And as the men disappeared along the tunnel towards the waiting ship with their crate, he took off his jacket and wrapped it around the two golden packages, apparently forgotten, still floating beside him.

'No. Absolutely not!' had been Pete Monroe's immediate response to Skater's suggestion that they smuggle Leo aboard the *Dragon*. 'It's illegal, it's dangerous, it's impossible. It's completely crazy.'

'Crazy, maybe,' corrected Jack Duggan. 'But it ain't impossible.'

'Whose side are you on?'

'Listen,' he continued. 'You know full well that getting him on board the ship ain't gonna be that difficult. It'd only take a couple of days to get something organised, search around for the right people to approach. Hell, it's what I'm gonna to be doing for myself anyways, to get me back to Earth.'

'Earth is five hours away. There are all sorts of ships going between here and there all the time. You can pretty much get there on anything as long as you've got a spacesuit and a fake ID. But we're talking about Mars. On a Zodiac.'

'Exactly. They're huge. So you smuggle him aboard and once you're under way he can come out and wander round like any other passenger. No one's even gonna suspect he don't belong. And if he does get found out, what they gonna do? They sure as hell ain't gonna to turn around and come all the way back here for one little stowaway.'

'But what about when we reach Mars?' Leo asked.

'Who cares?' Jack said. 'You're on Mars, which is exactly where you wanna be, right? Sure, they'll deport you, and if you're real lucky it might even be on the *Dragon's* return journey. So that gives you, what, three, four weeks on Mars? That sounds okay to me. Plenty time to do a bit of detective work before they kick you back home. Right?'

'Definitely,' Skater said.

Pete glared at her. 'And once he gets back home,' he said. 'What then? There's going to be a whole heap of trouble waiting for him, whether it's from the authorities here, or back on Earth, or maybe from our friend Aitchison, and whoever it is he's really working for.'

'So what?' Leo snapped. 'I don't care what they do to me. Nothing will ever be as bad as the fact that my mum's been kidnapped. And what can they do to me anyway? Send me back to Earth? Big deal. They're going to do that anyway as soon as you've left.'

'Dad, listen,' Skater said, taking his hand and lowering her voice as if she didn't want the others to hear. 'I know you're mad at me, and think this was all my idea. But it really wasn't. Leo's determined to go to Mars and if we don't help him you know he'll keep trying, and no doubt end up doing something really stupid – '

'*This* is really stupid, Skater.'

'Alright, even stupider.'

'I can still hear you, you know,' Leo said, offended. Skater ignored him.

'At least if we help him we can do it right. You told me this sort of thing happens all the time, people shipping out on freighters and stuff, and I bet you know exactly how to swing it so we can get him on board without anyone finding out.'

'Just because I could, it doesn't mean I should.'

'What if it was me that was missing? What if I'd been the one that was kidnapped? You'd do everything you could to find me, wouldn't you? Even if it was dangerous, or illegal or whatever?'

'You know I would. But this is different.'

'How?'

'Please,' Leo said. 'Just help me get on board. After that I promise you won't have to have anything else to do with me. I'll disappear.'

For a moment Pete said nothing. He stared at Skater, then turned to look at Leo and slowly shook his head. 'I'm not going to let a fifteen-year-old boy try and smuggle himself to Mars.'

'But Dad,' Skater began, but Pete continued.

'Not on his own. It's far too dangerous. And Skater's right. If we left you on your own, you'd only go and do something stupid and dangerous.'

'So we're going to help him?'

'Yes,' Pete said with a resigned sigh. 'We're going to help him.'

'Yes!' screamed Skater, and she wrapped her arms around her father, squeezing him tightly and nearly knocking both of them over. 'I love you, Dad.'

'But it had better be a one hundred per cent foolproof plan,' he added, looking across at Jack. 'If I think it's too risky, we abandon the whole thing and think again. Agreed?'

'Agreed,' said Jack.

'Agreed,' said Leo and Skater.

But the plan had been foolproof. And it had worked perfectly. Or at least so far, Leo thought, as he lay curled up inside the tiny, dark space that had been his home for the past hour or so — and might well be for the next few hours as well. They'd made it as comfortable as possible, but once the face mask and emergency air supply had gone in, there wasn't space for anything except a pillow and a couple of bottles of water. He could move around just enough to stop himself getting cramp, but actually he found that this wasn't nearly as much of a problem as it might have been thanks to the lack of gravity.

No, the real problem had been the panic. That first time they'd sealed him in, when the darkness had closed around him and he'd realised he couldn't just push up the lid and climb out, he'd kicked and shouted and hammered his fists until Pete had been forced to open the crate back up to calm him down. After that they'd taken it more slowly, getting him to spend five minutes, then ten, in the darkness, building up gradually until he could cope without trying to destroy the crate each time.

If only he could have kept his slate he could have stayed nice and calm for hours playing games. It might even have been fun. But Pete had said no. Any electronic activity would be picked up in the customs scan. That would result in a top-to-bottom search, and that would be the end of the adventure right there.

'Why not just go to sleep?' Skater had suggested.

'Yeah, right,' he told her, staring miserably down at his tiny, dark tomb. 'As if that's ever going to happen.'

Pete had seen to the crate. There were plenty lying around in the MarsMine depot at the shuttleport and he hadn't even needed to sign for it. The guys knew he was off to Mars and assumed he was doing a bit of importing on the side, as a favour to someone at the other end. Constructing the hidden compartment in the base had also been his job and that had been slightly more tricky. They'd had to assume the crate might be taken off and stored in one of the holds until departure and it was possible Leo might have had to stay in there for anything up to twenty-four hours before they could get access. So in had gone the breathing kit, the pillow – for when the gravity kicked in – and an extra empty water bottle. For emergencies.

But it sounded as if none of it would be needed – or at least not for the moment. Leo heard a knock on the side of the crate: two taps, two taps, two taps. It meant everything was fine and the crate was being unpacked. Had it really been that easy?

He squinted against the light as the lid was lifted from his tiny compartment.

'It's okay, Leo,' he heard Pete say. 'Everything's fine.'

'Well,' he said, twisting over onto his hands and knees and stretching his back. 'That was a lot quicker than I was expecting.' He sat up, looking out over the top of the crate, and found himself in a smaller, more compact version of Pete and Skater's hotel room. 'This is your cabin?' he asked. 'Nice.'

'This? This is probably the smallest cabin on the ship. You should see the ones I couldn't afford.'

'Well it's still a lot nicer than mine.'

'Yeah, I guess that's true. So how are you feeling?'

'That depends. Do I have to get back inside?'

'Sadly, yes. They're not letting passengers on board until

tomorrow morning, and we still have to have the crate checked over by the Candimen. Jack's down with them at the moment, sorting out the paperwork. He'll ping me when they're on their way. We've probably got about ten minutes or so, and I thought you might like to stretch your legs for a while.'

'Is there a toilet?'

Pete laughed. 'Through there,' he said, pointing to a door.

When Leo returned, Pete was looking through the belongings he'd pulled out of the crate and which were now floating above one of the beds like a small junk cloud. He reached in and pulled out a statue of what was possibly a Greek god. 'Where did you get all this stuff?'

'Don't blame me,' Leo replied. 'That one was Skater's idea. Actually, so was most of the other stuff as well.'

He and Skater had been responsible for stocking the crate. They'd put in all his own possessions along with some of hers, but that hadn't been nearly enough. So Skater had taken them on a shopping trip to Flea Market, and it was amazing how much she'd been able to buy on such a small budget. There were jackets, dresses, shoes, and an old sun hat that took up a lot of space because Skater insisted it couldn't be squashed. And there were books, dozens of them, although mostly these had gone in because Skater wanted to read them herself. And then there were the ornaments...

There was a beeping from Pete's pocket. 'Sorry, Leo,' he announced. 'That's the signal. It means Jack's on his way up with the Candies so we have to get you back into your den. Sorry it couldn't have been a longer break.'

'That's okay. I don't mind so much, now I know we're already on the ship.' Leo climbed back inside the crate. 'Thanks, Pete.'

'No problem.'

'I mean, thanks for everything. You and Skater have been brilliant, looking after me and sorting all this out. You know I couldn't have done any of it without you.'

'I know. And I also know that if we get caught we'll all be in a whole heap of trouble, most of which I can't even imagine. But I also know that something really big is going on, and in ten years' time I want to be able to look back and know that whatever happens, I did the right thing.'

'Are we doing the right thing?'

'You having second thoughts?'

'Not really. It's just. . .there's so much going on, so much to think about.'

'Well, there's nothing you can do until tomorrow morning, so try not to worry too much, okay? Try to get some sleep.'

Yeah, right, Leo thought, and remembered Skater making the exact same suggestion the previous afternoon. Why, he wondered, did everyone assume that wedging yourself into a cramped dark space was no different to lying in a nice comfortable bed. Sleep really wasn't going to be an option for the next few hours. He tucked himself back down into the bottom of the crate.

And then Pete closed the lid and the darkness and the fear squeezed in around him once again.

12

FOND FAREWELLS

AT LAST THE *DRAGON* fired its auxiliary engines, beginning the slow process of generating a full, Earth-level artificial gravity for the five thousand passengers and crew who would soon be hurtling across the Solar System to Mars. Tiny jets of blue-white crystals shot out from the several dozen exhaust ports evenly spaced around the ship's five kilometre circumference, so that for a few minutes the ship resembled a giant, slowly spinning Catherine wheel.

In the main departure hall of the Atlantis Spaceport, Agent Aitchison sat drinking a disappointing caff-carton and watching the *Dragon's* departure on one of the giant vid screens set up like windows along the far wall. They just couldn't get the coffee right, he thought, sadly. It was one of the two things he really missed whenever he was away from Earth: decent coffee and proper showers. Human beings really weren't designed to live on places like Luna, or to spend weeks cooped up in tiny metal cans speeding through space at tens of thousands of kilometres an hour. And yet so many of them did it, all the time, and even claimed to enjoy it. Madness.

Aitchison was not his real name. It was one of many he'd gone by over the years, and right now it suited him to use it. He wasn't a policeman either. In fact, officially he wasn't anything at all. He was whatever he needed to be, whenever he needed to be it. He was simply an agent, working for a very small organisation that, in turn, worked for a very large government. Some people might have called him a spy, others an assassin. Actually, he was both, but much more besides.

And for now he was happy enough being nothing more than a detective. What he'd said to Leo was true – that finding Leo's mother was his number one priority, though perhaps not for the reason he'd led Leo to believe. True, she was an important piece of the puzzle, and he would try to rescue her if he could, but he would also happily leave her right where she was if he thought that would better serve his aims. He hadn't been able to say that to Leo, of course. He'd had to lie, to promise he would do everything in his power to get her back. But that hadn't been a problem for him. Lying was part of his job, and he was very good at his job.

His phone rang. He clipped it to his ear and brought the tiny screen round in front of his right eye. He was expecting the call. 'Mei,' he said as a young woman's face appeared. 'What have you got for me?'

'You were right. Leo Fischer didn't keep his appointment. No one at the hotel remembers seeing him since yesterday and Monroe paid for both rooms when he checked out this morning. As he and his daughter are confirmed on the *Dragon*, our best guess is that they managed to sneak Fischer aboard somehow.'

'I guess so.'

'You don't sound surprised.'

'Do I ever?'

'Well anyway, the *Dragon* hasn't left yet. We could hold her back and do a top-to-bottom. If he is on board, we would have him back within a couple of hours.'

Aitchison looked up at the view screens with his free eye. 'She's already spinning up. I doubt they'd take too kindly to a couple of hours' delay at this point. No, let's not worry about it.'

'Really?'

'Really. Let's cut the boy some slack. He's been through a lot in the past few days and I'd say he deserves a holiday, wouldn't you?'

'By which you mean you think he's on to something and you want to see where he's going with it?'

'Exactly. He's obviously found some reason for abandoning Luna and moving his search to Mars, and I'm curious to know what it is. In fact, I think it's probably time I paid the Red Planet a visit myself.'

'On the *Dragon*?'

Aitchison let out a snort of laughter. 'God, no. Find me something a lot smaller and a lot faster. And without passengers. But I'll need updates on Fischer and his new friends, and I want someone who can keep an eye on him. Who do we have on board?'

'Let me check. Shall I call you back?'

'I'll hold.'

Aitchison liked Leo. For a fifteen-year-old boy he was dealing with the situation incredibly calmly and sensibly. And he was actually doing something about it. A lot of kids would have been on the first shuttle back to Earth, in floods of tears and desperate to be somewhere familiar, not sneaking aboard a ship to Mars. And he was intelligent, too. Aitchison had spent some time finding out all he could about the professor and her son, and what he'd discovered made for fascinating reading. Leo Fischer was definitely worth keeping an eye on. Perhaps one day he might even be interested in working for a very small organisation that worked for a very large government.

The phone screen flicked back to life. 'Well,' Mei said. 'Two of the crew are people we've dealt with before, but only unofficially. One's a junior officer, ex-military, and probably quite reliable. But I think our best bet might well be one of the passengers.'

'A passenger?'

'It's very interesting. Quite a coincidence.'

'You know I hate coincidences.'

Mei smiled. 'I'll zip you her details. You can see for yourself.'

'Fine. But give the junior officer a heads-up anyway. No matter how interesting your passenger is, she'll be no use to us if the crew discover they've got a stowaway on board.'

He finished the call, put away his phone and briefly considered buying another caff-carton before remembering just how bad the last one had been. Instead he gazed across at the view screens, watching the *Dragon* slowly spinning itself to full gravity.

'Good bye, Leo,' he told the screen. 'And good luck. Something tells me you're going to need it.'

PART TWO

THE
DRAGON

13
LIFE ON THE RING

TIME WAS RUNNING OUT. Lieutenant Tom 'Dynamo' Dillon zoned out the orders being barked through the comms system and pushed the stick as far forward as it would go, powering his fighter towards the enemy formation. Bright bursts of laser fire exploded around him but he ignored them, spinning his ship onto its side and returning fire, destroying one of the enemy craft with his second shot. 'Yahoo!' he screamed, a broad grin spreading across his handsome, chiselled face. 'It's payback time!' Two more shots took out two more of the hopelessly outclassed enemy craft, and suddenly he was through the first line of defence and the alien mother ship loomed in front of him.

'You're crazy,' bellowed the angry voice in Dynamo's ear. 'I ordered you to wait for back-up.'

Dynamo flicked off the comms between bursts of laser fire and the voice was silenced mid-sentence. 'Well, then I guess you'll just have to court-martial me when I get back.' And he spun his agile craft around, aiming directly towards the giant ship's bridge.

Now I really need the toilet, Leo told himself. He'd needed to go for a while, but had been hoping he could hold on until the end of the film, even though it really wasn't worth holding on for. He hated leaving films early, no matter how bad they were. It was a point of pride that he could sit through anything – and he'd sat through some truly awful offerings in his time to prove his point – but it was also the embarrassment of having to get up and struggle past a row of tutting viewers to reach the exit. Well, at least that wasn't going to be a problem today. There were only ten of them in the entire cinepod and he had his row all to himself, so *Space Avengers VI* was about to join the very short list of films so unbelievably bad that even he couldn't bear to see them through to the bitter end – even if it was being shown in 'amazing Holo-D'.

So as the alien mother ship finally erupted in an implausibly loud and colourful explosion, he slipped off his holo-visor and crept towards the rear doors. As it turned out, none of the other viewers paid him the slightest bit of attention. In fact, the first person he passed seemed to be fast asleep behind his visor, despite the barrage of sound and light bursting from the screens. Five minutes later, Leo was out on the Ring, relieved in both mind and body.

Sometimes it was hard to remember that he was on a spaceship, millions of kilometres from the nearest planet. The return to Earth-level gravity made life so much easier and more natural than it had been on Luna – as his visit to the toilet had just reminded him – and he could imagine he was back in any of the dozens of similar places he used to visit in Cambridge or London. It was only during his occasional trips to one of the viewing lounges that he truly remembered where he was. Space. Away from the glow of Earth, the vast, endless starscape was so amazingly detailed and full and beautiful, and when he gazed at the stars, the cold emptiness that had swallowed up the *Dragon* after it left Luna didn't seem quite so cold and empty after all. It was easy to see why people came out from Earth once and never returned.

But even if he did occasionally forget where he was, Leo could never forget why he was there. He thought about his mother all the time. Where was she? How was she being treated? Who had taken her, and why? Would she be working with her captors? Would she be trying to escape? He had no idea, no answers. But whatever else she might be doing, Leo hoped she would be doing whatever she could to stay alive. He had no brothers or sisters, no father. She was all the family he'd ever had and he couldn't imagine life without her. Sure, she'd sent him off to boarding school as soon as he was old enough, and even in the holidays her work meant she wasn't always around, but that wasn't the point. She loved him. In an odd, forgetful sort of way maybe, a way other people found hard to understand, but it was definitely love. And he was certain that if things were the other way round and it was he that had been kidnapped, she would now be doing everything in her power to get him back.

But none of this stopped him from enjoying himself at the same time. As long as he knew he was doing everything he possibly could to track down his mother, he saw no reason why he shouldn't be making the most of his first, and possibly only ever, trip on a luxury cruiser at the same time. And to be honest, there wasn't that much he could be doing for her right now anyway, except getting to Mars as quickly as possible. If he had to do it in style, then so be it.

And the *Dragon* really was amazing. Leo had imagined he'd be spending most of his cruise tucked away in the cabin, but Pete had said that the best way to go unnoticed was to be in plain sight right from the start. That way, after a few days the other passengers and crew would be used to seeing him around and he'd be able to wander the ship like any holiday-maker on his way to Mars. As long as he stayed out of trouble. Being seen around was one thing, but bringing himself to the attention of the security staff would not, Pete was keen to point out, go down so well. So he and Skater had dedicated their first few days to exploring the ship – or at least those parts of it they had access to – and had visited every shop, every restaurant and every leisure facility they could in an attempt to be seen by as many people as possible.

For Leo it had been almost unbearable. Even at the best of times he hated being the centre of attention, preferring to spend his time reading or playing on the computer, ideally tucked away in a corner where he wasn't in anyone's way and where he might possibly be forgotten and left in peace for hours on end. But of course, Skater was never going to let that happen. Even though she was happy to do all the talking, she'd still insisted on introducing him to every nice old lady they found themselves sitting next to on the transit shuttle, every helpful shop assistant and waiter who served them and even the honeymooning couple who happened to be sitting next to them one morning at breakfast.

But finally things had calmed down, and by the end of the first week Leo even found himself getting bored from time to time. Being with Skater was a lot of fun, but sometimes he felt like he just wanted to sit quietly and work his way through everything that had happened in those two seemingly endless weeks since he'd left Earth, and what was likely to happen once they reached Mars. Also, even though Pete hadn't said anything, and almost certainly never would, Leo suspected that part of him was wishing he could just enjoy the simple holiday with his daughter he'd been hoping for, without the added burden of having to babysit another teenager – especially one who brought so many problems with him.

Which was why he'd decided to waste two hours of his life sitting through *Space Avengers VI*, so that Pete and Skater could spend some quality time together. He only hoped they'd had a more interesting time than he had.

Assuming they would still be off having fun, Leo decided to head back to the cabin and get Daisy to teach him some more about Mars. He knew a fair bit already because they'd had to study it in school, but mostly just about the planet's geology and the history of its colonisation. When it came to current politics and economics, he was even more clueless than about the same things back on Earth. He knew Mars had its own government and that the planet was little more than a giant mining project, but after that, nothing. It had never seemed important enough to bother learning. Now, suddenly, maybe it was.

'Leo!'

Leo paused at the bottom of the stairway and looked back towards the main floor of the Ring. The shuttle had just pulled up and Skater jumped off and motioned for him to come over. When he reached her she gave him a smile and two large bags of shopping – mostly clothes and souvenirs by the look of it.

'I've just had the most ultra time. I'm going to tell you all about it and you're going to listen and be so sick jealous.'

'Yeah,' said Leo, holding up the bags. 'I can see there was no stopping you. Do you actually need any of this stuff, or are you just getting your Christmas shopping in early?'

'Oh, no, no, no.' She turned to the elderly woman who was standing quietly beside her. 'This is Miss...'

'Rodriguez Serrano,' the woman said. 'But please, call me Ana. Miss Rodriguez Serrano makes me sound like an old spinster. And really, you needn't bother with the bags. I'm quite capable of carrying them myself, you know.'

'No grief,' Skater replied before Leo could hand back the shopping. 'We're happy to help. This is Leo, by the way. He's my brother.'

'Well I'm very pleased to meet you, Leo, and thank you for carrying my things. But do take care of the blue one; it has the breakables in.'

Leo gave her a polite smile. 'I'll be careful.' And here we go again, he thought. Today it's carrying her shopping, tomorrow it'll be inviting us in to watch endless vids of her grandchildren over a nice cup of tea. Sometimes he really wished Skater wasn't so... Skaterish.

'Ana was saying this is her first time to Mars,' Skater said, steering Leo towards the escalator. 'Just like you. She's off to visit her son—'

'Nephew.'

'—nephew, who's out in Avalon. I've not been to Avalon. We only stayed in Lowell City when Dad and I were there last time, because that's where he was working. We didn't have time to travel round much, but I've heard Avalon's really nice. Maybe we'll go this time.'

'Well, you're certainly very lucky being able to do all this at your age,' Ana said with a smile. 'It's taken me sixty years to get around to it. Still, I do intend to enjoy it all the same.' She turned to Leo. 'But this is your first time is it, Leo? How was it your sister got to go all the way to Mars while you were left behind? That seems awfully unfair if you ask me.'

Leo shot a nervous glance across at Skater, unsure of how to reply. Apart from being siblings, they hadn't worked out a detailed back story yet and he had no idea what she'd already told the old woman. Fortunately, she carried straight on with her own, typically stupid, explanation. 'Back then we never used to let him out of the cage. And besides, he'd never have made it through quarantine.'

'I'm sorry?'

'Joke. He's my step-brother. His mum married my dad last year, which is why I now have to let him tag along with me. Still, he's handy enough when you need someone to carry your bags.'

'Well, I think he's a perfect gentleman,' said Ana, stopping outside her cabin and giving Leo an affectionate pat on the head. 'And I hope to see you both again soon. It's been lovely talking to you.'

14
ANGRY WORDS

'**Way, way too nosey**,' Leo said, once he and Skater were back in their own cabin. 'I thought the whole point was for us to be seen but not heard.'

'Seen but not heard?' Skater looked puzzled. 'How does that work, exactly? You want we should be doing a mime or something?'

'You know what I mean. Talk to people, yes. Just don't go giving them your entire made-up life story the first time they ask you a question.'

'Come on, Leo. She's like, a hundred years old, and I only met her for the first time about half an hour ago. You think she's some kind of evil kidnapper?'

'No, of course not. But she doesn't have to be an evil kidnapper to figure out I'm not exactly who we say I am, does she? And then all she has to do is mention it to one of the crew who decides to go and check, and then suddenly I'm sitting in a shuttle being escorted back to Luna under armed guard. Or whatever.'

Skater sat down sulkily in the room's one comfy seat and put her feet up on the built-in desk. 'You could at least thank me for coming up with such a good story at, like, zero notice whatsoever.'

'Thank you, step-sister,' said Leo, lifting up Skater's boots and sliding Daisy out from underneath them. 'And what are you going to tell her next time when she asks why my mum isn't with us, huh?'

'I could say she's all tied up at work?'

'Not funny, Skater.'

'Sorry. Bad joke. But come on, lighten up a bit, won't you? I'm just trying to make the trip a bit more fun. You can't expect me to go for five weeks without talking to anybody except you. I'd go insane.'

'-er.'

'What?'

'Insane-er.'

'What?'

'You'd go insan*er*. More insane.'

Skater looked blank.

'Oh, forget it,' said Leo. 'My humour is wasted on you.'

'So, how was your film?' Skater asked after a pause.

'About as bad as my jokes, apparently. I was half-tempted to ask for my credit back.'

'It was free, wasn't it?'

'Well then I was half-tempted to ask for my time back. Honestly, I was robbed.'

There was another pause.

'So are you going to ask me what I did?'

'Does it matter? You're going to tell me anyway, aren't you?'

'Yes, I am!' Skater said excitedly, dragging her boots off the table and sitting forward in her chair. Leo was glad he'd just moved Daisy out of the way. 'It was completely buzzing. Dad and I went on a tour of the hub.'

'Really,' said Leo, genuinely interested. 'How did you manage that? I thought it was off limits to all passengers?'

'All normal passengers,' said Skater with a smug smile. 'But Dad's a pilot, remember, and pilots are always happy to do each other little favours because you never know when it might be handy to get one in return. So he asked very nicely and they said yes.'

'Go on then,' said Leo. 'Tell me all about it.'

'Beyond wow,' said Skater. 'First of all you have to go through to the crew area, which is a separate bit on the other side of this ring. That's where all the day-to-day running of the ship and looking after the passengers gets done. They have offices and workshops and stuff and that's where the staff live. Oh, and they even have a security office in there with its own holding cell. You know, for when they catch stowaways and have to lock them up.'

'Ha, ha. Very funny.'

'Anyway, from inside there you can go up in one of the lifts that run along the spokes and by the time you get to the Hub there's no gravity any more and you're actually floating upside down. That was kind of weird. The Hub itself doesn't spin, by the way, except for the big motor section in the middle which is how they get the rings turning in the first place. Anyway, the back bit is just the engines and fuel and even we weren't allowed to go there. Then there's the ring motors, then the cargo bays, which are huge but kind of dull, and then at the front is where all the really interesting stuff is.'

'Like what?'

'Well, the bridge mainly and the comms centre, and a few other bits and pieces. And underneath is the shuttle bay, which is just huge. You could pretty much park a truss-bus in there if you wanted, except they've got two of their own shuttles in there already. And they're armed as well, just in case any pirates come snooping around. Oh, and I forgot, the bit that you'd really like. They have this special little room behind the bridge which is like their computer centre, and they have three AIs in there.'

'Actually, it's only two AIs,' Leo said.

'No,' Skater corrected him. 'The guy showing us around told me. They have two main ones that run the ship and a back-up for emergencies.'

'The back-up isn't an AI. It's an AIA.'

'A what?'

'Autonomous Intelligent Agent. Basically, it's a really clever self-learning computer that isn't quite on the same level as an actual AI. Interestingly, a lot of ships that claim to have their own AI don't actually have one at all, all they really have is an AIA.'

'Great. Well *a*, who cares? And *b*, how do you know? Have you been down there? Have you seen them?'

'I care. I'd much rather know how many AIs run the ship than how big the shuttle bay is. And I know about the AIs because Daisy's been talking to them.'

'What?' shouted Skater, taken aback. 'You have a go at me for chatting to some nice old lady who's just looking for a bit of company and then you go and let your computer talk to the ship. Don't you think that's just a teeny bit hypocritical? And dangerous? And stupid?'

'Why?'

'Why? Because the first thing the ship's AIs are going to do is report that there's another AI on board. Or, I don't know, scan it or something and find out all about us.'

'No, they won't. First of all, it's no big deal that there's another AI on board. Daisy is properly registered so I have every right to bring her wherever I want. With all these rich, important passengers, the chances are at least a couple of them will have brought their own AIs as well. And for your information, Daisy can't just be scanned. She's like a person. If she doesn't want to tell you something, or if she wants to keep something secret, it's up to her. Except that she's actually better at keeping secrets than a human would be because she'll never say anything by accident and she can't be bribed or forced or anything.'

'It's a computer.'

'No, she's not. She's an artificial intelligence. Calling her a computer is like saying a human being is the same thing as a monkey.'

'Well, maybe some of them are, jungle boy.'

'Oh, grow up!' Leo snapped.

Skater stood up.

'Fine. Whatever. Well, seeing as *she's* so great, maybe I should just leave the two of you to enjoy yourselves while I go and wander around on my own and not talk to anyone in case I accidentally tell them that you're a stowaway and should be locked up, because I'm not *intelligent* enough to keep my mouth shut. I mean, it's not like it's actually my holiday or anything, is it? And it would be an absolute disaster if I actually went and enjoyed myself for once, wouldn't it?'

And with that she stormed out, doing her best to slam the hydraulically controlled door behind her.

'Fine,' Leo said to the door. 'Go. See if I care.' But in fact he did care, and he also knew he was in the wrong. Skater was right that some old woman who happened to live down the corridor was no real threat. As for the stuff about the AIs, he didn't know why he'd made such a big thing of it. What did it matter if Skater couldn't tell the difference between an AI and an AIA? There weren't many people who could.

He knew he should follow her and apologise – it would save

a whole lot of grief later — but he also knew he was too proud, or possibly too scared. Instead, he powered up Daisy and while she gave him a detailed history of the development of MarsMine as a system-wide mega-corporation he ignored everything she was saying, replaying the argument with Skater in his mind until he'd ended up saying all the right things at just the right time and the scene ended the way he would have liked it to, not with the failed slam of a door, but with an apologetic kiss.

15

WHITTAKER MAKES PLANS

ALTHOUGH IT WAS HARD to tell from the eyes hidden behind dark glasses and the mouth twisted into a permanent sneer, Mr Archer was excited. He had news and it was the kind of news that would make the Old Man very happy. And in Mr Archer's view, there were few things better than making the Old Man happy.

Carlton Whittaker was arguing with the holo-screen hovering above his desk as Mr Archer entered the office, and Mr Archer knew better than to interrupt, even for something as important as this. He recognised the face on the screen. It was one of the Defence Force generals. One who certainly wouldn't be keeping his job — and possibly his life — for very much longer. 'But three attacks in the past month,' Whittaker argued. 'I call that a damned sight more than a minor inconvenience. My men are miners, not soldiers, remember. They can see off the odd band of nomad scavengers when they have to, but they are not equipped to deal with these co-ordinated pirate raids. They're even using orbiters on us, goddammit.'

'We're doing everything we can,' protested the voice.

'It's not enough!' Whittaker bellowed. 'Not nearly enough. I was promised a military presence large enough to deter these outlaws from coming anywhere near my mines. Instead I get an occasional fly-over that does nothing except help the pirates know which mines to target, because they know you won't be back again for several days.'

'We just don't have the resources...'

'But I do.'

'What, your convoy escorts? You know you can't operate them in-atmosphere. It would violate the Defence Code.'

Whittaker sat forward and thrust his angry face at the screen. 'Listen to me, you jumped-up tin-pot toy soldier. Either you find the ships you need to protect my mines by the end of this cycle, or I'm bringing down my own fleet to do the job, Code or not. Understand?' He slammed his fist on the control panel and the screen vanished before the other man had a chance to reply, then he sat back in his chair, his anger gone. 'That went well,' he said, turning to Mr Archer with a smile. 'I do enjoy putting that man in his place. Just as I shall enjoy removing him from that place very soon. But shouting bothers my throat. Pour me a water, and help yourself.'

Mr Archer took two crystal glasses from the sideboard and filled them with ice-cold water from the dispenser. The Old Man refused to drink anything but Terran spring water, which he imported in huge quantities. To be honest, Mr Archer couldn't taste any difference between this and the recycled water available to everyone else on Mars, but if the Old Man told him to help himself, that's what he would do.

'What if he finds the resources somehow?' he asked in the harsh, rasping voice which no amount of water would ever soften.

'He won't. Our dear friend the alcoholic admiral will see to that. But arrange for one or two more raids, just to be on the safe side. Maybe something out in the *Marineris*. That should frustrate him.'

'I have news,' Mr Archer said after a slight pause.

'Good, I hope?'

'We picked up the old pilot, Duggan.'

'Ah, splendid. And?'

'He still had the files on him, but it seems he made a copy and passed it on.'

'Disappointing.'

'Perhaps not.' He handed a slate across to Whittaker. 'This is who he gave it to.'

Whittaker studied the screen for a few seconds and then looked up in surprise. 'Fischer? The professor's son?'

'Yes. They met, apparently by accident, on Luna and now the boy is on his way here on one of the cruisers. Due in four weeks.'

'On his own?'

Mr Archer indicated for Whittaker to scroll onto the next page. 'He has teamed up with some pilot and his daughter who were already booked on the cruise. Just random holidaymakers as far as I can tell, although the father is a company man as well so it may be there was some previous connection.'

'How very interesting. Well, having the son as our guest would certainly give the mother an added incentive to achieve results, don't you think? They still have nothing to show for their efforts, I gather?'

Mr Archer shook his head. 'Not yet, no. She's proving quite stubborn, but then I haven't put much effort into persuading her yet. You told me to be nice. But if you let me have the boy...' He left the sentence hanging.

'Maybe. Maybe,' Whittaker said, reading more carefully through the two pages Mr Archer had presented to him. 'It says here he's already something of an expert with computers as well. That could be useful.' He closed his eyes and sat back quietly for a moment, turning ideas over in his mind and absently drumming his fingers on the desk. 'And this pilot the boy is with, he's a company man you say? Do we own him?'

'No. He works out of Luna. Comes here occasionally, but wouldn't be involved in any of our special operations.'

'Pity. How convenient that would have been. But no matter.' He drained the rest of his water and held up the empty glass, turning it slowly so that the ornate patterns carved into the crystal caught the light. 'Very well,' he said at last. 'Let's go and acquire him.'

'Acquire him?'

'These pirates, they're becoming more and more daring every day, don't you think? What if a few of them got together and decided to have a crack at a nice, juicy cruiser full of rich tourists? Not only would something like that give us the cover we need to go in and pick up the boy, but it would also be an absolute disaster for the government. Just the sort of negative publicity they can ill afford – what with the election so close now. And besides, it will also provide the perfect excuse for us to take matters of on-world security into our own hands.'

'It's one of the Zodiacs. And it would be right in the shipping lanes.'

'All the better. Can you manage it?'

Mr Archer nodded. 'Of course.'

'Good. Then get started. But make sure the attack comes in Martian space. I don't want any Terran intervention if I can avoid it.'

'Understood.'

'And Mr Archer, I think I can manage without you for a while. Perhaps you might like to oversee this one personally?'

A crooked smile crept across the stony face.

'Understood.'

16

TEARS AND APOLOGIES

AFTER A DAY of awkward silences and snide comments, Pete had clearly had enough. He sat Leo down at the table, forced Skater to sit opposite and stood staring at the pair of them. 'Right. Leo, Lisa Kate, I'm off to breakfast. I'm going to sit at one of those nice tables with its own external monitor screen and gaze out at the stars while I enjoy a very pleasant and very peaceful meal with plenty of coffee. If you can sort out this stupid argument, you're more than welcome to join me and hear what I have planned for the rest of the day. If not, you can sit here like this until you do. And if that means you're still here tonight, you can sleep like that for all I care. Understood?' He put on his jacket and left the two of them to it.

After a few moments of staring at the table, Leo tried to break the silence. 'Listen,' he said. But he got no further. Skater held up her hand to cut him off while she talked over the top of him.

'I can't think of any sentence that needs to come out of your mouth right now that doesn't start with the word, sorry.'

'What?'

'No, not what. Sorry.'

'But why do I...'

'Not why either. Sorry.'

'Fine. Sorry.'

'Sorry for what?'

'For arguing with you.'

'Not good enough.'

'Then what?' demanded Leo, who could feel the anger building up inside him once more and who thought he was already being generous enough in admitting it was his fault in the first place.

'For being rude and mean and spoiling what was one of the best things I've done in ages by not being interested in anything I said except the fact that I don't know the difference between an AI and a whatever the other thing was. I mean, honestly, does it really matter?'

Leo looked back down at the table, unable to speak. He was so angry now. Angry and frustrated and helpless. He could feel his throat tightening up and his face growing red and he knew he was going to start crying in about five seconds' time and that just made him more angry and ashamed and he wished he was anywhere at all except right there in the room with Skater.

'Well,' she demanded. 'Does it?'

'Yes!' he screamed, unable to stop the tears and suddenly not caring. 'It matters to me. Because everything in my life is horrible and everyone thinks I'm just a sad nerd who's more interested in computers than people. And it's true, I am. Because I understand computers, and they make sense, and I don't understand other people, and every time I try I get it wrong and end up saying the wrong thing. And the only person who really understands me is my mum, and I have no idea where she is or even if she's still alive. And I'm scared. I'm really scared, because I don't know what's going to happen and there's nothing I can do about it even if I did know, and it's...it's all just too much.' He buried his face in his hands and continued sobbing.

Skater said nothing. After a moment she got up and went round to the other side of the table, knelt down beside Leo and put her arms around him. 'I'm sorry,' she whispered.

Leo wiped his face and sniffed. 'And now I feel like a stupid little boy who bursts into tears whenever he's told off, and I wish I could crawl away and hide in the corner forever.'

Skater gave him a reassuring smile but Leo turned away, still too embarrassed to look her in the face. 'You know what I think? I think you're really brave. And I'd be worried if you didn't cry after everything you've been through.'

'Easy for you to say. You're not a teenage boy. We aren't supposed to cry.'

'Really? Well I know plenty that do. Anyway, most teenage boys don't have to go through what you're going through. And they certainly don't have to do it with some horrible grumpy, naggy, fake step-sister going all madam on them at the same time. I'll try to remember that from now on.' She took a deep breath. 'There. Now we've both apologised to each other, so we're all good, yes?'

Leo smeared the last of his tears across his face with his sleeve. 'Just so you know,' he sniffed. 'What you just said. Technically it was an admission of guilt, not an apology. They're not the same thing.'

'Well it's all you're getting, so don't push it. Now, friends?'

Leo managed to find a smile. 'Friends.'

'Good,' said Skater, standing up. 'Let's go and get some breakfast. Not apologising always makes me hungry.'

Leo shook his head slowly. 'You're unbelievable.'

'I know,' Skater replied, giving Leo her biggest, cheesiest grin. 'It's true. But, why, exactly?'

'The way you just get over things so quickly. I'm still a complete pile of angry and upset and embarrassed and...and god knows what else, and there you are, over the whole thing and just thinking about your stomach.'

'Stomachs are important. She dropped her smile and tried to look serious for a moment. 'But seriously, the truth is that still waters run deep.'

'What?'

'It's a saying.'

'Yeah, I know. And yes, I do know what it means. It's just...'

'Just what?'

'Nothing. Forget it.'

'You don't think my waters run deep?'

'No, I'm sure they do run deep. Way deeper than mine, even. It's just – and please don't take this the wrong way and force me to say sorry again – but I wouldn't exactly call them still.'

Skater laughed. 'Okay, fair point. Come on.'

'Listen. Please don't tell your dad about this, okay? I mean about me crying and everything. Can we just say we talked about it and sorted everything out?'

Skater looked at him. 'Okay. But in return you have to promise me something.'

'What?'

'To wash the streaks of snot off your face before we go. It'll really put me off my breakfast otherwise.'

Leo did, and ten minutes later the two of them found Pete in the breakfast room. He didn't seem surprised to see them and simply offered them the two empty seats at the table. 'So, any plans?' he asked, once they had both filled a collection of plates, bowls and glasses from the buffet counter.

'Be nice to each other,' Leo said with a weak smile.

'Well, that's a good start,' said Pete. 'Because I've come up with a little plan to keep the two of you occupied and out of trouble – at least for a couple of hours a day, anyway.'

'Let me guess,' said Skater. 'You've discovered that one of the other passengers is a teacher who would love to spend her time giving private lessons to bored kids.'

'As a matter of fact, yes. Sort of.'

'No! I was joking. I'd rather throw myself out the airlock than school-up my holiday. I absolutely refuse. Listen, me and Leo have made friends. We'll go off and do stuff on our own and keep out of your way, won't we Leo? All day if need be. I promise we won't be annoying and...and you're winding, aren't you? You haven't really found someone who wants to be our teacher, because you wouldn't be that mean. Would you?'

'Would you like me to explain?'

'As long as the explanation doesn't involve school, yes.'

'I've arranged for you to have piloting lessons.'

Skater stared. 'No. Way.'

'Really?' asked Leo, nervously. 'Piloting lessons, like flying shuttles?'

'Don't worry. I'm not about to set you loose in a real shuttle.'

'Oh,' said Skater, clearly disappointed.

'No. In a simulator. They have one for crew training and Lieutenant Tolliver has very kindly offered to give you lessons in it. After our tour the other day, when you went to find Leo, we got chatting and it turns out we're both Sentinel reservists. We had a great time swapping stories and I was telling him about how you want to train as a pilot after college and how I'd already run you through the basics in a Lunar hopper. He said he could probably fix you up with a few sessions in the simulator if you wanted and said he'd look into it. Well, he has and it's been okayed by the Captain, so you're good to go. To be honest, I think Tolliver was glad of the excuse to spend more time in there himself. Apparently there's not a lot for a pilot to do on this thing. It pretty much looks after itself.'

'Dad,' said Skater, beaming. 'I love you. You are by far the best dad I have ever had and I completely forgive you for calling me Lisa Kate in front of Leo earlier.'

'What about me?' asked Leo. 'You didn't tell him about me, did you?'

'No. I just said you were a friend of Skater's who would love to come along as well. But it's up to you. I just thought you might think it was fun.'

'He does,' said Skater. 'He's coming.' She looked at Leo and gave him a pleading smile. 'Yes?'

Leo gave a shrug. 'Sure, why not? Maybe I'll discover a hidden talent.'

17
PILOT TRAINING

IT BECAME VERY CLEAR, very quickly, that Leo did not, in fact, have a hidden talent for piloting. Had he been training in a fighter, racing his way through cluttered asteroid fields while enemy craft took pot-shots at him, possibly his thousands of hours inside his holo-game console might have counted for something, but the slow business of carefully docking and undocking from orbiting stations seemed to be completely beyond him.

Skater was a natural, of course, and although she wasn't the most patient of students, once she was in the control seat it was clear she knew what she was doing and could do it well. Leo was impressed, and so was Tolliver. 'I don't suppose it's all that surprising,' he said, 'what with your dad being a pilot and all, but I gotta say, Skater, you handle this thing pretty darned well for a beginner. Your dad says you're wanting to go on and be a pilot too. That right?'

'Definitely,' Skater replied. 'But we've got this deal. He wants me to go to college first and if I still want to be a pilot when I've finished – which I so definitely will – he'll pay for me to go and train.'

'Not a bad idea. There's a whole lot more to being a pilot than just knowing how to steer. A good degree'll set you up pretty well if you want to make a career for yourself, especially in the Navy or the Diplomatic.'

'Nah. I figure I'll be a free trader.'

'A trader? That's a pretty lonely profession for a youngster like you. Most traders are older folk – restless types who can't seem to settle down anywhere. I'd say you'd be better off leaving trading till you've tried a fair few other things first.'

Skater gave a non-committal nod and turned back to the controls and Leo suspected this was an argument she'd had with her dad many times and which she didn't want to get into again. He smiled to himself. From what he already knew about Skater, if she wanted to be a free trader, then that was almost certainly what she was going to end up being.

By the end of their first week, Tolliver was so impressed with Skater's progress he decided to try out her landing skills. 'Up here you're piloting,' he explained. 'And even though you're whizzing along at thousands of kilometres an hour, it feels like you're moving in slow motion, doesn't it? You just match speeds with your target and then it's all gentle nudges and delicate bursts until you're locked on. But once you drop down in-atmosphere, well, that's proper flying, and its a whole different ball game. Things come at you a lot faster, even though you're really going much slower, and when you're coming in to land you've got a whole host of things to remember to do all at the same time.'

'But doesn't the ship do most of that for you?' asked Leo from his usual seat at the navigation console.

'Well, I guess that depends on the ship. On the one hand you've got your fully automated cargo shuttles that go straight up and straight back down again. Now they still need a pilot, mind, but he generally gets to sit at base and fly remote. And yeah, he's mostly there for show. But at the other end of the scale you've got some antique piece of junk that's been cobbled together by some salvager — or free trader — who can't afford anything better. And believe me, with some of them you're lucky if you get two wings, never mind a computer.'

'So,' said Skater, impatient to attempt her first landing. 'Shall we give it a go?'

'Sure,' Tolliver replied, reaching across and selecting one of the landing programs. 'And seeing as how we're still on Earth gravity, let's start with an Earth landing.'

'Oh, why not Mars?'

'Because, little lady, landing a shuttle on Mars is the kind of thing you get to do after five years of good hard training, not after five sessions in a simulator. Now, let's give Earth a go and see how you do.'

She crashed, and they all died. Even though the whole thing was little more than a series of unpleasant bumps, Leo found it unsettling to watch the monitor screens as the runway grew closer and closer, then suddenly flipped over and disappeared in a huge ball of flame.

'Oops,' said Skater, looking sheepish.

'Well, that's why we have simulators.'

'Can I try it again? Please?'

Tolliver looked back at Leo. 'How about you, Leo? You want a turn?'

'God, no!' said Leo. 'I can't even park the thing properly in space. I'm quite happy sitting here and watching, thanks.'

Tolliver checked his watch. 'Okay. Once more and then we need to wrap things up till tomorrow. But I'll co-pilot. My back's not up to another one of your landings.'

This time Skater was much better. Tolliver guided her through the early stages of re-entry with a lot of talk about aft steering jets and available aerosurfaces, most of which went over Leo's head. He could understand the numbers, however, and he followed the descent on his station monitor, watching the decrease in speed and altitude and trying to imagine that it really was the Atlantic Ocean whizzing past beneath them. 'Okay,' said Tolliver. 'Here we go. Switching to manual.'

The next five minutes were filled with a constant stream of instruction, punctuated by the occasional swear word and apology from Skater, but finally the shuttle had come to a standstill, only slightly beyond the end of the runway, and Skater let out a whoop of delight. 'I rock!'

'Well, there's still some space for improvement,' said Tolliver. 'But yeah, I'd say you rock. Nice job.'

Later, over lunch, Skater went through the whole thing again for Pete, and even though he'd carried out the procedure himself, for real, well over a thousand times, she insisted on explaining every step to him in minute detail by successfully landing a mini-baguette onto a cutlery runway that stretched across the table. She did not, Leo noticed, choose to drive her bread off the end of the runway and onto the floor.

'How about you, Leo?' Pete asked. 'How are your piloting skills coming along?'

'They're not. I tried, but the simulator wasn't having any of it. I think it could smell my fear or something because every time I sat in the seat things went wrong. I still enjoy it, though,' he added quickly, in case Pete took this as a sign he wanted to stop the lessons.

'It's fun watching Skater do it and I kind of like the navigation side of things. I love plotting routes into the astro-charts and tracking the other local ships and stuff.'

'Well, that's a pretty good skill to learn as well.' He looked at Skater. 'Piloting's not all just take-offs and landings, you know. You have to be able to get where you want to go as well.'

'Yeah, but I can leave all that to the computer.'

'And what if the computer stops working?'

'Well then,' she said with a wink at Leo. 'Wonder-boy can fix it for me.'

'And what if he stops working?' Leo asked.

'Bad things,' she said sternly, and took a large bite out of her shuttle.

18

MISTER ARCHER MAKES HIS MOVE

TWO DAYS AFTER the *Dragon* crossed into Martian space, Mr Archer launched his attack.

From a distance his ship appeared to be nothing more than a medium freighter, patched up and modified in typical pirate fashion with a single, low-frequency energy weapon mounted beneath the main hull. But all this was just a shell, by way of disguise, and inside lay a state-of-the-art rapid-attack frigate with enough firepower to destroy the *Dragon* several times over. The greedy and ambitious admiral who had turned a blind eye to the ship's current mission as a 'personal favour' to the Old Man was no friend of his, but Mr Archer had to admit that he had provided them with everything they could possibly need for the task in hand.

As well as an impressive collection of energy weapons, rocket torpedoes and some traditional cannon for work in-atmosphere, the ship also came equipped with a fully automated, AI-controlled targeting system, a vast array of sensor and communications jammers, a retractable, kevlar-bonded boarding tunnel and some truly impressive laser-cutting equipment that could slice through the hull of a civilian cruise ship in minutes if necessary. Even the cabins were large and comfortable. As the frigate raced towards its prey, Mr Archer decided he would definitely keep it for himself once the Old Man's plans had come to fruition and the admiral was no longer an issue.

'They're hailing us, Captain,' called one of the crew from the far side of the bridge. 'Requesting ident.'

'Ignore them,' Mr Archer replied, watching the *Dragon*'s progress on the main monitor screen.

'They say they will be forced to defend themselves if we don't respond or alter course.'

'Good.' As he continued to watch, two tiny dots emerged from the front of the *Dragon*'s hub and sped towards him.

'They've launched fighters, Captain.'

'They don't have fighters,' Mr Archer replied with a sneer. 'They're lightly armed shuttles – nothing more. Target them, and transfer fire-control to me.' As the computer locked onto the two targets and tracked their approach, Mr Archer tapped in the code to disable the weapon safety protocols and sat back to wait.

The shuttles opened fire as soon as they were in range, their unseen laser beams burning their way into the outer shell of the disguised frigate. Several members of the bridge crew looked nervously towards Mr Archer, but the giant man's face was as emotionless as ever. He tracked the craft as they sped past on either side of the frigate but made no move to return fire. Instead he concentrated on the *Dragon* itself, looming ever closer ahead of them. 'Tag it,' he said quietly.

The man sitting beside him tapped on his console for a few

seconds, then waited, watching his monitor. For thirty seconds nothing happened and then the monitor began flashing up new information. 'Tagged, sir,' the man said with obvious relief.

Just then the frigate was rocked by more fire from the shuttles as they came in for their second attack run. This time a large chunk was blasted free from the side plating, but Mr Archer knew there was no danger of the shuttles' weapons causing anything more than minor surface damage to the military armour hidden beneath. 'Confirm the tag,' he said, calmly.

'Confirmed.'

'Good.' He pressed the fire button his finger had been hovering over and felt the ship shudder as globes of super-heated plasma, many times more powerful than the shuttle lasers, shot out from hidden recesses on either side of the frigate. The two small craft didn't stand a chance. For one instant they blossomed like miniature suns, and the next they were gone. Mr Archer didn't even bother to watch. 'Start the clock,' he said. 'We have twelve hours. After that we have to assume help will arrive and I want to be long gone before it does.'

The man sitting beside him looked up from his monitor. 'Surely we don't need to worry about other ships, sir? Hell, in this little beauty we could take on a whole squadron of Sentinels and come out on top.'

Mr Archer said nothing. But suddenly he sprang from his seat and in one swift movement had spun round and brought his foot down on the man's arm. It was a difficult manoeuvre to make in zero gravity, but even so, the blow came down with such force that there was a definite snap of bone. The man let out a howl and drifted backwards out of his seat, but before he could find his balance, Mr Archer had reached across with one of his huge hands and grabbed him by the throat, pulling him up until their faces were almost touching. 'Do not question my orders,' he said in his harsh growl. 'Ever. Now, do as I say and start the clock.'

The man let out another howl of pain as Mr Archer grabbed the broken arm and forced it down to the control panel, using it to tap out the sequence that began the countdown. Once the clock was running he heaved the whimpering man across the room and turned his attention to the main screen. 'Take him away,' he ordered. Immediately two of the other crew members freed themselves from their seats and collected the limp and drifting body. 'And make sure he's the first one across when we board. Now, someone else get me a link to the captain of that ship. Audio only at this end.'

Two minutes later a view of the *Dragon*'s bridge appeared on the main screen. A nervous captain was seated in the command chair and three senior officers were standing behind him. 'This is Captain Henrik Iversen of the Zodiac Cruise Ship, *Dragon*. To whom am I speaking?'

Mr Archer studied the face of the captain, searching for any clue to whether or not he was a fighter. All he saw was fear. He was a tired old man who was probably thinking about a family somewhere, about retirement, about getting out of this situation as quickly and painlessly as possible. He wouldn't put up a fight unless he was forced into it, and Mr Archer had no intention of doing that. He was here to cause disruption, to make people afraid, and to ruffle a lot of important feathers on Mars, but not for any unnecessary killing that might attract unwanted attention from Earth.

'Hello?' asked Captain Iversen. 'Who's there? What ship is that?'

'My ship does not have a name,' Mr Archer replied, finally. 'And neither do I.'

'Can I at least see who it is I'm talking to?'

'No. You'll see me soon enough.'

'Well, sir, I am duty-bound to inform you that the Zodiac Corporation has a strict policy of non-negotiation with hostage-takers. And furthermore, the Corporation will seek the apprehension and prosecution of all perpetrators of...'

'Yes, yes,' cut in Mr Archer impatiently. 'Fine. But now I want you to stop talking and listen to me. You are aware, I assume, that we have tagged your ship, yes?'

'Yes,' confirmed Captain Iversen.

'Good. And you will also be aware that our ship is much faster and more heavily armed than yours, yes?'

'Yes.'

'So listen to me very carefully, Captain Henrik Iversen. I want you to maintain your present course and speed. If you try to run I will catch you and I will slice your ship into so many tiny pieces that your precious corporation will never be able to put it back together again. I mean to dock with you in just under one hour from now and I expect to find no resistance of any sort. If I do, I will kill you and every one of your officers, slowly and painfully, and I will take a great deal of pleasure in doing so. Is that clear?'

There was not even a moment's hesitation. 'Yes.'

'Good. You will also have crew, passenger and cargo manifests waiting for me and I expect all those passengers to be tucked away inside their cabins where they will not cause any trouble.'

He cut the link.

19
PIRATES!

SKATER WAS ON final approach on her next landing attempt when Lieutenant Tolliver received the emergency call. The moment it finished, he shut down the simulator. 'Session's over,' he said abruptly.

'Hey,' Skater complained. 'So not fair. That was going to be my best landing yet.'

'I'm sure it would've been,' Tolliver said, ignoring her complaints. 'But right now I've got to go. Sorry.'

Leo saw the worried look on the lieutenant's face. 'What is it?' he asked.

'Don't know. Could be nothing, could be... Listen, you kids ought to go back and find your parents for now. We'll pick this up again tomorrow.'

On their way back to the cabin, Leo couldn't help noticing that the whole crew area had become a hive of activity. Several officers, including Tolliver, had made their way to the access lift and were heading for the Hub, while in every room they passed, stewards were putting on their uniforms, or being given hurried instructions by their supervisors, or crowding round any available monitor and discussing whatever it was they were watching. Leo tried to step into one of the rooms to take a look for himself, but he was politely turned around and pushed back out into the corridor.

Their own cabin was empty, but after a quick search of the Ring, Leo and Skater found Pete sitting quietly in one of the main lounges reading his slate. 'Hey, guys,' he said as they approached. 'Finished already?'

'Tolliver got called away,' Skater told him. 'Something's happened but he wouldn't tell us what. And all the crew seem to be rushing around getting ready for something.'

Pete scanned the lounge. There were three stewards on duty, but all three were clustered together and deep in conversation. 'I'll go and ask, see if there's anything they can tell me.'

'Hey guys, look,' called Leo. He was standing by one of the large viewing screens that served as windows, which gave a clear view of the front of the Hub. 'They're opening the docking bay.' Skater, Pete and the stewards all rushed over and were in time to see the two shuttles launch. 'That's not good,' said Pete. He turned to the stewards. 'What's going on?' They looked at each other uncertainly. 'Come on, dammit. I'm a pilot. I know you don't launch both your shuttles unless there's some serious problem.'

'We've picked up a pirate,' one of the stewards said quietly. 'We've been told not to panic the passengers and to stand by for further information. That's all we know.'

Pete turned back to the screen, following the shuttles' path. 'There!' he said, pointing to a distant patch of space. 'You can just make out its lights. It's big, but at least it looks like it's on its own.'

'Can the shuttles deal with it?' Leo asked.

Pete shook his head. 'From this distance I can't tell what kind of weapons it's got. We'll find out soon enough though.'

'The shuttles have lasers, right?' Skater asked. 'Will we see when they open fire?'

'Shhh!' muttered one of the stewards, looking round to see if any other passengers had heard. But the lounge was not busy and no one seemed to be paying any attention.

'You won't see it,' Pete explained, 'but you can guarantee they'll have been firing from the moment they were in range.'

'Can they destroy it?' one of the other stewards asked.

'Well, that's another matter. The shuttles are mostly there as a deterrent for chasing away small raiders, and that thing is way bigger than your average pirate ship. But they've got to be crazy to try attacking something this big right in the middle of the shipping lanes. The Sentinels will be all over the place by this time tomorrow. There's no way they'll get away with it.'

'They're making another run,' said Skater. 'And I'm sure I saw something like a hull panel being knocked off the big ship.'

But then the pirate ship returned fire. Two bright dots shot out from the front of the ship, found the shuttles, and destroyed both in a single incandescent instant. 'What the Sol was that?' Skater screamed, and this time no one bothered to tell her to be quiet. 'It just blew them to pieces with one shot.'

'We're in trouble,' said Pete quietly. 'Big trouble.'

More people were beginning to gather, staring at the rapidly approaching ship and asking questions none of the stewards could answer. What would happen now? Could the *Dragon* outrun it? Had they sent out a distress call? Would the pirates try to board? What then? Skater looked questioningly at her father but he shook his head and held her close. He didn't have the answers either.

The ship's public address system gave a loud warning tone that brought the room to silence.

Ladies and gentlemen, this is your captain speaking. I am sorry to have to announce that due to circumstances beyond our control we are obliged to request that all passengers return to their cabins immediately and remain there until further notice. I would like to stress that the ship is not in any danger, there is no cause for alarm, and we hope to have the situation remedied very soon. Staff members will be on hand to assist in any way possible and you will be informed the moment all public areas are re-opened. Thank you for your co-operation.

The shouting began at once, with everyone trying to be heard above everyone else. The stewards did what they could to calm people, but they knew no more than the passengers and were just as frightened. Pete took hold of Skater and Leo and steered them back towards their cabin, pushing past groups of worried passengers and desperate stewards. Once inside he sat them down and spoke to them sternly. 'I want you to stay here and lock the door after me. I'll be back as soon as I can.'

'Where are you going?' Skater asked.

'I have to see if there's anything I can do to help.'

'What? No you don't. You have to stay here with us. You're a passenger on this trip, remember, not a pilot.'

'I'm also a reservist, which means I have a responsibility to help out in situations like this.'

'Then I'm coming too,' Skater said, leaping to her feet.

'No!' Pete snapped, cutting her off. 'Absolutely not. This is not some fun adventure I'm going on. This is serious. From what the captain said, it sounds like he's got no choice but to let the pirates come aboard.'

'What?'

'You saw how powerful their weapons were. If he tries to fight or run they'll destroy the ship. His only choice is to surrender and let them do whatever they want. My guess is they'll leave the passengers alone and go for the things they need — weapons, fuel, supplies, stuff like that — so you'll be fine.' Pete drew Skater close and gave her a kiss on the forehead. 'But just in case anyone does come snooping around, you give them anything they want, understand? No heroics. I don't give a damn about any of this stuff, just you.' He looked down at Leo. 'And that goes for you too, Leo. Look after each other and don't do anything stupid.'

'Dad!' said Skater as Pete reached the door. He turned and she ran over and flung her arms around him. 'You too, okay? Nothing stupid. Promise?'

'I promise. I'll check in with Tolliver, let him know I'm available and see what I can find out. I'll be back before you know it.'

And so they waited, pacing around the small cabin and barely saying a word to each other. Leo powered up Daisy to see if she could find out what was going on but there was nothing she could tell them except that the ship had been successfully tagged and that they were preparing one of the external airlocks as the hostile ship was too big to fit into the shuttle bay.

'What does "successfully tagged" mean?' Skater asked.

A tag is an electromagnetic signal fired from one vessel to another in order to establish a forced communications link between them. If successfully established, the tag allows the tagging vessel access to all flight and navigation data from the tagged vessel and, provided the tagging vessel is the faster, will allow that vessel to plot a corresponding intercept course.

'So you're saying we can't run away?'

There are three technically accepted methods available for overriding or negating a tag. Would you like me to explain them to you?

'No. Shut up and keep listening to the ship's computers.'

'So what are they like?' Leo asked. 'Pirates, I mean. I'm guessing you know a lot more about them than I do.'

'It depends,' Skater said. 'Some people call any unregistered ship a pirate, but that's just dumb. There are plenty of adventurers or explorers or traders that aren't registered and they're probably more scared of pirates than anyone. As far as I can tell, proper pirates are quite rare, even out around Saturn and Jupiter. Either there are too many ships and it's too risky to attack them, because of the Sentinels and stuff, or else there aren't enough ships around to make pirating worth doing in the first place. Dad's been attacked a couple of times.'

'Really?'

'Yeah, but nothing serious. Once he ran away and once he chased them off. It sounds cool, doesn't it, but he says it was no biggy.'

'But what about all the stories of pirates ripping ships apart and killing everyone on board?'

'I don't know. That's what I heard, too, but Dad says it's never happened to anyone he knows. Maybe it's all just made up.'

'God, I hope so. Watching those shuttles get blown up was seriously scary. Do you think Tolliver was in one of them?'

Skater looked shocked. 'I don't know. I hadn't thought of that. No. Surely they would have had pilots already there, on standby, wouldn't they?'

'I don't know.'

Suddenly there was a noise at the door, startling them both. Someone was using a pass key to try and open it from the outside. 'Dad,' Skater said with relief and ran over to release the inside lock but Leo grabbed her hand and pulled her back.

'Wait,' he whispered. 'Check first.'

Skater nodded. 'Who is it?' she called out.

'Ah, miss? My name is Arthur. I'm one of the stewards and I was wondering if you could open the door for me.'

'Why?'

'Because there are...ah...some people here who want to speak to you.'

'Who?'

'Well, they're...'

There was an almighty crash and the door burst inwards, shattering the lock and knocking Skater backwards onto the floor. Leo jumped forward to help her but was brought to a stop by the barrel of a laser rifle pressed against his chest. Skater screamed and scrabbled away from the door, grabbing Leo's hand and pressing herself against the side of the bed as the man behind the gun stepped into the room. A second man remained in the doorway with the steward.

They were dressed in black, light-weight environment suits, minus hoods and air packs. On top they wore military-style armoured jackets. Around the first man's waist was a belt from which hung a holstered pistol and a vicious-looking, unsheathed knife. Keeping the rifle firmly pointed at Leo he scanned the cabin then looked down at Skater. 'Lisa Kate Monroe?' he asked.

'Yes,' Skater whispered.

'Where's your dad?'

'I don't know.'

'What do you mean, you don't know?'

'He went to see if there was anything he could do to help the crew. He never came back.'

The man stared at them for a moment then turned to his companion. 'Take the steward and go find him. Peter Monroe. And when you do, take him up to the bridge. I can manage here.'

The other two hurried off and the man turned his attention back to the room. 'And you must be the Fischer boy, yes?' Leo nodded. 'Don't look so surprised. We know all about you, Leonard Fischer. Or is it Lenny?'

'Leo.'

'Leo. Nice. Well it's your lucky day, Leo, 'cos you're coming with me. It seems our skipper's very keen to make your acquaintance.'

'Me? Why?'

The man jabbed his gun towards Leo's face. 'I didn't ask, 'cos it's none of my business. I just do what I'm told, see. If the boss says bring this kid to me, I do it. And if he says shoot this kid for me, I'll do that as well. Got it? Now, you've got two minutes to find a bag and pack.'

'Pack?' Leo asked, confused.

'Yes, pack. No more pleasure cruise for you, lad. You'll be our guest from now on. Go!'

Leo grabbed his backpack and began to stuff in whatever clothes he could see lying around.

'What about me?' Skater asked.

'You're not invited,' the man replied. 'But I think I'll take you as far as the bridge in case the boss has changed his mind. On your feet.'

When Leo was ready the man backed slowly out into the passageway, keeping his rifle trained on Leo. Leo slung the rucksack over his shoulder, took Skater's hand and noticed she was shaking. He tried to give her a reassuring smile but he was as terrified as she was and couldn't manage it. 'Sorry,' he whispered. 'For all this.' She said nothing, just squeezed his hand as tightly as she could.

'Come on,' the man said. 'I 'aven't got—' And then he lowered his rifle and stared at them with a puzzled look. His eyes lost their focus, and after a long, silent second, his legs buckled and he toppled forward, falling heavily to the floor. And in his place stood Ana Rodriguez Serrano.

20

AN ESCAPE PLAN

SKATER STARED AT the old woman then down at the heavily armed man sprawled on the floor. 'Ana?' was all she could manage to say.

'You two will have to drag him inside,' Ana said by way of reply. 'He's much too heavy for me.'

'Is he dead?' Leo asked.

Ana looked at the man. Already a small pool of blood was forming at the back of his neck. 'Yes, he's dead. Unfortunately, once you get to my age, killing someone becomes a lot easier than rendering them unconscious.'

'Oh my sweet Sol,' Skater moaned and sank down onto the bed, horrified by what she saw but unable to take her eyes off the body.

'Pull yourself together, girl,' Ana snapped, all signs of the friendliness of their previous meeting replaced with a ruthless efficiency. 'He was a thug and a killer and the Solar System is a lot better off without him. Now unless you want to join him, I suggest you get over your squeamishness and help Leo get him inside before his friends come looking for him.'

Leo took hold of the man's arms, and with Skater's reluctant help, managed to drag him until he was inside the cabin. Ana found a towel and wiped up the blood. The steward's pass key was still pushed into the now-broken door lock and she took it, closed the door and wedged the dead man's legs against it to keep it shut. When she was satisfied with her efforts she turned her attention to the rest of the body, searching it for anything useful and removing the weapons.

'Who are you?' Leo asked, surprised by his own calmness.

'I'm exactly who I said I was,' Ana replied. 'I'm an old lady enjoying a nice cruise on her way to see her nephew on Mars.'

'Old ladies don't kill pirates,' Skater said.

'These aren't pirates, they're mercenaries. And believe me, that's far more worrying. And I wasn't always an old lady, Skater. For a long time I worked for one of the governments back on Terra – or at least a very special, very secret part of that government.'

'Doing what?'

Ana looked down at the dead man. 'Doing the kind of work it appears you're never really allowed to retire from.'

'This is all about me, isn't it?' said Leo. 'I'm not even supposed to be on this ship, but he knew my name and exactly where to find me.'

'Actually, as far as I can tell, it's all about your mother. Unfortunately, both of you – and now the Monroes as well – have become caught up in things that are bigger than you can imagine. I don't really know what's going on myself, only what my contact has been kind enough to tell me, which was that you had hidden yourself on board and that I was to do whatever was necessary to make sure you arrived safely on Mars.' Ana sighed. 'Which I rather naively assumed would involve nothing more complicated than ensuring the crew didn't find out you were a stowaway and transfer you onto the first passing ship back to Earth. I wasn't expecting anything like this, I can tell you.'

'So what happens now?' asked Leo. 'They're bound to come looking for this guy soon, and when they find him like this they'll know we did it.'

'Which is exactly why we need to get you off this ship. She handed Leo his backpack. 'Finish packing. Add whatever food you have in the cabin and wear something warm. You too, Skater.'

'Off the ship?' said Skater. 'Are you crazy? We're in the middle of like, a billion kloms of nothing in every direction.'

'Right now it's your only hope. If you stay here, they'll kill you. If you try and hide, they'll find you and then kill you. But if they can't find you in the next few hours they'll have to abandon the search and run, otherwise they'll have the Sentinels to deal with, and no matter how powerful their ship is, they won't want that.'

'So how do we get off the ship?'

'Pack!'

While Skater put on her jacket and boots, Leo went to the fridge and emptied the contents of the minibar into his bag. As an afterthought, he unplugged Daisy, wrapped her in his jacket and squeezed her into the now-full rucksack. As he did so, something fell out of his pocket and Ana reached down and picked it up. For a moment she studied it, then smiled and handed it back. It was the plastic call-card Aitchison had given him on Luna. He'd completely forgotten about it and would happily have left it behind, but Ana insisted he bring it. 'Keep this safe. It may prove useful sometime. Now, let's walk and talk.'

They stepped carefully around the body, Ana pulled the door closed behind them as best she could and the three of them made their way cautiously along the deserted corridor, heading in the opposite direction to the crew section. There were surveillance cameras in the corridors, but there was nothing they could do about that except hope no one was watching.

'The escape pods,' Skater said, once she realised where Ana was taking them.

'Precisely.'

'But they'll detect the launch and come straight after us.'

'No they won't. I'll see to that.'

'Then they'll pick up the beacon.'

'Not if you're not transmitting.'

'But we have to transmit. It's automatic.'

'Young woman,' Ana growled. 'Is there anything you don't know?'

'My dad's a pilot. I know a lot about spaceships.'

'Indeed.'

Ana stopped in front of a door marked *Emergency Access Only*, and opened it with the pass key she'd removed from the cabin door. Metal steps led down to a long, narrow passageway with a row of air lock doors on either side. 'Now listen to me very carefully,' she said. 'I need you to get inside a pod. Seal yourselves in but do not, I repeat, do not under any circumstances turn on the power. I shall release you from this end and you'll quickly drift away from the ship. After half an hour or so you'll be undetectable.'

'Yeah,' interrupted Skater. 'And then as soon as we power up, the beacon will kick in and they'll spot us.'

'Which is exactly why you won't power up.'

'What? This is crazy. How are we going to survive without power?'

Ana used the swipe card to unlock the closest air lock and motioned for them to get inside. 'Look, it's huge. These things are designed for ten people. There's enough air to last the two of you several days before it will begin to feel stuffy and I doubt you'll notice it getting any colder at all. In twenty-four hours our visitors will be long gone and there will be a score of friendly craft out looking for you, so all I'm asking you to do is remain dark until then. After twenty-four hours you can power up and I promise you'll be picked up in no time.'

Skater shook her head. 'No. We can hide out here on the ship if it's only for twenty-four hours. There's hundreds of places where they'd never find us in that time.'

'Then be my guest,' Ana snapped. 'And good luck avoiding all the cameras and heat sensors and roving search parties. I'll be in my cabin being a nice harmless old lady if you need me.'

'Wait,' said Leo. 'We'll do it.'

'What?' Skater replied, shocked. 'No we won't.'

Leo stepped through the air lock and took hold of the inner door. 'Yes, we will. I'm not being taken prisoner by pirates, or mercenaries, or whoever they are, and your friend is right. If we stay on the ship they'll find us. And if it's only me they want, what's to say they won't kill you in revenge for killing one of their own? Sorry, Skater, but I really think this is our only choice, and I'm closing this door in ten seconds.' Skater looked desperately at Leo and then back at Ana. 'Nine, eight, seven...'

'What about my dad?' Skater demanded.

'He'll be fine and I'll explain everything to him.'

'Six, five, four, three...'

Skater kicked the side of the air lock and let out a roar of anger. Then she clambered through to Leo, gave him a hard slap across the face and stormed to the far end of the escape pod where she strapped herself into one of the seats and sat staring at the wall. Leo closed the door and sealed it shut.

Ana closed the airlock's outer door then spent more time than she would have liked struggling with the manual release for the pod. Her arms were weak and the lever was heavy, but finally she forced it down and there was a hiss as the restraining clamps released and the pod was pushed gently away from the ship. Satisfied, she made her way back to the main passageway and quickly along to her cabin.

Aitchison, she thought, remembering the call-card Leo had dropped. H.S.N. It was such an old joke, but clearly someone at the Network still had an old-fashioned sense of humour. Well, whoever this particular Aitchison was, he would definitely be contacting her again once the *Dragon* arrived at Mars and she could explain to him exactly how much trouble she had been put to for his benefit. Surely the very least they could do in return would be to offer her one of those rather lovely Ambassador Class cabins for the return trip to Earth.

At the door to her cabin she paused, drew out the percussion knife she had used to kill the mercenary earlier, and held it against the fire alarm on the wall. When she pressed the release there was a faint pop and then the deafening blare of sirens. Quickly she locked herself into her room, lay on her bed and waited for the mayhem.

21

ALONE IN THE DARK

AS LEO SHUT THE DOOR, the darkness closed in around him. There were no windows in the pod and he hadn't thought to look around and work out where anything was before sealing the two of them inside, or bring anything as simple and obvious as a torch for that matter. Reaching out cautiously into the blackness, he felt around until he found a seat and strapped himself in. Escape was their first priority and after the pod separated from the ship they would quickly lose the artificial gravity that was keeping him the right way up.

His face was stinging where Skater had slapped him. She could hit really hard when she wanted to, and the blow had come with all the fear and frustration and anger that had built up inside her with nowhere to go. He didn't blame her – he knew just how she felt – but that didn't stop it from hurting.

'Are you strapped in?' he asked.

There was no reply, not even the sound of a movement. He looked across, but the darkness was total, and even though he knew she was just a few feet away, the feeling of isolation was so great he might as well have been in the pod by himself.

Was she right? Was the plan crazy? A few minutes ago it had made perfect sense. But now he was starting to have second thoughts. Huge big second thoughts. Maybe they could have hidden somewhere on board like Skater had suggested. It would only have been for a few hours and there were hundreds of places down on the Ring. Surely the pirates would have run out of time long before they could have searched the whole ship, even with scanning equipment? Why had he trusted the word of a complete stranger? Because she was an old woman and sounded so convincing? Because he'd seen her kill someone right in front of his eyes? No. It was because she'd said they would kill Skater if they caught her and one look at Ana's face had told him she knew exactly what she was talking about.

He felt sick and realised they were losing their gravity as they separated from the ship. He clenched his fists, took a deep breath and desperately hoped he wasn't going to throw up. Twenty-four hours of sudden weightlessness and total darkness was going to be bad enough, but it would be unbearable with a cloud of vomit floating around in there as well. But the queasiness passed after a few seconds and he was pleased to see how well his body had adapted to space travel in the weeks since he'd left Earth. He thought back to that shuttle journey, when he'd first experienced weightlessness and when he'd first met Skater. How simple everything had seemed. Simple and exciting and childish. He'd imagined it was going to be the greatest adventure of his life. Unfortunately, that was exactly what it had become.

'We've left the ship,' he said. 'We're on our own now.' There was still no reply. 'Skater?'

'Leave me alone,' she said, quietly.

'I just...' he began. And then stopped. Just what, he thought? Just wanted to protect her? Just wanted to make everything right? So far every time he'd tried he'd actually made things worse. She was right; he should leave her alone. 'Nothing,' he mumbled.

As he sat turning things over in his mind, it suddenly occurred to him that he had, in fact, brought a torch with him. In one of the side compartments of his rucksack was his pocket slate. He didn't use it for anything except playing games, but it had a nice bright screen that would do as an emergency light source – assuming it had any charge. But finding his rucksack was not so easy. He'd put it down beside his seat, but once they separated from the *Dragon* it must have drifted off. He unfastened his seat restraint and carefully stood up, feeling around with his arms outstretched so as not to crash into anything, and after a moment the rucksack nudged him in the side of the head.

The light came as a huge relief. Leo hadn't realised how nervous the darkness was making him, even though he knew there couldn't possibly be anything to be afraid of inside the pod. Skater turned to see what was going on and he held up the slate and smiled. 'Well, the good news is we have light. The bad news is the battery's on twenty-eight percent, but at least it'll give me enough time to have a look around.'

Skater didn't reply, but she didn't turn away again either. She watched as Leo made his way around the pod, checking the control panels to make sure he knew how to power up the ship when the time came and searching the storage compartments beneath the seats for anything useful. There wasn't much, just some small pillows and blankets, but finally his searching paid off and he discovered two fully charged emergency torches clipped into panels on either side of the door. He let one of them rest against the roof and finally there was enough light to show them the entire pod.

It was quite small. It would certainly have been a tight squeeze for the ten people it was designed for, but for Leo and Skater it was like being in their own private shuttle. There was space to lie down, as long as they could find some way of stopping themselves from drifting, and Leo was relieved to see that there was even a toilet attachment behind a small sliding screen. It wasn't much, but it would save them a lot of awkwardness and embarrassment later on.

With nothing else to do, Leo pulled himself back into his seat. He looked across at Skater but she had wrapped herself in one of the blankets, possibly to try to get some sleep or possibly just so that she didn't have to look at him. Either way, she clearly wasn't in the mood for talking. Great, Leo thought. Nothing to do, nowhere to go, and the only other person for thousands of kilometres hates me and refuses to speak to me. Life doesn't get any better than this.

He was restless and uncomfortable and bored. He thought about using the toilet but changed his mind and decided to make a bed for himself instead. This he managed to do eventually by tying two of the blankets to the arms of his chair so that he had something like a sleeping bag that wouldn't drift off across the pod while he was asleep. Not that there was any chance of him getting any sleep. He was much too wound up for that. But he took off his boots, climbed inside and made himself as comfortable as possible – mostly because he couldn't think of anything else to do.

'What do you think's happening on the *Dragon*?' Skater asked a few minutes later. The sudden noise made Leo jump. He'd begun to think that maybe Skater had decided not to say anything to him until they were rescued and he was relieved to discover this wasn't the case.

'They'll be searching for us,' he told her. 'They're bound to have found the body by now.' For a while Skater stayed silent and Leo wondered whether that was all she was going to say. 'But I guess they didn't spot us leaving,' he continued, desperate to keep her talking. 'They would have come after us and picked us up by now if they had.'

'I can't believe I actually saw someone being killed right in front of my eyes.'

'I know. I've never even seen a dead body before.'

'I didn't know it was going to be like this.'

'What was?'

'Helping you find your mum. I thought it was going to be some great adventure where we'd be the brilliant kids who solved the whole case and the police would be like, wow, you guys are amazing, we couldn't have done it without you. And you'd have your mum back and we'd all be great friends and go off and do loads of other stuff together. I never thought people were going to die.'

'You heard what Ana said. If anyone deserved to die, it was him.'

'But what about the shuttle pilots? They were just two innocent guys who had no idea what was going on and were just trying to do their job. It was our fault they were killed.'

'Not our fault,' Leo said. 'My fault.'

'No, *our* fault. If it hadn't been for me thinking I could be some great detective none of this would have happened. You'd have gone back to Earth on a shuttle and I'd be off enjoying my holidays like any normal fifteen-year-old girl.'

'And my mum would still be missing.'

Skater fell silent again, but Leo had the feeling she still had a lot to say so he kept quiet and waited for it to come pouring out.

'They're going to kill my dad, aren't they?' she said at last.

'That's not what Ana said.'

'Ana said exactly what she needed to say to get us off the ship. I don't care what kind of super-spy she used to be, she has no idea what they'll do when they can't find us. She's just doing her job, which is to protect you. And you know what I hate? I hate the way everyone seems to know what's going on except us. They all say things like, this is big, bigger than you can imagine. Well, what is? What's so damn important about some stupid high-tech spaceship that means people have to be killed for knowing anything about it? Honestly, what? What?' She was shouting now and Leo didn't dare say anything in reply. He simply sat in his makeshift bed, silently agreeing with everything she was saying.

The torch on the roof began to dim. 'What's going on?' Skater asked.

'The charge is going,' Leo replied. 'We've probably only got a couple of minutes before it goes completely and I don't want to use the other one until we come to power up tomorrow.' He looked across to the corner. 'There's a toilet over there if you need to go while there's still light. The hose won't be working of course, but at least it's something.'

Skater looked at the tiny cubicle and grimaced. 'I'll be fine... fortunately. Hungry though.'

'Ah, well you're in luck then,' Leo said. 'Because we have chocolate.' He pulled over his rucksack and opened the top to get at the supplies he'd taken from the minibar, firing two of the bars across the room to her. Then the torch faded out completely so they sat in the darkness and ate chocolate, talking quietly but actually saying very little. Skater's anger had faded with the light and now Leo thought she just sounded sad.

'Do you like me, Leo?' she asked.

'Yeah. Of course I do,' Leo replied.

'Why?'

'Why? Because you're...' Leo paused, trying to decide what to say and blushing in the darkness. '...Likeable. I don't know, you're just easy to be with.'

'Really? As far as I can see I'm constantly bossy, constantly grumpy, and so far I've managed to reduce you to tears and I've slapped you round the face. Sorry for that, by the way.'

'It's fine,' Leo said, smiling to himself. 'It hardly hurts at all now.'

'No, but really. What's to like?'

'I'll tell you what it is,' Leo said after a pause. 'When I'm with you I enjoy being me. You don't care that I'm a computer geek and you never tell me I should be wearing on-trend clothes or listening to different bands or anything, even if that's what you actually think.'

'I think you shouldn't ever have to pretend to be someone you're not, especially if it's to impress someone else. Trust me, I've been there and it never works.'

'Yeah,' he replied. 'I know.'

They spoke less and less, and after a while they fell silent again. After an even longer while Leo finally began to feel tired and despite everything, he thought he might actually be able to get some sleep. It was all still present — the fear and the worry and the horror — but there in the dark, with Skater somewhere close by, he felt strangely safe and happy.

'Are you sleepy?' he whispered. He waited, but there was no reply so he pulled the blanket up around his neck and turned onto his side. 'Good night, Lisa Kate Monroe. Sweet dreams.'

22

FINDERS, KEEPERS

LEO WOKE WITH A START from a dream in which a huge, black-clad figure was standing over him, pointing a gun in his face and shouting, *knock-knock, knock-knock*, over and over. He opened his eyes and panic flooded in as he discovered that he couldn't see or feel anything. He reached out but there was nothing, and only after several terrified seconds did he remember where he was and calm down enough to realise he must have slipped out from his blankets in his sleep.

Suddenly there was a loud grating noise and the whole pod lurched sideways. Something hard caught him on the front of the head and sent him spinning away with a grunt of pain.

'Leo?' Skater shouted. 'What's going on?'

'I don't know. Where are you?'

'Here. I'm here. I'm trying to find you.'

Leo reached out into the darkness, found something to grab

hold of and pulled himself towards it. It was one of the control panels and it was upside down. 'Did we hit something?' he asked.

'I don't know,' Skater said. 'Either that or someone's grabbed us.'

Leo spun around and pulled himself across the pod until he reached the door and the second torch. As soon as there was light Skater pushed towards him and grabbed his hand. 'Sweet Sol,' she said, staring at the cut on his forehead. 'You're bleeding.'

'I'm fine. Shhh!'

They floated silently, straining to listen for any further noise. Leo's heart was pounding, his head was throbbing and he could barely hear anything over the sound of his breathing. There was another jolt and he grabbed the door to prevent them being hurled across the pod.

'Someone's got us.'

'The pirates?'

'I don't know. How long's it been since we left the ship?'

Skater checked her watch. 'Nine. No, nearly ten hours. That's nowhere near enough time for us to be safe. They must have found out what happened.'

'But we're not transmitting. How could they find us?'

'I don't know. But I'm scared, Leo. Really scared.'

'Me too.'

There was nothing to do but wait, and the waiting went on and on. After a while, Leo found his fear was being replaced by impatience and he began to feel foolish, pressed against the side wall of the pod like a frightened animal, ready to spring away at the first sign of danger. 'What are they doing?' he asked. 'Why don't they come in?'

'Setting up an airlock,' Skater replied. 'It'll take a while to pump the air in and check it's secure.'

'Well at least they're probably not going to kill us then. If they were going to do that, they wouldn't bother with an airlock. But this is crazy. I'm starting to get bored, waiting to be captured by pirates.'

Skater let out a snort of laughter. 'Sorry,' she said. 'That sounded kind of funny.'

Leo grinned. It was true, it did sound funny. And it seemed like such a long time since either of them had had anything to laugh about. Maybe now was an odd time to start again, but he had to admit that the whole situation was starting to get totally surreal. 'Hey,' he shouted. 'I don't suppose you could hurry it up at all, could you?'

'Yeah,' bellowed Skater, with another snort. 'Get a move on!'

Now Leo was laughing, too. It just came flooding out and there was nothing he could do about it. It wasn't even that funny, but every time he tried to stop he looked at Skater and they started up again.

There was a clang of metal on the far side of the door and Skater screamed. Immediately, the laughter died and the fear was back. Slowly, the lock began to rotate and Leo and Skater pushed themselves to the far side of the pod. Skater gripped Leo's arm and he gripped the torch, holding it in front of them as if it might provide some sort of protection.

The door swung open and Leo caught a glimpse of someone in a bulky environment suit filling the doorway. Then the figure pointed a much brighter torch into Leo's face and he was forced to shield his eyes. But that glimpse had told him one thing – the person did not appear to be carrying a gun.

The torch panned slowly around the pod and only when the figure was satisfied that no one else was hiding in the darkness did it step through the doorway. Leaving the torch floating, the figure released the safety catch and removed its helmet, revealing someone so unlikely to be a pirate that Leo felt suddenly weak as the tension drained away and relief flooded in.

The man facing them was at least sixty years old. He was almost completely bald, but had a straggly white beard that disappeared down into his spacesuit and wore a pair of small round spectacles that hooked around his ears to keep them in place. He looked so comically small and frail inside the huge suit that Leo wanted to laugh once more, but instead he held up his hand and gave a small wave.

'Hi,' said Skater quietly.

'Who the heck are you?' the man asked. 'And why the heck have you switched off all your power?'

'That,' replied Leo, 'is a really long story.'

'You off the *Dragon*?'

'Yes.'

The man nodded. 'Thought so. And you in some kind of trouble?'

'Yes.'

'Thought that, too. Well, you don't look dangerous. You want to come aboard and tell this really long story to me, or you want me to close up and leave you alone again?'

'Please,' said Skater, feeling foolish but needing to ask anyway. 'You're not a pirate are you?'

The man gave a quick laugh. 'Ha! Pirate? You better ask the rest of my crew about that.'

His name was Solomon, though these days people just called him Old Man Sol, and the rest of his crew was made up of his wife, Li, and a lazy old cat they called Early Warning. They were free traders who mostly made short runs between Mars and the Belt stations but also, like now, the occasional trip all the way to Earth for luxury goods or engine parts. Their ship, *Beautiful Moment*, was technically an old-style cargo flute, but with so many replacements and alterations over the years that it was no longer much of anything in particular. All this Leo and Skater learned within the first few minutes of coming aboard, and it was clear both Sol and Li were happy to have someone to share their story with.

Their own story took much longer to tell, and was told over a very welcome meal Li quickly put together for them. Fresh bread, cheese, real tomatoes and apples, even some thin strips of cured ham. Clearly not all the luxury goods they'd picked up on Earth were for trading. And for once it was Leo who did most of the talking. Skater seemed distracted, barely saying anything except in reply to direct questions, and occasionally not even then. When the story, and the meal, came to an end, Li looked pointedly at her husband. 'Sol, why don't you take Leo over to the pod for a while and get it powered up? Skater, you stick here with me and we'll see if we can get a message through to the *Dragon*, eh?'

Skater was suddenly more alert. 'Really? Can you do that? Will it be safe?'

'Oh, sure,' Li replied, patting Skater's arm reassuringly. 'We already spoke with her a few times over the past three or four days – just routine navigation stuff – so they won't think it's anything strange if we call again.'

'But what about the pirates? You'll be telling them exactly where you are.'

Li smiled. 'Don't you worry yourself. We've been doing this for plenty long enough to have learned how to deal with pirates. Come on, let's go see what we can find out.' She led Skater towards the front of the ship and Leo followed Sol back into the escape pod.

'Will it be safe to power up?' Leo asked. 'What about the homing beacon? If the pirates are still in the area and they detect it, they're bound to follow it.' Sol gave him a sly smile. 'Watch and learn, my boy. And hold my torch.' Sol searched the pod until he found the particular control panel he was looking for and carefully removed the front. 'These days it's all labelled so any fool can find his way around. Not like back when you actually had to know about things. See?' He held up a collection of variously coloured wires. Along each one, in tiny lettering, was printed its function. 'Of course, you have to be able to read tiny and I'm not so good at that now, even with these things on. Here, you look. Which one says beacon on it?'

Leo stared at the wires. 'This one says, Emergency Location Transponder,' he said helpfully.

'The blue one? Good, good, good. Now, we follow it back to that little box there and very carefully we pop it out, like so. We could just cut it, of course, but this way we can put it back later.'

'Do we need to?'

'Sure we do. Recovery rights. Zodiac will pay us a nice fat reward for bringing this baby in, but only if it hasn't been tampered with. We can keep it running for as long as the power holds out — that's fine — but one single cut wire or missing circuit board and it's bye-bye reward.' Sol replaced the front of the panel and went through the start-up procedure. Tiny red and green lights appeared as the various control panels came to life and after another minute the main generator started up, filling the pod with bright light and filtered air. 'So. Easy, no?'

'Yeah,' said Leo. 'I wish I'd known how to do that yesterday.'

They spent a few more minutes checking over the pod, and despite Sol's insistence that nothing was to be tampered with, he seemed happy enough to help himself to the pillows and blankets and a large collection of sachets of liquid food that Leo had missed during his own search. They were about to make their way back with their spoils when they heard Skater let out a scream from the main ship. Sol paused and looked at Leo. 'That a good scream, or a bad scream?'

Leo listened as Skater let out a whoop of joy at her dad. 'It's okay,' he replied, beaming. 'That's a good scream.' And he rushed through to join in the conversation and find out exactly what had happened.

Ana's plan had worked perfectly. The fire alarm had caused panic and hundreds of passengers had streamed out of their cabins and towards the assembly points. The crew hadn't known whether to go and help or to obey the raiders' instructions and remain in the crew area, and the raiders hadn't known what to do when most of the crew decided to ignore them and go to the passengers. In all the confusion it was hardly surprising that no one noticed the launch of a single, unpowered escape pod.

The dead man was discovered, but not until much later. And that, Pete explained, had been when his problems really began. When the raiders came aboard he'd been with Tolliver in the Hub and had been forced into one of the cargo holds along with the rest of the flight crew, where they were kept under armed guard. 'Then one of them appeared and said I was to go with him,' Pete said. 'He told me he had you and Leo, and we were all off to see their captain. But just as we arrived at the docking bay the fire alarms went off and I was left standing around while everyone else tried to work out what was going on. I probably could have snuck away, but I was sure you'd be arriving any second and I didn't want to miss you so I just waited and waited. But of course you weren't going to be turning up – you were already off the ship by then – and eventually their captain appeared from inside their ship and demanded to know where you were.

'He was this huge great bull of a man and he kept his visor

pulled almost all the way down so I never got to see his face, but he had this horrible rasping voice like a snake's hiss, and I definitely won't be forgetting that in a hurry. I told him I had no idea where you were and that I thought his men had you and were on their way to bring you to him. Then, when he told me you'd killed the guard and escaped, I was sure he was going to shoot me there and then.'

'But we didn't kill him,' Skater said.

'I know. I know. Your friend Ana came and found me as soon as the pirates left and explained the whole thing. I have to say I was furious with her for sending you off like that and I told her so as well, but everything's turned out okay so I guess she was right. I'm just so glad you're safe.'

'So how did you get away?' Leo asked.

'He let me go. I don't really understand it myself, but that's what happened. They searched the ship for a few hours and when they couldn't find you he seemed to lose interest and ordered his men to start looting stuff.' Pete looked around to make sure no one was close to him before turning back to the screen. 'Obviously this wasn't a proper pirate attack. It's all to do with your other business, Leo, I'm sure of it. My guess is that the man let me go because he figured this was the best way of finding you later, knowing that we'd meet up again once we reach Mars. I don't know.'

'Yeah,' Leo said. 'That would make sense, I guess. So maybe Ana's plan wasn't such a bad one after all. I mean, we're all still here, aren't we? Even if here isn't actually there, if you see what I mean.'

'Wait a sec,' said Skater. 'What do you mean, we'll meet up again once we're on Mars? Why aren't we meeting up now?'

'Well,' said Pete. 'That's another problem.'

'What is?'

'The fact that we're not stopping to pick you up.'

'What?' demanded Skater. 'Why not?'

'Captain Iversen says he needs to get to Mars as quickly as possible now and can't spare the time or the fuel to slow down enough to let you catch up. If you were still drifting in the pod that would be one thing, but seeing as how you've been picked up and are on your way to Mars anyway, he says it's out of the question.'

'But—'

'Listen, Skater. I don't like it any more than you, but there's nothing I can do about it. And believe me, I tried. If we still had the shuttles I could have come and picked you up. But we don't. So I'm going to have to carry on to Mars without you and sort things out for when you arrive. At this speed we'll be there in less than a week, and I guess you'll arrive about a week after that. That still gives us plenty of time on Mars before the return trip to Luna. I'll do what I can to make up for it, but to be honest, I can't see us getting much sightseeing done now. There's too much other stuff that needs sorting out. Sorry.'

'Dad!' Skater protested. 'I don't give a damn about the sightseeing. I just want to be back with you; that's all. Promise me that whatever it is that needs sorting out, we'll do it together, okay? No more going off and leaving me on my own.'

'I promise.'

'And you'll call me every day from now on?'

'Twice a day. More. As often as I can.'

'Dad?'

'Yes, sweetheart?'

'I love you.'

'I love you too.'

Leo stood to one side, feeling slightly awkward as they said their goodbyes and wondering when, if ever, he might get to have his own family reunion. Right now, the possibility seemed further away than ever.

23

THE COMING STORM

THE CALL FROM THE OLD MAN came much sooner than Mr Archer would have liked. Ideally he would have liked it not to come at all, but he knew that sooner or later he would have to explain that his mission had been a failure. At least this way the Old Man couldn't throw anything at him.

'Ah, Mr Archer,' Carlton Whittaker said. 'Already on your way home, I take it?' He was smiling, but as Mr Archer well knew, that didn't mean he was happy, only that the mind behind the smile was busy planning something. And that something could be extremely painful for someone. On the wall screen behind Whittaker, huge waves crashed onto a wind-swept beach while dark clouds filled the sky above. Ominous.

'Yes, sir.'

'Well I must say, you've certainly stirred up a hornets' nest back here in Minerva. The people are horrified and terrified in equal measure.'

'You have the details already?'

'Naturally. You know what they say; good news travels faster than a spaceship.'

'But I do not have good news. I failed to locate the boy.'

'Oh, never mind the boy,' Whittaker said with a dismissive wave of his hand. 'He's old news. I'll get to that later. It was the raid itself that was important and that's played out wonderfully. Imagine, pirates so bold as to attack a cruise ship on an established route. A Zodiac, no less. People are asking where it will end. The Belt stations? Phobos and Deimos? Perhaps even Mars itself is no longer safe? I've already mobilised the fleet to protect our mines and not only is there absolutely nothing those fools in government can do about it, half of them don't seem to care.' He motioned to the screen behind him. 'As you can see, Mr Archer, there's a storm coming. And it's my storm. One way or another, I will have this planet as my own and I do not intend to wait much longer before I get it.'

'Of course.'

'Now,' said Whittaker. 'Tell me how the boy managed to slip through your fingers and I shall tell you something interesting about the mother.'

'He is more resourceful than his report led me to believe. He killed one of my men.'

'Really? A teenage boy? Fascinating. Go on.'

'He went to ground. There wasn't time for a detailed search of the ship and the scanners gave us nothing. In the end I took the decision to forget him and concentrate on the primary objective. If this was wrong, I apologise.'

'No need. After all, he was only ever going to be the carrot to your stick where the good professor was concerned, and it appears we no longer require either. Professional curiosity has finally got the better of her, as I knew it would, and she has begun to work with our technicians. Perhaps not as enthusiastically as on one of her own projects, but nevertheless, she has taken the first step.'

'With results?'

'Patience, Mr Archer. Patience. Give her time and a little freedom and I'm quite sure she'll make remarkable discoveries soon enough. The trick will be making sure she shares them with us. That's where having the boy might have proved useful. But no matter. He seems to be heading straight towards us as fast as he can anyway, so once he arrives we can arrange for the two of them to be reunited. In the meantime, you and I have plenty to be keeping us busy. How do you like your new ship, by the way?'

Mr Archer curled the side of his mouth into a smile. 'It suffices.'

'Good. Well, you'd better bring it back safe and sound. The admiral suspects we haven't been entirely honest with him and he's been calling me day and night trying to find out what we've done with it. Really, he's becoming quite tiresome.'

'Would you like me to kill him?'

'Now, now, Mr Archer,' said Whittaker with a small laugh. 'The admiral is a useful weapon in our armoury for now. I would hate to see him replaced by someone less...accommodating. But believe me, when I change my mind you shall certainly be the first to know.'

Mr Archer nodded, satisfied.

'Now,' Whittaker announced. 'To work. I have an election to win and some generals to bribe. And you, Mr Archer, have more acts of piracy to commit.'

Once the connection was broken, Mr Archer leant back in his chair and let out a sigh of relief. Smiles and laughter — that had been unexpected. He'd been prepared for anger, criticism, even cold disappointment, and he would have taken everything the Old Man threw at him in humble silence. But to have his failure dismissed as irrelevant? That was almost an insult in itself.

It was the boy, Mr Archer thought. Just fifteen years old, a schoolboy, and yet Leo Fischer had made a fool of him, made him look sloppy and amateur, and this was not something he was going to forget. If the Old Man wanted the boy alive, then he would do as the Old Man said. But once their business was finished, once he became surplus to requirements, he would teach Leo Fischer the lesson he was due — a lesson he would certainly not live to regret for very long.

He flicked the intercom and one of his lieutenants appeared on the screen. 'Find me a ship,' Mr Archer growled at the man. 'And find it quick. I need to kill something.'

24

BEAUTIFUL MOMENT

BEAUTIFUL MOMENT WAS TOO SMALL to carry passengers and it was explained to Leo and Skater, in the politest possible way, that they would be expected to help out until they arrived at Mars.

For Leo this meant two wonderful weeks of tinkering with the ship's computers and electronic systems with Sol, each of them taking great delight in showing off their particular skills to the other. Sol had been a trader for nearly forty years and knew his ship inside out, having single-handedly replaced pretty much everything on board at one point or another. 'Parts are not always easy to come by,' he had explained. 'So you have to know how to borrow from one system to mend another without having the whole thing fall apart around your ears.'

Leo was like a sponge, soaking up everything Sol taught him and thoroughly enjoying himself in the process. He learnt how to make an emergency fuel cell and a solar panel, how to cold-solder and how to put together an essential tool kit from everyday objects. But when it came to computers, Sol was totally out of his depth. He could just about rebuild one if he could find the right parts, but programming was beyond him and always would be, so Leo set about earning his keep by doing what he did best – playing with computers.

First he introduced Sol to Daisy and within a few hours they had her linked to the main computer, updating the navigation database and installing whatever new software she felt would be useful or, in several cases, essential for the safe and efficient running of the ship. By the third day Daisy was in full control and Leo was able to work on the system core itself. It was ludicrously out of date and Leo found himself spending more and more time each day sitting in front of the main console, inputting and testing new code until he could barely keep his eyes open. Sometimes he would be so caught up in his work that for a short while he even forgot about the grief and worry and uncertainty waiting for him once they reached Mars.

For Skater, helping out was not so straightforward. After two days of enthusiastic disasters in the galley she was forced to accept that she was no cook – something the others were quick to agree with – and nor was she anything like tidy enough to keep the place tidy. In the end Sol promoted her to Communications Officer and made her responsible for maintaining contact with the *Dragon* so that they could use the larger ship's more sophisticated sensors to keep a lookout for any further potential pirate attacks. As this basically meant talking to her father for an hour or so whenever he was free, she was more than happy to accept her new role, especially as it kept her from feeling completely useless.

But she also had another, more surprising function. Almost from the moment they had come aboard, the ship's cat, Early Warning, had taken a liking to her and was now convinced she was a more reliable source of biscuits and caresses than either of his usual providers. This pleased Skater no end and she had taken to wandering around with Early Warning either draped across her shoulders or floating beside her. As far as she was concerned, the constant company was well worth the inconvenience of taking him to the cat toilet three times a day.

Towards the end of their first week, while Leo and Sol were still busy reprogramming the ship's computers, Skater was in the hold with Li, helping her sort the cargo and divide the goods they had brought from Earth into smaller crates and containers, ready for delivery to the locations across Mars where they planned to stop off.

'What's it like?' Skater asked. 'Being a free trader, I mean.'

Li thought for a moment and shrugged. 'Lonely.'

'Really? But surely you can go anywhere you want? Any planet, any station. Aren't you meeting new people all the time?'

'Meeting, yes. But not making friends. Sure, there are people we see every time we go to a particular station or outpost. Some we've known for years and I suppose we do look forward to spending time with them. But we're there for two, maybe three days and then we're gone. They go back to their own lives and forget about us and we move on to our next delivery. They're not really friends — just good clients.'

'But don't you have a home, like a base somewhere you can go when you want to rest for a while?'

'Not really. When we're on-planet we're travelling mostly, going from market to market or stopping only to drop off a delivery. Thimble Rock, where we're headed first, I guess that's the closest we have to somewhere we could call home. It's where we lived before we became traders, where Sol was born, in fact. But we haven't stayed more than a week for well over twenty years now and we don't feel we belong there any more.'

'Don't you have family?'

'Nope. Just me and Sol.'

'You never had kids?'

'We...' Li paused in her packing and looked across at Skater. 'Did you ever wonder why we called our ship *Beautiful Moment*?'

'Well I was going to ask,' replied Skater with a smile. 'But I thought it might be something to do with you and Sol. You know, something personal.'

'You mean you thought it was to do with sex?'

'Well, yeah, maybe.'

'In a way I suppose it is.' For a while Li said nothing more but sat staring at the far bulkhead, lost in memory. Then she closed the crate she was working on and motioned for Skater to come and perch beside her.

'When I first met Sol he was a very handsome man. Strong, too. He used to come to the farm where I worked and do jobs around the place, fixing up vehicles when they broke down, repairing air scrubbers or rad-shields or whatever. He was always good with machines. Well, we got to know each other and we fell in love and straight off I knew this was the man I wanted to spend the rest of my life with. So we got married and we moved into Thimble Rock and Sol set up business as a repair man. Things like that were easy back then. The government was desperate to get people out of the cities and into the mining regions and they gave us everything we needed to open up a small workshop.

'Anyway, life was not so bad and we were doing okay and after a while we decided to start a family. Well, that wasn't so easy and it took a while, but eventually it happened and we were blessed with a beautiful little daughter. We named her Bao, which means treasure in old Chinese, and she was our special treasure.

'But we knew even before the birth that there was something the matter with her. Her heart was made wrong and the doctors told us that even with surgery, they couldn't guarantee she would survive. They suggested we...you know...end the pregnancy. Try again.'

'But you said no.'

'We both said no. We couldn't do that.'

'And she did survive after all?'

'They operated, and she survived the birth. Then they operated again, and again. But then...' Li held out her empty hands. 'It was too much. Too much for all of us. So we stopped. We took our little treasure home and tried to forget she was sick. We poured our love into her every day and every night for six months. Then one day, while I was holding her and she was smiling up at me, she died, right there in my arms. So happy and innocent and loving.' Li paused, but it was clear she had more to say. Skater blinked away a tear and watched it float out in front of her face while she waited for Li to continue.

'To lose a baby is a terrible thing, but not to have had one in the first place — that would have been much worse. I thought that at the time, and I still think that now. Those six months are more precious than everything else in our lives put together. They are our beautiful moment. We say Bao died of a broken heart, because that's what it was, but hers wasn't the only heart that broke. Sol and me, we were never the same afterwards. We didn't want to stay in Thimble Rock, didn't even much care for Mars itself, so we packed up, sold everything we could and borrowed what we didn't have and bought ourselves this ship. We needed to get away from everything for a while. But the longer we stayed away the less we wanted to go back, and eventually we decided to stay out here and make a living any way we could. That's how we ended up becoming traders and we never found anything we wanted to do as much.'

'Will you ever retire?'

'What, settle down somewhere?' Li shook her head. 'I don't think we could. We've been out here so long we wouldn't know what to do with ourselves staying in one place. No, I think we will live out here and we will die out here. And when that day comes, I hope to be able to die happy, with a smile on my face, just like my little Bao.'

There was so much more Skater wanted to ask, about life as a free trader, about the places they'd travelled to and the adventures they'd had, but it felt like now was not the time. Instead they went back to work sorting the deliveries and saying very little. After a while, Sol popped his head around the door and announced that her father was calling.

'You okay, sweetheart?' Pete asked as Skater took her seat in front of the screen. 'You look down.'

Skater managed a weak smile. 'I'm fine. Just missing you. Where are you?'

'In Minerva. We docked earlier this morning and I was on the first shuttle down. The place is in an uproar about the attack and apparently there have been some others, even closer in. The military are sending out patrols all over the place and MarsMine have even brought in their own fleet to protect their mines, though that's technically against the law out here. I tell you what, this holiday is going from bad to worse. Not only do we have all…the other business, but we seem to have picked the worst possible time to have a holiday on Mars. I'm trying to keep a low profile with the Company in case someone decides to cancel my leave and reassign me to duty out here.'

'Can they do that?'

'Sure they can, if they decide they need me.'

'Well, don't let them know you're there.'

Pete shook his head. 'I'm not going to volunteer, if that's what you mean. But as soon as I went through immigration their records would have been automatically updated. If they put out a call, I'll have to answer.'

'Hmph!'

'But listen. Things aren't that bad yet. Nowhere near. And I've still got a week before you get here so I'll sort out as much as I can before then and I promise we'll get this holiday back on track.'

'What about Leo?'

'Honestly? I think Leo needs more help than we can give him from now on,' Pete said, defensively. 'He needs someone local on the case, otherwise he'll get nowhere. I'll talk to the police here, fill them in on everything and make sure they take him seriously, not just dismiss him as some crazy kid.'

'And after that we just abandon him, is that it?'

'No, of course not. I just don't know what else we can do for him; that's all.'

'We could help him find his mum.'

'How? Where?'

'I don't know. You're the dad. I thought you always knew everything.'

Pete smiled. 'And you're the teenage girl. I thought you were the one with all the answers. Listen, we'll do what we can for Leo, okay? All I'm saying is that from now on, I don't think there is much we can do for him.'

Leo was thinking about Mars. He'd been gazing at it earlier, and considering they were only a few days away it had still seemed quite small and lonely, with only one of its tiny moons visible to keep it company in the darkness. He didn't know which one it had been —

Deimos or Phobos – and he didn't care. All that mattered now was getting onto the surface of the planet and continuing the search for his mother. He'd meant to spend his time on board the *Dragon* working out a plan of action for when he reached Mars, but so much had happened, he hadn't ever settled down to any serious thinking. Now he was days away and was still no closer to knowing what he was going to do once he got there.

And on top of everything, it seemed like he was going to be blundering around without even Skater for company. He'd overheard her conversation with Pete earlier; not deliberately – or at least not at first – and it seemed pretty clear that Pete would rather not have anything else to do with the whole business. And maybe Skater was starting to feel the same, which was fair enough, he had to admit. On Luna it had seemed so exciting. They were finding clues, making connections, getting somewhere. But since then she'd seen someone killed in front of her, been marooned in a pitch-black escape pod and been convinced her father was dead. Leo couldn't blame her for wanting to get back to her normal life after that. He would definitely do the same if he could. He didn't want to be a detective or a hero; he just wanted to be a boy with a mother again.

So, what could he do? His only solid lead was the *Arcadian*, the old pile of junk that had been swapped out for the mysterious black ship he'd seen on Duggan's video file. It had recently been transferred to one of the big museums in Minerva. If he could get a look at it, maybe he'd find something, or someone, that could help. It was a terrible plan and he knew it. The *Arcadian* was a decoy, a distraction. It wouldn't hold any clues, and even if it did, he probably wouldn't recognise them anyway. And all that was assuming he managed to get anywhere near the ship in the first place, which was unlikely.

Plan B, then. He took out the small call-card he'd been carrying since their escape from the *Dragon*. It was plain white except for the embossed name, Aitchison. He hadn't trusted the man on Luna and he didn't trust him now, but something about the way Ana had insisted he keep the card safe made him think again. Did she know him? And so what if she did? At this point Leo had no idea whose side she was on, or even if there were sides. So many people seemed to be involved in different ways and for different reasons and he didn't even know what it was they were all involved in. But Aitchison hadn't kidnapped his mother and he seemed genuinely interested in finding her. That would have to do.

Leo was alone in the escape pod, which now doubled as his bedroom. Skater would spend time there during the day – especially as Early Warning enjoyed investigating it – but Li had insisted the two of them sleep in separate parts of the ship, just in case. 'In case what?' Skater had asked, with a wink at Leo, and he'd blushed so much that thinking about it now made him start again.

It took him ten minutes to hook up his phone to the pod's communications console, and another half hour to devise a method for getting it to read the information embedded in Aitchison's card. The call was answered almost immediately. 'Hello, Leo. Nice to hear from you at last. You've been keeping busy, I gather.'

'I guess,' Leo answered. 'And I guess Ana told you about our adventures on the *Dragon*?'

'Who?'

'Ana. She was the passenger who...' Leo paused. There was barely any time lag between them, he realised. 'Are you on Mars?'

'You really are a detective.'

'But how did you know?'

'It's my business to know.'

'Are you here to help me, or to bring me back?'

'Which would you like?'

'Your help, obviously. You are still looking for my mother, aren't you?'

'Among other things.'

'Like the mystery ship that isn't really the *Arcadian*?'

'Among other things.'

'So when I get to Mars, where can I find you?'

'You can't. I'll find you.'

'Yes, but where? I'm not even—'

The connection went dead. He called again, but there was no reply. 'Great,' muttered Leo. 'More secrecy.' But it was something. It was a lifeline so that he wouldn't be completely alone once Pete and Skater left him to get on with their holiday. There were fifty million people on Mars, and apart from Pete and Skater he knew exactly one of them. No – not one: two. Because he was now convinced that somewhere down there was his mother. And he was not going to leave without her.

PART THREE

MARS

25

THE FACILITY

THE MAN TRIPPED AND FELL, bouncing across the rocky ground and sending up clouds of brown dust that hung in the air around him. For a moment he lay stunned, but then, remembering why he was running, he staggered back to his feet and stumbled towards the rocky outcrop fifty metres ahead. If he could make it to the rocks he would be safe – perhaps not forever, but at least for long enough to catch his breath, take his bearings, and work out his next move .

The plas-glass visor on his helmet was misty with condensation and he could barely see where he was going, but he staggered on, making random direction changes and kicking up dust to make himself a more difficult target. Even in the low Martian atmosphere, someone would have to be a trained marksman to stand much chance of hitting him at this range. Or very lucky, he thought, as the patch of ground beside him erupted in a shower of stone and dirt, knocking him to the ground once more.

A sharp pain in his right arm told him he'd been hit and he looked down to see a tear in his environment suit. A jagged piece of rock protruded from his arm and blood was beginning to drip from the wound, but right now that was nowhere near as important as the air leaking out. If he didn't deal with that right now, he wouldn't need to worry about stopping to catch his breath — he wouldn't have any breath left to catch.

Again he staggered to his feet and continued his erratic dash towards the rocks. Another shot hit the ground in front of him and then another ricocheted off a large rock just as he managed to throw himself safely behind it. Three more shots hit the rock, ripping out chunks of stone in tiny, almost silent explosions, before the shooter finally gave up and the running man was able to turn his attention to his injury. Gritting his teeth, he pulled the jagged piece of stone from his arm and sealed the tear with one of the quick-seal repair pads that came with the suit. The wound would have to look after itself until he could stop for long enough to set up a proper air-shield and stitch himself back together.

They would come looking for him. Of course they would, with fliers, skimmers, ground vehicles, everything they had. But he'd already disabled his suit's transponder, and once he was safely inside the canyon, and with nightfall only an hour or so away, there wasn't a chance in hell of them finding him. Most likely they'd give up the hunt after twenty-four hours, assuming his air would have run out, but they didn't know about the supply drops he'd set up along the canyon bed. These would keep him going for the three or four days he'd need to reach safety. He checked to make sure the patch on his arm was airtight. Good. A couple more minutes to gather his strength and then he would continue.

Suddenly the rock disappeared, along with the man hiding behind it. One instant they were there, and the next, with a silent sucking-in of the thin atmosphere, the whole area collapsed in on itself, leaving nothing but a shallow, perfectly smooth crater and a cloud of slowly drifting dust.

Mr Archer used the weapon's zoom sight to bring the scene up close. As the dust cleared and he was able to examine the crater in detail, he gave a grunt of satisfaction.

'Wow!' Dr Randhawa's voice cut in over his suit's comms system. 'That was some shooting, my friend. We definitely need to upgrade you from Mr Archer after that. You should be Mr Rifleman at least.' He laughed at his own joke. 'Or Mr Sniper, maybe.'

Mr Archer looked disdainfully at the other man for a moment, then turned back to examine the cannon. 'It's an effective weapon, Dr Randhawa. Still, I would rather have finished him with the rifle.'

'I'm sure you would. But he was already well beyond the rifle's maximum effective range. And he was zigzagging all over the place. I doubt anyone could have made a kill shot at that range, even with such an amazing weapon.'

Mr Archer said nothing.

The men stood on the roof of a tall, narrow, featureless building, in the middle of a sprawling compound the size of a small town. Until recently it had been MarsMine's main centre for research and development – and in a sense it still was – but MarsMine had changed quite a lot over the past few years and what was now being researched and developed in the compound had little to do with system-wide ore mining. Beyond the high-security fence that snaked its way around the complex, the rocky and lifeless Martian desert stretched to the horizon in all directions. The thin, arrow-straight silver scar of the monorail was the only sign that the settlement ever had any contact with the world beyond.

With a nod from the scientist, the group of technicians who had been standing a little way off came forward and set to work dismantling the cannon and collecting the other weapons scattered around. Dr Randhawa followed Mr Archer and the two of them made their way to the airlock that led back into the building. 'As I say, an effective weapon, but impractical,' Mr Archer continued, once they were out of their environment suits. 'Power-up and targeting still take too long.'

'That's because I didn't design it for such wriggly little targets,' Dr Randhawa replied, sounding offended. 'The cannon is primarily a shuttle weapon. You know, for mounting on a spaceship and shooting other spaceships and stuff. Okay, so it can be used in-atmos, as you so elegantly demonstrated, but in that case I see it not so much as an anti-personnel weapon but more as an anti-much-bigger-things weapon. A siege weapon, maybe.'

'A siege weapon?' Mr Archer made the rasping sound at the back of his throat that was the closest he ever came to a laugh. 'And do you think we will have much call for siege weapons in the coming months?'

Dr Randhawa shrugged. 'You tell me.'

Mr Archer looked at him. He had to admit that Dr Randhawa had done an excellent job of creating these weapons in such a short time, but admiring his technical skills was certainly not the same as liking him, and Mr Archer really did not like him. He was too young, barely in his mid-twenties, and he behaved like an excitable child with a box of new toys. Also, he didn't seem in the least bit unnerved by his – Mr Archer's – scarred face and looming presence, and this was something Mr Archer was not used to. He liked people to be nervous around him – fear was such a good controller – and it bothered him that this boy showed no signs of nervousness or fear. Or respect. Still, he thought with an inward smile, he probably wouldn't be needed forever.

'So. How does it work?' he asked, as they left the airlock.

'You want the idiot's guide, or the fifty gigabyte version?'

Mr Archer sighed. 'By the time I reach the lift.'

'Okay. Antiparticles.'

'Antiparticles?'

'Antiparticles. And a little bit of top-secret technical know-how that manages to generate said antiparticles, store them and deliver them to a target area without requiring them to travel through the intervening space to get there – which would, obviously, destroy them en route – and spadoosh! No more target area.'

'Clever.'

'Oh, you don't know the half of it. But it's a short corridor so I doubt you ever will.' He smiled. 'Just make sure you point it in the right direction before you pull the trigger and you'll be fine.'

'And just you make sure you can stabilise the prototypes and get them sent to production as soon as possible,' replied Mr Archer. 'Or else you won't be.'

'Idiot,' Mr Archer added as the lift doors closed in front of him.

'Imbecile,' Dr Randhawa muttered as he made his way along the corridor to his workshops.

The lift stopped at the ground floor, but after Mr Archer pressed his thumb on the control panel it continued down for several more floors, finally opening into a cavernous hangar not much smaller than the entire compound above. Small and medium-sized craft – mostly shuttles and patrol ships in various stages of repair – had been cleared away against the side walls, and the entire space was taken up with the partially dismantled carcass of a giant black spaceship, together with the more familiar cranes, cutting tools and other equipment that surrounded it. Even the quickest of glances would have told Leo and Skater that this was the very ship encountered by Jack Duggan and *Erebus* almost a year earlier – the one they, and many others, were so desperately trying to locate.

But Mr Archer passed along the length of the ship without giving it even that quickest of glances and continued to a guarded doorway beyond. The two men on duty snapped to attention and one of them unlocked the door without question. Inside was a large workshop, mostly abandoned and empty except for the near corner, where a comfortable workspace had been set up. A man and woman, both in their early twenties, were staring at computer screens. They looked up as Mr Archer entered, then quickly turned back to their screens. A third person, a woman some thirty years older, who was sitting on a sofa surrounded by computer slates and piles of papers, also looked up at the sound of the door but then continued to stare at the new arrival.

Mr Archer walked across and stood in front of her. 'Professor,' he said by way of a greeting.

'Jailer,' she replied, coldly.

'May I sit down?'

'It's your sofa. And you're the one with the gun.'

For a few seconds the two stared at each other in silence and then, reluctantly, the woman moved a pile of papers from the far end of the sofa, allowing Mr Archer just enough space to perch on the edge of the seat. 'So what is it this time?' she asked. 'Not a progress report, clearly.'

'Why not?'

'Oh come on,' the woman replied. 'Any fool can tell you're monitoring everything we do from upstairs.'

'We monitor everything everybody does here, even the work of our own technicians. It's standard procedure.'

'Yes. For someone as paranoid as you, I'm sure it is. Though I don't know why you bother. None of your so-called experts will have the faintest idea whether we're making progress or not. Isn't that why you had to kidnap us in the first place, because no one else knows how to do this stuff?'

'Perhaps,' Mr Archer conceded. 'But in your case it is enough for me to know you're working, even if I don't understand the work. Isn't this way so much easier than before, when you were refusing to work for me?'

'Yes, well,' the woman said with a weak smile. 'Starvation and sleep deprivation can be wonderful motivators when used so lavishly.'

Mr Archer picked up the top page from one of the piles of papers beside him and began to read, but without any real interest. 'And do you have any progress to report?'

'Some. Not much. Certainly nothing worth you coming all the way down here for.' She reached over, took the page from Mr Archer and replaced it on the pile. 'If only you and your thugs had had the sense to kidnap my computers as well as my assistants, we might have been finished by now and on our way home.' She paused, before adding, 'But something tells me sending us home is not exactly high on your to-do list, is it?'

Mr Archer stood up to leave. 'I'll do what I'm told,' he said. 'If I'm told to let you go, I'll see you onto the shuttle and make sure you have a safe journey home. If I'm told to kill you, I'll gut you without a second thought.'

'My, how well-trained they've got you.'

'My suggestion to you is this. Try to keep the man whose decision it will be as happy as possible. Give him some results. Soon.' In the doorway he paused. 'Oh, Professor, I nearly forgot. There was something else I wanted to tell you.'

'Go on,' she said.

'I thought you might like to know that your son has recently arrived on Mars.'

The shock hit the professor like a blow. 'What?' she stammered. 'Leo? How?'

'It seems he's come here looking for his mother. Should I help him find her?'

'No!' she screamed, leaping up and scattering papers in all directions. 'You leave him alone.' She ran towards the door and launched herself at Mr Archer, but he simply stood his ground and took the full force of her attack. Without effort he took hold of her wrists, pinned them together in one of his huge, powerful fists and pushed her to the floor. The two assistants ran forward and between them they managed to hold her back as she struggled to renew her pointless assault. 'You leave him alone, you hear?' she screamed. 'If you lay one finger on him, if you so much as come anywhere near him, then so help me I'll rip you apart with my bare hands.'

'Results,' Mr Archer said as he closed the door. 'Soon.'

The professor broke free and dashed after him, but the door was already locked. For a few seconds they stared at each other through the glass panel. Then Mr Archer turned away, muttered instructions to the guards and wandered back through the hangar towards the lift.

In the workshop, after having endured week after week of physical and emotional torture with nothing but silent determination and rage, Professor Lillian Fischer collapsed to the floor, helpless amid the flood of tears she could do nothing to stem. 'Leo,' she sobbed. 'I thought you were safe. I wanted you to stay safe. Oh, Leo, what are you doing all the way out here? What in heaven's name are you doing?'

26

FIRST STEPS ON A NEW WORLD

'**WHAT AM I SUPPOSED** to be doing?' asked Leo.

'Just watch the screen,' replied Sol without taking his eyes from the tiny plas-glass window in front of him. 'And if any numbers go red, tell me which ones.'

'Right.' A few seconds later Leo's screen went blank. 'Uh, Sol...'

Sol cast a quick look behind him. 'Hit it.' Leo gave the screen a gentle nudge and when that had no effect, a more determined whack. The numbers reappeared and they were all still green. 'We're good.'

Although technically a freighter, *Beautiful Moment* was so old and small she had been reclassified as a heavy shuttle and so was permitted to travel in-atmosphere. This meant there was no need to dock in orbit and transfer their cargo onto one of the local ferries every time they came to Mars, and avoiding this extra bureaucracy was one of the main reasons Sol had never upgraded to a more modern ship. 'That,' he had explained to Leo earlier, 'and the fact that Li would throw me out the airlock for even suggesting such a thing.'

Despite this, they had still spent almost a day in orbit. Their first stop had been to return the escape pod to the *Dragon*. This had taken longer than expected and Leo suspected much of the delay had been down to Sol's haggling over the salvage fee. After that, there was the unavoidable inspection from the Customs and Immigration officer that Leo had been dreading for days. Having been a stowaway on board the *Dragon*, he was convinced the Martian authorities would refuse him entry and order him onto the next ship heading for Earth, but the inspecting officer showed no interest in him at all. He simply scanned all five of them, Early Warning included, and when the system confirmed that they were cleared for entry onto Mars he turned his attention to the cargo hold.

And finally they were cleared to land. As a special treat Skater was allowed to sit up front in the co-pilot's seat, and as Sol guided *Beautiful Moment* down through the Martian atmosphere, she mimicked his every action on her own controls, with as much skill and attention as she would have shown had she been flying the ship herself.

'Mars is a pig,' Sol said as he wrestled with the controls. 'It's got enough gravity to pull you down like a speeding lump of lead, but the atmosphere's so thin there's nothing for you to glide in on. So it's boosters all the way down.'

'Yeah,' replied Skater, mimicking Sol's adjustments on her own controls. 'I get that.'

Behind them Leo smiled to himself. It was true, Sol was bringing the ship in and it would be Sol that got them down in the right place and with a – hopefully – soft landing, but it was Daisy who was really controlling the ship. She was regulating the thrusters, keeping them descending at something like the right speed and angle, and she could even override manual control if safe operating parameters were exceeded by more than five percent. So far this hadn't happened. After all, Sol was a hugely experienced pilot who'd done all this many times. Even so, Leo was glad of the safety net.

In fact, the landing was perfectly soft as well as perfectly safe. Sol brought them in towards the settlement of Thimble Rock from the north, so they could fly over the tall outcrop that gave the town its name, before coming in to land near the far edge of the spaceport's almost deserted landing area. 'Sorry,' Sol said in response to Li's questioning look. 'But they said they're having to keep the main area clear for some military stuff due in tomorrow.'

'Military?' Li said. 'What could the military possibly want out here in Thimble Rock?'

Skater looked across at Leo. 'Maybe it's to do with us?'

'I doubt it,' Sol said. 'If they'd wanted to pick you up they'd have done it up top, while we were waiting. Nope. My guess would be it's just routine manoeuvres or whatever, and it's our bad timing to get here on the same day, but I'll ask around once we're inside. There's bound to be someone I know on duty. Come on, let's go explore.'

With Li's help, Leo and Skater had spent the last couple of days sorting out spare environment suits for themselves from the vast collection of spares Sol kept 'just in case' and although they weren't exactly state-of-the-art, they were strong and reliable and not, in Li's words, likely to pop at the first drop. Leo had offered to pay for them but Li had laughed and said she would be glad to be rid of some of Sol's old clutter.

Now, as the four of them were squeezed into the airlock at the back of the ship, Leo checked the seal on his face-plate for the tenth time. 'Are you sure this is really all we need? I mean, it's kind of...well...thin.'

'Relax, kiddo,' came Skater's voice over the comms. She turned him around so he could see her smiling at him through their helmets. 'It's plenty. Mars has an atmosphere these days. This nerd I know told me all about it. How they've been terraforming the planet and building up the atmosphere for years and years and how soon we won't need our E-suits at all.'

'Yeah,' Leo replied. 'In about five thousand years' time it'll be a lovely place to go for a picnic. But in the meantime, we're all being slowly cooked by solar radiation.'

'You'll be fine,' said Sol, patting him on the shoulder. 'All the buildings above ground are shielded. Just don't stay in the open too long.'

The airlock door hissed open and one after another they stepped into the Martian evening. Five steps later, Leo stopped. 'What's up?' Skater asked. For a few seconds Leo didn't say anything. He just stood and stared around him. 'I'm standing on Mars,' he finally managed.

'Pretty buzz, huh? Though technically, you're not on Mars yet, you're still on the concrete landing pad. Does that count as Mars, or do you need to be standing on the actual dirt? Although now that I think about it, it's obviously Martian concrete, made from Martian...whatever concrete is made from...rocks and stuff, so I guess it probably does count after all. Doesn't it?'

'Skater.'

'What?'

'Shut up please. Let me enjoy the moment.'

'Okay, I'm shutting up. But I have to tell you, this is nothing compared to some of the stuff you'll get to see. I mean, if you think about it, this is just a spaceport. It could be anywhere. Wait till you get out into the desert. That's when it gets really awesome.'

'The sun is blue,' Leo said, ignoring her.

'Yep,' said Sol. 'And night is cold. Come on, and let's enjoy it from inside.'

As they made their way towards the terminal building, Leo was surprised by how easy he found walking. He had imagined there would be a fair bit of stumbling and picking himself off the floor, as there had been during his first days on Luna, but after two weeks of weightlessness on board *Beautiful Moment*, the Martian gravity felt just right. And his stomach thought so, too. Not only had he managed to keep his lunch where it belonged, but he was looking forward to his first encounter with Martian cuisine which, hopefully, was not too far away.

Skater was still talking, but Leo could tell it was the sort of talking that wasn't exactly a conversation and that didn't need any input from him except the occasional noise to show he was still there. Instead, he spent his time marvelling at the strange new world around him, where the sky was yellow and the sun turned blue at sunset, where the air was poison and nothing grew, but where you could walk about wearing just the thinnest of environment suits. And unlike on Luna, where almost everything was underground, here they'd built up as well as down. Thimble Rock was only a small town and from what he'd seen as they flew above it, there wasn't much that was above two, or maybe three, storeys high. But Minerva and the other capitals were true metropolises, with real skyscrapers and sealed domes that stretched over entire blocks, and skyways connecting them so you could live a perfectly normal indoor life and almost believe you were back on Earth — at least until you looked out of the window at the cloudless yellow sky and the empty brown land beneath it.

Once inside the spaceport airlock, Sol showed them how to detach and fold their helmets so they could be tucked inside a pouch on the front of the suit. 'You're in and out of buildings all the time,' he explained, 'so it's best to keep the suit on and just stow the hood.' He tapped one of the air packs on his belt. 'And always remember to keep these guys topped up, just in case. Most public places will have their own refill stations, but if you get desperate, just ask. No one's going to refuse you a couple of hours of air, though they might charge you for it if they're feeling unfriendly.'

The terminal itself was tiny, with no more than a couple of dozen passengers and members of staff to keep it from looking abandoned. As the airlock doors hissed open an old man in an even older uniform jacket stood waiting to greet them. 'Hey, Sol. Hey Li. Good to see you again.'

'Zach Hedermeyer,' said Sol, shaking hands. 'You still alive?'

'Last time I checked,' Zach replied. 'You in town for long?'

'The usual few days. Maybe stopping back a while later as well.'

'And with company,' Zach said, looking at Leo and Skater. 'Let me guess. This would be a Miss Monroe and a Mr Fischer, I presume?'

'That's right,' said Skater, looking excited. 'Have you got a message for us?'

'I do. Came through earlier, from a Pete Monroe. That would be your father, I'm guessing? He says you're booked on the overnight mono to Minerva, and all being well he'll be there to meet you at the station tomorrow morning.'

'All being well?' Skater asked.

Zach turned back to Sol. 'I guess you won't have heard yet, but things are all kinds of messed up over there right now. Ever since the news about those pirate attacks, folks have been in an uproar, what with strikes and demonstrations and whatever else. Most flights from Minerva have been cancelled these past two days — that's why this place is so quiet — and even the mono's gone down to just the overnight. We even had some business here in town. Not much, mind, this far out, but there's a lot of talk about change. They're saying the government won't even last till the elections at this rate and it looks to me like Old Man Whittaker's already got the presidency in the bag.'

'Carlton Whittaker?' Sol asked. 'Mr MarsMine?'

'The very same.' Zach pointed to one of the walls, where every few seconds a large screen was repeating a clip of Carlton Whittaker smiling and waving. *Martian, heart and soul*, Leo read as the words appeared across the bottom of the image. *Vote Whittaker and help create a future to be proud of.*

'You really think he can do it?' Li asked.

'Why not? MarsMine pretty much runs the provinces already and they've come out strong over these past couple of weeks. And, you know, sometimes people just like change. Hell, I might vote for him myself.'

Zach led them to a small desk where he scanned their fingerprints, swiped their ID cards and confirmed they were cleared to enter. 'There,' he announced. 'Welcome to Thimble Rock.'

'That's it?' Leo asked.

Zach waved at the desk dismissively. 'There's plenty of other stuff if you want, but to be honest it's a waste of time and energy. If the computer says you're allowed in, that's fine by me.' He looked at the others. 'Well, you were the last ship due in so that's me done for the night. What say we go grab a bite to eat and I'll fill you in on everything? There's still a good three hours till the mono leaves, and that's assuming it gets here on time, which these days is no sure thing.'

27
AWKWARD

THE MONORAIL TRAIN did not arrive on time, but then neither did Leo and Skater. Their meal with Zach went on much longer than anyone had expected, partly because he wouldn't stop talking, but mostly because what he was saying was so interesting, and then they had spent far too long at the ship, sorting out their possessions and saying goodbye to Sol and Li. Their two weeks on board *Beautiful Moment* had come as a much-needed break from their worries and they had learned a lot, but now it was clear they were both impatient to move on — Skater to be with her father and Leo to continue the desperate and probably fruitless search for his mother. But by the time the mono finally pulled away, Leo and Skater were settled into their compartment, their back-packs and environment suits were stowed, and Leo was busy on his slate, studying their planned route across Mars.

'Well, this is a lot nicer than the last time we travelled together, huh?' Skater asked.

Leo looked up briefly. 'Is it?'

'Yeah, you know, in the escape pod. At least this time we can actually see each other.'

'Oh, yeah. Right,' Leo replied, and went back to studying his screen. Thimble Rock was south of Minerva, one of the last stops on the main line coming up from Ptolemy, and as far as he could tell, there wasn't anything between them and the capital except a couple of small farming settlements and a lot of rocky desert. He zoomed in on one of the farms. There was a single large building built around the monorail track and then, stretching out for mile after mile on either side, giant hydroponics domes where food was grown. There were thousands of farms like this all across Mars – especially near the big cities – and they were so efficient that Mars was now producing enough food to feed its own population and supply the outer colonies as well. He even knew which sorts of food were grown locally and which still needed to be imported from Earth, how long they took to grow, and what media they could be grown in. It was all useless information, but Martian agriculture had been one of the things Daisy had taught him, during one of his rare quiet days back on the *Dragon*, and like most things, once the information was in his head, it tended to stay there.

Skater was saying something. After a few seconds Leo's brain finally caught up with his ears and he looked up, puzzled. 'What? Who would be shot?'

'Boring people,' said Skater. 'Especially nerds. When I'm president of Mars I'm going to round them all up and shoot them. Or maybe just torture them for a bit, until they learn how to be a bit more socially interactive.' She reached over, grabbed Leo's slate and switched it off.

'Hey! I was using that to plot our route.'

She gave him a pitying look. 'We're on a train, Leo. It goes in a straight line, through a lot of sand, and there's nothing to see in either direction except maybe, if you're really lucky, a rock. Also, in case you hadn't noticed, it's nighttime. So there's really, *really* nothing to see. So here's an idea. How about you try taking part in a conversation instead? These last few days you've hardly said a word to me and now, when it's just the two of us and we have the perfect opportunity to talk about all the stuff that's been going on, you ignore me so you can stare at a train line in the middle of a desert on a computer all night.'

It was true. Ever since Leo had overheard Skater talking to her father about leaving him in the hands of the Martian authorities so that the two of them could get on with their holiday, he hadn't known what to say to her. What was there to say? To help him get halfway across the Solar System and then abandon him when he needed them most seemed like a betrayal. Okay, so it had been Pete's idea, not Skater's, and she had at least sounded like she was unhappy with the decision, but could he honestly expect her to go against her father's wishes to help somebody she'd only known for a few weeks? And did he even want to?

'Fine,' he mumbled. 'So what do you want to talk about?'

'Honestly,' she said, staring at him. 'Is that the best you can do? Look, if you don't want to talk that's fine. But tell me, so I can stop making a fool of myself trying to be all friendly and chatty. I'll go off somewhere else and we can maybe try again in the morning.' She stood up to leave but Leo reached out and grabbed her arm to stop her.

'I'm just preoccupied,' he said. 'Thinking about my mum. You know how it is.'

Skater looked down at him and smiled, but didn't sit back down. 'I'm a girl,' she said.

'Uh, yeah. I know,' Leo replied, not sure what that had to do with anything.

'You can't lie to a girl about emotional stuff. It doesn't work. I know you're worried about your mum, and I know you spend a lot of time thinking about her and trying to decide what to do about finding her and everything, but that's not what you're doing right now. You're thinking about something completely different and trying to pretend you're not by lying to me and using your mum as an excuse. You know it and I know it and now you know that I know it. And whatever it is, you obviously don't want to talk about it to me, do you? So, good night, Leo.'

'Where are you going?'

'It's a long train. I'll go explore for a bit.'

Leo let her go. He knew from experience that if he tried to defend himself any more, it would only make matters worse. Anyway, she was right. He had used his mother as an excuse. He still wanted to find her, more than anything, but recently he'd also found himself getting cross with her, blaming her even, for having got him into this whole mess. He knew it was unfair, but he also knew that was just how he felt and there wasn't a whole lot he could do about it. In fact, if he was being honest, there were times when he wasn't thinking about her at all. He would be doing something completely different and would suddenly realise he hadn't thought about her for hours. And the worst thing was, it was getting to the point where he didn't even feel guilty about it.

Because the fact was, he would rather be thinking about Skater. He was much too sensible – or maybe shy – to ever admit to being in love, but sometimes he did wonder whether that's what it was. She'd certainly become his closest friend. No contest there. But that didn't necessarily make her his girlfriend. Did it? They'd been through so much over the past few weeks, but he'd never had the guts to tell her how he felt about her and now it looked as if he never would. Soon — maybe even tomorrow — he would be handed into the care of some government official or other, and Skater would head off with Pete to finally enjoy the holiday he had so successfully ruined for them. And that would be that. Probably they'd keep in touch for a while. Maybe they'd even meet up again, back on Earth, but sooner or later he knew he'd stop being a part of her life and all of this would become just a great story for her to tell to some new friends.

Leo moved to the window and pressed his forehead against the cool glass. Somewhere outside was the Martian desert, whizzing past at hundreds of kilometres an hour, but the darkness was so complete he could see nothing of the dead world except his own, miserable reflection.

'So,' he asked the face in the glass. 'Now what?'

After an hour of indecision, Leo finally went to look for Skater. It was indeed a long train and he had made his way through ten or eleven darkened and almost empty carriages when he caught sight of her coming towards him. She stopped in front of him and waited, either for an apology or for him to get out of the way so she could carry on back to their compartment. She probably didn't really care which.

Leo was shaking. His throat was dry and his heart was pounding but he'd decided what it was he needed to do and he knew if he didn't do it now he never would. He stepped forward, put his hands on Skater's shoulders and kissed her on the lips. He expected her to pull away and give him another good hard slap across the cheek. But she didn't, she just stared at him.

'It was you,' Leo managed at last, unable to look her in the eye. 'I've been thinking about you.'

'Oh,' Skater said after a few seconds of heavy silence. 'Well, now I feel like Queen Bitch of the Universe. Again.'

'Sorry,' Leo said, taking his hands away from her shoulders. 'I should have said—'

'Yes, you really should have. Ages ago.'

'Really? Like, when?'

Skater just looked at him and shook her head slowly. 'Boys. Honestly.'

Leo hadn't planned what he would do after the kiss and he felt slightly foolish as he followed Skater back to their compartment. He thought perhaps he ought to hold her hand, or put his arm around her or something, but the aisle was too narrow for them to walk side-by-side and so they walked back in silence, Skater occasionally glancing around to make sure he was still behind her.

'Now what?' Skater asked once they were back in their compartment.

Leo sat down beside her. 'I could kiss you again,' he offered, smiling slightly foolishly, but Skater held up her hand like a shield between them. 'Not right now,' she said. 'How about we just talk for a while?'

'Okay,' Leo said, relieved that Skater was so calm and was taking control of the situation. It made the whole thing much less awkward.

So they talked. About the overheard conversation with Pete and the call to Aitchison; about what they would do once they reached Minerva and when they might go their separate ways; about everything that had happened since that first meeting on board the shuttle to Luna and how it had changed them in ways they still didn't understand; and further back, to their lives on Earth before they knew each other. Leo told Skater about the exclusive boarding school that was more a home to him than the empty house in Cambridge where he spent his holidays, and how he'd decided to study computers because they were so much easier to deal with than other kids, who were only interested in you if you wore the right designer clothes, listened to the right music and knew everything there was to know about every sport ever invented.

In return, Skater told him what it was like to live in a tiny apartment where every day seemed to start, and end, with an argument. 'Mum hates Dad,' she explained. 'And she hates space. And she hates that I love both of them so much. Sometimes I think she hates me as well. She never says so, but sometimes she gets this look in her eyes, like I'm beyond filth, not worth speaking to or even shouting at. And I know she blames me for the divorce, even though it was nothing to do with me. She was the one who made life unbearable for all of us, with her shouting and arguing and never-ending bad moods. She had an affair once as well, one of the first times Dad was away on Luna. She thinks I don't know about it but she was so useless at keeping it secret I'm surprised the whole building didn't find out. I'll never forgive her for that. Never.'

'And there was me thinking you had the perfect life because your dad was a shuttle pilot and you got to go to Luna twice a year.'

'Yeah, well you were wrong. These bits – when I'm with Dad – they're perfect in every way except that they're never long enough.'

'Couldn't you live with your dad all the time?'

'Oh, if only. And don't think I haven't suggested it like a billion times, but it just isn't going to happen. Not unless he gives up piloting and settles down somewhere and I wouldn't let him do that. It's his whole life. No, I'll just stick it out with Mum for another year until I've finished school and then I'll walk out the door and never look back.'

'Well, at least you have a dad you can run away to.'

'And at least you have a mum you don't need to run away from.'

'Hopefully,' Leo replied, after a pause.

'Yeah,' Skater replied softly. 'Hopefully.' She yawned and checked the time. 'Sweet Sol, it's late. So late, in fact, it's now technically early, and I really need to get some sleep. Something tells me we've got a looooong day ahead of us.'

'Listen, sorry about earlier, with the kiss and everything. I just... well...I just wanted to show you how I felt.'

'It was definitely very brave of you,' she said, smiling, as she clambered up into one of the sleeping pods above the seats. 'And kind of nice, too. Maybe I'll let you do it again sometime.' And with that she pulled the slide across, leaving Leo to blush in private.

Leo was much too wired to sleep. He thought about the kiss, replaying the moment over and over in his mind and remembering the soft, tingling warmth of Skater's lips against his, but it wasn't this that kept him away from his bed so much as the excitement he felt at being on Mars after so many long weeks in space. He was impatient to get going, even though he didn't know where it was he was going, but at least now it looked as if Skater wasn't going to abandon him after all. She'd said she would tell Pete she didn't care about the holiday. All she wanted was to help Leo, in any way she could and for as long as she could, before they had to head back to Luna.

Then there was Aitchison. Leo had so many questions he wanted to ask but he knew he'd never get a straight answer to any of them. Who was Aitchison really? Why were three kidnapped scientists so important? How, and why, had he managed to get to Mars so quickly? And what use could he possibly have for a fifteen-year-old boy who was blundering around the Solar System trying to find his mother? Too many questions without answers. But whoever he is,

Leo thought, if he's here on Mars, then right now, Mars is the place to be. He rubbed his eyes. Perhaps he was tired after all.

Sunrise was fast approaching. Already it was light enough to pick out the silhouette of distant rock formations against the purple sky, and every passing minute added depth to the pale landscape between them and the train. Wisps of ice cloud glowed briefly blue as they were carried across the sky by a faint breeze, before fading away into the dull brown of the early morning sky. And then, without warning, the tiny sun rose up from behind the distant hills, and the empty plains became a sea of orange and red and brown.

It was Leo's first Martian sunrise, and although it wasn't anything like as stunning as a desert sunrise would have been on Earth, in its own way it was still beautiful. But slumped in his seat, with his head wedged between window and headrest, he slept through the whole thing.

28

SIGHTSEEING ON MARS

LEO WASN'T GOOD AT REUNIONS — all that hugging and gushing was kind of unnecessary, and so unbelievably cringeworthy. And this particular reunion was especially difficult because he still wasn't entirely sure how he felt about Pete. Skater had promised him he was wrong, that neither she nor her father was going to abandon him just so they could go off and have a nice holiday without him. But even so, Leo felt that in some inexplicable way his relationship with Pete had changed since the last time they'd all been together on the *Dragon*, and rushing up and giving him a hug seemed like so completely the wrong thing to do.

Not that there was much chance of him doing it anyway, even if he'd wanted to. Skater attached herself to her father the moment the train doors slid open, practically knocking him over in her enthusiasm and relief at the two of them being back together, and she was showing no signs of ever wanting to let go. So Leo smiled and nodded to Pete from a distance and hung back, unwilling to get involved in this way-too-public display of emotion.

A chime from his pocket told him he'd received a message on his phone. He knew it would be to tell him he was now linked into the local network, but checking it gave him something to do and stopped him feeling so out of place beside the mass of words and waving arms that Skater had become. He clipped the phone to his ear, brought the screen round and checked messages. Sure enough, he was greeted by a smiling facsimile of a young woman who welcomed him to Mars Global and explained just how surprisingly expensive it was going to be if he intended to contact anyone outside Minerva. There was even an option to send one-way messages to anywhere in the Solar System, as long as there was someone or something at the other end to receive them, but while this might have been technically feasible it was, as far as Leo was concerned, financially impossible.

Another message came in and Leo watched as the same woman appeared. But this time she had a different message. *Mars Global hopes you have a long and pleasant stay here in Minerva. While you're here, why not take the time to visit some of the city's top tourist attractions. We particularly recommend The Mars Montgomerie Museum, where you can see their newest acquisition, the hundred-and-fifty-year-old space-exploration vessel,* Arcadian. *To avoid the expected crowds, we recommend you plan your visit to this most informative of exhibitions for tomorrow, at exactly twelve local.*

Aitchison. Leo smiled. How fitting he'd chosen *Arcadian* as the place to meet. Was there actually something there worth seeing, or was it just his idea of a joke? Either way, he'd find out soon enough. And besides, the Montgomerie had been the one place he'd planned on visiting anyway.

'All okay?' Pete asked, making a gap for himself in Skater's detailed recounting of their adventures by gently putting his hand over her mouth.

'Hey, not fair!' she mumbled, but then paused to hear what Leo had to say.

'It's a message from Aitchison. He wants us to meet him tomorrow lunchtime. And guess where?' he said, smiling at Skater. 'In a museum.'

'Oh joy!'

'Aitchison?' Pete asked, surprised. 'That so-called policeman from back on Luna? What's he doing on Mars? And what the hell are you doing agreeing to meet up with him tomorrow? I thought the whole point of smuggling you aboard the *Dragon* was to get you away from him?'

'Yeah, it was. But then I thought...well I thought that...' Leo's explanation ground to a halt and he looked across to Skater for support.

'Leo overheard us talking and thought we were going to dump him once we got here so we could go off and enjoy our holiday without him. He called the guy because he still had his card and he didn't know what else to do and it turned out he was already on Mars and had pretty much known Leo was on his way here anyway and had been waiting for him to call. But I've told Leo he was completely wrong about us and we're not going to leave him. And I have to say I'm a bit unimpressed he even thought we would do such a below low thing, but anyway, now we can all go and meet Aitchison together and see if he's got any news for us, right?'

Leo looked sheepishly across at Pete. 'Sorry,' he said, but Pete just smiled.

'Don't worry about it. Honestly, at this point, I really don't know if there's much we can do for you, and I do think getting help from someone local is the best plan, even if that someone local turns out to be this Aitchison guy. But believe me, when the time finally comes for us to say goodbye, it'll be because there's literally no other option.'

'Or because we've succeeded in finding your mum,' Skater added helpfully.

'Exactly. Now, how about we head to the hotel I've booked us into.' He looked at Leo, still crumpled from his few hours sleep in his seat. 'You may want to freshen up a bit, then maybe we can talk through some ideas for this meeting tomorrow over some...what? Breakfast? Lunch?'

'Breakfast,' said Leo.

'Both,' said Skater.

'Fine. Both it is.'

'But is there any chance we can do the eating without the tactics talk?' Leo added. 'Can't we just wait and see what Aitchison has to say first? I'd really like just one day of enjoying being on Mars without letting all the other stuff come in and ruin it. A day of sightseeing, or hanging out doing nothing much except soaking up the atmosphere—'

'There isn't any atmosphere, dummy,' Skater said, looking particularly pleased with herself.

'—or whatever.'

'Just like a real holiday,' Pete said.

'Exactly.'

'Sounds good to me.'

'So anyway,' Skater said as they made their way down to the subway to find a pod to take them to the hotel. 'Where was I? Oh yes, just after we were rescued...'

The day turned out to be a huge success. Having been to Minerva many times before, Pete knew his way around and had a good idea of where to take two excited teenagers who wanted to do as much as possible in a very short time. First up, after a stop at the hotel for a shower and change of clothes, was Max's Stax, 'World Famous on every World', for their special-recipe pancakes and forty different toppings. It was Pete's favourite breakfast destination whenever he was in town, and Leo and Skater — who both ate far more than they needed to — could see why.

Next was the Sky Walk, a seven-kilometre-long enclosed walkway that wound its way around the central part of the city, twenty storeys above ground. 'It's become a tradition to walk the whole thing in one go,' Pete explained. 'But that would take us most of the rest of the day. And to be honest, once you've walked a couple of the sections, you've pretty much got the idea. We can do the section from Wallace Street to the University Tower. It's not so popular with the tourists because you don't get such good views of the desert, but you do get a pretty good view of the city itself. And you can see the shipyards,' he added for Skater's benefit.

'Barely,' she complained, later, as she pressed her face against the glass wall and peered between two skyscrapers at the spaceships that could just about be seen in the distance. 'I can see, like, two ships.'

'Well, you used to get a good view of the shipyards, back when I first came up here and before they kept building up and up. But anyway, depending on what happens tomorrow at our meeting, we can head out there afterwards and do the full tour if you both want.'

'Of course we both want. Don't we, Leo?'

Leo wasn't really listening. Having discovered he was 'a little uncomfortable' with heights, he was too busy concentrating on trying to control the tingling down the back of his legs by keeping as far back from the outer walls as possible, though given that the floor was made of the same clear plas-glass, he was failing miserably.

His only relief came when the Sky Walk passed alongside one of its supporting buildings, which were disturbingly few and far between.

'Don't we, Leo?' Skater repeated.

'What? Yes. Definitely,' he said distractedly, trying not to look down. Or sideways.

'Excellent,' said Skater. 'Let's carry on then.'

'I don't suppose this thing has ever fallen down, has it?' Leo asked Pete, in what he hoped sounded like a voice without fear. Pete laughed. 'Not so far.'

'And it is shielded?'

'As far as I know, yes.'

'Well,' Leo muttered to himself. 'I suppose that's something.'

As promised, and much to Leo's relief, they abandoned the Sky Walk at the university and spent a long while wandering inside the huge dome that engulfed the main campus. Mars Minerva University was famous throughout the System for two things. The first was its stunning architecture, which relied on state-of-the-art construction methods and the low Martian gravity to create a series of stylish interlinked buildings that all but floated above their own elegantly landscaped zen-inspired gardens and which had, as far as Leo could remember, won pretty much every single architectural award there was.

The other thing MMU was famous for was being far and away the most exclusive, and expensive, university in the system. 'I feel like any minute now they're going to kick us out just for walking on their paths,' Skater said. 'In fact, I'm surprised they're even letting us breathe the air. It's probably double-filtered or something special like that,' and she took a deep breath and filled her lungs just in case.

'I thought about applying to come here,' Leo said quietly.

'Really?' Skater looked genuinely shocked. 'Are you serious? I mean, I know you're clever and all that, but how could you afford it? It's like a gazillion dollars a week to come here. Isn't it?'

'I've got an open scholarship to go to whichever university I want. It's something Mum arranged for me with Delphix. Basically, they pay me to study and I go and work for them once I've finished – which is fine with me, seeing as how I was kind of thinking of going to work for them anyway.'

'You can't have a scholarship already. You're fifteen years old. You haven't even done your Mids yet.'

'Actually, I have,' Leo replied. 'Well, a few of them, anyway.'

Skater looked at him suspiciously. 'How many?'

'Eight.'

'Eight? Sweet Sol, that's more than I was planning on getting in total, and you've done them already? That's just wrong.'

'Yeah well,' Leo said, beginning to feel embarrassed. 'You're fifteen and you're already a pretty good shuttle pilot. Certainly way better than I'm ever going to be.' Skater turned to her father with a huge grin. 'It's true; I am. And he really, really isn't.'

'Well I'm delighted to hear it,' Pete said. 'But you know the deal. You still go to college first. Just...maybe not this one, all right?'

'Anyway, I doubt I'll actually end up here,' Leo added. 'Mum says the computer science department is full of idiots and incompetents who couldn't even build an intelligent computer that could build itself. Most likely I'll end up staying in Cambridge, or maybe going to Beijing.'

'Good. Because if you go to university here, I am never, ever coming to visit you. It's just so...expensively vile.'

'Pretty impressive buildings though.'

'Meh,' Skater said, with a dismissive wave of her hand. 'Most of the walls don't even go all the way down to the ground.'

Unsurprisingly, the day ended with another large meal. As MMU was close to one of the more interesting shopping districts, Skater insisted they stop off to 'look for bargains', and after two hours of wandering in and out of every second-hand book and clothes shop they could find, Leo and Pete were ready for a long sit-down, far away from anywhere that might possibly sell second-hand anything. Pete knew just the place.

The Cavern was quite possibly the most way-beyond-amazing place Skater had ever been in her entire life that didn't have anything to do with spaceships. It was an actual cave that had been dug out during the initial excavations for the early sub-levels of Minerva but then abandoned. After several decades functioning as a storage yard for old mining vehicles, it had been bought by one of Minerva's more enterprising businessmen, who had transformed it into the Solar System's largest restaurant.

There were exactly four things on The Cavern's menu – and that was all there ever would be. There was piping hot pizza (meat-style or standard veg) and ice cold drink (light beer or double-filtered water). The food was delicious, the drinks were refreshing, the service was fast and the prices were low, and as a result The Cavern was never anything except a gigantic, bustling hive of activity.

Afterwards, on the way back to the hotel, Leo found a moment for a quiet word with Pete while Skater was enjoying a completely unnecessary ice cream she had acquired along the way. 'Thanks, Pete. It was a great day.'

'Just what the doctor ordered, eh?'

'It feels like that, yeah. I know tomorrow's going to be different. Maybe every day will be from now on, but at least my first day on

Mars will always be worth remembering.'

'Well, just remember that I have a lot to thank you for as well. These last two weeks, I've done nothing but sit here twiddling my thumbs and worrying myself sick waiting for Skater to turn up. It really meant a lot to me to know she had you looking after her.'

'Honestly, I think she was the one doing the looking after. All I ever seem to do is get her into trouble in the first place.'

'Well, you're here now, and you're both safe, and that's good enough for me.'

'And tomorrow?'

'Tomorrow?' Skater piped up from behind them. 'Tomorrow we'll have more pancakes for breakfast.'

29
THE WHOLE STORY

AFTER HIS FIRST FULL DAY in Minerva, Leo's overriding opinion was that it was a city waiting to be filled. Everything was so much bigger, or wider, or taller than it needed to be for such a small population. But Mars being what it was, there was no shortage of land to build on or material to build with. And there was clearly no shortage of money to pay for it either. The only thing missing was the people, but Leo guessed that in fifty or a hundred years, it would be just as over-crowded as any of Earth's mega-capitals.

The Mars Montgomerie Museum was no exception. The three main entrances, *Mariner*, *Viking* and *Phoenix*, each had its own subway station and the museum ran a shuttle service between them. The exhibits were housed over twelve floors, four below ground and eight above, and each floor seemed to go on forever.

'How can they possibly find enough junk to fill the place?' Skater asked.

'Amazing, isn't it?' Leo replied, gazing up at the various examples of ancient space hardware suspended from the ceiling.

Skater glanced up and shrugged. 'If you say so. But remember, we're here because we've got a job to do, not to waste time museumising.'

'We can do both.'

'No, we can't,' she said firmly, pushing him along towards the nearest lifts. 'Especially if we're going to have time to do the shipyards afterwards.'

'Skater! This is exactly what you did to me on Luna, at MOSS, remember? As soon as we got there you wanted to drag me off somewhere else. Now you want to do the same thing here. Honestly, museums aren't anything like as boring as you think they are. Not ones like this, anyway.'

Skater looked at him with a puzzled expression for several seconds. 'Shipyards?'

Leo tried again. 'You may not realise this, but the human race has achieved a lot more in the past thousand years than strapping someone to a tube full of explosives and pointing them towards the black bit full of stars.'

Skater gave him an idiotic smile. 'Shipyards,' she repeated, then turned and wandered off. Leo looked at Pete for support but he just shrugged. 'What can I say? The girl likes spaceships.'

Once on the right floor, Skater led them in as direct a line as possible to where the *Arcadian* was on display and Leo made a mental note of three different areas they passed that he was absolutely, definitely, going to go back to later, no matter what Skater thought.

The new exhibit was doing brisk business, with a stream of visitors making their way up the steps and along the walkway surrounding the hanging ship. The craft was not that impressive to look at, but the story of the *Arcadian*'s return to the Solar System and subsequent recovery had captured the public imagination and it seemed as if most of Minerva was suddenly eager to vid-snap themselves standing in front of it. Leo, Skater and Pete joined the queue and edged forward, but it was only when the elderly tourists ahead of them had finished listening to everything their virtual guide had to say and shuffled off to find the next item on their tour map that they could finally come face-to-face with the ship that had, in so many ways, been the cause of all their problems.

'Wow,' said Skater sarcastically. 'It's so beautiful.'

'Remember it's a hundred and fifty years old,' said Pete. 'Spaceship design has come a long way since then.'

'Clearly.'

'Also,' added Leo. 'It was never meant to be a proper spaceship. It was just a mobile science lab really.'

'An ugly mobile science lab.'

There were plenty of people around so Leo lowered his voice. 'Anyway,' he said. 'We don't even know if it really is a hundred-and-fifty-year-old spaceship or just something MarsMine put together six months ago in some secret dock somewhere.'

'Well, it looks genuine enough,' said Pete. 'And I doubt they'd have let it end up here, on view to the public, if it wasn't.'

'Oh, it's quite genuine,' said a voice behind them. Leo turned and Aitchison gave a small nod of his head by way of a greeting. 'There's no way you could fool these clever Montgomerie folks with something you put together six months ago in some secret dock somewhere.'

'But the whole thing is still a hoax, right?' Leo said. 'There was a different ship, wasn't there?'

Aitchison tutted, looked disapprovingly at Leo for a moment and then motioned over his shoulder. 'There's a small food stall over there where they sell something claiming to be coffee. Against my better judgement I think I'll pick up a cup and sit at one of those empty tables where I could, if needs be, have a nice, quiet, *private* chat.'

They followed him over, bought themselves a selection of over-priced snacks and drinks and joined him at his table. Aitchison took a sip of his coffee and grimaced. 'Eugh! That is spectacularly bad coffee. Ah well, my fault for suggesting we meet here, I suppose.' He took four rods of sugar and pushed them, one after another, through the slot in the top of his cup.

'Well?' Leo asked, impatiently.

'Better,' Aitchison answered, tasting the coffee once more. 'But still not perfect by a long way.'

'I mean the spaceship. Is it the real *Arcadian* or not?'

'Not. As far as we can tell the real *Arcadian* is still speeding through deep space, and will continue to do so for the next thirty thousand years or so, at which point it will finally pass too close to a nearby star and be destroyed. That thing over there is most likely a working prototype that was built at the same time as the original. They would have been identical, so you can see how it would be easy to deceive the Montgomerie experts into believing it was the genuine article. After all, they were only looking to authenticate its age, not investigate it as a possible hoax. When all's said and done, it is still a one-hundred-and-fifty-year-old spacecraft. It's just that the farthest this one ever made it from Mars was a few million kilometres, to where it was so conveniently discovered last year. How MarsMine got hold of it is still a mystery, but we're working on that.' Aitchison turned to Leo. 'Welcome to Mars, by the way. I gather the trip was not exactly uneventful.'

'You knew he was aboard the *Dragon* all along?' Pete asked.

'I did.'

'Then why didn't you stop me?' Leo asked.

'Because you were doing such a fine job of helping me with my investigation. I knew you'd found out something on Luna and I was curious to see what it was. Also, I wanted to see who else might be interested in your little trip.'

'So basically, you were using me as bait?'

Aitchison ignored the question and took another sip of coffee. 'Shall I tell you the whole story? It's long and confusing and sadly, it doesn't have an ending yet, but we're working on that as well.' He paused while Skater took a loud mouthful of her Krispi-Bix. 'Everything begins with your old friend Captain Duggan and his ship, *Erebus*. A year ago, as you know, he encountered an unidentified vessel while he was out beyond Jupiter and, luckily for us, he had the good sense to record the incident and call it in.'

'The mysterious black ship.'

'We call it the *Interloper*. It seems appropriate. Anyway, rather quickly the incident came to the attention of Duggan's superiors, some of whom, I'm sorry to say, are not the fine, upstanding citizens they should be.'

'You mean MarsMine?'

'MarsMine is many things. And many people.' He looked across at Pete. 'Not all of it is bad by any means, but if I were you I might start thinking about changing employers. But more about that later. For the moment let's just say someone fairly high up in the company found out about our visitor and realised what it was and how important it could be.'

'And what is it?'

Aitchison sat back and regarded the others with a look of amusement. 'You still don't know?'

'We have our suspicions,' Pete replied. 'Something military. Very new, very secret.'

'Not military,' Aitchison replied. 'Alien.'

'Alien?' Pete asked, after a long pause. 'As in, from outside the Solar System? Are you serious?'

'Completely.'

'You'll forgive me if I find that a little bit hard to swallow.'

'Why?'

'Because it's crazy. That's why.'

'Why?'

'Because aliens don't exist.'

'Actually, they almost certainly do,' said Leo apologetically. 'At least somewhere in the universe they probably do. But it doesn't really matter whether they do or not because wherever they are, they're so far away we're never going to meet any.'

'Unless they can travel really fast and set off a really long time ago,' Aitchison replied.

'And you think they did?'

'Please believe me when I say that some of the best minds in the System have been studying that clip of the *Erebus* encounter for well over half a Terran Standard year now. And when I say minds, I mean both human and artificial. I'm not a technician so I can't tell you what exactly they've been doing, but I can guarantee that they've had unlimited access to the largest databases and most advanced technology available. And each time they come to a conclusion it's always the same. Our *Interloper* did not originate anywhere within the Solar System and is not the product of human endeavour.'

'My God,' Pete muttered. 'Aliens? This is huge.'

'Not aliens,' Aitchison corrected him. 'An alien ship. Alien technology. I very much doubt there were any little green men on board.'

'So,' said Skater cheerfully. 'No alien invasion just yet then, huh?'

'But you can't prove it, can you?' Leo said, ignoring her. 'You can't prove anything, because you don't have the ship.'

'Exactly.'

'MarsMine has it hidden away somewhere.' Leo was growing more and more enthusiastic as he began to piece everything together. Aitchison let him continue. 'And they're not going to go public until they've got all the information they can from it, are they? Having it before anyone else would be worth trillions to them. And that's why they kidnapped my mum, isn't it? They want her to find some way of accessing the alien computer systems. Without that, they've got nothing.'

'Could she do it?'

'Honestly, I don't know. I guess it all depends on just how alien your aliens are. I mean, if they're super-advanced they might not even use computers. But assuming they do, accessing them probably wouldn't be too difficult. It's just a question of working out how to power them up safely and finding some way to understand whatever comes out the other end. That'll be the tricky bit — the translation — and that's not really Mum's area.'

'But it is yours,' Aitchison said calmly. 'Isn't it, Leo?'

'Sort of, yeah.'

Skater looked across at Leo, but neither he nor Aitchison seemed to be joking. 'What? You really think Leo could translate alien?'

Aitchison looked at Leo. 'Could you?'

'No. Well, not the way you mean, anyway. But given access to enough material I could maybe make a start. I mean, it's all pretty obvious really. You look for anything mathematical, because maths is a universal language. What I mean is, no matter where you are in the universe, the relationship between the radius and circumference of a circle will always be the same, and the square on the hypotenuse will always be equal to the other two squares in a right-angled triangle. Or the concept of prime numbers. These things can never change. So you look for these and you use them as the starting blocks for building up your knowledge of how the alien minds work, and this will help you to understand how their language works. Well, that's the theory, anyway.'

'And how long would it take?'

'To get access to the data? A few weeks I guess, assuming you had the right equipment. But to be able to translate it and understand it? Who knows? Maybe months if you're incredibly lucky. Maybe never.'

'Okay,' Pete said. 'So let's assume, for argument's sake, that it really is an alien ship and someone at MarsMine was clever enough to realise this before news got out. Are you really saying that they're covering up the greatest discovery in the history of the human race just so they can be the first to get their hands on some new technology?'

'Yes, I am.'

'It's insane.'

Aitchison leaned forward and lowered his voice, even though there was no one else nearby. 'Most of what I've just told you, you either knew already or could have worked out for yourselves. But really that's only part of the story, and in some ways not even the most important part.'

'Yeah, right,' snorted Skater. 'Because discovering aliens isn't that big a deal really, is it?'

'I've been working on this case for over five years, and for most of that time it's had nothing whatsoever to do with the so-called *Arcadian* incident, or the discovery of an extra-systemic intelligence, or even the search for your mother, Leo. It's been about MarsMine, and more particularly, about Carlton Whittaker.'

'Carlton Whittaker?' Leo asked, confused. 'You think he's behind all this?'

'Almost certainly.'

'But he's about to become president of Mars, isn't he?'

'Again, almost certainly. And much more besides if he gets his way.'

'What do you mean, much more besides?' Pete asked. 'How much more is there once you're president of Mars?'

'Whittaker doesn't just want to be president, he wants to rule Mars, completely and permanently. He wants to own it.'

'I thought he already did,' said Pete. 'He's the richest man in existence, and everyone knows the only reason Mars can continue to function is because MarsMine is basically funding it.'

'Well, clearly that isn't enough for him. Because for several years he's been pursuing a policy of expansion and development that has transformed MarsMine from a hugely successful mining corporation into the Solar System's sixth-largest military force. And over the past few months, the pace has picked up alarmingly. Once he's president, once he controls MarsMine and the government, I don't think it will be long before we see Mars declaring itself independent and breaking away from the Unity.'

'What?' said Leo. 'But that's crazy. Earth would just come and take it back.'

'Would they? With what? Have you ever tried getting an invasion force large enough to conquer a planet through two hundred million kilometres of hostile space? It's not that easy.'

'Then what? We sit back and let him get away with it?' Skater asked.

'Not at all. There are other options.'

'Such as?'

'Oh, the usual. Diplomatic negotiation, the threat of sanctions—'

'In other words, letting him get away with it.'

'—inciting civil unrest. Terrorism. Assassination.'

'So is that why you're here?' Leo asked.

'I'm here to help you get your mother back,' Aitchison replied, smiling his unnerving smile.

'Then where is she?'

'I don't know.'

'But you're still looking?'

'Yes, I'm looking,' Aitchison snapped. It was the first time Leo had ever seen him be anything except calm and aloof and it was unnerving. 'But MarsMine suddenly seems to have become a very difficult organisation to infiltrate. Twice now I've tried to get someone onto the staff at the compound where I think she's being held, but both times my contact failed to report back once they were inside. I can only assume they were expected and are now dead. I'm reluctant to try a third time. No, what I need is someone who's already on the inside.' He looked across at Pete. 'Someone who has a good enough reason for being there not to arouse suspicions.'

'No, no, no, no, no.' Pete held up his hands in protest. 'No way. I'm a pilot, not a spy. And just because I wear the uniform it doesn't mean I can wander in to any MarsMine compound I like and act as if I own the place. If there's no good reason for me to be there, I'll be no better off than those other poor fools you sent in already. If you want me to shuttle you there, I will. If you want me to fly recon for you, I will. It's not cowardice stopping me from saying yes — it's common sense.'

'Don't worry,' Aitchison said, his smile returning. 'It was simply wishful thinking on my part. After your little encounter with those so-called pirates on the *Dragon*, I think it's safe to say that Whittaker and his men already know all about you and your mission here on Mars. I imagine they'll let you keep going for now, to see how much you know, but be warned. If they think you've become any sort of threat, they'll kill you. So watch your back.'

Aitchison got up to leave. 'Wait,' Leo said. 'What happens now?

What are we supposed to do?'

Aitchison shrugged. 'Think about everything I've said. There's a lot to take in. And get on with enjoying your holiday. I understand at least one of you wants to pay a visit to the shipyards.'

'At least tell us where you think my mother's being kept.'

'Nowhere you'd want to add to your holiday itinerary.'

'Why can't I decide that for myself?'

'Because if you manage to find out where it is, and storm off there on your own, you'll get yourself killed. And that would be...a waste. I'll contact you again if I think you need it.' He turned to Pete. 'And for your information, those two people I lost, they were highly skilled and extremely brave agents, not fools.'

There was, indeed, a lot to take in. Pete, Leo and Skater stayed sitting at the table for a long time after Aitchison had gone, discussing everything he'd told them. Aliens? Civil war? It was all too unbelievable. And yet Leo was certain that every word of it was the truth. And he wanted to believe it, too. It meant his mother really was here on Mars, somewhere close, somewhere the authorities knew about, even if they couldn't get inside. What was it Aitchison had said? He needed someone who had a good enough reason for being there. Pete had assumed he'd meant him, because he'd been a MarsMine employee for years and so might not arouse suspicions. But what if it had been him, Leo, that Aitchison had been talking about? He thought about it, and the more he thought about it, the more he realised exactly what Aitchison wanted. And what he wanted, too.

When he announced he would rather stay and look around the Montgomerie than go to the shipyards, he was sure the others would know what he was planning and refuse to leave him alone. He tried to make it sound as if he didn't really care either way, but that there were so many interesting things in the museum that he would probably never get the chance to see again and, to tell the truth, he wasn't so interested in wandering around inside a collection of half-finished spaceships.

'Are you sure?' Pete asked, concerned. 'We could all stay here and do the shipyards another day if you want.'

'Dad!' Skater pleaded desperately. 'You said we were booked in.'

'Well, that is true,' Pete replied, and it was clear he was every bit as keen to go as Skater.

'Listen, I'll be fine,' Leo said. 'There's more than enough stuff here to keep me occupied until closing time.'

'The Montgomerie doesn't have a closing time. It's open round the clock.'

Leo smiled. 'I know. But I promise I'll drag myself away in time to meet you back at the hotel for dinner. And I have my phone. I can call if there's a problem.'

'See,' Skater said, already tugging at Pete's sleeve. 'He's happy, he has his phone, and we'll see him at dinner. It's a great plan.'

'I'll take lots of vid-snaps for you,' Leo called out as they parted.

'I won't look at them.'

They left, and Leo watched and smiled until they were out of sight. Almost at once he found Aitchison standing beside him.

'Well, that didn't take long,' Aitchison said. 'Well done.'

'How did you know I'd figure it out?'

'Because you're a clever young man.'

'But how did you know I'd agree to do it?'

'Because I'm a clever old man. Now, come on. We've got a lot to do in a very short time.'

30

A WILLING CAPTIVE

MR ARCHER WAS WATCHING Carlton Whittaker on the wall screen. It was a live broadcast from the Downtown Dome, where the Old Man was holding an election rally, and he was playing the crowd perfectly: shaking hands, stopping to exchange a few words here and there, waving to those further back. At one point he really did kiss a baby. And all the while the broad smile never left his face. It was a smile of openness, of warmth, of confidence. It was the smile of a winner.

But Mr Archer was less interested in the Old Man than in the people around him. It had been agreed – reluctantly on Mr Archer's part – that he should not accompany Whittaker while he was out campaigning. It sent the wrong message to the voters, implying that here was a man who was in need of protection, a man who couldn't get close to his own people. And besides, the truth was that Mr Archer scared people. Especially babies.

So now Whittaker was out on his own, with only his personal assistants to keep him moving towards the podium. It was some consolation to Mr Archer, however, that the two women in question were both highly experienced bodyguards, trained by him and carrying enough concealed weaponry to see off anything short of a tank.

A call came through on his desk monitor and he took it without looking. 'What?'

'Morton, sir, from the front desk. I'm sorry for disturbing you, but there's a young boy down here asking to speak to Mr Whittaker.'

'Send him Downtown.'

'Yes, sir. I did. But then he said that if Mr Whittaker wasn't available, I was to inform the...well, he gave a description of someone who could only have been you, sir. He said to tell you his name was Leo Fischer.'

Instantly Mr Archer's head flipped round to the screen. 'Show me.' The security guard spun his camera around until it showed Leo, standing nervously on the far side of the desk. Mr Archer stared at him for a while, genuinely surprised, before making up his mind. 'He's alone?'

'Yes, sir.'

'Escort him to one of the waiting rooms downstairs. Keep him on his own. Search him thoroughly and never leave him unguarded. Understand?' The security guard looked surprised but knew enough to obey Mr Archer without question. 'Yes, sir. Understood.'

Mr Archer turned back to the wall screen. The Old Man was still working the crowd. He watched for several minutes, flicking between the available cameras so he could see the scene from all angles, but always it was the people in the crowd he was interested in, not Whittaker. That was where the danger lay. Every one of those adoring supporters, cheering and waving and holding out their hands, was a potential assassin. It was Mr Archer's job to make sure that none of that potential was realised.

As Whittaker finished with the crowd and made his way onto the platform, Mr Archer tapped the tiny headset in his ear. 'Kalina. I have something I have to deal with. You're running the show from now on. Clear?' On the screen, one of Whittaker's assistants turned briefly towards the following camera and gave a slight nod. 'Good. And make sure you keep him to schedule. Out.'

Leo was scared. Despite the air-conditioning in the waiting room and the cold glass of water the security guard had offered him, he was sweating and he could feel his legs shaking against the chair. The guard had been pleasant enough, apologising for having to search him and explaining that it was standard procedure, but somehow Leo got the feeling he was being treated as anything but standard. Not that it mattered. All being well, there was much worse to come.

After a long wait the door opened and Mr Archer stepped in. Leo knew what to expect – Aitchison had shown him plenty of holos – but being in the same room was absolutely terrifying and Leo began to wonder whether this whole plan had been a really, really bad idea. He stood up, his legs still shaking, but even so Mr Archer towered over him, staring down from behind his jet-black glasses, his mouth twisted into its permanent sneer by the thick scar running down his face.

'Sit down.' Leo sat back down and Mr Archer turned to the guard. 'You searched him?'

'Yes, sir.' The guard stepped over and placed Leo's wallet, wrist computer and phone-set on the small table beside Mr Archer.

'Good. You can leave us now.' The security guard nodded and

left, clearly glad to be out of the room. Leo knew how he felt.

Mr Archer picked up Leo's wallet and emptied it, carefully checking each section. There were several credit cards, his Standard ID as well as another from his school, a Lunaburger loyalty token and some odd scraps of paper with appointment times, or phone numbers, or other obscure notes scribbled on them. There was also an old-fashioned, paper-printed photograph of his mother. Mr Archer looked at it for a few seconds, tucked it back into the wallet and handed the wallet to Leo. The cards he put in his own pocket, along with the phone-set and computer. 'Where are the others?' he asked.

'What others?' Leo's throat was dry and he took a long gulp of water.

'Monroe and his daughter.'

'They don't know I'm here.'

'Where are they?'

'The shipyards. They're sightseeing.'

There was another long pause.

'You know who I am?'

'Yes.'

'How?'

'I searched. I was searching for my mother and the trail led me here.'

'What trail?'

Leo had to be careful. He'd gone through with Aitchison everything he was allowed to say and everything he should forget he knew. He could mention the ship, of course, as they knew about his meeting with Jack Duggan on Luna, and he could even say how he'd worked out it originated from outside the Solar System. But he was to say nothing about the situation on Mars or Whittaker's plans to take over the planet, and under no circumstances was he to say anything about having had contact with Aitchison.

'I know about the ship.' Leo paused, waiting to see if his words would have any effect, but Mr Archer remained stony-faced and silent. 'The real ship, I mean, not the *Arcadian*. I know you're hiding it somewhere here on Mars and I know you kidnapped my mum so you could force her to unlock its computers.'

'You know nothing,' Mr Archer said after a long pause.

'I know the ship is alien.' This time the pause went on so long Leo began to wonder whether Mr Archer had heard him. With the dark glasses covering his eyes, he could even have fallen asleep for all Leo knew. But he doubted it.

'This room is shielded,' Mr Archer said, finally. 'And you were scanned while you were waiting so I know you have no transmitters on you. Nothing we say here will ever be heard by anyone else. This is lucky for you.' He leaned in close and Leo instinctively drew back. 'But if you ever say that word again I will rip the tongue right out of your head so that I don't have to listen to you screaming while I tear the rest of you apart, as slowly and painfully as possible.'

'Please,' Leo whispered. 'I just want my mum.'

'You're a very resourceful boy to get all the way to Mars on your own.'

'But I wasn't on my own. I had help.'

'Yes, I know. First from Duggan and then from Monroe. How convenient to have found such helpful friends just when you needed them. And it was just coincidence, I suppose, that both these new friends happened to work for MarsMine.'

'Yes.'

'Who else?'

'No one.'

Mr Archer suddenly slammed his fist down on the table, knocking over the empty glass. 'Don't lie to me, boy. Who are you working with?'

'No one,' Leo pleaded, desperate to explain. 'I met Lisa Kate Monroe on the shuttle up from Earth. She was sitting beside me and we just started chatting and when we got to Luna and I found out my mum had been taken, her dad offered to look after me. I met Captain Duggan by accident. He was following me because he'd overheard me talking about my mum and he thought maybe I could help him find out about the...you know...the other ship.'

'And they just decided to smuggle you to Mars?'

'Yes. No. It was my idea, but they helped, yes.'

There was another long pause. Leo was shaking. He wanted to pick up the glass and set it back the right way up but he was worried that if he tried he would knock it to the floor and smash it. He took a deep breath and tried to calm himself, wondering if Mr Archer believed his story. At least he wasn't having to lie, which made it much easier to sound convincing. So far everything he'd said was the truth – it just wasn't the whole truth.

'Who killed one of my men on board the cruise ship?'

Damn. Well, so much for sticking to the truth, thought Leo. 'They were your men?' he asked, trying to sound surprised. 'I thought they were pirates.'

'Who killed him?'

'I did,' Leo said quietly. 'I had to.'

'A trained professional. Armed. And you killed him with a single blow to the back of the head?'

'He attacked Skater – Lisa Kate – and I thought he was going to kill her. They were struggling and he dropped his knife and it was the only way I could think of to stop him. Afterwards I knew the others would come looking for us so we ran and hid until they'd gone.'

'I don't believe you,' said Mr Archer. 'And I don't trust you. As

245

far as I'm concerned you're a problem. If it was my decision, I'd deal with you right here and now. But luckily for you, it is not my decision. Instead I'm going to give you what you want. Come.'

'My mum?' Leo asked. 'Is she here? Are you taking me to her?' He could feel the sudden excitement building inside him, even though he knew it was unlikely. Aitchison had said she wasn't in Minerva, but was almost certainly being held at some research site in the middle of the desert. Was that where Mr Archer was taking him now?

Mr Archer said nothing. He led Leo out of the room and along to the lifts, where they went several floors deeper into the building. Leo was allowed to walk freely, with Mr Archer directing him from behind, and Leo suspected this was not only because there was nowhere to run, but because one of those big, powerful, crushing hands could be around his throat before he'd gone more than two or three paces.

They eventually stopped at a code-locked door. Beyond it was a darkened room that appeared to be a surveillance centre. On one wall was a bank of monitors showing locations in and around the MarsMine building, and across the room was a long desk at which two technicians sat, scanning the screens and occasionally inputting data into terminals. They looked up when Mr Archer pushed Leo into the room but showed no surprise and went straight back to their work. Leo was led over to a smaller desk on the far side of the room where there was another monitor.

'Sit.' He sat. Mr Archer powered up the screen and after a few seconds of staring at an empty chair at the other end, someone in a white lab coat appeared and sat down. 'Yes, sir?' the man said as soon as he recognised Mr Archer.

'Bring me the professor. I have something I want her to see.'

The man nodded and walked off. Mr Archer turned to Leo.

'You wanted to see your mother. Well, you can see her.' He flicked a switch on the side of the monitor. 'No talking though.'

Leo waited. A minute went by, and then another. He was too excited, too nervous, to wait. After all these weeks of worry, of not knowing whether his mother was still alive, he was finally going to get to see her. Would she be happy? Or angry that he'd risked himself to find her? He didn't care. Just so long as he could see her. And no matter how much he wanted to, or how much she needed it, he wouldn't give any hint that being here was part of a plan to get her out. If all went well, that would happen soon enough.

And suddenly there she was, staring into the screen, not knowing why she'd been summoned away from her work. 'Mum!' Leo screamed, jumping up from his seat and grabbing the monitor on both sides. 'Mum! You're okay.' She couldn't hear him, he knew that, but saying the words out loud felt better. 'I love you,' he cried. 'I love you. I love you.'

She looked thin and frail, like a dry twig that might snap at any minute, and Leo could only imagine what she must have suffered over the past weeks. He smiled, trying to reassure her that everything would be okay, and she smiled back, even though he could see tears streaming down her cheeks. Slowly she shook her head from side to side. *Why?* she mouthed.

'Because I had to.'

Lillian Fischer reached out and pressed her palm against the screen and Leo did the same. It was warm and he could almost imagine it was his mother's hand he was touching instead of the glass. She mouthed something else and he blinked away his own tears to see more clearly. *Stay safe.* He nodded to show he'd understood. 'You too.'

Mr Archer pulled him away from the monitor. For a few seconds he stared at the professor and then held up a piece of paper on which he had written a single word in large letters. RESULTS. Then he switched off the screen.

He led Leo back through the building and up one floor to a small accommodation room. It looked comfortable enough. It was still below ground so there was no window, but there was a perfectly nice-looking bed, a desk and a small bathroom off to one side. There was even a wall screen, but Leo guessed it was only there to receive, not to transmit. 'You'll stay here,' Mr Archer said.

'For how long?'

'For as long as I say.'

'Please,' Leo said desperately as Mr Archer was about to close the door. 'I'll work for you if you want. I'm really good with computers, with programming and artificial systems and things like that. That's why I was going to Luna in the first place, to work with my mum. Just ask her and she'll tell you. I can already do loads of stuff even some of her students don't know how to do. Please, just let me be with her and I promise I'll do everything I can to help her. And I'm sure she'll work better as well, knowing I'm safe. Please.'

Mr Archer wasn't listening. He locked the door and made his way back to his office. On the wall screen, Carlton Whittaker was still making his speech and his two assistants were still scanning the crowd with their restless eyes. Satisfied that everything was in order, Mr Archer took out his phone-set and made a call.

Yes?

'How soon can you be at the shipyards?'

The shipyards? Within the hour.

'Equipped?'

Within reason.

'Good. I'll send through the information. Do it somewhere out in the desert. I'll leave the details up to you, but I would rather the bodies were never found.'

Understood.

Mr Archer hung up and nodded to himself with satisfaction. It was turning out to be a very successful day. The Old Man would be pleased.

31
THE HOLIDAY COMES
TO AN END

'SO,' PETE ASKED. 'If you could pick any one of these ships to be yours, which one would it be?' He and Skater were standing on a raised walkway looking out at a vast and varied collection of spaceships, either fixed to the floor below them or suspended from the dome above. One or two were newly built, state-of-the-art private cruisers and tourers, but there were also many old favourites that Skater recognised: the long-serving Atlas Shuttle-bus; the Xinkai Rockhopper; an old P84 fighter. In all, there were maybe thirty or thirty-five craft squeezed into this one large dome they called the Museum Wing.

'Well?'

'Well,' Skater replied after a while, pointing up to a small, elegantly curved silver craft near the ceiling. 'I'd probably go for the Crescent Moon, I guess.'

'Really?' Pete asked. 'The flying croissant?'

Skater nudged him in the side. 'It's not a croissant, it's a classic. It's one of the buzzest ships ever designed.'

'And one of the most uncomfortable as well,' Pete added. 'Not to mention slow and notoriously difficult to handle in-atmos.'

'And how would you know? Have you ever flown one?'

'I sat in one once. That was enough for me.'

'Okay then. Which one would you pick?'

'That one,' Pete said at once, pointing to one of the brand new luxury cruisers.

'Yeuch! Honestly, Dad. That's, like, easily the ugliest thing in here.'

'So? Who cares what it looks like? When you get to my age, comfort on the inside becomes a whole lot more important than style on the outside.'

'You have no soul,' said Skater. 'And anyway, it was an unfair question. They haven't got the ship I really want.'

'Let me guess. A Wayfarer?'

'Exactly.'

'So, still set on becoming a trader then?'

'Yep.'

'Wandering from planet to planet and station to station, constantly trying to scrape together enough credit to pay for the upkeep of your battered old ship and hoping you never bump into any pirates? It's a hard life, you know.'

'Dad! You promised.'

'I know, I know. And I'll stick to it, too. Just so long as you stick to your part of the deal. I'm just saying, it's a hard, lonely, unforgiving sort of life.'

'Not necessarily lonely.'

'Oh? You thinking of bringing someone along with you now?'

'I just mean you don't have to be on your own. Look at Sol and

Li, for example.'

'So you have been thinking of bringing someone else along?'

'Maybe.'

'Leo?'

'Maybe.'

Pete gave Skater a knowing smile and she felt herself obliged to dig him in the ribs with her elbow once again. 'It's not like that,' she said, defensively. 'Well, not exactly like that. Not yet, anyway.'

'Do you like him?'

'Yes, of course I like him.'

'But do you *like* him?'

Skater paused, thinking of all the stupid and annoying things Leo had said and done over the past few weeks. 'Yes,' she said with a smile. 'I figure I do.'

'And does he *like* you?'

Skater laughed. 'Oh yes.'

'Good. He's a nice lad. Clever, too. And sensible.'

'Not much of a kisser though.'

'Lisa Kate, please! There are some things I don't need to know.'

'I'm just saying.'

Somewhere in the background there was an announcement over the public-address system that the two of them ignored until they heard their own name mentioned. Pete held up his hand for Skater to be quiet and the two of them listened carefully. 'Report to the Information Desk?' Pete said, once the announcement had finished. 'What for? And how did anyone know we were here?'

'Leo knew. Maybe he's found out something.'

'Maybe,' Pete replied, but he didn't seem entirely convinced. And when they saw the policeman waiting for them at the Information Desk, Skater was even less convinced.

'Mr Peter Monroe?' the policeman asked as they approached.

'I'm sorry to have to tell you this, sir, but there was an incident a little while ago, a traffic accident, involving a Mr Leonard Fischer. I was given to understand you are currently acting as his guardian, yes?'

'What happened?' Skater demanded. 'Is he okay?'

'I'm afraid not, Miss. He was hit quite bad and had to be rushed to hospital. I was told to come and find you here and bring you over to be with him. I have the car waiting if you'll follow me.'

Skater grabbed hold of Pete's hand and the two of them hurried along beside the policeman with Skater firing off questions at him as they went. 'How did it happen? Was he pushed? What injuries?' But the policeman knew nothing. He'd simply been on patrol nearby and been told to pick them up and get them to the hospital. They would find out what they needed to know once they were there.

At the main entrance they paused to fix the hoods onto their environment suits and then the policeman led them out across the vehicle park to his waiting car. As soon as they were all inside, he started the engines and the car rose into the air. Despite her worries for Leo, Skater felt a jolt of excitement as the car left the ground. She had never been in a police skimmer before and she only wished her first time could have been under more pleasant circumstances.

After a few seconds a green light appeared on the front control panel to indicate that the air was now breathable and they took off their hoods. 'Where did they take him?' Pete asked, looking out his window and trying to identify where they were.

'Don't worry,' the policeman answered calmly. 'We'll be there in no time.'

'But which hospital?'

The policeman didn't reply.

'Why didn't he come with us?' Skater said, more to herself than

her father. 'I knew it was a bad idea to let him go off on his own.'
Pete said nothing. Skater leaned in close beside him and whispered.
'What if it wasn't an accident? What if it was someone trying to
kill him? He could still be in serious danger. We all could.'

'I think we already are,' Pete replied. He leaned forward. 'We
don't seem to be heading towards any hospital I know. Where are
we actually going? And how come you're on your own? I thought
there were always meant to be two officers for each patrol car.' By
way of reply, the policeman pressed a button on the panel beside
him and a transparent screen shot up right in front of Pete, sealing
off the back part of the car.

'Hood!' Pete screamed over the hiss of escaping air as both side
windows began to slide open. Skater grabbed the hood she had
only just taken off and yanked it back over her head, clipping it into
place and hitting the switch on her wrist pad to start the flow of air.
She checked her gauge – almost full. So either they were going to fly
around in circles for the next five hours or the man in the front of
the car, whoever he might be, was going to have to find some other
way to kill them.

More out of desperation than because she thought it would
work, Skater leant back and gave the panel in front of her a vicious
kick with the heel of her boot. Nothing, not even a scratch. It was
made from some sort of reinforced plastic that was probably bullet-
proof. It was certainly boot-proof anyway, and that was all she had.
She looked out of the window, in case there was any possibility of
jumping, but they were too high, and travelling much too fast, for
that to be anything but a very last resort. She sat back and gave the
panel another kick, just for the sake of it.

'Dad,' she said over the suit's intercom. 'What's going on?'

'I guess someone's decided we're getting too close for comfort.'
He patted Skater on the leg. 'From the look of it we're heading out

of town, so I guess we've got a little bit of time before...whatever's going to happen will happen.'

'He's going to kill us?'

'I think that's the plan, yes.'

She reached over and took his hand.

'And we're going to stop him, right?'

'I guess we'll have to.'

'How?'

Pete shook his head. 'I don't know, sweetheart. But we'll think of something.'

They fell silent. Soon they began to leave the city behind and after a few minutes there was nothing to see except the dull brown monotony of the rocky desert. Skater looked around for something – anything – they might be able to use to smash the reinforced plastic panel. She checked the floor, the roof, around the edges of the doors. She even leaned out of the open window to see if there was anything on the outside of the car, but there was nothing. She thrust her hands into the gap along the back of the seat, hoping that maybe some previous occupant had dropped something useful, but again there was nothing.

Wait. There was something. She forced her hand further in and felt around until she found it again. A small lever of some sort. Of course, she thought excitedly. It was the release catch for the seat. It wasn't much, not much at all, but it was all they had.

'Dad. Help me.'

Pete shuffled forward, and while Skater pulled the lever he tugged at the seat until it swung away from the back rest. The man in the front looked round to see what they were doing and Skater glared back at him.

'Just ignore him,' Pete told her. 'There's nothing he can do without lowering the screen, and the minute he does that I'll be in there at his throat. I'll watch him; you keep looking.'

Skater clambered over the upended seat and searched the space beneath but there was nothing, just the metal base of the car itself. She looked up at Pete and shook her head. But there had to be something. Maybe not a convenient metal bar they could break the panel with, but maybe some other way of stopping the car. And then she had an idea. She dived back down and pushed herself as far under the seat as she could, until she worried that if she squeezed any further she might tear her suit. She reached out, feeling around in the empty space until she found what she'd been searching for. Wires.

The police skimmer's main engine was up front, but once in the air it was kept aloft and controlled by four thrusters, one at each corner. The two rear ones were connected to the engine by a mass of cables and wires running along the side walls of the car and now Skater had one set of these wires grasped in her fist.

'Hang on to something,' Skater called and she tugged at the handful of wires.

Nothing happened. Skater cursed, twisted herself around so she could get both her hands around the wires and tugged again, this time with all her strength. Some of the wires came loose. She tugged again and a few more came away in her hand and suddenly the car gave a lurch as one of the rear thrusters lost power. Up front, the driver was struggling to keep control and he dropped down until they were whizzing along no more than a few metres above the ground. But even with only three thrusters it was clear he was going to be able to control the vehicle enough to land it safely. The car began to slow down. Skater twisted round and felt for the wires running along the other side wall.

'Skater. No!' Pete shouted desperately, but it was too late. She tugged, the wires came loose at the first pull, and this time there was no way the driver could keep control. As the second thruster cut out, the front of the car shot upwards and then the whole thing flipped over and crashed back down into the hard ground, throwing up great clouds of dust and rock and bouncing end over end several times before finally coming to a stop, nose down in the dirt.

Skater lay in bed and tried to decide whether it was time to get up. She felt dizzy, but also warm and comfortable and she was sure no one would mind if she gave herself another half-hour's sleep. Had she been dreaming? She couldn't remember. Already the images had faded, but maybe they would come back if she thought really hard. If only it wasn't so noisy. Who was making all that noise at this time of the morning? And why was her bed so uncomfortable? She tried to turn over, but a sharp pain sliced through the fog in her head and suddenly everything came back to her; the policeman, the car, the crash.

She was lying on her side, wedged beneath the rear seat that had swung back on top of her. Her left shoulder was a mass of pain when she tried to move, but the terror of thinking she was trapped was even worse and she pushed against the seat, screaming as the pain flooded through her body. The seat swung away and the Martian sunlight seeped back in, along with a certain amount of relief. But not much.

She could breathe okay, and there was no tell-tale hiss of escaping air, so the suit had survived intact. That was something. And it meant that whatever was wrong with her shoulder, it wasn't something sticking into it, as that would have torn the suit as well. She silently thanked Li for having given her such a good, strong suit. It had almost certainly saved her life.

But what about the others? 'Dad?' she called over the comms. She could see he wasn't in the back of the car. 'Dad? Where are you?' There was no reply. Was he okay? Had he made it out of the wreck? And what about the policeman? From where she was lying she couldn't see the front of the car so she couldn't see if he was in his seat, although she did notice that the crash had finally cracked the reinforced panel. Was he waiting for her outside? Had she survived the crash only to be shot the moment she showed her head?

She had to get up. She took a deep breath, gritted her teeth and used her right arm to pull herself slowly up into a sitting position. Every second was agony. Her shoulder felt like it was on fire and if she didn't keep it completely still, waves of pain shot through her chest. Twice she had to stop to take a breath before carrying on, but finally she was free of the cramped space. She sat, propped on the upturned seat and gasping for breath. Sweat was pouring down her face and her legs were shaking, but she had succeeded without passing out or throwing up and things would be much easier from now on.

Then she saw the driver. He was still strapped in, but his seat was now twisted and buckled and his body was wedged tight against the control panel. She couldn't see his head, but the shattered helmet and the long smear of blood across the controls told her everything she needed to know. She turned away.

'Dad!' she called again. She looked out into the desert, but from where she was sitting she could only see a small area to each side and there was nothing except a few twisted pieces of metal. She slid along the seat until she could reach the door but found it was locked, so she pushed her legs through the open window, took hold of the handhold above the door with her good arm and lowered herself as slowly as possible down onto the ground.

Her father was lying face down about twenty metres behind the wrecked car. She staggered towards him as quickly as her weak legs would let her, and ignoring another wave of pain from her shoulder, she rolled him onto his back. His visor was badly scratched but still intact and she couldn't see any obvious tears in his suit, but there was a bad gash on his forehead and blood had run down as far as his mouth. She watched for several seconds until she was convinced he was still breathing and then moved until she was shading his face from the sun.

For the moment that was all she could do. She was too weak to move, and too stunned to think properly. When the tears came there was nothing she could do to stop them. Each sob sent a jolt of pain through her, but the pain just made her sob all the more and she was making so much noise she missed the moment when Pete's eyes flickered open and he coughed the blood out of his mouth. It was only when he reached up and put his hand on hers that she realised he had regained consciousness.

32
NIGHT WALKING

THE SHOULDER WAS ONLY dislocated, not broken, and Pete explained that the best thing to do was to pop it back into place as soon as possible.

'Pop?' Skater shook her head. 'I don't think so. As long as I don't move it I can manage the pain. We can save the popping till we're back in Minerva and somewhere where they have serious pain drugs.'

'We're not going back to Minerva,' Pete said.

'What? Why not?'

'Because it's too dangerous. We were lucky this time, but once they find out we survived this, they'll come again, and again, until they succeed. And Minerva is their city. We'd never be safe there.'

'But where else is there? We're in the middle of the desert. On Mars. We have...what? Four hours of air left. That's not going to get us far.'

'You're right. It wouldn't even get us back to Minerva.'

'So we stay here until we're rescued then?'

'And who's going to be the first to come looking? The real police or this guy's friends?'

'Then what are we supposed to do?'

'Well, first off, this.' Without warning, Pete took hold of Skater's arm and tugged. Skater screamed and sank to her knees as the pain tore through her, but even as the shock wore off she could tell her shoulder was back in its right place. Pete knelt down and put his arms around her. 'I'm sorry, sweetheart. But it had to be done. The longer we left it, the worse it would have become.'

'I know,' Skater muttered, blinking away the tears. And then she threw up.

Skater hated throwing up at the best of times, but throwing up in a sealed environment suit — especially one she had no way of taking off for the next few hours — was so much worse. The smell was unbearable, the brown smear on the inside of her visor was annoying and the revolting sticky squelching down the front of her suit was just gross. Pete left her sitting on a rock, complaining to herself, while he went to examine the wreck of the car.

'So what are we going to do?' she asked over the comms.

'Well, that kind of depends on what I can find in here. The good news is, it's a real police car, so it's pretty well equipped. Or at least it was, before the crash. We'll take whatever we can and use it to get as far as one of the Life Lines. After that, all we have to do is keep going till we hit the first depot.'

'Life Lines?'

'They're trails across the desert. Sometimes, if the ground is hard enough, there might be an actual track, or sometimes it's just the route of a fuel pipe or power line. But at regular intervals there are emergency supply points. Some might be nothing more than an air supply and a comms kit. Some are actual shelters. But either way the idea is they'll keep you alive until you can make it to a proper settlement.'

'But what about *them*? Won't that be the first place they go looking for us?'

'Possibly. Probably. But there's not a whole lot we can do about that. We'll just have to keep our eyes peeled for trouble and hope we've got a few hours' head start.'

Skater looked towards her father through her smeared visor. 'Keeping my eyes peeled. Mmm, that should be fun.'

A few minutes later Pete brought over everything he had been able to salvage. 'Medi-kit,' he said. 'Not much use until we can find an airtight shelter, but at least it comes with a handy shoulder strap.' He placed the strap over Skater's hood and carefully lifted her left arm so that it was resting along the top of the kit. 'As for air,' he continued, 'we have two full spare packs and one that's part-used.'

'Part-used?'

Pete glanced back at the car. 'He's not going to need it.'

'Oh. Right.'

'That will give us well over ten hours of air each, which should be more than enough. We have one small bottle of water and no food. Again, for a few hours that won't be a problem, but come tomorrow, we'll start to need water pretty quickly. We'll have to hope we find a well-stocked depot nice and quick. As for the car, the comms was completely smashed, but actually that's a good thing. I doubt I'd have been able to take it out anyway and if the car isn't transmitting, it'll be harder for anyone to locate it. Or us.'

'I still have my phone,' said Skater helpfully.

'Me too. I'd rather not use them unless we have to as they're bound to be tracking them, but it's good to know they're there in case we get desperate.'

Skater motioned with her right hand. 'Doesn't this count as desperate yet?'

'Come on,' Pete said, helping her up. 'Let's not be here when they come looking.'

As she stood up, Skater noticed that Pete had also taken the policeman's pistol, along with his gun belt and what appeared to be plenty of spare ammunition. 'I guess he won't be needing those, either?'

'And hopefully, neither will we. But I'm not counting on it.'

'So which way are we going?'

'That way,' Pete replied, pointing out into the emptiness. 'It's away from Minerva and it's pretty much due north, which is the right direction.'

'Right direction for what?'

'For the Life Lines. And after that, for someone who might be able to help us.'

'Help us do what?'

'Find a way out of this mess.'

'And who might this person be?'

'An old friend. Maybe.'

Pete clearly didn't want to say more and for once Skater was happy to walk in silence. For a start, she hated walking. Her shoulder was still killing her, her back was sore, her legs were weak and she was still shaky from the crash. Also, the smell inside her suit was terrible, she was uncomfortable and itchy and she was already thirsty. And cold. And fairly soon she was going to need the toilet. It was not the evening for a pleasant chat.

So they walked in silence, both lost in their own thoughts. Occasionally Pete would forge on ahead and clamber onto a rock to get a better view, and sometimes he would fall into step beside Skater and give her a reassuring smile, but generally they kept to themselves. And they didn't stop. Skater was exhausted and sore but she knew there was no point in resting. She wouldn't be able to drink, or fall asleep, and she would find it all the more difficult to get up again afterwards. Plodding on, even at their snail's pace, was the only thing they could do until they came to something man-made.

Sunset was long and they kept the last of the light for a good while after the tiny sun had disappeared beyond the horizon. But eventually it became too dark to see more than a few steps ahead and after Skater had stumbled on loose rocks for the second time, Pete slowed down and the two of them walked hand in hand to avoid losing each other in the darkness.

Pete was running out of air. Skater could hear him over the comms, taking slower, deeper breaths and wheezing slightly, and now that she thought about it, her own lungs felt as if there was something pressing against them each time she breathed in. 'Dad,' she said, breaking the long silence. 'I think it might be time to change our air.'

Pete took out the torch from the policeman's belt and examined the dials on their air packs. Skater's was showing four percent remaining, his was flashing zero. 'I guess so,' he laughed.

Skater took a deep breath and held it while Pete unclipped her air feed and reattached it to the second pack. The difference was startling. The new air felt clean and fresh and she felt stronger, more awake. She hadn't realised how drowsy the stale air had been making her feel and she was amazed her dad had been able to struggle on for as long as he had.

'You doing okay?' Pete asked her.

'Not really, no. You?'

'I've had better days. Don't think I've ever had a headache this bad before. Still, we're alive, and that's something. Come on, let's not stand around wasting air.'

They set off again more confidently. Phobos had risen and was giving them just enough light that they could pick out the ground ahead. It was less sandy now, easier to walk on, and in the distance they could see the silhouette of a low ridge. 'Let's have a look up there,' Pete said. 'It'll give us as good a view as we're likely to get of the surrounding area.'

'Dad?' Skater asked, after they had gone a little further.

'Yes, sweetheart.'

'Leo's dead, isn't he?'

There was a pause before Pete replied. 'What makes you say that?'

'I've been thinking about it. What that policeman said.'

'You don't really think Leo was run over by a bus, do you? That was just the story to get us to go along with him.'

'I know. But he knew Leo's name. And Leo was the only one who knew we'd be at the shipyards, so they must have got to him. And if they were prepared to kill us, why not him as well?'

Pete took Skater's hand. 'Honestly? I don't know. I've been thinking about it as well. Yes, they've got Leo. I think you're right about that. But that doesn't mean they're going to kill him. Remember it's him they're interested in, not us. He's important to them. They want to use the fact that they've got him as a hold over his mother, and if that's the case, they'll keep him alive.'

'For as long as they need him.'

'Well, let's hope they keep needing him for long enough to give us time to rescue him.'

'Rescue *him*?' Skater gave a hopeless laugh. 'Rescue him? Who's going to rescue *us* first?'

'Who needs rescuing? Look.'

They had reached the crest of the ridge. Skater looked over onto the far side and stopped, unable to understand what she was seeing. They were on the edge of a shallow crater that stretched away for as far as she could see. But the slope in front of her was filled with strange dark shapes, long and low and angled up from the ground. There were hundreds, thousands maybe, set out in neat rows down the sides of the crater like the seats in some bizarre, giant amphitheatre. And where the stage should have been was a huge, low dome, dark against the darkness around it, but picked out by bright blue beacon lights running along its spine.

'What in Sol's name is that?' Skater asked.

'Salvation,' Pete replied, with obvious relief.

'Yeah, but what sort of salvation?'

'It's a farm,' Pete said as they set off, down through the solar panels. 'A sun farm.'

It took them fifteen minutes to make their way down to the dome, another ten to work out how to access the automated air lock and a further thirty until someone inside was awake enough to come and investigate. Even then, it took a fair amount of discussion before the man inside was prepared to open the inner door. There was a camera link and he could clearly see that Pete was both covered in blood and carrying a gun, and it was only when Skater began to cry with desperation that he relented and let them in.

'Here,' Pete said, unclipping his belt and handing it to the man as soon as they were inside. 'You keep it.' The man looked at the pistol, at the Police Authority belt buckle, and didn't seem any more reassured. 'You'd best come on down,' he said in a thick Russian accent. 'I'll wake others, then we see if we can get you patched up.'

'Thank you,' Pete said. 'And sorry for all the trouble.'

'Pah!' the man said with a wave of his hand. 'Is most exciting thing happening in months. I should be thanking you.' And he led the way downstairs.

33

A FAMILY REUNION

LEO WAS KEPT IN HIS NEW ROOM for three days. He was allowed to sleep as long as he wanted, was brought perfectly nice meals at regular intervals — always by the same polite but uncommunicative guard — and for the rest of the time there was television. He had access to ten channels. Nine of them were clearly designed to drive him slowly insane with their dizzying mix of children's cartoons, ancient films, embarrassingly bad game-shows and endless documentaries about the difficulties of life in the Martian farming regions. Three weren't even in English. But the final channel was Leo's saviour. *Non-Stop 9 News*. It was dull and repetitive, and so unbelievably positive in its outlook that after three days of watching, Leo was starting to believe that nothing bad ever happened on the planet. But it did tell him everything he needed to know about the coming elections, and about MarsMine boss and presidential front-runner, Carlton Whittaker.

Whenever Whittaker appeared, Leo watched. Mostly it was just the odd minute of headlines covering a rally or walkabout, or a soundbite from a particularly rousing speech. But occasionally they would have a longer piece, an 'election special', or even, once, an exclusive interview. Leo watched and listened and studied as if revising for an exam. This was the man who had kidnapped his mother, who had forced her to work for him, and who would order her death the moment she was of no more use. And it didn't matter what he said, or how much he smiled, or how many hands he shook. Leo knew, with every ounce of his being, that the man was pure evil and had to be stopped.

But after three days locked inside the room, Leo had started to feel that things were going disastrously wrong. It had all seemed so straightforward when Aitchison had explained it to him. He would give himself up, offer to help them in return for being taken to his mother and then…well, he wouldn't think about that right now. It hadn't occurred to him that they would simply lock him up and ignore him.

And what about Skater and Pete? Aitchison had said it was better if they didn't know what was being planned, that he would think of something to tell them so that they weren't worrying. But what? That he'd decided to give up the search for his mother and go home? As if. They were probably wandering around Minerva right now, looking for him. They might even have come here, to MarsMine, for all the good it would have done them.

The door opened and the guard arrived with his lunch. 'Eat it quickly,' he said. 'And be ready to leave in fifteen minutes. Wear your E-suit.'

Leo's heart began to pound. Finally, something was happening. And being told to wear the environment suit meant they would be going outside. For a second, it occurred to him that they might be taking him somewhere remote to shoot him, but he remembered something Mr Archer had told him the other day, that he could have killed him there and then in the waiting room and no one would have raised a finger to stop him. Or they could have poisoned him with the food. No, this had to be because they were finally taking him to his mother.

Leo shovelled down some food, made sure he had his wallet and put on his environment suit. He was sitting on the bed when the guard returned. This time when they took the lift they went to the top floor, where Leo was handed over to another guard, already suited up, who led him up a stairway and along a mobile corridor on the roof of the building to a shuttle waiting for them on the hoverpad. It was long and sleek and shiny, and looked fast and expensive. It could have been Whittaker's own private craft for all Leo knew.

'Wow,' Leo said, after he had been led through into the main cabin. 'Nice.' The guard followed him, sealed the door and directed him to one of the large, soft chairs that were more like personal sofas. 'Sit,' he ordered. 'Strap yourself in, keep your mouth shut and touch nothing.'

'No,' said a familiar, rasping voice from behind him. 'Touch what you like.' Leo spun his seat around. Mr Archer, sitting further along the cabin, did the same so that they were facing each other. 'Eat some fruit, have a drink. You may even watch television if you like.'

'I'm fine.'

'As you wish.' He ordered the guard to sit up front with the pilot and then helped himself to something Leo didn't recognise from the fruit bowl.

'So,' Leo asked, looking around the luxurious cabin. 'This belong to Mr Whittaker?'

'The entire building belongs to Mr Whittaker.'

'But, I mean, is this his private shuttle?'

'Sometimes.'

There was a very gentle rocking as the shuttle took to the air. Leo hadn't even been aware of the engines starting up. 'Are you taking me to my mother?'

'Yes.'

'Did she provide you with the results you wanted?'

'She appears to be trying very hard.'

'I meant it, you know, what I said the other day about being willing to help if I could be with her.' Mr Archer nodded but remained silent. He picked up the slate he had been scrolling through and paid Leo no more attention. Leo helped himself to a drink, even though he wasn't thirsty, and stared out of the window at the rapidly disappearing skyscrapers and domes of Minerva. The shuttle was fast. He couldn't tell if it was designed for orbit or not, but on this journey they were clearly going to be staying in-atmosphere. Presumably that meant their destination was not too far away. Good. Already he could feel the anticipation building inside him.

'What's it like?' he asked. Mr Archer looked up from his slate. 'The ship,' Leo added. 'How...strange is it?' He remembered Mr Archer's threat of what would happen if he ever mentioned the word *alien* again. It had probably just been to scare him, but he wasn't prepared to test out his theory.

'I'm not a technician.'

'But you must have seen inside it. I mean, from the outside it didn't look anything special, but presumably on the inside it's just completely...different.'

'You're like your mother. At first she refused to help us, refused even to talk. But when she discovered what we had for her, she soon changed her mind. You could see it in her eyes. More than professional curiosity. It was a hunger, a compulsion. A challenge.'

'Yeah,' said Leo. 'I can imagine.'

'You'll see for yourself soon enough.'

The journey took three hours and Leo soon grew tired of trying to talk to Mr Archer, who grew equally tired of having to answer his constant questions. At one point Leo dozed, his soft, comfortable seat proving too much even for his excitement, but for the last part of the journey he sat staring out at the endless desert landscape. Sometimes it was easy to forget he was actually on Mars. He had grown so used to the low gravity that it seemed natural now, and he could only imagine how difficult it was going to be getting used to his proper weight again once he made it back to Earth. When, or if, he ever did.

The shuttle had begun its descent before Leo spotted the compound. Even from this high up it looked impressive, with several tall buildings surrounding a huge central tower and dozens of one- and two-storey structures spreading out from this central core. A large landing area and vehicle park were off to one side and Leo was surprised to see the place even had its own monorail station. As they dropped lower, Leo also noticed that the compound was surrounded by a tall security fence, giving it a distinctly military feel, and there were several guard vehicles stationed beside the two points where the fence was broken; a double gate that provided the only vehicle access, and the monorail terminus. The monorail cut through the rocky landscape behind them in a straight line as far as Leo could see.

Suddenly Mr Archer was standing beside him. 'If you try to escape, the guards will kill you. If you manage to sneak past them, the desert will kill you. The nearest settlement is over a hundred kilometres away and if by some miracle you make it that far, all that will happen is that they will send you straight back. And then

I will kill you.'

'Remember,' Leo said, trying to sound much more confident than he felt. 'I was the one who asked to come here. I'm not planning on leaving just yet.' Mr Archer gave a grunt, as if he wasn't entirely convinced, but said nothing more.

Leo had expected the shuttle to put down in the landing area, but it came to rest on top of the central tower. The moment its engines powered down, two workers ran out another mobile corridor, identical to the one in Minerva, allowing them to enter the building without having to suit up. Once inside Mr Archer led him down and down until they came to the great hangar where the remains of the black ship lay, buried among the more familiar equipment and machinery that had been used to dismantle it.

'Is this really it?' Leo asked in amazement, walking over so that he could run his hand along the smooth black surface. 'Why are you breaking it up?'

'It is more useful to us like this,' Mr Archer replied. 'But we can rebuild it if we choose to. Come.' He led Leo over to a guarded doorway and peered through a glass panel on the door. 'I see the professor. Where are the other two?'

'They've finished for the day,' one of the guards explained. 'But she always works late on her own these days.'

'You see,' Mr Archer said to Leo. 'Amazing what you can achieve with the right motivation.'

Leo was too excited to reply. He was staring at his mother's back, willing her to turn around. Even now, he wasn't sure if Mr Archer intended to let him go to her, or whether he had brought him here as a means of tormenting her. But when the guard unlocked the door Mr Archer stood to one side. 'Go on,' he said. 'Have your precious family reunion. I will talk to you both in the morning.' He pushed Leo forward and closed the door behind him.

His mother was lost in her work and hadn't bothered to turn around at the sound of the door. 'Mum,' Leo called, but his mouth was so dry the word came out as a whisper, and he had to swallow and try again. 'Mum.' This time she turned, and as Leo ran towards her she leapt up, knocking over her seat, and wrapped her arms around him.

The hug went on and on, neither wanting to let go. When Leo felt tears welling up, he let them come. 'Leo,' his mother whispered through her own tears. 'Leo. Leo.' Finally she pulled away, holding him at arm's length so she could see his face. 'Oh, Leo. I'm so happy to see you and know you're safe. I've been worried sick ever since they told me you were on Mars. And when I knew they'd picked you up I thought they'd keep you away from me and never let me see you. Oh, I'm so happy.'

She paused and glanced up at one of the cameras set into the ceiling before leading Leo across to the sofa. 'I knew you'd try to find me,' she continued. 'But I never thought you'd make it this far. How in heaven's name did you get all the way to Mars?' She reached forward and hugged him again, whispering in his ear as she did. 'Be careful. They can hear everything we say.'

Leo sniffed and wiped his eyes and nose on the sleeve of his environment suit. Back on Earth his mum would have said something, but here she barely seemed to notice. She looked different. Not just tired and thin but somehow weaker, as if some inner fire had been extinguished; as if she had already been defeated. Would it return, he wondered, now that he was with her, or was it gone forever?

'It's a very long story,' he said. And one day soon he would be able to tell it to her. All of it. But for now he would stick to those parts that Whittaker and Archer already knew. And as painful as it would be for his mother, he would also have to keep playing the part of willing captive for a while yet.

'Take your time,' Aitchison had told him. 'They'll be expecting you to try something in the first few days, so don't even think about being anything except what you claim to be – a boy who wants to be reunited with his mother at all costs – until you've been there at least a week.'

'But I can explain things to her, surely?'

'Absolutely not. She has to believe the story completely, just like everyone else. No explanations. No hints. Nothing.'

'She'll blame herself. It'll make her feel terrible.'

'Well, let her. It'll be good for your cover. You can apologise and tell her the truth once you're both safely out of there. Trust me, that's the way it has to be.'

And so Leo followed instructions and only told his mother half his story. Even so, there was plenty to tell and the two of them had been sitting together on the sofa for well over an hour by the time Leo reached the part where he went to the MarsMine building to give himself up.

'Why?' Lillian asked. 'Why put yourself in such danger?' She looked up at the camera once again. 'You must have known what sort of people we're dealing with. They're killers, pure and simple, and as soon as they've got everything they can from us, they'll throw us away like any other piece of worn-out equipment. More than anything, I hate them for that. If they'd asked me to come and sworn me to secrecy, I probably would have done it anyway. It's a once-in-a-lifetime opportunity. But they didn't have the sense to see that. All they see is a job that needs doing and the person who can do it, so they force the two together any which way until the job's done. And they're going to do the same with you, because you were fool enough to let them.'

Leo desperately wanted to tell his mother the truth, even give her the smallest of hints, so that she wouldn't be so disappointed in him. It was the same whenever he got into trouble at school. What bothered him wasn't that she was cross, because she never really was, but that she was disappointed. She had expected more and he had let her down. 'I'm sorry,' he said, convincing himself that he really was. 'I just wanted to help. I just wanted to be with you.'

Lillian squeezed his hand. 'Well, you're here now, and even though I wish you weren't, I'm glad you are.'

'That makes no sense, Mum.'

'It makes perfect sense. And if you'd spent less time gallivanting around the Solar System over the past few weeks and more time studying some logic, you'd see that it does.'

Leo smiled. She was already beginning to sound like the mother he remembered. Perhaps the inner fire was still burning after all.

PART FOUR

MARS ALONE

34
PRESIDENT WHITTAKER

'**LADIES AND GENTLEMEN.** Welcome to a whole new Mars.' A huge cheer went up from the five thousand or so people squeezed into the auditorium, and Carlton Whittaker, newly elected president of the Martian Territories, let the cheering and clapping go on for as long as it wanted to. He gazed around at his audience, smiling and waving at those he recognised in the first few rows, but also making a point of sharing the smile with the clusters of news cameras hovering around the dome, which would be transmitting his speech across the whole of the planet – and well beyond.

'Mars,' he continued, once the noise had died down to a manageable level. 'Two hundred years ago, she was just a baby, home to a handful of hardy astronauts and scientists stuck in the underground caves of Alba Station. One hundred years ago, she was still a child, but a child who was growing quickly. She was strong and confident. Already there were settlements, towns, even a fledgling city. And there were mines. Huge mines that worked day and night to provide Earth with precious ores and minerals. And we were happy to do it. We owed our very survival to Earth, with her water, and her settlers, and her technology, and it was only right that we repaid her generosity.

'But let's move on another hundred years, to here and now. Now Mars is no longer a child. Now she's all grown up, with her own cities and her own population, her own industries and her own government. And those same mines are bigger and more productive than ever. Today this beautiful planet has become the workhorse of the Solar System, providing those ores and minerals not just for Earth, but for every single one of the colonies and settlements and outposts and bases the human race has built.'

Another loud cheer filled the hall, and the whistles and applause went on and on. Whittaker looked out with pride at the sea of blue and orange from the thousands of tiny waved flags. His colours. And soon they would be more than simply the colours of his presidential campaign. A new Mars – a Mars that could stand apart from Earth, could stand alone against the grasping hands of all those Terran governments – would need a new flag. Something to symbolise its status as an independent planet. Something all Martians could rally behind, take pride in, look up to. Blue and orange – his blue and orange – would do nicely.

'And yet!' Whittaker shouted, holding up his hand to silence the crowd. 'And yet the governments of Earth still insist on treating us like the child we were a hundred years ago. Yes, we have our own government. But for what? So we can better organise our shipments of cargo back *home*? So we can administer our industries more efficiently, allowing us to produce more and more for that ever-hungry planet? So we can force our people to work for them and keep them in line when they grow unhappy? No! Not any more.

We've been doing that for a hundred years and the time has come to get something in return. And what is it we want? Nothing much. Just a chance to be listened to.

'Mars has a voice, and for too long Earth has ignored it. For too long we've asked...no, begged, for the power to control our own planet, for the right to have an equal say in the running of this system we are so generously supplying, for the right to be treated as more than another colony. But each time we ask, Earth ignores us. Well, Earth is not going to ignore us any longer. Mars has a voice, a powerful voice, and the time has come for us to use it. So I say to you now, to all of you, and in a voice loud enough to reach the farthest regions of the Solar System...' Whittaker paused, raised his fist defiantly and stared up at the roof of the dome, as though looking directly at Earth itself. And then in an angry roar that was carefully and deliberately magnified by the technicians operating the sound system, he bellowed, 'The time has come for you to listen to Mars. Because from this day forward...Mars stands alone.' The audience leapt to their feet, shouting and cheering and waving their flags. 'Mars alone!' Whittaker repeated, 'Mars alone!' and the chant was taken up by the audience. Whittaker stepped out from behind his lectern, walked to the front of the stage and raised both arms in a show of defiance and victory. The chanting grew louder.

'For god's sake, turn that damned thing off,' Whittaker said, in a subdued and slightly hoarse voice as he entered the room. Mr Archer, who had been watching the speech on the wall screen, instantly stood up and switched it off.

The Old Man looked exhausted. Hardly surprising, Mr Archer thought, considering the punishment he'd put his body through over the past few days: little or no proper sleep, food only when it was forced on him and a cocktail of drugs to keep him awake and alert for the succession of rallies, speeches and meetings he'd had to endure to win the election. It had been close, much closer than either of them had expected, and the strain was visible in the lined features of his face. He needed rest, proper food and a good long sleep, but Mr Archer could see that now was not the time to suggest it. The eyes still burned with their fierce energy and the mind behind them was nowhere near ready for sleep.

Whittaker sat on one of the large, luxurious seats and allowed his body to sink into the soft leather. Mr Archer brought him a glass of Scotch and waited to hear what the Old Man had to say. Whittaker gulped down the whole thing and let out a long, satisfied sigh. 'It was a terrible speech,' he said at last. 'Nothing but crap and cliché. The sooner we can stop all this crowd-pleasing rubbish the better.'

'They seemed to like it well enough.'

'I don't give a damn if they liked it. They're nothing but cattle, and soon enough I'll make sure they know it. I want to know what the Terrans thought of it.' Mr Archer picked up a slate and offered it to Whittaker, but he waved it away. 'Not now. Just give me a run-down.'

'It's as expected. The Lat-Ams and the African Confed were quick to come out in support, but only because they hope to benefit from any new trade concessions. The North Atlantics are generally "disappointed" but say it's probably just empty talk. The Chinese are out-and-out hostile, already threatening sanctions. Luna has nothing to say for itself as usual and it's still too early to expect anything from the Outer Colonies.'

'So, the North Atlantics are disappointed, are they? They'll be more than disappointed by the time I've finished. They'll be on their knees, begging for any scraps I care to throw them and offering me anything I want in return. As for the Chinese...' He held out his glass for another drink. 'Are we ready for war?'

'Defensively?' Mr Archer replied. 'Certainly. We have been for some time. Even without our new weapons we could see off anything the Chinese send against us. With them, I'd say even the United Fleet would struggle.'

'And offensively?'

Mr Archer shook his head. 'Two years before we have effective strike capability. At least five for a full invasion, and that's assuming significant local support.'

'Hmm.' Whittaker sat back and closed his eyes, but to think, not sleep. 'Then we advance our schedule. Have the news channels play up this Chinese aggression. Lie if necessary, although knowing the Chinese, you won't have to. I want it to sound like they really might consider a pre-emptive attack – and soon. Then set up a meeting with the chiefs of staff. I'll use the threat as justification for a temporary suspension of the Council and we can move to an emergency military government. We can worry about something more permanent once everything is up and running. You have my list of who stays and who goes. Implement it.'

'Yes, sir.'

'Now. Tell me about our other little project.'

'The boy appears genuine,' Mr Archer said. 'He's working alongside the professor and her attitude has improved.'

'See,' Whittaker said with a triumphant grin. 'What did I tell you?'

'I still don't trust him.'

'Of course not. You don't trust anyone, and that's why I need you. I'm getting too soft in my old age. Too forgiving. I need you to be suspicious for me.'

'But you over-ruled me with the boy.'

'Because I need him.' Mr Archer said nothing. 'You disagree,' Whittaker continued. 'I can tell. But you would never say so to my face.'

'No.'

'Why not?'

'Because you always have your reasons, and I don't always know what they are.'

'Very true,' said Whittaker. 'But what is it about our little Leo Fischer that bothers you? That he chose to come over to us voluntarily, or that he managed to kill one of your men?'

'The man was nothing.'

'The boy's a genius, you know?'

'So I've read.'

'And I need people like that, just as much as I need people like you. You may have got your nice new weapons, but there are plenty more secrets locked away inside our mystery ship, and I intend to unlock every last one. If the two of them are working hard and getting results, let them work. But by all means keep the boy on a tight leash. Teenagers can be so headstrong and foolhardy, and it would be a shame to have to lose him because of his own stupidity. I won't have the ship or the facility compromised, but beyond that I don't mind him being given a certain degree of freedom. Use your judgement, of course, but for now I would like you to give him the benefit of the doubt. Who knows, perhaps in time you might even come to trust him a little.'

'Perhaps.'

Whittaker yawned. 'My body betrays me. I need to do something about it.'

'A few hours sleep?'

'I was thinking of something of a more medicinal nature.

There'll be plenty of time for sleeping when I'm old.'

'I'll have something sent up.'

'With coffee,' Whittaker added as he slowly pulled himself to his feet and made for the door to his inner office. 'And a nice pastry, perhaps.'

'Yes, sir,' Mr Archer said. And after a slight pause, he added, 'Mr President.'

35
MORGAN

AS THE MONORAIL TRACK continued for a further forty kilometres before terminating at a small scientific research station at the foot of the Jesper Hills, the town of Gilgamesh was not, technically speaking, the end of the line. But it might as well have been. Once it had been a prosperous centre for the region's vast mining operations, but as supplies of precious ores had run down, so had the town. People packed up and left for the bigger towns and cities. Buildings were closed up or simply abandoned, and the desert crept back into the outer districts, covering them in a thick layer of dark dust that went ignored by the ever-decreasing number who chose to remain. Now, the official population stood at 8,324.

'Don't pay no attention to that,' said the woman behind the information desk, motioning towards the welcome screen that Skater was reading. 'That old thing hasn't been updated in months. At the rate folks is moving out, I'd say there's no more than half that number left.'

Skater walked over to the booth to say hello.

'You here on your own, missy?' the woman asked.

'No,' Skater said, pointing across to the small food stall where Pete was buying breakfast. 'With my dad.'

'Business or pleasure?'

'We're visiting an old friend of his. So, pleasure, I guess.'

'Figures. No one comes here for business no more. Well, welcome to Gilgamesh. Enjoy your stay.'

'Thanks.'

Skater wandered over and sat on one of the many spare seats, rubbing the cold out of her sore shoulder. She no longer needed to keep the arm in a sling, but it still bothered her, especially after yet another uncomfortable night on the mono.

It had been an eventful week, starting with three days at the solar farm. Mikhail, the chief engineer, had refused to let them go anywhere until they were rested and recovered, and they'd been in no position to argue. Pete had the gash on his forehead clipped and sprayed, and Skater had her shoulder properly bound up before they were both found comfortable beds. Skater had slept for twenty-four hours straight, staggering out on the second day to be presented with a huge breakfast of pancakes and syrup, while Pete was plied with good, strong, real Russian coffee and a string of questions from Mikhail and the three other workers who made up the farm's workforce.

Pete hadn't wanted to lie to someone who had just saved his life, but there was no way he could tell Mikhail and the others the whole story: the kidnapping of Leo's mother; the so-called pirate attack during the journey from Luna; Whittaker's conspiracy. It was way too dangerous to be sharing any of that with strangers. And as for the alien ship? He was still having trouble believing that one himself. Instead he told them about a contract killing they had accidentally witnessed and a crime boss who wanted them 'taken care of'. To Pete this story seemed almost as far-fetched as the truth, but Mikhail accepted it, keeping any doubts to himself. Skater had said nothing.

Later, Pete spent some time locating, and then calling, the old friend who could hopefully provide them with somewhere to hide until they could work out how to get off-planet and back to Earth.

'Who is this mysterious old friend?' Skater asked. 'Anyone I know?'

'Just someone I used to work with a while back,' was the only reply she got.

Late afternoon on the third day, Mikhail called them up to the control room to show them a view of the desert on one of the monitor screens. A small shuttle was circling in the yellow sky. 'Someone has found crash site, I think.'

'And you think they'll come looking for us here?'

'Is only place for many, many kilometres. They will come for sure. But not today. Is too late now.'

'Then we need to leave as soon as it's dark.'

'I think so.'

'And tomorrow, when they come, what will you tell them?'

Mikhail had made a show of looking shocked. 'Will tell them truth, of course.'

'And which truth will that be?' Skater asked.

'We see nothing,' Mikhail said with a shrug. 'Here is always same. Nothing ever happening. No one ever visiting.'

That night they had left. A tall, bearded and taciturn Finn named Jussi had driven them to the nearest settlement in the farm's old solar-powered buggy. It was a long, uncomfortable ride with the three of them squashed into the driver's compartment, but all

Skater could think of was how much more pleasant it was than her last journey through the Martian desert and how grateful she was to whichever of them had cleaned up her E-suit. At one point she had tried to doze, but without success.

It was still dark when they arrived at Ariel, a tiny settlement of small buildings that clung desperately to the side of the monorail track. Jussi explained that the train only stopped on request but that Mikhail had called through to arrange for the morning supply train to pick them up. He left them in the small station building with a large pack of food and provisions, and was gone well before the train arrived.

Three long days, three uncomfortable nights and several easily forgotten settlements later and here they were: Gilgamesh. The end of the line. Almost.

'Hungry?' Pete asked, taking the seat beside her and holding out a thin sandwich with a dubious filling.

'That depends,' she said cautiously. 'What is it?'

'Paste, of course. Meat-flavoured paste. There may be some cheese as well.' Skater unwrapped the sandwich, bit, shrugged and finished it in three mouthfuls. 'And some water,' Pete added, holding out a small bottle. 'But don't drink it all, that's for both of us. And that was the last of the credit Mikhail gave us as well, so we'd better hope Morgan's in when we call, otherwise we could be in for a long, thirsty wait.'

'Morgan? He's your old friend, right? How come you've never talked about him? I remember loads of people you used to work with but I can't remember you ever mentioning a Morgan. Was he a Sentinel?'

Pete let out a small laugh.

'What?' Skater asked. 'What's so funny?'

'No,' Pete said. 'I think it's safe to say that Morgan Fourie was never a Sentinel.'

'Then what? Is he MarsMine?'

'Come on,' Pete said, getting up and shouldering the pack. 'The sooner we get there the sooner you'll have your questions answered. And the sooner we can get something decent to eat.'

They took the Metro heading east from the centre of town, but as they approached the fifth stop there was an announcement to say that it would be the last, the stations beyond being no longer in service. 'Great,' muttered Skater as they suited up and left the station. 'More walking.'

This part of town was still occupied – at least for the most part. Here and there Skater saw the occasional building boarded up and without power, but plenty weren't and even at this time of the morning there were a few people up and about. But as they walked further from the centre there were fewer people, fewer functioning buildings and more and more signs of abandonment. 'Are you sure this is the right way?' she asked after Pete had stopped to check directions for the third time. 'It's starting to look kind of ghost-townish, don't you think?'

By way of reply, Pete simply nodded and carried on, turning one corner after another until he came to a long, low building that looked every bit as abandoned as many of the others they had passed. From what Skater could tell it had been some sort of showroom, but the once-elegant entrance hall was closed up and dark, and dust dunes had piled up against the steel and glass all along the front. A sign above the main doors had broken in two, leaving only the word *Motors* hanging down at an angle. The other part was lying face-down in the dust.

'This the place?' Skater asked. 'I like it. Friendly and inviting.'

'Let's try round back,' Pete suggested.

At the rear was another entrance, clearly still in use. Two large automatic doors were set into an otherwise featureless wall and there were fresh vehicle tracks leading up to them. To one side was a smaller, equally uninviting doorway that had had the dust swept away around it. The whole area, Skater noticed, was monitored by security cameras.

Pete pressed the call button on the small door's access panel and after a few seconds the door slid open to allow them into the airlock. Once they had their helmets off, Skater noticed that Pete was looking nervous.

'What is it you're not telling me about this guy, Dad?'

The inner door opened before Pete could reply and Skater found herself looking up into the face of a very tall woman. She was dressed in dirty work overalls and her dark hair was carelessly tied back from her face in a ponytail, much like Skater's own. She had the thin, angular features of a Martian-born but without any of their typical sallowness of complexion, and though it was hard to tell, Skater guessed she was probably in her late thirties or early forties. There was a large dark grease smear across one side of her face. 'Well, well,' she said. 'Pete Monroe. Long time.'

'Long time indeed,' Pete replied. 'How you doing, Morgan?'

'What?' Skater said, staring at the woman in disbelief. '*This* is Morgan Fourie? I was expecting some old guy you used to fly shuttle with, not...well, not this.'

Morgan smiled. 'I guess your dad never mentioned me then, huh? Well, he certainly told me all about you.' She wiped her hand across one of the cleaner parts of her overalls and held it out. 'Nice to meet you, Lisa Kate.'

'You too.'

'So,' Morgan said, turning to Pete. 'Do we shake hands as well, or what?'

Pete stepped forward and gave her a quick peck on the cheek —

the one without the grease on it. 'Hi, Morgan.'

Morgan smiled. 'You call that a greeting?'

Pete reached round and put his hand on the back of Morgan's neck, pulling her gently towards him and giving her a proper, much longer, kiss. Skater felt a pang as she remembered the kiss Leo had given her, that night on the monorail, and for a moment she pictured his sweet face, wondering if she would ever see it again for real. But there was a time and a place for these things, and as far as she was concerned, this was neither. 'Guys!' she pleaded. 'Other people present.'

Pete broke away from Morgan, looking embarrassed. 'I guess I've got some explaining to do, haven't I?'

'And not just to her,' Morgan said. 'I'd like to know why I hear nothing from you for four years then suddenly here you are, your daughter in tow, and some story about how you're on the run and your lives are in danger.'

'It's a long story,' said Skater. 'Please can we tell it over breakfast?'

Morgan let out a laugh. 'Her father's daughter,' she said, leading Skater inside. 'Come on. Let's see what we can find.'

'So there she was, trying to sell me this buggy, with no idea it was me she'd stolen it from two days earlier.'

Morgan smiled. 'Yeah, that was pretty dumb of me all right. I should have known there was a good reason you were looking to buy a buggy in such a hurry.'

'So what happened?' Skater asked. She was having the time of her life, discovering a whole new side to her father. 'Did you call the police?'

'Of course not,' said Pete. 'She was much too good-looking for that. No. I haggled for a while, got a good price on the buggy, and asked her out for a drink. It was only later, once we were better acquainted, that I told her it had been my buggy in the first place.'

'And you never asked for your money back?'

'Honestly, after Morgan had had it for those first two days, the engine always ran smoother and quieter.'

'Just like its owner,' Morgan added. Pete smiled.

'So come on,' Skater said. 'You two were together for, like, years. You're obviously still good friends now. How come you haven't seen each other for four years?' Morgan's smile fell and Pete looked away awkwardly. Skater realised she'd said the wrong thing. 'Oops.'

'I was in prison,' Morgan said after a while. 'For two years.'

'For stealing buggies?'

'Pretty much. Only when you do it off-planet they call it piracy.'

'Oh.'

'You were never a pirate,' said Pete, defensively. 'You were a smuggler. Who sometimes stole things.'

'Yes. I believe they call that piracy.'

'And you never went to visit her?' Skater asked.

'Of course I did. Well, I tried.'

'I refused to see him.'

'Why?'

'Embarrassment. Shame. Pete was part of a different life. A life I couldn't share, and it hurt to be reminded of it. Anyway, I figured he'd forget about me soon enough – get on with his own life. He was on Luna so much of the time, and you were already booked to come out on one of your first visits. What was the point of trying to keep in touch when I was in prison and he was the other side of the Solar System?'

Skater looked at Pete. 'But you never even mentioned her.'

'I was worried your mother would find out. She wouldn't have let you come and stay with me if she'd known.' He looked at Morgan. 'When I found out you'd been released I thought about coming to see you, but as far as I was concerned, the ball was in your court. I was waiting for you to call and you never did, so I assumed that was that.'

'When I got out, I needed some time on my own. I guess in some ways I still do.'

'You have this place all to yourself?' Skater asked.

'Why not? You probably noticed there's no shortage of space around here these days. I can't afford to keep the main showroom area aired up so I just use it for storage, but this part's plenty big enough for me anyway.'

'You still in business?' Pete asked.

Morgan paused before answering. 'Not like in the old days, no. Mostly I'm legit now.'

'Mostly?'

'Just some customs-running now and then. Electronics mostly. It helps to pay the bills.'

'And what about helping a couple of fugitives get off-planet?'

'Does that pay the bills?'

Pete shook his head. 'I can't use my cards – they'll be tracking them – and we have nothing except what you see. Everything we had with us is still stuck in Minerva and we had to rely on Russian hospitality to get this far. But you know I'll give you anything I can, as soon as I can.'

'I know,' Morgan said, kindly. 'And I have every intention of letting you. It'll take some time to sort out though, even for an old pirate like me, so it looks like you're going to have to call this place home for a while. And home doesn't come for free.'

'Just say what you want us to do and it'll be done.'

Morgan smiled. 'I like the sound of that. Well, why not start by sorting out one of the spare rooms.' She turned to Skater. 'There's a shower of sorts, if you want to freshen up, and you're welcome to anything you can find in the wardrobe, though it's all going to be way too big. We can head out and pick up something more suitable later, but I've got some bits and pieces to finish off first. I was halfway through an engine when you called.' She left them with the empty breakfast plates and went back to her workshop through a set of swing doors.

'Oh. My. Actual. Fiery. Sunbeams,' Skater said as soon as the doors had closed.

'What?'

'Dad, she is so *beyond* amazingly…amazing. I can't believe you never told me about her. And I can't believe you ever let her go, either.'

'You heard the story. I didn't have much say in the matter.'

'Maybe not. But you do now.'

'And what's that supposed to mean?'

'It means that you're here now, she's beyond pleased to see you and it sure doesn't look like there's anyone else on the scene.'

'What? We don't know that,' Pete said. Skater gave him a pitying look. 'Well we don't,' he said, defensively, but she continued with the look until he gave up and began to collect the dirty dishes. 'Go and have a shower,' he said. 'I'll wash up.'

Skater shook her head. 'There really is no hope for you, is there?'

'And once I'm done in the kitchen,' Pete added as Skater reached the door, 'maybe I'll wander through and see what Morgan's up to.'

Skater smiled to herself. And in the next room, with her face pressed against the crack in the swing doors and her curiosity satisfied, Morgan smiled too.

36

SETTING THE WHEELS
IN MOTION

TRUE TO HIS PROMISE to Agent Aitchison, Leo did nothing out of the ordinary for the first week of his new captivity. The first two days were easy. They were all about catching up, going over the details of his mother's kidnapping and learning what her life had been like during those past three long and miserable months, and recounting his own adventures once more. Each time his mother would ask him more penetrating questions and seem less convinced by his answers, and Leo suspected she knew he was keeping something from her. But she never asked directly, and he never volunteered, and so the part of his story that included Aitchison remained unspoken.

He got to know Sam and Samira, the research assistants who had also been taken from the base on Luna. They were in their early twenties and although physically they were in better condition than his mother, their ordeal had clearly taken a great deal out of them.

They were pleasant enough, and helped to make Leo feel welcome, but as the days passed Leo noticed they spent nearly all of their time off somewhere together and rarely talked to his mother about anything except work.

'It's been hard for them,' Lillian explained to Leo when he asked her about it. 'Especially Samira. She had a breakdown not long after we arrived and spent a week barely able to get out of bed. She's a lot better now though. Sam nursed her through it and a while ago the two of them finally...got together, if you know what I mean. Since then she's seemed much stronger and happier.'

'So that's why they're always off together?'

'Partly. But also they feel uncomfortable around me. Perhaps it's because, technically, I'm still their boss, but I also think they blame me for what happened.'

'You? But how is this your fault? It's not as if you asked to be kidnapped, is it?' Unlike me, Leo thought, awkwardly.

'No, but it's because of me they're here. Perhaps they think I should have done more to try to get them released, that I should have traded my services for their freedom. I don't know. It's obviously not something they would ever say to me, so I get on with my work and let them get on with theirs however they want. And now they have each other. That's something. But they know there's only one way this can end and I don't think either of them is ready for that. They're so young.' She looked at Leo and shook her head slowly. 'So young.'

That was when Leo had come closest to giving away his secret. It was so close to the surface, so desperate to spill out and give him away. He closed his eyes, took a deep breath and said nothing. Not then. Instead, he changed the subject, asking her about the ship, what she had learnt and how her work was going, and gave all his concentration to what she said in reply. Before long, the secret was safely buried away once more.

The ship was a marvel. Leo spent long hours amid the mysterious alien machinery, running his hands along the flawless outer shell and imagining what its creators might look like. Did they know their ship had been discovered by another species? Would they send another? Would there be more contact in the future?

It was clear this ship was nothing more than a scout. Despite its size, there were no internal compartments suitable for lifeforms of any sort. Any space that had not been taken up with engines and fuel cells had been filled with equipment, mostly computers and sensors. And weapons. Leo wasn't sure why a deep-space explorer would even need weapons, and possibly they were nothing more than an automated defence system against cosmic debris, but for Dr Randhawa and his technicians they had been the most important aspect of the entire ship. And whether the system had originally been designed as an offensive weapon or not, that was what it had now been turned into.

Breaking down the alien weapons and reusing the technology was one thing, but understanding their computers and accessing the data stored on them was another matter entirely. After much careful experimenting, Lillian and her assistants had succeeded in powering up the alien computers and even linking them to the facility's network, but this had simply provided them with endless screens of unintelligible language that they were only now beginning to decipher.

'We started with the obvious,' she explained to Leo as they sat on the sofa surrounded by print-outs and handwritten notes. 'Mathematical constants, geometric points of reference, trying to identify which symbols represented numbers rather than letters.'

'I guess it was too much to hope that they used binary?'

'Yes it was, sadly. In fact, one of our major hurdles has been that as far as we can tell, they don't use any base system at all. It would appear they have a separate, unique symbol for every single number – or at least all the ones we think we've identified so far, which is maybe three or four thousand.'

'Really? That's pretty complex.'

'Indeed. So either there's some fundamental concept we've overlooked in their number system...'

'...or it's artificially created.'

'Precisely.'

'Which would imply they have pretty advanced AI.'

'Suggest, not imply.'

'So presumably our computers haven't been able to translate it?'

Lillian looked at the equipment sitting on the nearest table and sneered. 'For a state-of-the-art science facility their computers are rather disappointing. All speed and processing power and no logic. We've had one of their fastest running a translation program non-stop for the past month but I doubt it's going to give us anything worthwhile for the next five years or so.'

'They don't have any AIs?'

'It is an AI. But it's never had to do anything this interesting before. All it seems to be capable of is designing bigger and bigger guns for the boys to play with.'

'I brought Daisy with me,' Leo said. 'I thought she might come in useful.'

'Really? Why didn't you tell me this before?'

'I don't know where she is. They confiscated her when I turned myself in and I haven't seen her since.'

'Well,' said Lillian, standing up. 'Let's see if we can find her, shall we?' She turned to the nearest monitoring camera. 'Hey, Jailer. Go find Archer and tell him we need the computer he took away from my son. Tell him if we get it, it could save us weeks, or perhaps even months of work, and we can start providing him with more of those precious results he's so desperate for.' She sat back down.

'Will that work?' Leo asked.

'I doubt it, but it's worth a try. In the meantime, we shall just have to make do with what we have.'

'What do you want me to do?'

Lillian pointed over to the table. 'Do what you do best. Go talk to a computer.'

Which is exactly what Leo did for the next five days. After all the excitement and adventure, it felt good to be sitting quietly in front of a screen. It was what he enjoyed, and in some strange way it made him feel safe, as if he was back at his own desk, in his own room, at home in Cambridge – especially as he only had to look up to see his mother, nestled among her papers on the sofa or sitting at a workbench dismantling some delicate piece of equipment and lost in her own world, just like she used to be back home.

She had never been a controlling parent and this was still true. She left him to work away, only interrupting him when she had something interesting or significant to share. She didn't force him to stop for breaks or meals, or to go to bed – possibly because she rarely remembered to do these things herself – but occasionally she would wander over and run a hand through his hair, or stroke his neck, while she leant forward to read whatever was on his screen.

Mr Archer visited them twice during the week. The first time was simply to tell them he was refusing their request for Daisy. If there was anything specific they needed, they could have occasional supervised access, but they could not use it day-to-day, no matter how much time they thought it could save. Lillian shouted at Mr Archer, accusing him of being an idiot and an incompetent, but to no avail. She was ignored, as usual, and Daisy remained locked away.

The second visit was much longer and this time Mr Archer was accompanied by two of Dr Randhawa's assistants. They looked over Leo's work, asked him some fairly technical and relatively sensible questions, and made detailed notes. After about an hour they left.

'Congratulations,' Lillian told him. 'It appears you've passed the exam.'

'They were testing me?'

'To see if you really are as clever as we say. They obviously find it hard to accept that a fifteen-year-old might know more than they do.'

'I haven't done that much yet.'

'Don't worry. You said a lot of things they didn't understand, and once they've gone away and found out what they mean, they'll stop pestering you.'

'Good.'

Leo went back to work and, as predicted, the remainder of the week passed with no more interruptions. He kept busy and kept to himself, working at his own desk and hardly saying a word, even to his mother. But not all his time was taken up with the work he had so patiently explained to the two scientists. A large amount was taken up with his own project – his and Aitchison's – and by lunchtime on the seventh day, it was ready to be put into action. Gathering the information had been easy. He had access to so much of what he needed anyway, and what he didn't have access to had been easy enough to steal from the facility's hopelessly under-protected main network. He had compressed it into a tiny software 'bullet' hidden deep within his work files, and now all he needed was to load it into the 'gun' that would fire it off to Aitchison – hopefully without anyone noticing.

He stood up and wandered over to the graveyard. This was the workbench where they kept the computers that had been opened up and pulled apart. It was littered with processors, circuit boards, wires and cables, abandoned monitor screens and casings, and a vast array of useful tools, ranging from the smallest of micro-drivers through to one very large and very unscientific mallet. Leo collected the things he needed.

'What's going on there?' his mother asked as he rooted through the spare parts.

'I just need to play for a while,' Leo replied with a smile.

'They get angry if you try to dismantle the wrong computers.'

'Don't worry,' Leo promised. 'I'll be good.'

When he sat back down, he made sure to move his chair slightly so that his back was towards the nearest camera, and he carefully placed an old monitor to hide his hands from another. He set to work on one of the cables he'd brought over, snipping off the connector at one end and stripping back the plastic covering until he had exposed the wires inside. Then, casually, he reached into his pocket, to his wallet, and took out the photograph he had put there for safe-keeping. It was an old-fashioned static photo of his mother, a close-up of her sitting at her desk but looking up and smiling. On the back was a hastily written note that read: *Missing you. Love, Mum.* The paper was worn along the edges, as if it had been carried around in a wallet for a long time and often brought out to be studied, but in fact Leo had never set eyes on it until a week ago, when it had been given to him by Aitchison, along with the instructions on how to use it.

Leo played with one corner of the photograph until he was able to peel off the back layer. Between the two layers of semi-rigid paper was a web of micro-circuitry. He taped the bare wires from his cable to the two clearly marked connection points, plugged the other end into his computer, and began the download of information.

It would take fifteen minutes. The download would be completed within a minute or so, but Aitchison had explained that he would need to charge up the tiny power cell by leaving it connected to a computer for at least that long. After that he would have no more than an hour to send the message, otherwise the charge would have run down and he would need to do the whole thing over again.

Leo had never realised how long fifteen minutes could take. Hours, it seemed. He tried to distract himself by looking through his notes but every sentence seemed to read: *How long now? How long now?* At one point the door behind him clunked open and his heart, already pounding furiously, felt as if it was going to burst out of his chest. As casually as he could, he glanced round, expecting to see the hulking form of Mr Archer storming towards him with his throat-crushing hands reaching out, but it was only Sam and Samira returning from their lunch break. They nodded a greeting as they passed but showed no interest in what he was working on. Relief flooding through him, Leo turned back to his computer, wiping his sweating palms down his trousers and wondering how many minutes had passed since he had last checked.

Finally it was done. Leo put the photo back together and tucked it loose into his pocket. Now came the hard part. Sending the signal would be simple, but to do so he would have to be above ground, and that was the problem he'd been wrestling with all week. The workshop, their living quarters and the other areas they were allowed access to were deep underground and well shielded. There was no chance of transmitting the message from down there. But what reason could he give for needing to be above ground? He was on Mars. It wasn't as if he could say he just needed some fresh air.

But Mr Archer's refusal to return Daisy had given him the opportunity he'd been looking for and now he strode over to the door with as much confidence as he could muster. 'I need to speak to Mr Archer,' he told the guard.

'He's not here,' the guard replied. 'He went back to Minerva.' Perfect, Leo thought.

'He said I was to be given access to my own AI if I needed it, so long as I was supervised. Well, I need it now.' The two guards looked at each other uncertainly. Leo smiled, innocently.

'Okay,' the first guard said at last. 'Come with me.' He led Leo through the main workshop to the lift at the far end, but they only rose one floor before he motioned for Leo to get out. This was a disaster. He had assumed Mr Archer was keeping Daisy in his own office, or some laboratory higher up in the building, not on the floor above him. That was still too far below ground to guarantee success.

The guard led him along an open corridor overlooking the main workshop from about twenty metres up. From this height, Leo could see the alien ship in all its glory and he wondered if they would ever try to rebuild it. Probably not, he guessed. These people were breakers, not makers. They weren't interested in the ship, only what they could get out of it. Anything that could make them more powerful.

The guard stopped at an office on the opposite side of the corridor, knocked, and motioned for Leo to follow him when a voice shouted for them to enter. It was one of the two scientists who had interviewed Leo earlier in the week. He was in the middle of a video call and clearly resented the interruption. 'What is it?' he barked.

'Sorry to bother you, sir,' the guard mumbled, 'but the lad says he needs access to his own computer. Mr Archer said he was to be allowed so long as he was supervised.'

'So, supervise him.'

'With respect, sir. I'm not qualified to do that. I wouldn't know what it was he was doing.'

'Well you'll just have to try and figure it out. I'm too busy right now.'

'I could come back later?' the guard offered.

The technician let out a scream of frustration. 'Out! Just watch what he does and if you don't like the look of it, shoot him.'

The guard closed the door. 'Git!'

'I agree,' Leo said, smiling. 'Listen. I won't be long and it's nothing complicated. I promise. Please.'

The guard shrugged. 'Come on then.' This time they went up above ground and after they left the lift the guard led them along a deserted corridor. As they passed a small window Leo stopped.

'What is it now?' the guard asked.

'Mars,' Leo replied. 'Sky and sunlight. I've been stuck downstairs for a whole week without seeing any of it.' Almost casually, he slipped his hand into his pocket and drew out the photo, making sure to keep it out of sight of the guard. 'Look. You can even see a huge great dust devil. Over there.'

The guard stepped up to the window and peered out. Leo felt for the tiny pressure pad that would transmit his message and pressed down, silently counting off the ten seconds Aitchison had recommended.

'That's nothing,' the guard said, unimpressed. 'I've seen bigger. Sometimes you get a whole group coming at the same time. That one'll be gone within the hour. Come on.'

'Actually,' Leo said, reaching ten and shoving the photo quickly back into his pocket, 'I've changed my mind. It's probably not a good idea to be doing this without proper supervision. We could both get into a lot of trouble and it's not that important anyway. Let's come back later.'

The guard looked at Leo and then slowly shook his head.

'Honestly. You lot are all the same. Can't ever make up your mind about anything. Well I'm not doing this again. Next time you want to go wasting everyone's time, wait till someone else is on duty first.'

'Sorry,' Leo said, trying not to grin as they headed back to the lift.

Finally, it was done. Help was on its way.

37
SKATER BECOMES A PIRATE

SKATER AND MORGAN SAT watching the news on a small monitor that had been set down in the middle of their breakfast plates. Pete was in the kitchen, making a second pot of excellent coffee – a farewell present from Mikhail – while Skater kept him updated.

'Some demonstrations,' she shouted through. 'But only small and peaceful. No more riots.'

'Well that's no surprise,' Morgan muttered through a mouthful of toast. 'Not after they sent in the army to shoot all the rioters the other day.'

'And there are still curfews in Peishan and Ptolemy,' Skater continued. 'But not in Minerva. What? You're kidding!'

Pete poked his head around the doorway. 'What?'

'Now they're actually having demonstrations *in support* of Whittaker.'

'Of course they are. Most people around here agree with him.'

He disappeared back into the kitchen.

'But he's a crazy, power-hungry madman. And insane.'

'Maybe,' said Morgan, mimicking the voice from the constant television adverts. 'But he's Martian, heart and soul.'

'And they don't mind that he's about to drag them into a war against the rest of the human race?'

'Obviously not.'

Pete came in, refilled the cups and pulled his seat towards Morgan's so he could get a better view of the screen. Quite casually, he put his arm around her and she nestled in against him. Skater smiled to herself but said nothing.

They continued to watch the news. Scores of Terran diplomats had been expelled from Mars, and Mars had recalled most of its own from Earth. All Earth-registered ships on or around Mars had been ordered to return home immediately or be impounded, and flight restrictions had been imposed for all non-military travel to or from the planet.

'Well,' said Morgan. 'So much for getting you back to Earth in a hurry.'

'I can think of worse things than staying on Mars for a while longer,' Pete said and gave Morgan's shoulder a squeeze.

'Even a Mars that's about to go to war?'

'I'm already fighting a war. Not very well, it has to be said, but fighting it anyway.'

'And what about Skater?' After some reluctance, Morgan had dropped the 'Lisa Kate'.

'Looks like it's my war as well. I'm in.'

'That's not what I meant. Don't you have a life back on Earth?'

Skater gave a snort. 'Not so's you'd notice,' she replied, glancing across at Pete. 'And not for much longer anyway. Hopefully.'

Morgan looked from one to the other but didn't probe further.

'So what?' she asked. 'Are you just going to stay here repairing buggies and fliers until demand runs out?'

'Are you?' Pete asked.

'Maybe.' She smiled. 'Then again, maybe not.'

'Go on.'

'Interesting times are coming. Possibilities. Opportunities. You can make a lot of credit during interesting times if you know how to find things – and the people who are looking for them.'

'Profiteering? Isn't that a little...un-noble?'

'Only if you want it to be. But I'd say it depends on where, and how, you acquire your goods and who you're prepared to trade them to.'

'Oh, I see. So it's a steal from the rich and give to the poor sort of thing?'

'Up to a point.'

'Steal from the crazy dictator and give to the desperate resistance?' Skater offered.

'Resistance?' Morgan laughed. 'What resistance? Any resistance was wiped out the day before yesterday when our dear president sent in the army to stop the looting and they shot eighteen people. Now everyone's too frightened to do anything except march in support of him.'

'So who are these people you're looking to trade with if they're not resistance?'

'Just people like us. Traders, farmers, miners. All the people who were promised a new life out here, only to be abandoned as soon as the mines ran dry. Whittaker may only have been president for a few days, but MarsMine has been chewing people up and spitting them out for decades. Especially around these parts. Just look at Gilgamesh. Another five years and it'll be a ghost town, and all because MarsMine decided to pull out the minute the local mines became uneconomic. But there's still plenty of ore in these hills. It's just that now mega-mining is uneconomical. You have to work more slowly, for smaller profits, and that's not what MarsMine is all about, is it? So us poor, forgotten people have to look after ourselves. And each other. Because, sure as hell, no one else is going to. Personally, I would happily put as big a dent as possible in MarsMine's profits in order to give us some extra scraps of comfort in our lives.'

When she had finished there was silence for a few seconds until Skater spoke up. 'Um, excuse me, but that sounds pretty much exactly like stealing from the rich to give to the poor.'

'I suppose it does,' Morgan admitted.

'You see,' Pete added. 'I always said you were too nice to be a pirate.'

'Maybe. But I'm not a charity either.'

'Seems to me,' Pete continued, 'that if you were to get involved in this sort of business, you could probably use a good shuttle pilot.'

'I already have one. Me.'

'I could offer you a better one.'

'Two,' Skater added. 'I can fly.'

Morgan looked questioningly at Pete, who shrugged. 'She's learning. She's pretty good.'

'She's fifteen years old. And you're suggesting turning her into a criminal?'

'Come on, Morgan. What choice do I have? Even if we do make it off-planet, there's no way we're going to find a ship that can get us away from Mars now. They've got the entire planet on lock-down.'

'Says the man who smuggled a boy out from Luna.'

'That was different. And anyway, we're already on Whittaker's personal hit list. Now that he's president that pretty much makes her a criminal already, wouldn't you say?'

'This is true,' said Skater. 'Plus, I'm actually nearly sixteen, so I'm old enough to make up my own mind. Plus, I know exactly what I'm letting myself in for. Plus, I really, really, *really* want to do whatever I can to pay them back for trying to kill me. Twice.'

'Plus,' said Pete, 'we have no other choice so we'll end up doing something like this anyway.'

'Only without me you'll make a complete mess of it.'

'Possibly.'

'And I suppose you do make pretty good coffee.'

'Definitely.'

'Fine. We'll work together.'

'Partners?' Pete held out his hand.

'Partners,' Morgan replied, taking the hand and pulling Pete towards her in order to give him a kiss. 'But only until the coffee runs out.'

'The coffee's already run out. That was the last of it.'

'Damn.'

'Yes!' shouted Skater. 'This is so buzz. I am officially a desperado. So what do we do now?'

'The washing-up,' said Morgan.

'Oh,' Skater said, deflated.

'And after that I'll take you both for a drive.'

Morgan kept her own fleet of buggies and fliers in the abandoned showroom. Some were old and damaged and clearly just for spare parts, but there were several in working order and she chose one of the larger, more rugged land vehicles for their trip. It was fast, too. Morgan kept to a modest speed as she navigated the deserted streets of Gilgamesh, but once free of the town she opened up the throttle and let it race across the hard ground towards the distant hills.

The journey took over an hour and could have been made in less than half the time in one of the fliers, but it was clear Morgan preferred to travel this way and it was also clear she wanted to show off her driving skills, as well as the power of the engine she had obviously customised. In places the ground became more uneven and the buggy was thrown about, spending more time off the ground than on it. Skater loved every minute.

With the hills looming, Morgan slowed and brought the buggy to a stop. 'You want a turn?' she asked Skater.

'Really?' She looked at Pete. 'Can I?'

'Don't ask me,' he replied with a shrug. 'You're nearly sixteen. Apparently that's old enough to make your own decisions. Just don't crash it, okay? It's a long walk back and I've had my fill of trudging through the desert after car crashes, thank you very much.'

Skater swapped places with Morgan, checked the controls, and set off with a lurch. 'Gently,' said Morgan. 'Take it nice and slow to start with.'

'Sorry,' said Skater. 'I have driven a buggy before, but only on Luna. Mum never lets me drive anything back on Earth. She says I'm too young, which is just dumb. Plenty of people my age can drive. And anyway, it seems kind of stupid to be allowed to pilot a shuttle but not to drive a buggy. Doesn't it?'

'They're different skills. But don't worry. You seem to be getting the hang of this. Just be careful. She's got a more powerful engine than most buggies her size.'

'Yeah,' said Skater with a smile. 'I noticed.' She drove on, more smoothly now, and more confidently with every passing minute. 'So,' she asked. 'Where to?'

'Aim for the end of that rock,' Morgan said, pointing. 'You'll see where we're headed when you get there.'

As they approached, Skater saw that the area was surrounded by an old wire fence, though sections had either collapsed or were half-buried by drifting sand. She slowed the buggy and drove past the two large gates, which were wide open and had clearly not been used for a long time. There was a sign on one but Skater couldn't see what it said.

'It's one of the old mines,' Morgan explained. 'There are half a dozen just like it dotted all over these hills. But this mine is mine.'

'Really? The whole thing?'

'Well, let's just say I'm looking after it until someone comes along and tells me to clear out.'

'So you're like a caretaker?'

Morgan smiled. 'Something like that.'

Skater followed an obvious track that led away from the gates and round the side of the rocky outcrop. There were more signs of life now: abandoned machinery; empty buildings and storage sites; a communications tower. They continued for another five minutes until the track swung round to the back of the outcrop and Skater found herself heading towards the main entrance to the mine. It was an enormous cavern, reaching right into the heart of the rock and stretching up for fifty or sixty metres. The rock walls were smooth and clearly machine-made, with stout, regularly spaced metal pillars for extra support. The ground, at least where the desert sand had not encroached, appeared to be reinforced concrete.

'Wow,' said Skater, switching on the buggy's headlights so she could see further into the dark cave. 'This place is huge.'

'Welcome to MarsMine Jesper One: Mixed Mineral Extraction and Processing Facility.'

'Catchy.'

'I call it the Hangar.'

'Good name,' said Pete, peering into the gloom. He could make out one shuttle craft parked nearby with something – possibly another – further away. 'What's that?' he asked.

'That,' replied Morgan, 'is a piece of junk.'

'Yeah, I can see that.'

'It's called *Ruby*. Or at least it was. But I've ripped so much out of it I'm not sure it still deserves to have a name. It was all I could get hold of after they released me.'

'I guess you never got *Hummingbird* back?'

'*Hummingbird*?' Skater asked.

'That was my ship, before I was sent to prison. They impounded it as evidence and that was that. I never saw it again. It's possible they put it to good use somewhere. It was pretty fast in-atmos and easy to handle, but my guess is they've got it locked away in some storage depot, and that's where it'll stay until it falls apart or gets scrapped because they need the space.'

'So what's that sitting over there in the shadows?' Pete asked. '*Hummingbird II*?'

'Come on,' Morgan said with a smile. 'Let me show you around. We'll have a look out here later.'

They suited up and made their way through the labyrinth of rooms and passages that made up the old mine. Morgan powered up the main generator but explained it was just for lighting. Pumping in air would take too long and be too expensive. They could top up their E-suit tanks before leaving.

'Sweet Sol, it just goes on and on,' Skater announced.

'The mine itself is pretty small,' Morgan explained as they walked. 'Most of this area was the processing plant, which is why the entrance is so big. They would've had freight fliers coming in and out to take the minerals to their factories in Minerva, or wherever. And mostly it would have been automated. My guess is there were no more than fifty or sixty people here at any one time.'

'That's still a lot, isn't it?'

'Not compared with some,' Pete said. 'I've been to a couple of surface mines down south that were like small towns, with hundreds or even thousands of people. Like Morgan said, this one was mostly automated, which is why it would have been so easy to shut it down when the ore ran out. All the big diggers, and even most of the processing equipment, would have been mobile, so all they needed to do was switch off the power and drive everything to the next site.'

'Exactly,' said Morgan. 'And from the amount of stuff they left behind, I guess they were in a hurry to be gone. All the big stuff went, but anything that would have taken time to dismantle or dig out they abandoned. Even now the living areas are still pretty much fully stocked. I stay out here whenever I'm working on the ship, but mostly it's a convenient place to fly from. I can get in and out without interfering with the traffic around Gilgamesh – not that there's too much of that these days – and it's conveniently far away from prying eyes. If your new friends come looking for you, this would be a safe place to hide out.'

'True,' said Pete. 'But let's hope we never need it. Now, when are you going to show us that ship?'

They returned to the main hangar, where Morgan switched on the overhead lighting and led them towards the ship.

'Sweet Sol,' Skater said as she looked across at the ship. 'That's a JetX Morningstar.'

Morgan looked impressed and turned to Pete. 'She really is your daughter, isn't she?'

'How the hell did you get your hands on that?' Pete asked.

'Oh,' Morgan said, dismissively. 'A friend of a friend.'

'I see you've made some changes.'

'One or two. I needed extra cargo space, and I've never thought that much of JetX's in-atmos thrusters so I swapped them out for Mostic 7s. Also, I had to lose the wing cannons, of course.'

'Did you keep hold of them?'

'Still thinking of your rebellion, huh?'

'Just wondering.'

They wandered over to where Skater was examining the craft up close.

'This is amazing,' she said. 'An actual Morningstar. That's just so supreme. Is it ready to fly?'

'Absolutely. It's been fully fixed up for about six months, and it runs beautifully. I take it out once or twice a month, whenever I have business off-planet, but I don't tend to stay away too long. I've been out to a couple of the Belt stations, but mostly it's just ship-to-ship stuff nearer in.'

'Can we take it for a flight?'

'What, right now?' Morgan laughed. 'I'm afraid not. But you can have a look inside if you want.' She tapped in the code on the security panel and the rear ramp began to descend. Skater leapt on and was halfway up before it had even touched the floor.

'Does it have a name?' Pete asked.

'Officially? Yes. But it's Chinese and I can't remember it. Or pronounce it, for that matter.'

'So why not re-register?'

'I can't think of a good enough name. And no, before you suggest it, I am not going to call it *Hummingbird II*.'

'No. It's not much of a hummingbird, is it? Pity though. I thought *Hummingbird* was a great name. And a great ship, too. I have some good memories of it.'

'Like that trip out to the Aten Orbital?'

Pete smiled. 'Yeah. Like that.'

'Well, maybe there'll be some good times on this one as well.'

'I hope so,' Pete said, turning to Morgan and taking her hand. 'I'd like that.'

Skater's head appeared at one of the small cockpit windows and her voice cut in over the environment suit comms.

'You guys do know I can hear every word you're saying, right? And I know perfectly well what you're talking about.'

That night, back in Gilgamesh, Skater lay in bed thinking up possible names for Morgan's ship. She came up with plenty, but none of them was right. They were too boring, or too long, or too stupid. Finally, with the ship still unnamed, she drifted off to sleep.

The following morning she woke early, and was not in the least bit surprised to discover she was alone in the room. Her father's bed was empty and had clearly not been slept in.

38
RESCUE

THE RAID BEGAN as soon as Phobos had set and the vast desert around the settlement had been swallowed up by the Martian night. Crouching figures emerged from their camouflaged shelters and raced towards the compound's security fence, no more than two hundred metres ahead. The first two to arrive pressed close against one of the fence's support columns, ignoring the pool of light that exposed them from above, and set to work bypassing the sensor array that monitored that section of the perimeter. After a few seconds the light blinked off, then back on, and one of the men gave the all-clear. Another figure emerged from the darkness and used a hand laser to melt a hole in the reinforced plastic mesh, then the assault team quickly filed through into the outer grounds of the compound. There were twenty of them. They were well-equipped, heavily armed, and knew exactly what they were doing.

Once everyone was inside, they split up into smaller groups, keeping to the shadows and staying away from the larger, central buildings where many of the lights were still burning. The facility appeared to rely mostly on automated security systems – cameras and motion sensors – and the infiltrators moved as if they knew exactly where these were and how to avoid them. The occasional two-man roving patrols were also easily avoided. They were not expecting trouble and paid little attention to anything except their own, in-suit conversations. But when a patrol wandered too close to one of the hidden groups, it was swiftly and efficiently dealt with.

After ten minutes, everything was set. Three teams had pushed further into the compound with a large supply of explosive charges, while the rest of the group took up position around one of the outlying buildings. On a signal from their commander, two men entered the building's airlock, overrode the electronic lock and forced their way inside.

The night watchman glanced up as he heard the hiss of escaping air and was shot twice through the head before he had a chance to see his killers. The commander and the rest of his squad followed, pausing briefly to seal the main doors behind them and to drag the watchman's body out of sight before descending a narrow staircase at the back of the now-deserted room.

Two technicians were working on the floor below, both with their backs to the staircase and unaware of the new arrivals until it was too late. Their throats were slit and their bodies bundled beneath their workstation. When the assault team were satisfied the area was secure, the commander motioned for his men to open their visors. 'Save your air,' he said. 'We may need it later.' He picked out two of his men. 'You two; rear guard. Set charges on the air pumps, then make sure the escape route stays open. Radio silence unless your position is compromised. Clear?'

'Clear.'

'The rest of you; with me.'

Twelve and a half minutes later, Leo woke with a start as someone shook him awake and clamped a thick-gloved hand across his mouth to stop him calling out. A surge of adrenalin flooded his body, banishing sleep, and he tried to pull at the hand. But almost at once his mind caught up with his body and he understood what was happening. He'd been expecting this moment for five days, ever since he'd sent the message to Aitchison, and he'd spent most of that time trying to guess when, and how, the rescue would come. Now he knew. He relaxed his grip, held up his hands in submission, and let his fear turn to relief.

'Leo Fischer?' the man whispered. Leo nodded. 'We're here to get you out. Do you understand?' Leo nodded again. 'Good.' The man took his hand away from Leo's mouth. 'I need you up and dressed as quickly as possible.'

'They took our E-suits,' he said as he leapt out of bed and felt for his clothes in the dark.

'Don't worry. We brought spares.'

Leo scrambled into his under-suit, all the time feeling his heart pounding in his chest. He had no idea what the escape plan was. Aitchison had said nothing about what was to happen after he'd sent the information, only that someone would come as soon as possible and for him to be prepared for anything. 'Done,' he said, slipping on his shoes.

'Good lad. Here, put this on.'

Leo felt the man slip something over his head and onto his eyes and suddenly the dark room was lit up in glowing shades of green.

He held up his hand in front of his face and waved it from side to side. 'Nice.'

'Let's go.'

Leo followed the man along the corridor into his mother's room. She was already up and dressed and was also wearing one of the night-vision visors. Another armed man watched over her while she collected her notes, but when she saw Leo she rushed across to him and took him in her arms. 'Leo. Are you okay? They're here to rescue us. We're going to get out of here.'

'I know.'

She paused and drew away so she could look at him directly, but in the strange green half-light, and with his eyes hidden behind the visors, Leo's face was giving nothing away. 'You knew they were coming, didn't you?' she asked. 'You've known all along?'

'Yeah, I've known all along,' he answered with a broad grin. After two weeks of keeping his secret, Leo felt a huge sense of relief in being able to say the words out loud and show his mother that giving himself up hadn't been the stupid, pointless act she'd thought. She would still be mad at him, telling him it had been too dangerous, that he should have kept himself safe, that he could have been killed. He didn't care. She could say what she liked. He knew he'd done the right thing.

But she didn't say anything. They both knew this wasn't the time or place to be having this conversation, and whatever they had to say could wait until they were somewhere safer. She simply smiled and ruffled his hair.

One of the men came over. 'I'm Captain Mackie. Is everything all right?'

'Yes, fine,' Lillian answered.

'Good. Let's get going then. The others are waiting.'

'Wait,' hissed Leo. 'What about all the stuff in the workshop?'

'More papers?'

'And the hardware.'

'Hardware?'

'Computers. Some of them are...irreplaceable. We have to bring them with us, otherwise this whole rescue mission will be for nothing.'

'Fine,' Mackie said, not even arguing the point. 'Two of my men will go with you. Show them what you need and they can carry it for you. But only absolute essentials, understand? We have to stay mobile. And hurry.'

'But there are cameras in there,' Lillian said. 'And microphones. And there are guards on the outer doors.'

The man shook his head. 'Not now there aren't. Get going.'

Leo headed back into the workshop, fascinated by the glowing green world he was inhabiting. He ignored his own computer, which was just an access terminal anyway. All the information was stored on the main system and there wasn't time for him to start downloading stuff. Instead, he went across to where the alien components had been set up and began disconnecting them. The main unit was huge – far too big and heavy for them to take – but some of the smaller ones would break down into manageable components. As quickly as he could, Leo began to dismantle the system his mother had spent so long setting up. He only hoped he'd remember how it fitted back together, once they were back on Earth and free to carry on their work. Always assuming that was where they ended up. Now that he thought about it, Aitchison hadn't said anything about what was going to happen, either to them or the alien technology, once they were free of Whittaker's clutches. Still, Leo thought, that was something to worry about later, not now.

One of the men produced a large rucksack and began to fill it with the pieces Leo handed to him. Once it was full he slung it effortlessly onto his back and motioned to Leo that it was time to go. Leo grabbed one final piece and followed him back out into the far corridor, just in time to see his mother clinging to a rope and being hauled up through an air vent in the ceiling at the far end.

Suddenly there was a commotion behind him and the door to the workshop swung open. For an instant Leo's green world glowed dazzlingly bright as light flooded in from the giant hangar beyond and it took several seconds for the glow to die down so he could see once more. Two of the assault squad came running over and spoke quietly to their commander.

'We've got company. There's a patrol on its way down. Four men.'

'Are we compromised?'

'Not yet. It's just routine, but they'll notice the missing guards and they're bound to come looking.'

'How long?'

'Two minutes, max.'

'Are the charges set?'

'All set.'

'Good. Then let's deal with the guards and get the hell out of here.'

While the two men took up firing positions, the commander turned to the man with the rucksack. 'You're up next. Warn them we've got trouble then make sure you get the civilians back to the extraction point, asap. Don't stop. Don't wait. We'll cover your back.'

The rope was dropped back down and the man was hauled up as soon as he'd taken hold of it. But at the top there was a delay. The rucksack made him too big to fit through the air vent and he was forced to slide back down, take off the pack and hand it up separately before he could climb through.

Leo felt himself starting to panic. He looked along the corridor, convinced that any second the door would burst open and the security patrol come charging through. He looked back up at the air vent. Where was the rope? What was going on? Why was it taking so long? His palms were sweaty and he wiped them on his jacket. Would he even be able to keep hold of the rope? The computer component he was holding meant he would only have one free hand and he could imagine himself slipping and falling, or dropping the computer with a deafening crash that would alert the patrol.

Finally the rope was dropped down. He wiped his free hand, twisted it round the rope and gripped as tightly as he could. The workshop door swung open. He held his breath. For one, two, three seconds, nothing happened. Then he felt the tug of the rope on his arm and at the same time he heard the soft thud-thud-thud of silenced weapons behind him. There was a crash, shouting, and suddenly he was at the vent and strong arms were pulling him through. 'That way,' a voice said, as he was forced onto his hands and knees and pushed along the low, narrow passageway. 'Follow the others.'

Leo scrambled. There was loud gunfire behind him as the patrol returned fire, then he was round the corner and the only thing he could hear was his own clumsy movements and the pounding in his chest. He caught up with the others. They seemed to be moving so slowly, as if they were on some Sunday afternoon stroll in the park, not trying to escape from a gunfight, and he wished he could give the whole line a shove and tell them to get a move on.

They continued for another few minutes, until they came to a small vent. It took a while for everyone to clamber through into the room beyond, then straightaway they had to climb a long metal ladder bolted to the wall. Leo looked across at his mother while they were waiting and she gave him a weak smile, but they were too nervous and preoccupied to say anything. And besides, thought Leo, what was there to say? Everything's going to be all right? We're safe now? It was way too soon for that.

He began to climb, awkwardly because of the bulky equipment he was carrying. Every two rungs, he had to grip the ladder with his fingertips and reach up with his free hand, take two steps and then hang on with his fingertips once more. At first it was fine, but by the time he was halfway up, his fingers were starting to hurt and his palms were too sweaty to hold on properly. He hooked his arm through one of the rungs and tried to rest for a minute, but now his legs were starting to shake as well and he knew he wasn't going to be able to hold on for much longer. He was about to call out, when he felt a supporting push from beneath him and Captain Mackie reached up and took the computer from him. 'Up you go,' he said, with a humourless smile. 'How about we save the resting for later on, huh?'

Leo nodded, took a firm grip with both hands and raced up to the top as fast as his weak legs could push him. Once there, he found himself in a large room full of humming machinery – much of it, Leo noticed, wired with explosives. His legs were shaking and he needed to sit down, but there was no time. One of the men handed him a spare environment suit and helped him to put it on. He could see his mother, Sam and Samira doing the same.

Once they were ready, Captain Mackie got everyone's attention. 'We've lost the element of surprise. The alarm's been raised and extraction will be under heavy fire. Civilians, each of you has been assigned a minder. You stick with your minder and do exactly what they tell you. Clear?'

The man beside Leo patted him on the shoulder. 'In your case, that'll be me.'

Leo nodded. 'Yes, sir.'

'Call me Mitch,' the man replied. 'We only call the captain sir.'

'If your minder goes down,' Mackie continued, 'you do not stop to help him. Keep going and attach yourself to one of the others. And understand this. If you do not do exactly what you're told to do, the second you're told to do it, you'll be putting your own lives, and the lives of my men, at risk. Clear?'

'Clear.'

'Good. Then seal suits and move out.'

They went up one more flight, onto the ground floor, and after a pause while his men took up their positions and checked their weapons, the commander's voice cut in over the comms. 'All teams. We are at Station One with all four packages. Commencing overland evac in ten seconds. I want lights out, detonations and covering fire in three...two...one...mark!'

Mitch urged Leo towards the doorway, this time ahead of the others. As they passed the front desk Leo had just enough time to notice some legs sticking out from beneath it and then everything went dark as the power was cut. He'd been forced to leave his night-vision visor behind as there was no way it would fit now that he was wearing the E-suit, but as soon as he was through the doorway and out into the compound he realised he wouldn't be needing it. Even with the power cut, the place was alive with light as silent explosions blossomed on the far side of the compound. And before they reached the first of the outlying buildings, back-up generators were already flooding the area with emergency lighting.

He ran on, sometimes keeping up with Mitch and sometimes falling behind as they wove their way across the hard ground and between the small structures dotted around them. Twice Mitch stopped to fire his weapon – Leo couldn't see the target – and once he was forced to pull Leo down into the cover of some machinery as a patrol buggy speeding along the road fired directly at them.

The bullets tore up chunks of concrete and ricocheted off the side of the machinery, but inside his helmet the only thing Leo could hear was the sound of his own breathing and the occasional order barked out over the comms. Everything happening around him was like a strange and silent dream.

Mitch returned fire – two short bursts – and the buggy swerved, bouncing off the road and flipping over and over until it crashed against a nearby building. At once they were on their feet, racing towards the perimeter fence. They passed a body lying face down on the ground with a stain spreading out from its chest, then another with swollen features gazing out in horror from behind a shattered face mask. Leo looked away quickly.

They didn't stop at the fence, but carried on into the desert beyond and it soon became difficult for Leo to see where he was going. There was still a glow from the compound, but the further they ran, the more Leo found himself stumbling as he tried to sprint across the rocky ground. His foot slipped on a rock and he went down. It wasn't too bad, and he managed to twist and land on his side, protecting the alien computer he was still clutching, but he knew he couldn't keep going at this pace. Sooner or later he would fall again and twist his ankle. Or worse. If he tore his suit or cracked his visor... He saw again the grotesque features of the body they had passed earlier and shuddered.

'I can't see where I'm going,' he hissed. 'We have to slow down.' Mitch hauled Leo back to his feet and Leo stared at him in horror. There was a large crack across the front of his visor and a small hole where air was clearly escaping. It hadn't shattered, but there was no telling when it might. 'Okay,' the man said. 'But not too slow, eh?'

They continued into the darkness.

39
RETALIATION

WHEN THE CALL CAME through, the overhead lights came on automatically and Mr Archer was immediately awake. He checked the time, saw that it was the middle of the night, and knew at once that something serious had happened. He leapt out of bed, clipped in his ear bud and began to dress.

'What is it?' he demanded.

'Sir,' came the voice in his ear. 'The research facility is under attack.'

'Details?'

'They're reporting a commando-style raid. Somewhere in the region of twenty to thirty assailants. There have been explosions and a significant number of casualties.'

Mr Archer was already out of his room, still dressing as he raced along the corridor. 'I want a shuttle, ready to leave as soon as possible.'

'Already done, sir.'

'Is it armed?'

'No, sir. It's the president's private jet. It's the only thing we have prepped for immediate take-off. But I've put out a call to Fort Greene and they're scrambling a fighter escort for you. They'll meet you en route.'

'Good. I'm on my way up now. I'll need a suit.'

'Everything is on board. The pilot is standing by.'

'Well, tell him to stand down. I'll fly it myself.'

'Yes, sir.'

'Have you told the president yet?'

'No, sir. You were the first to be informed.'

'Good. Don't. I'll tell him myself. And set up a secure link to the facility. They can give me the details on the way.'

Waiting for the lift, Mr Archer was perfectly calm. He knew when to rush and when there was no point, and he knew that bashing the call button over and over was not going to make the lift appear any sooner. Besides, it gave him time to think. Mars, and especially its president, had made new enemies over the past two weeks. The Old Man had plenty of old enemies too, for that matter – any number of whom would be happy to launch an attack against MarsMine and its facilities. But not so many with the capability. The chances were they would discover the identity of the attackers soon enough, one way or another.

But it was the timing that bothered him. He wasn't so naïve as to believe the alien ship's existence was still as closely guarded a secret as the Old Man believed. There had already been at least two attempts to infiltrate the facility, and an attack like this was bound to have happened sooner or later. But why now? He already knew the answer, of course. It was obvious. And it wasn't any of the generals, or politicians, or rival corporations they counted among their enemies who had succeeded in breaching their defences, it was a fifteen-year-old boy who was simply trying to get his mother back. It would be funny if it wasn't so inconvenient. The lift arrived. Mr Archer pressed the button for the top floor.

The prisoners would be long gone by the time he reached the facility – he knew that. But they wouldn't get far, no matter how much help they were being given, because there wasn't anywhere they could go that would be far enough. He would track them, hunt them, harass them, until there was nowhere left to hide. And when he had them in his grasp, he would kill them. No ceremony, no delay, no torture. He would take out his gun and shoot them, one at a time, through the back of the head. The professor, her assistants, the boy. And after that he would get on with his work and not give them another second's thought.

But until then, Leo Fischer would be very much in his thoughts.

40

RUNNING INTO A SPOT OF BOTHER

THE FURTHER LEO GOT from the compound, the more his fear turned to relief. He knew they weren't safe yet — not while they were out in the middle of the desert — but the shooting had stopped and they seemed to be making good time towards their evacuation point, despite the rocky ground.

'Over there,' Mitch said, pointing to the dark, looming shape of a rocky outcrop. 'Not far now.'

Leo glanced across at him. He had stuck an emergency suit patch across the side of his helmet to cover the hole in his cracked visor. It wasn't perfect, but it would probably get him as far as the rocks, assuming the rest of the visor didn't shatter. Back in the compound he'd saved Leo's life, pulling him out of the path of the speeding buggy, and Leo wished he could repay the debt. But given that he didn't have a spare helmet to offer, running as quickly and carefully as he could was all he could think of. So that was what he did.

It was only when they came to a stop beside the rocks that Leo realised they weren't rocks at all. They were vehicles, partially dug into the ground and covered with camouflage sheeting that the assault team quickly set about removing. Beneath were two military-style transport cars — a bit like armoured buses, Leo thought — but on tracks rather than wheels. He stood to one side and caught his breath while he waited for the vehicles to start up and for the rest of the party to arrive.

His mother was next in, gasping for breath but otherwise fine. She gave him a long hug then collapsed onto the sand, exhausted. A minute later Samira appeared, followed by two soldiers who were supporting Sam between them. 'Leg wound,' one of them explained over the comms. 'We patched up the suit but he's still bleeding.'

'Get him inside Number One,' said another voice. 'I'll take a look as soon as we're sealed and pumped. Go!' The rear doors were now open and the men carried Sam into the nearer one. Samira went with him, along with most of the waiting troops. The door was sealed and almost at once the transport trundled off, its tracks throwing up a cloud of sand as it went.

'We'd best get inside as well,' Mitch said, helping Lillian onto her feet. 'We'll be off as soon as the others get here.'

They clambered into the back of the second transport. A dull red light picked out a row of bucket seats running down each side of the interior. Mitch made sure Leo and Lillian were strapped in to the two seats furthest from the door, then reached into a storage locker above their heads and took out a spare helmet. With practised skill, he popped open the seals on the old one, took a deep breath, screwed his eyes closed and swapped helmets. Ten seconds later he came back over the comms. 'Christ, I hate doing that. I know the facts, about the atmosphere and all, but every time I do it, I'm convinced my head's going to explode or my eyeballs are going to melt or something. And damn, but it's cold, too.'

'Exactly how many times have you had to do it?' Lillian asked.

The man laughed. 'It's part of our training. We train a lot.'

The conversation was interrupted by the next arrivals — two of the troops, dragging the body of a third between them. They laid him gently on the floor then one of them grabbed a large medi-kit from the overhead lockers, spilling the contents in a desperate search for what he needed. The wounded man was bleeding badly, but Leo knew there was little anyone could do until they could get his suit off.

Three more men climbed in and the last, Captain Mackie, closed the door. 'We're sealed,' he shouted to the driver over the comms. 'Pump and run!' The transport gave a lurch and began to lumber across the desert, rocking as it picked up speed. While the compartment was being flooded with air, the two soldiers set to work on their injured comrade, stripping away his body armour and cutting through the environment suit and clothing to reveal a mass of blood and torn flesh across his abdomen. The medic pressed a large pad onto the wound and immediately it began to turn red.

'Keep that pressed down,' he told his assistant calmly and shot an injection into the top of the injured man's leg. But as he moved back to the wound, the man reached up and gripped his arm. Slowly he rocked his helmet from side to side, then his strength left him and his arm sank back down. The medic gave him a second injection and sat back. By the time the overhead lighting changed from red to white to show that the compartment was fully pressurized and filled with air, the man was dead.

Leo and Lillian took off their suit hoods and the others opened up their visors. The medic folded the dead man's environment suit back across the wound. He left the visor closed.

'How many men did you lose?' Leo asked.

Captain Mackie looked at him and then down at the body. 'That makes four,' he said.

'One for each of us. I'm sorry.'

'It's our job. We know the risks.'

'So what happens now?' Lillian asked.

'There's a flyer waiting a few klicks out, well out of missile range of the base. We'll transfer onto that and get you somewhere you can rest up for a while. Once you're there, that's my job done. Someone else will sort out getting you back to Earth.'

'Aitchison?' Leo asked.

'I guess.' The captain turned back to his men, snapping out orders that sent them scuttling about the transport, refilling air packs, reloading weapons, bagging up the dead body.

Lillian looked at Leo. 'Who's Aitchison?'

Leo paused. It was a good question, and one he still couldn't really answer. Policeman? Secret agent? If he worked for the government, Leo didn't know which government that was. 'He's my contact.'

'Your contact? Your contact with who? Who exactly are these people?'

'The good guys,' Leo said, and left it at that.

They continued in silence. Captain Mackie had accessed a computer console built into the back of the cabin and from time to time he would say something over the comms, either to their own driver or to the other transport, which was still several minutes ahead. But without his hood on Leo could hear only half of what was being said and it made little sense. At one point Mitch handed him a small plastic box that contained a sandwich, a carton of juice and a thin bar of something sweet. Leo ate it all and was surprised by how hungry he was. But mostly there was nothing to do except wait and hope and try not to think about the body bag stretched out by his feet.

Mackie stiffened, staring at his console screen. 'We have company,' he called out. 'Two signals, coming in fast from behind. Confirmed hostile. Driver, find us some cover. Do it now.'

The transport swerved violently and Leo felt himself being pressed into his seat. Quickly he pulled on his hood, checked his air packs were full and pulled his safety harness as tight as it would go. The ground outside had become more rocky and the vehicle was being thrown from side to side as its armoured tracks crashed over ever larger rocks.

There was a huge bump, followed by a moment of weightlessness, then the vehicle came back down with a jarring smash that sent a jolt of pain up Leo's spine. 'We're hit! We're hit!' someone was shouting, but another voice – the driver's, Leo assumed – cut in over the top.

'Negative. We are not hit. That was just the terrain.' It was true, they were still moving. But now they were tilted downwards, as if racing downhill. 'We're in a canyon. It'll be bumpy for a while but it'll give us—'

There was another, more powerful crash and this time the transport was flipped upside-down as it skidded and tumbled down the side of the canyon. Everything seemed to be happening in slow motion. Somewhere deep down, beneath the fear and panic, Leo was fascinated by what was happening. People who survived crashes often claimed that it felt as if everything had happened in slow motion and he'd always wondered what they meant. Now he knew. He pressed himself into his seat, trying to stop his head crashing from side to side, and looked across at his mother. She was curled up with her hands around her head to protect it from the pieces of equipment flying around the cabin. Someone had forgotten to restore the medi-kit and Leo watched it glide across in front of him, bounce against the end wall beside his head and spin off towards the rear door. There was a lot of shouting over the comms, but he couldn't make out any words. It was just noise. And then he was startled by the sight of the black body bag by his feet starting to move. It rose up, spun round and hurled itself directly towards him. Then, thankfully, everything went silent.

The noise came back much too quickly.

'Leo! Leo!' That was his mother. Why was she being so loud? He was right here in front of her, not half a mile away.

'He's fine. Just stunned. Give him a minute.' And that was... someone else. But who? A doctor? In black body armour with a rifle slung across his chest? Unlikely. A soldier. The crash. The escape. Mars. Slowly it all came back as his head began to clear. He gave a groan. 'My moupf hurpf.'

'You bit your tongue,' the man said, offering him a squeeze tube of clear liquid. 'Drink this. It'll help.'

Leo took a sip, gasped with pain, then squeezed the whole thing quickly down his throat. It was only then that he realised he was no longer wearing his hood. The lights were still on and there was obviously air in the cabin. The man with the gun nodded and moved away to treat someone else. Lillian took his place. She offered Leo a carton of water. 'This will help as well,' she said, quietly.

Leo took it and squeezed jets of water into the back of his throat, avoiding the tongue. 'Whap happened?' he mumbled.

'A near miss. We were knocked into the canyon, but we didn't fall too far from the look of things. We're still in one piece and they say we'll be almost impossible to spot from the air. They're trying to make contact with someone, but no one seems to be answering.'

'Sorry,' he said.

'For this?' Lillian asked, indicating the chaos all around them. 'Don't be.'

'But...'

Lillian held up her hand. 'Don't talk. Give the anaesthetic time to kick in. Just listen, okay?' Leo nodded. 'When they came and took me, back on Luna, I thought I was going to die. I was terrified. I had no idea what was going on and all I could think was that these people were going to take me somewhere and kill me. Every day was the same. I didn't know where I was, or why they'd taken me, but I knew they were going to kill me. Later on, when I understood what they had planned for me, it was no different. I knew no matter what these people said, there would never be any chance of them letting me go. It was as if I'd been sentenced to death and it was just a question of when that sentence would be carried out.

'I gave up hoping, because it was too painful. And after a while, I even gave up being angry. I just did what they told me and each day I wondered if it would be my last. Some days I hoped it would be, because I was so tired of the whole thing. Then, one day, they brought me into a room and there you were on the screen, and I realised how much worse things could be. Because you didn't bring me hope, or happiness, or comfort. You just made things even more difficult and painful.'

'Mum...'

She held up her hand again. 'No. Let me finish. That's how I felt when you arrived, and how I've felt all this past week. Right up until tonight, when I was dragged out of bed and told I was going home. Right then the hope started growing again. I didn't want it to, because a part of me thought — still thinks — that we may not make it back home. But I can't help it. It's just there. And you know what? I'm glad. I realise now that living without hope is not living at all, it's just existing. And that's not enough.'

'Mum...'

'So I want to say thank you, Leo. Thank you for giving me back my hope. I'm sorry I ever doubted you.'

'Mum!'

'What?'

Leo motioned for her to look behind her. 'I think the Captain wants to say something.'

'Oh, I'm sorry,' she said, shifting to one side and looking slightly foolish. 'Please.'

'Are you all right?' Captain Mackie asked. Leo carefully stuck out his tongue. 'It'll heal,' Mackie said, dismissively.

'Can we help at all?' Lillian asked.

'I understand you're good with computers.'

'Well, that depends on what's wrong with them.'

'As far as I can tell, nothing. But we need someone to come and get us out of here pretty damn soon and I can't raise anyone on the short-range comms.'

'Exactly how short is your short range?'

'Fifty kilometres, give or take.'

'So what about the other transport, or the flier? Why can't you contact them?'

'They're gone,' he said in a matter-of-fact voice.

'What? Are you saying they've already left without us?'

'No. I'm saying they're gone. Destroyed. We know the other transport came under fire at the same time we did. As I haven't heard anything since, I can only assume there are no survivors. As for the flier, I have no idea. Maybe it got away, maybe not. But it's gone now, so either way, we're on our own.' He paused. 'I'm sorry about your friends.'

Lillian closed her eyes.

Leo thought of Sam and Samira and tried not to picture them torn and mangled in the ruins of their wrecked vehicle. After all they'd been through, all they'd suffered, to have everything stolen away just when they thought they were finally safe. It was cruel, and stupid, and senseless, and one more thing he would add to the list of Carlton Whittaker's crimes. Maybe he was super-powerful, and maybe he was the president of Mars, but that wouldn't save him once he, Leo Fischer, was ready to take his revenge.

But that would have to wait. For now he needed to think about his current situation, which was beginning to look a little desperate. He took a deep breath and pressed his tongue against the top of his mouth to make sure the pain was completely numbed. 'So what do you need us to do?'

'I need to know if you can boost our signal somehow.'

'Why can't you just use a phone?' Lillian asked.

'Because they control all the comms satellites and they're jamming the network to stop us getting a message out. We're stuck with what we've got on board, and what we've got on board can't transmit far enough.'

'How long before the air runs out?'

'Air's not the problem,' Mackie said. 'As long as we stay inside and don't open up the back, we're carrying enough for a couple of days at least. No, our problem is that we've only got another four hours of darkness left. Once the sun comes up, we'll be sitting ducks for anyone out looking for us.'

'Four hours?' Lillian shook her head. 'To do the work, send the signal and give someone time to get back here to rescue us? It can't be done.'

'Do you have a better idea?'

'Wait,' said Leo, excitedly. 'I do.'

He slipped his arm inside the top of his environment suit and felt around for his wallet. He took out the photograph of his mother and held it up triumphantly. 'I'll need fifteen minutes,' he announced.

The others stared at him, completely puzzled.

41
RESCUING THE RESCUERS

THE FIRST TIME the phone rang, Skater covered her head with a pillow until the noise stopped. When it immediately rang again, curiosity got the better of her and she fumbled around in the dark until she found it and clipped it on.

'You?' she said as Agent Aitchison's face appeared on the screen. 'What do you want? It's the middle of the night.'

Aitchison was clearly in no mood to chat. 'I need to speak to your father, right now. Wake him up if you have to.'

'I'll say it again. It's the middle of the night. I'm not going to... Oh, wait. Is this about Leo?' She was awake now, excited.

'Yes.'

'Sweet Sol! Where is he? Is he okay? Someone told us he'd been involved in an accident, but he turned out to be a hired killer, not a policeman, so we didn't know if he was telling the truth or not. Is he okay?'

'Miss Monroe. Listen to me. I really need to speak with—'

'Is he okay?' she shouted.

'Yes,' Aitchison said, the frustration beginning to show. 'For now. But that "now" is getting shorter by the minute so please, go and wake your father.'

Skater leapt out of bed and ran to Morgan's bedroom. At the door she hesitated for a moment, wondering whether to knock, but decided she was being stupid and barged in, waving on the lights as she went. 'Dad!' she screamed. 'It's Aitchison. He's found Leo.'

Pete and Morgan were awake at once, too startled to be embarrassed, and Skater thrust the phone at her father. 'He needs to speak to you urgently.'

'What is it?' Pete asked, as soon as the phone was in place.

'I need your help,' Aitchison said. 'Yours and Miss Fourie's.'

'What?' Pete was startled. 'You know where I am? You know about Morgan? How?'

'Because it's my job to know. Now listen carefully. We have Leo and his mother. We rescued them earlier tonight but the extraction team ran into problems and they're trapped in the desert. MarsMine security teams are searching for them and once daylight comes we'll have no chance to get them out. We need someone to go in and pick them up before then, and right now, Miss Fourie's ship is the only asset I have access to that can get there in time.'

'Then maybe you should be talking to her, not me.'

'Leo's life, and many others, depend on her co-operation. I was hoping you might persuade her.'

'All right. Call me back in ten minutes.' He hung up. 'Skater. Get dressed and suit up. Two minutes. Go! Morgan...'

'Let me guess,' she said, already reaching for her clothes. 'You need to borrow the ship?'

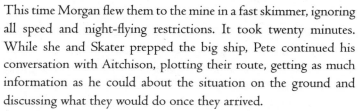

This time Morgan flew them to the mine in a fast skimmer, ignoring all speed and night-flying restrictions. It took twenty minutes. While she and Skater prepped the big ship, Pete continued his conversation with Aitchison, plotting their route, getting as much information as he could about the situation on the ground and discussing what they would do once they arrived.

'Just remember we're civilians,' he told Aitchison. 'And pretty much unarmed. We're there to get your people out, not fight a battle for you.'

'Understood. The plan is to be in and out before their ground forces are organised, but you will have to deal with any fliers they still have in the area.'

'I'm sure we'll come up with something.'

'I'm sure you will. You're a highly resourceful and experienced individual. I've read your file, remember.'

'Don't confuse me with that guy. He was far too young and far too reckless.'

'He was also an exceptional pilot.'

'Yeah, maybe. But don't get your hopes up. Today he's almost certainly going to be riding shotgun.'

'Damn straight,' said Morgan, cutting in over the comms as she strapped herself into the pilot's seat. 'Nobody gets to fly this ship except me. And we are now prepped and ready for launch.'

'Good luck,' said Aitchison. 'And thank you.'

'Don't thank me,' Morgan replied. 'Pay me.'

There was a shudder as the secondary thrusters kicked in and the ship began to rise off the ground, heading towards the giant hangar's mouth. Once clear of the rocks, Morgan increased the power and the ship rose effortlessly into the night sky.

Skater sat at the rear of the cockpit, staring at a pair of monitors linked to the external cameras, and wishing it could be her up front piloting the craft. 'How come you're not going sub-orbital?' she asked, once it became clear Morgan had no intention of firing the main engines. 'Wouldn't that get us there loads quicker?'

'It would. But I can only carry enough fuel for one round trip, and something tells me I may need to save it for a quick getaway.'

'Oh, right. Of course.' Skater felt slightly foolish and completely useless. Pete and Morgan knew exactly what they were doing and could do it without any help. In fact, she wasn't even sure why her dad had allowed her to come along, except that the extra pair of hands had been useful prepping the ship in such a hurry.

'So, what's the plan?' she asked.

'The plan,' Pete replied, 'is that Morgan flies us in, I do whatever needs to be done on the ground and then Morgan flies us out again. That's it.'

'And me?'

'You stay there and keep out of trouble until we've got everyone safely on board and we're back in the air again. After that, you'll be on passenger duty.'

'Passenger duty?'

'Who knows what state they'll be in when they arrive? Some of them might need medical attention, or maybe just a drink and a change of air. Either way, it'll be your job to sort them out with whatever they need.'

'Passenger duty. Right,' said Skater sarcastically. 'Then I'd better dig out my badge that says, *Hi, I'm Skater*, and start working on my big cheesy smile.'

'Would you rather I'd left you back at the mine? I brought you along because I thought you'd earned the right to have me to stop treating you like a child. But the first thing you need to do is learn to follow orders, no matter how unexciting they might be; otherwise it's going to be a long while before I feel I can bring you out on another one of these little adventures.'

'Okay, point taken. I'll be good and do what I'm told. Promise.'

'That's my girl.'

'So, there are going to be more adventures?'

Pete looked across at Morgan. 'I'd say it's more than likely.'

'Supreme.'

'Besides,' Pete added with a smile, 'This way you'll get to spend the whole of the return journey with Leo.'

Yes, thought Skater. *I will indeed.*

So Leo had finally managed to get his mother back. She was happy for him – of course she was – but she was jealous as well. Ever since she'd first met Leo, on the shuttle from Earth, they'd done everything together: solving those first clues on Luna and finding Captain Duggan; their escape from the *Dragon*; their time with Sol and Li; even their first days on Mars. She'd been a part of it all, and it would have been nice to have been there for the reunion. It had been their adventure, together, and it didn't seem right that he'd got to carry on without her. Although, she reminded herself, she'd had her fair share of adventures since she last saw Leo. There would be plenty of catching up to do on both sides. And from the look of it, they were at least going to be together for the last act.

They flew on, and little by little it began to get light. Sunrise was still a way off, but so was their destination and it soon became clear that they would be carrying out the evacuation in daylight.

'I'll be dropping down low in a little while,' Morgan said, finally. 'Maybe now would be a good time to go get ready.' Pete gave her a questioning look, but he knew perfectly well what she meant.

Morgan engaged the auto-pilot and when she was satisfied it was in full control of the ship she got up and left the cockpit.

She was back after a couple of minutes, now wearing some sort of light armoured vest and with a pistol strapped to her leg. 'Here,' she said, handing Skater an identical vest. 'Put this on. It's a bit heavy, but if we run into trouble you may be glad you were wearing it.'

In fact the vest was lighter than Skater had expected and nothing like the solid, heavy things she'd seen soldiers wearing back on Earth, or the one Morgan had just given to Pete. She also handed him a gun belt and pistol, like her own, and another, much larger weapon – some sort of rifle. He took them without question.

'So,' Skater asked, trying to lighten the mood. 'Are we there yet?'

'Almost.' Morgan took back control of the ship and let it drop down until they were racing along no more than twenty or thirty metres above the surface. Pete scanned the area ahead for other craft. 'Nothing,' he said. 'Either they haven't got there yet, or they're already on the ground. But either way, it doesn't look as if they've got air support.'

'Good,' Morgan said with a satisfied nod. 'That gives us one less thing to worry about, eh?' She glanced at the head-up display. 'We're about five minutes out. Better let them know we're friendly, in case they get a bit trigger-happy.'

Pete made the call, using the radio frequency and call signs Aitchison had passed on to him. 'Ground One. Ground One. This is Air Rescue. We are inbound on your position, ETA five minutes. Do you copy? Over.'

For several seconds there was nothing but static. Pete repeated the message and waited, and then finally a reply came through. 'Air Rescue. This is Ground One. Message received and understood.

Glad you could make it. We are situated near the east end of the canyon, about half a click in, but be advised that there are hostiles in the area, with more approaching from the south.'

'Fliers?'

'One shuttle, on the ground. There were two fighters earlier, but we haven't seen them for a while. They're possibly back refuelling.'

'Acknowledged.'

'We'll put down on the north side,' Morgan added. 'But we can't get too close to the canyon in case the ground's unstable. You'll have to make a run for it.'

'Shouldn't be a problem. Just glad for the ride. Out.'

Morgan saw the canyon directly ahead and fired the forward thrusters to slow the ship down. The sun was still not up but there was light to see by and she chose a solid-looking patch of rocky ground about a hundred metres from the canyon's edge. 'There,' she said. 'That'll do. Hold tight.' More thrusters kicked in until the ship had lost all momentum and was hovering high above the ground. Then slowly, slowly it began to creep downwards.

'Come on, come on,' Skater muttered, urging the ship to get a move on. But she knew there was nothing Morgan could do to speed things up. The thrusters were computer-controlled and the system was designed to get the ship down without damaging the landing gear. One single buckled foot and there might well be no chance of taking off again. She flicked between cameras, watching the ground, then the lip of the canyon, then the area on the far side where a distant cloud of dust marked the approach of more enemy vehicles.

Just before the swirling clouds of sand engulfed the ship, Skater caught a movement at the canyon and saw the first small figures clambering out. 'I see them!' she shouted. 'They're coming.'

Pete was on his feet. Before he pulled down his hood and sealed his suit he stepped across to Skater and kissed her on the forehead. 'Stay inside. Stay safe.' He picked up his rifle, left the cockpit and made his way through the ship to the airlock at the back of the cargo bay.

'You too,' Skater said. But it was too late for him to hear.

42

A FLY IN THE OINTMENT

BY OVERRIDING THE SAFETY protocols and keeping the shuttle's engines burning at full power, Mr Archer had made the journey from Minerva to the research facility in well under two hours. While he had stopped to assess the situation in the compound, his escort – two state-of-the-art military fighters – had gone ahead to intercept the escaping raiders and any vehicles waiting for them. Twenty minutes later they reported the destruction of two tracked vehicles and a transport flier. Ten minutes after that they reported no further movement.

The facility was a shambles. The monorail terminus, two of the power generators and the air-purification plant had all been badly damaged, as had three of the facility's four large all-terrain transport vehicles. Several smaller buggies and four security posts had been destroyed. Thirty-four people were dead.

But none of this interested Mr Archer. The facility could run on reserve power for weeks if necessary. The damage could be repaired and the dead personnel replaced. But two things did interest him. The first was that the research laboratories, where the new weapon prototypes were stored, had gone unnoticed and were undamaged. The second was the miraculous survival of the alien ship. The main hangar had clearly been the raid's primary target and the area itself was a scene of devastation. Several huge craters had been gouged out of the concrete floor and were filled with the twisted and broken remains of most of the spacecraft and machinery that had been in the hangar. One entire section of workshops had been demolished. But the alien ship, or at least those parts that had not already been dismantled, had resisted the blast to an amazing degree – a fact that would be worth investigating more thoroughly as soon as the facility was back up and running.

Much of the delicate alien technology had been lost, of course, either destroyed along with the workshops or carried off with the scientists and their rescuers. But when the news came in that these same scientists were now scattered across the Martian desert in little pieces, Mr Archer decided the night had ended up very far from the disaster it could have been. He might even fly straight back to Minerva and give his report to the Old Man in person. But not before he had satisfied himself that the professor and that annoying brat of hers were well and truly dead. He took two security teams – a dozen men in total – and set off in the shuttle to investigate whatever wreckage the fighters had left behind.

When he caught sight of the rescue ship coming in to land, Mr Archer was disappointed, but not overly surprised. The raiders were well-equipped and resourceful and he had been expecting some sort of rescue attempt ever since his men had located the damaged transport vehicle in the canyon, they had disembarked to investigate, and the shooting had begun. His own reinforcements were still twenty minutes away, and at this rate the battle would be over and the enemy safely airborne long before they arrived. He had two choices. Either he could get back to his shuttle, wait for the other ship to leave and shadow it until he could call in fighter support, or he could get out there right now and deal with the ship personally, while it was on the ground and at its most vulnerable. For Mr Archer, it was an easy choice.

'Press forward with the attack,' he shouted over the comms. 'I'm going for the ship.' He grabbed his assault rifle, fired off a few shots and broke from cover , sprinting away from the action as best he could in the low gravity and trusting that the early morning gloom would afford him some protection while he was out in the open.

He didn't really expect anything from his men. They were security guards, up against highly trained and better-equipped professionals, and several had already managed to get themselves killed. But at least they were a distraction. They were forcing the raiders to keep their heads down, to move slowly, and this would give him more time to reach the ship and deal with the crew before they knew what was happening.

The ship was churning up clouds of sand as it settled onto the ground and this gave Mr Archer the cover he needed to get right up to it without being spotted. For a moment he was disoriented as the sand swallowed him up and he could barely see even to the end of his rifle. Suddenly a figure appeared in front of him and he fired automatically, hitting it over and over and knocking it back into the swirling sand. He crouched and edged forward until he found his victim. It was one of the soldiers, his body armour torn to shreds by the powerful rifle blasts.

As he stood up again another figure bumped into him. With no space to bring up and fire his rifle, he used it as a club instead, smashing it upwards against the side of the man's head and knocking him back out of sight. He brought the rifle round and tried to shoot, but the blow must have damaged the weapon's mechanism because it wouldn't fire. He threw it away, drew out one of his pistols, and carried on towards the ship. After a few seconds he located the waiting airlock and stepped inside.

As soon as the inner door hissed open, he saw a figure hurrying towards him from the far side of the cargo bay – a girl, by the look of it. He shot her in the chest and she went straight down. Someone else came running in from the front of the ship. This time it was a woman and she was armed. She fired once, hitting the bulkhead beside his head and Mr Archer made sure that was the only chance she got. He clicked over to automatic and fired, spraying the doorway with bullets and hitting her several times before his gun was empty and she was able to stagger backwards and seal the door through to the rest of the ship. He would have to deal with her later.

He slipped another clip into his pistol and a thought suddenly occurred to him. *Of course*, he told himself, as he realized who it was he'd just killed. *The Monroe girl.* The thought pleased him. It was one fewer loose end.

A blue light came on behind him to indicate the airlock was in use. He pushed himself out of sight against the bulkhead and waited for the inner doors to open, and when they did, he couldn't help but give a grunt of satisfaction. First out was the professor, followed by Leo. Even in their suits they were easy to recognise, because of their size and shape and because they were clutching hardware from the alien ship rather than guns. There was a third person with them – one of the raiders. Mr Archer stepped forward, thrust his pistol into the man's armpit, above his body armour, and shot him twice through the heart, then quickly locked the airlock to prevent any further interruptions.

Lillian screamed. Leo staggered backwards as the dead body toppled against him. He dropped the computer and began to back away. Mr Archer shook his head, then held up his pistol and motioned for the two of them to remove their hoods. Once they were off, he released the catches on his own helmet and carefully removed it.

'Well, well,' he said, and smiled his crooked smile.

43
NOWHERE LEFT TO HIDE

AN ICY FEAR CLUTCHED at Leo's heart. He already knew who the man was, even before he'd taken off his dark helmet. His size, the way he carried himself; there was only one person it could be. And in that moment Leo knew with absolute certainty that he and his mother were about to die.

'Well, well,' Mr Archer said, and smiled his crooked smile. 'So here we are.' For once, he was not wearing his glasses and Leo stared, horrified, at the mass of scar tissue and electronics that took the place of the man's right eye. No effort had been made to disguise the injury, or to graft new skin onto the raw flesh surrounding it. They had simply filled the empty socket with a complex lens array and, from the look of it, wired it directly into his brain.

Lillian wrapped her arms around Leo, trying to back away. But there was nowhere to go. 'So, what now?' she asked. 'Are you going to kill us?'

'Of course I am.'

'And what about Whittaker? What are you going to say to him when he asks what you've done with his two favourite prisoners?'

'After everything that has happened tonight, I'm sure Mr Whittaker will be more than happy with my actions. You think you're special? Indispensable? Well, you're not. You're nothing. Do you want to know why we chose you? Because you were convenient; that's all. There were a dozen others we could have picked, but you were already on Luna and taking you seemed the easiest option. Next time we will be more careful in our selection process.'

'Next time?' said Lillian defiantly. 'There won't be a next time. It's all gone now. Everything was destroyed. You have nothing.'

Mr Archer let out a low laugh. 'That's where you're wrong. Your attack was hopelessly ineffective. The ship is not destroyed. Far from it. And look,' he said, waving his pistol towards the large backpack still strapped to the dead man. 'You didn't even have the sense to destroy your own research, did you? No, Professor. We still have everything. It's you who has nothing.'

Someone began hammering on the airlock door and Leo's heart leapt with sudden hope. Was there any way it could be opened from the outside? Mr Archer clearly didn't think so. He didn't even bother to turn and check, just continued to stare at the two of them with his hideous machine eye. 'Enough talk,' he said. 'I don't want to keep the others waiting any longer than necessary. Both of you, turn around and get down on your knees.'

Leo obeyed, too scared to stare death in the face and too ashamed, even now, to show his tears. He wanted to run, but there was nowhere to run to. He wanted to fight, but he had barely enough strength to keep from collapsing onto the floor. All he could do was kneel down and wait.

As Mr Archer stepped forward, Lillian pleaded with him one

last time. 'Please,' she begged. 'Just me. Not Leo. None of this is his fault. Kill me if you must, but please, not him as well. Just me.'

'You're wrong, Professor. It is his fault. This whole mess is his fault. He tried to play the hero and he failed. Now it is time for him to pay the price.' He leant down and put his mouth close to Leo's ear. 'One final thing,' he said in his harsh, grating whisper. 'There's no need for you to worry about the Monroe girl; she's already dead. I killed her myself, not five minutes ago. And that was your fault as well.'

Mr Archer stood back up and placed his pistol against the back of Leo's head. Leo took a deep breath, shut his eyes and tried to think of nothing. But there she was, right there with him, with her tangle of blonde hair tied up with string and her mad green lips and her wonderful big smile. He was glad he'd had the chance to meet her, to get to know her, even to love her. And he was glad that she would be the last thing he thought of. 'Skater,' he whispered.

The shot rang out and Leo felt his body jerk forwards like a coiled spring, suddenly released. There was no pain, only a red dizziness that wrapped itself around him. Then nothing.

The shot hit Mr Archer in the top of the leg, punching through and tearing its way out the far side. He spun around, ignoring the pain and firing several shots into the airlock door before he realised it was still sealed. He dropped into a crouch, trying to work out where the shot had come from. The far door was still sealed. There was no other way in. He glanced towards the dead soldier, just in case. But the body was still there, just as it had fallen, only now it was lying in a pool of dark blood. But something was wrong. The man's pistol was missing from his belt. Where was it? Realisation suddenly dawned on Mr Archer. He turned around.

And at that instant, Skater shot him again, this time right between the eyes.

The giant body slipped backwards, a look of shock fixed on the hideous, scarred face. Lillian leapt up and ran to Leo. Skater slumped back against one of the empty cargo crates, the pistol suddenly too heavy for her to hold. She tried to call out, but the pain in her chest stopped her from taking a deep enough breath and all she managed was a weak whisper. 'Leo?'

Lillian was too busy with Leo to hear and Skater was forced to hammer the pistol against the side of the crate to attract her attention. Finally Lillian rose and came across, stepping around the dead bulk of Mr Archer.

'Leo?' Skater tried once more.

'He's fine,' Lillian said, kneeling beside her with tears streaming down her face. 'He fainted from the shock, that's all.'

'That's good,' Skater said with a weak smile. 'I think...I'll do the same. Maybe you could let the others in...'

EPILOGUE
SIX WEEKS LATER

LEO WAS RUNNING some more tests. Or, to be more exact, the sprawling mass of hardware scattered across his desk was running the tests while he sat in front of a monitor, eagerly watching the arrival of the shuttle into the mine's main hangar, two floors above.

'Leo,' his mother called across. 'Pay attention to your work.'

'I am paying attention to my work,' he replied, defensively. 'Just not right at this very minute.'

Lillian looked up from her own, equally cluttered desk and noticed the image on his monitor. 'Are you running more diagnostics?'

'I am.'

'Can they look after themselves for a while?'

'They can.'

'Go on then,' she said with a smile. 'I'll finish up here.' Leo was off his seat and heading for the door before his mother had time to change her mind. 'And say hello from me,' she called as the door swung shut behind him.

Leo made his way quickly towards the staircase, stopping briefly to stick his head around one of the other doors along the way.

Captain Mackie was sitting at a long table, stripping and cleaning a row of rifles. Like Leo and Lillian, he was now one of the mine's temporary residents, as were the three surviving members of his original squad and the dozen or so others who had arrived a few weeks ago, together with a substantial amount of specialist equipment and supplies. With little chance of making it back to Earth in the near future, they had no choice but to remain on Mars, and had agreed with Agent Aitchison that they should set up a field base at the mine, helping out where they could. So every week or so the group would suit up, load into one of the shuttles and disappear, returning a day or two later, looking slightly the worse for wear but refusing to say more than that they had been 'out scouting'.

'Shuttle's in,' Leo said.

'So I see,' Mackie replied. 'I'll be up in a while.'

Leo left him to his work. There were others living at the mine now as well, friends of Morgan's hounded out of their homes because of their opposition to the new regime, or 'business associates' who were grateful for a safe place to rest up between their ever more risky journeys off-planet. Leo passed a couple of them on the stairs. They were carrying a large crate and he had to squeeze to one side to let them past.

'Shuttle's in,' one of them said, giving Leo a knowing wink as he went.

'So I see,' Leo replied.

Morgan still kept the showroom and warehouse in Gilgamesh for herself, and Pete and Skater had moved in with her. Leo had visited a couple of times early on, but recently they had all agreed that maybe it wasn't such a good idea — at least until things had calmed down a little. Gilgamesh was so small and insignificant that the military authorities had done nothing more than install a token garrison in an abandoned building close to the monorail station. They rarely ventured further than a few blocks from this base and never sent out patrols into the desert, but even so, Leo and Lillian were still fugitives and one unlucky encounter was all it would take to jeopardise everything. Instead, Skater had started spending more and more of her free time with Leo at the mine. There wasn't a lot to do except sit and talk, but the two of them found that this was enough. They had a lot to talk about.

By the time Leo reached his own room, Skater was waiting for him. 'Hey, birthday girl,' he said as she got slowly up from her chair. 'How's it feel to be sixteen?'

'Meh. Pretty much the same as it did yesterday.'

He put his arms carefully around her shoulders and they shared a long, passionate kiss. He didn't even blush.

'Mmm,' he said. 'Nice. I've never kissed a sixteen-year-old before.'

'No, me neither. Oh wait,' she added with a sly smile. 'I still haven't.'

Leo sighed. He still had nearly three more months of this to put up with before his own birthday. 'How are the ribs?'

'Fine. I'm drugged up.'

'I saw you coming in. Were you flying solo?'

'Pretty much. Dad still likes to be on hand while we're flying over the town, but the landing was all mine. And Morgan made it up here today as well. The two of them are off doing something birthdayish for me.'

'Which reminds me,' Leo announced. He reached into his pocket and pulled out a scrunched up ball of paper. 'Happy birthday.'

'For me? You shouldn't have. It's what I've always wanted.'

'That's the wrapping, dummy.'

'I knew that.' Skater opened up the paper and took out a small, dull lump of yellow-green crystal. 'Ooh, that's...something.'

'It's a magnesium iron silicate. Goes by the name of olivine. I was going to do a bit more with it, like polish it and shape it and stuff but, you know, I didn't. I thought you might be able to find someone in Gilgamesh who could make it into something proper and put it on a chain or something. Finding presents is difficult out here and at least I dug it out myself. It was either that, or write you a happy birthday subroutine for the translation program.'

'You are so nerdishly sweet.' She gave him another kiss. 'And I'll treasure it always – especially if you let me keep the crumpled paper as well.'

'It has nerd stuff written on it.'

'All the better. Come on, let's go see what hideously beyond-embarrassing things the others are devising for me.'

They found Pete and Morgan in the dining area. Pete had set out a birthday cake and some plates and was in the middle of trying to hang a string of small triangular plastic flags across one of the walls. Morgan was sitting as comfortably as possible in a cushioned chair and being highly entertained by the spectacle. Her right arm was still in a sling and she had a walking stick tucked by the side of her chair.

'Leo,' Pete called out. 'Perfect timing. Come and give me a hand with this, will you? Where's your mum?'

'Downstairs, finishing off my work for me. She'll be up soon.'

'How is she?'

'She's good. She still talks about home quite a bit, but I think she's coming round to the idea that we might be stuck here for a while. Work's going well anyway, and that always helps with Mum.'

'And having you here. I guess that helps, too?'

'Yeah. That too.'

'So what about you? How are things with you?'

'I'm good.'

'Really?'

Leo paused, glanced across at the others and lowered his voice. 'I'm still having the nightmares. Not every night, but still more often than not. Always the same thing. That horrible eye, staring down at me. The voice, and the gun against the back of my head. Then the shot. It always ends with the shot.'

'It was a terrifying thing to have to go through,' Pete said. 'I'm not surprised it's still giving you nightmares.'

'But I feel like such a fraud. All I did was faint when someone put a gun to my head. It wasn't like I was shot, or beaten, like the rest of you.'

'You weren't shot, it's true. But in some ways you came a lot closer to death than anyone else. And just because your wounds are on the inside, not the outside, it doesn't mean they're going to heal any quicker. These things take time.'

'Well, that's something I've got plenty of. I don't see us being able to go home until this whole independent Mars thing dies down, and that doesn't look like happening for a good long while.'

'No, you're right about that.' Pete looked across the room. Skater was showing Morgan her lump of olivine and the two of them were sharing some secret joke. 'And maybe not even then. This is my home now. And Skater's, I think. I won't stop her if she wants to go back, but—'

'She doesn't,' Leo said.

'No. I guess not.'

'And I don't even know if I want to either,' Leo added. 'Everything's changed now. Earth. Mars. Aliens. It's never going to go back to the way it used to be, is it? How can I go back to school after all this? I'm not that person any more. That life seems like it was a thousand years ago.'

'And yet it seems like no time at all since Skater was introducing you to me, that very first time back on Luna.'

'Do you ever wish she'd ended up sitting somewhere else on the shuttle that day, that she'd never met me?'

Pete didn't even hesitate. 'Never. And before you ask, neither does she.'

'Thanks,' Leo said. And then he couldn't think of anything else to say. Fortunately, Skater came to his rescue.

'Yap, yap, yap,' she called across to them. 'How about you boys stop gassing and come over and cut us invalids some cake?'

'That', said Lillian, appearing in the doorway, 'sounds like an excellent idea.'

So the cake was cut up and passed around and enjoyed, and Skater let everyone sing *Happy Birthday* to her, even though she was sixteen now and way too old for things like that. But sometimes, she said, you just had to go with the flow.

Two floors below, buried among the hard drives and monitors and cables cluttering Leo's desk, was a small silver cube of alien origin. It had been one of the few items Leo had been able to bring from the compound, but even now, he wasn't sure what it was for. Even with power, even hooked up to his own computer system, it had refused to show any signs of activity. The two rows of intricately shaped red lights set into the top had remained dull and lifeless.

Until now.

ACKNOWLEDGEMENTS

I would like to thank the following people for their support, advice and encouragement in getting me to this point on my literary journey. In something like chronological order...

James Marshall, an inspirational teacher and the man who kickstarted my lifelong love of science fiction by introducing me to the work of that genius and legend, John Wyndham. Leigh Chambers and her fabulous Angles Writing Group in Cambridge, who have steered me away from so many creative blunders over the years — too numerous to mention individually, but you know who you are. Kate Scott, a truly wonderful children's author and my very first professional reader. Iain Hood and Melissa Fu, talented authors both, whose invaluable feedback was always spot-on and of whose own novels I am immensely jealous. Adrian Sullivan, one of the world's great gatherers of magic and my science fiction/fantasy partner in crime. My editor, Simon Edge, who is as sharp and incisive with his editing as he is when carving his own words. Dan Hiscocks and the entire team at Eye/Lightning Books, who have taken an unknown writer and turned him into a proud novelist, and Ifan Bates, my cover artist, who makes my work look so good even I want to go out and buy a copy.

I would also like to give a special mention to my early Young Adult readers, Nick Wingate, Imogen Hood and Struan Gardiner, whose constant enthusiasm and insatiable hunger for more make writing so rewarding. And especially to Ezra Heydtmann, who not only devoured everything I sent him, but also took the time to write me such a thoughtful, insightful and charming response.

And finally my thanks and love to Helen, James and David, who have already shared their home with Leo and Skater for many years, and who will no doubt be required to do so for many more.

If you have enjoyed *The Arcadian Incident*, do please help us spread the word – by putting a review online; by posting something on social media; or in the old-fashioned way by simply telling your friends or family about it.

Book publishing is a very competitive business these days, in a saturated market, and small independent publishers such as ourselves are often crowded out by the big houses. Support from readers like you can make all the difference to a book's success.

Many thanks.

Dan Hiscocks
Publisher
Lightning Books

Leo and Skater return in *Escape to Midas*, the second part of the *Mars Alone Trilogy*, published by Lightning Books in August 2023.